THE GIRL IN ROOM 12

BOOKS BY KATHRYN CROFT

The Girl With No Past

The Girl You Lost

While You Were Sleeping

Silent Lies

The Warning

The Suspect

The Lie

The Wedding Guest

The Lying Wife

The Neighbour Upstairs

The Other Husband

The Mother's Secret

Kathryn Croft

THE GIRL IN ROOM 12

bookouture

Published by Bookouture in 2024

An imprint of Storyfire Ltd.
Carmelite House
50 Victoria Embankment
London EC4Y 0DZ

www.bookouture.com

ISBN: 978-1-83790-982-7
eBook ISBN: 978-1-83790-981-0

For Lucy

PROLOGUE

Extract from the *Wandsworth Times* online:

> Police have launched a murder investigation after a woman's body was discovered in a hotel room in Putney, southwest London.
>
> The body was discovered in a room at the River Walk Hotel, but it's not yet clear how long the woman had been there before she was found by housekeeping staff.
>
> The manager of the hotel, Claire Sands, said she was deeply saddened by what has happened, and is fully cooperating with police to help establish the facts.
>
> Police are appealing for witnesses. If you have any information about this incident, please contact the Metropolitan Police on 020 8870 9011 or tweet @MPSWestPutney.

ONE

'Where's Daddy?' Poppy asks for the hundredth time this evening.

I stop stirring the risotto and crouch down to her eye level. She's five now, and quite tall for her age, but right now she looks as tiny as one of her dolls. She's wearing her favourite rainbow-coloured jumper over her navy school sweater, despite the heating being on. I haven't said a word – I learnt long ago to let my daughter's clothing choices go.

'He'll be here soon,' I assure Poppy, moving a strand of chocolate-brown hair that's fallen across her dark eyes. As quickly as these words leave my mouth, I admonish myself for making my daughter this promise. The truth is, I have no idea when Max will be home.

Until a few months ago, he would always message to let us know when he was likely to be back; but somehow that routine has become extinguished, and neither of us has addressed why. But I'm acutely aware that a new normality has seeped into our life together.

I leave the pan of risotto simmering and rush to the living room to check outside again, with Poppy close on my heels. We live on one of the quieter roads in Putney, so on a winter evening like this it could just as easily be midnight outside as six p.m.

No one is out there, and there's no sign of Max's BMW. My red Toyota Yaris sits alone on the drive.

Poppy tugs on my dress. 'Daddy's *always* at work,' she complains. 'Or angry.' She glances out of the window and sighs.

For a second, I don't register what she's saying. The words are so alien: how can they apply to Max? The man who's always been a loving and kind husband and father. The sort of father who will get down on the floor and unselfconsciously play any game his daughter requests. Until all of that stopped abruptly.

'Remember we talked about how Daddy's a bit stressed at work at the moment?' I say. 'Sometimes when adults have a lot of difficult things to do in their jobs, it can make us... well, a bit grumpy at home.'

Poppy frowns as her five-year-old brain scrambles to make sense of what I'm explaining. 'But *you're* not. And you work too.'

I smile. How can I explain to my daughter that it's different for me? Owning an independent bookshop brings its own issues, but it's my passion so it rarely feels like work. I relish the challenges that come with being a business owner. Taking over from my mum six years ago was one of the best decisions I've ever made. Whispering Pages gives me an identity outside of being a wife and mother and, as much as I love those aspects of my life, I thrive on running the bookshop. And offering a sanctuary to anyone in the community who wanders inside. Like stepping into the past. Time seems to pause within those walls, and I think that appeals to people wanting just a few minutes to escape their hectic lives.

'We have very different jobs,' I tell Poppy.

'I know.' She rolls her eyes. 'Daddy does numbers. And they're super hard.'

Max is a financial analyst for a global technology company, and he would work twenty-four hours a day if he didn't need to sleep. Is this why his stress levels have been so high lately? I sense that it's more than that – he's had demanding jobs since I met him, so what's changed now?

I hug Poppy, and we turn back to the window. 'Come on,' I say. 'Let's go and check that risotto before it ends up sticking to the pan.'

By the time I've dished up dinner, there's still no sign of Max. I check my phone and there's no message letting me know he'll be late. I leave his plate empty and join Poppy at the table.

I lose myself in her chatter about school, and try to ignore the niggling sense that something is wrong.

We finish eating and I tell Poppy she needs to have her bath.

'But I'm waiting for Daddy!'

'I know. And he'll be here soon. Wouldn't it be nice if you were all ready for bed when he got home? Then he can read you a story.' Again, I'm making a promise I might not be able to keep.

'Okay,' she says reluctantly, slowly getting up and making her way upstairs.

Poppy's finished in the bath and is in her pyjamas when I hear a key turn in the front door. She glances at me, waiting for me to nod before she rushes downstairs to greet Max. A few weeks ago, she never would have sought my approval for this.

I hold my breath and go downstairs. I don't want to admit this to myself, but it's like waiting for a stranger to get home. *Which version of Max will it be tonight?*

Max holds Poppy in his arms. 'I know I promised I'd be home before dinner,' he says, easing her down. 'Sorry.' His voice is gentle. Soft. It belongs to the Max I married.

I smile, studying him carefully. There are no frown lines across his tanned face, and he looks handsome in his navy suit. It's the one I got him for his birthday and risked choosing myself, even though he's as fussy as his daughter when it comes to clothes.

I kiss him. 'I can warm your dinner up.'

'I can do it,' he says, pulling off his suit jacket.

Like a shadow, Poppy hovers behind him. Perhaps she, too, can sense that tonight he might just be himself again.

'Can I stay down here while you eat?' Poppy asks. '*Please?* Just this once.'

'It's already past bedtime,' I warn. 'And it's a school night.' Perhaps I'm worried that anything might set Max off. It doesn't take much to irritate him at the moment.

Poppy glances at Max. 'Please,' she begs, her voice quieter this time.

He ruffles her hair. 'Just this once, then.'

She squeals and throws her arms around him.

'I had ice cream,' Poppy tells him, as we make our way to the kitchen.

Max smiles. 'Did you now? I hope you saved some for me.'

'You can have some.' Poppy laughs. 'But only if you eat all your dinner first.'

Max laughs and picks her up, spinning her around.

Everything is normal.

'How was your day?' I venture, placing Max's plate in front of him.

He scoops up some rice with his fork before answering. 'Yeah, good.'

I glance at Poppy, who is now playing with her Polly Pocket toy on the floor, but she's not listening. She doesn't seem to notice the bluntness of his response. Or that normally we can't stop him talking about work.

Max looks up. 'How was yours?'

I nod, and fill the awkwardness. 'Katy was late again. Thankfully Cole was happy to take over in the coffee bar till she got in.' I don't add that it took a lot of persuasion on my part, along with a promise that he could leave early. Of course he didn't take me up on this offer, though. He never does. Sometimes I think Cole's whole life is tied up in the bookshop.

Max raises his thick, dark eyebrows. 'And how many times has she been late so far this year? Fifteen? Twenty? You seriously need to rethink your staffing arrangements, Hannah.'

Normally I would argue my case, and point out that it's *my* business to run and I'll do it however I see fit, but this evening I keep my mouth clamped shut. And neither do I admit that I've lost count of the times Katy's strolled in late, full of apologies and promises that it won't happen again. Until the next time it does. She's only twenty-four, still finding herself, she tells everyone. Can I blame her for not being committed to the bookshop?

'I'm still hungry. Can I have fruit?' Poppy asks. 'An apple without the core and skin.'

I nod and get up to fetch her an apple. Even though I'm not looking at him, I can feel Max's eyes on me, and I know he's silently questioning why I haven't responded to his comment. Why I haven't taken the bait. Am I becoming as much a stranger to him as he is to me?

'Just say it!' he suddenly snaps, staring at me.

'What?'

'I know you want to have a go at me for being late. Just get it over with. Nothing stops you normally.'

I glance at Poppy, who's staring at Max, her eyes wide circles.

'Why are you shouting, Daddy?' Poppy asks, shrinking back against the wall.

He rushes to her and pats her arm. 'I'm sorry, sweetheart. I wasn't shouting. I just... Daddy's had a long day.' He turns to me. 'I'm sorry.'

Poppy jumps up and rushes over to me, throwing her arms around me.

I hold her close and kiss the top of her head. 'Everything's okay. Come on, let's peel this apple.'

She shakes her head. 'I don't want it now.'

I put the apple back in the fruit bowl.

'I can put Poppy to bed,' Max says, rising from the table. 'You've been working all day too. And you made this.' He gestures to the barely touched risotto on his plate. 'It was lovely.'

My face crinkles – I don't know how to deal with this abrupt turnaround. And as I watch them disappear upstairs, Max clutching Poppy's hand, a flurry of questions crashes around my head. *What the hell is going on with him?*

Once Max has read Poppy a story and tucked her into bed, I go up to say goodnight. By the time I come back downstairs, Max is sitting on the sofa in the kitchen, staring through the bifold doors. He's holding his phone but not looking at it.

'Poppy's drifting off,' I say.

Max flicks his head. He's a million miles away and I don't know how to reach him. Silently, I pour us both a glass of red wine and take them over to the sofa, sitting beside him. Instinctively, I go to reach for him, but something stops me.

He takes a glass and places it on the coffee table. 'Thanks.'

'Want to talk about it?' I offer. I've had enough of being kept in the dark. Something's going on with him and I need to know what it is. *For better or worse.* Isn't that what we promised each other six years ago?

He shrugs, and continues to stare out at the dark. There are smudges on the lower half of the doors – Poppy's handprints – and I doubt he even notices them. 'I've got a crushing headache, that's all,' Max says. 'Work has been... relentless. I'm still carrying Peter's workload. It's doing my head in that they still haven't replaced him. It's been months. This is all just...' He sighs. 'Untenable.'

'I know.' I reach for his hand. 'Can I do anything?'

He laughs. 'Only if you've suddenly become an expert in finance overnight.' He strokes my cheek. 'I'm just joking.'

'I run a successful business, Max. Don't be patronising.' I might have little idea about all the forecasting and analysis he has to do each day, but equally he doesn't know everything it takes to run a business, especially in this uncertain climate.

'I didn't mean—'

'I can listen,' I suggest. 'If you want to talk about anything. Sometimes it's not about having your problem solved, but just being able to let it out.'

'Now who's being patronising?' He turns away.

My closest friend, Sarah, is always quick to point out how men don't like to talk, and how trying to make them is like expecting to squeeze apple juice from a grapefruit. Max isn't like that, though. That's why I fell for him. Even at the beginning, he never put on any pretences – what you saw was what you got.

When I worked in the HR department of the company he still works for, we'd meet at lunchtimes and sit on the roof terrace, taking in the sprawling views of Southbank. To some people, London is bleak, grey and dirty, but I only ever see the beauty in it. The life. The history. The diversity of its inhabitants.

Max would share so much in those early days as we immersed ourselves in the London landscape, marvelling at how we are all just tiny specks going about our business. Sometimes it was like talking to a female friend.

I didn't see him as anything else until one lunchtime I felt the strong urge to kiss him. We'd been laughing about something and our heads were buried closely together. To this day, neither of us is sure who made the first move. He claims it was me. I beg to differ. Perhaps it was both of us simultaneously.

What does it matter, anyway? From that moment we never looked back.

And even when he opened up to me about the incident in his past, I never saw glimpses of that unfamiliar person. *Is that what I'm seeing now?*

We've had our challenges, like when Poppy arrived and I wasn't prepared for life with a newborn. Max took it all in his stride, seamlessly navigating this new world of parenting, while also managing to stay focused on his work. He patiently stood by me while I was too shattered to give him a second of my time. I know it must have been hard for him, but he threw every ounce of energy he had into being a dad to Poppy. In the end we found our feet. Since then, for the most part we've sailed along smoothly. Until now.

Max shakes his head. 'I'm fine. I don't need to talk. I just need my workload to ease.'

'They'll replace Peter, won't they?' I venture. 'Then things will settle.'

He nods. 'Eventually. It takes time to recruit, though. It's not like you deciding to give someone a job in your shop. Like Katy.'

Without another word, I stand up and leave the room, taking my glass of wine with me. Over the last few months, I've learnt to keep my distance when Max decides he wants to pick a fight.

Upstairs, I check on Poppy then head to my bedroom and sit on the bed. While I sip my wine, I flick through Facebook.

I click on the local Putney community page, aimlessly scrolling until something catches my attention. A discussion about a woman's body being found in the River Walk Hotel. I immediately click on the link that takes me to the local news story.

The hotel is walking distance from our house. I've never paid much attention to it, even though I must have wandered past it a thousand times on my way to the Tube station. I study the photo of the girl. She's young and vibrant, and in the photo she's smiling, her piercing blue eyes shining for whoever snapped the photo. Her long dark-blonde hair is tied in a ponytail, and aviator sunglasses rest on top of her head.

A stab of recognition hits me. I stare at the photo, willing something to come to me, but it doesn't. Perhaps I've seen her posting in the local Facebook group? Or she could have bought a book in the shop.

I keep reading. The police are appealing for information. There are contact numbers and ways to help. It's strange that I feel uneasy when I don't know anything about it. All I know is that this young woman feels familiar.

Her name was Alice. A classic, pretty name. A name that belongs in a fairy tale, not a murder news story. Somewhere, at this moment, parents will be aching for their daughter. It's heartbreaking that she's dead, but to be left in a hotel room like that makes it even more tragic. Dying alone in a soulless place. A place that belongs to no one and has no meaning. The last person she would have spoken to, spent any time with, was her murderer.

I abandon my phone and rush to Poppy's room. Kneeling on the floor bedside her bed, I watch the gentle rise and fall of the duvet. The assurance of life.

I'm still in here when Max comes upstairs. He peers into Poppy's room, squinting into the darkness, but stays silent for a moment. As if he can't quite see me. Or doesn't want to.

'What are you doing?' he asks. He's right to question me; it's been years since either of us has had to sit with Poppy to help her drift to sleep. How can I explain why the death of a stranger is affecting me this way?

'I'm coming,' I say, standing and wiping at my watering eyes. I feel foolish now. I don't know Alice Hughes. I'm not sure why she felt so familiar when I've never even met her. Everyone in my life is safe and well.

Max watches me. He's changed into jeans and a khaki T-shirt. 'Need to do some work,' he says. 'It will be a long night. Don't wait up for me.'

This means he'll be out in the garden office. Although we have four bedrooms, we had it built years ago when Max was struggling to work with a sleep-averse baby in the house. But since Poppy got older, he's rarely used it until the last few weeks, usually preferring to stay late at work. Now, it's the first place I check when I know he's at home but can't locate him.

'Okay,' I say, watching him head downstairs.

My phone rings – a WhatsApp call from Sarah. Although I'm tempted to let it ring out, to message and tell her I'll call her tomorrow, I could never ignore her call. She's been my closest friend since we met at our NCT group when we were both pregnant. We immediately bonded, and although the other women were pleasant, Sarah and I hit it off immediately, and I knew straight away she'd be a lifelong friend.

'Hey. You okay?' I force my voice to sound cheerful.

'What's the matter?' she asks. 'You sound... weird.'

I've never considered myself as being easy to read. I like to think there's a part of me that no one can quite fathom, but somehow Sarah has me all worked out. 'I'm fine,' I tell her. 'Just... did you hear about that woman at the River Walk?'

'Yeah. It's awful. That's why I'm calling, actually. It makes you cherish the people in your life, doesn't it? When something like this happens. She was around our age, I think.'

'A few years younger. It said she was thirty.' I head into our bedroom, pulling the door closed so I don't wake Poppy, and flop down on the bed.

'What was she doing there?' Sarah says, as if she expects me to have an answer for that. 'She only lived in Roehampton. That's walking distance. Why would she need to stay in a hotel

so close to her house? What was she doing? It's all a bit weird.'
She pauses. 'It's just really hit me. I don't know why.'

'Because it's right on our doorstep. It could have been—'

'Don't say it!' Sarah warns. 'I don't think either of us would
have been in a hotel room like that, would we? Well, I hope not
anyway. And it's not a cheap one, either. Besides, you're a
married woman and I know I'm not, but...' She trails off. It's still
hard for her to talk about Dean. It's been over five years since he
left her when she was pregnant with Ivy, writing them both out
of his life.

'How's Ivy?' I ask.

'She's okay. But I've been thinking about Christmas. And
how Dean will be with his wife and other kids, while Ivy barely
knows of his existence.' She pauses. It always hits Sarah especially hard at this time of year. 'I'd never wish Ivy away, but I
curse the day I met that man. Nasty liar. To me and his oblivious wife. Sorry. You don't want to hear all this.'

'Yes, I do,' I remind Sarah. 'That's what I'm here for, right?
Plus, it's only November. There's a bit of time to go.'

She sighs. 'Yeah. I know. What would I do without you?
How are you guys, anyway? Poppy okay? Max feeling less
stressed?'

Normally I wouldn't hold back from spilling everything in
my life to Sarah, but right now that's impossible when I don't
understand it myself. 'Poppy's fine. Max is still stressed. He's
got a lot on his plate at work. I told you about his colleague
leaving and Max having to take on his workload?'

'Yeah. That's harsh. And I know exactly how it feels.'

'How are things at the hospital?' As a nurse in A & E, Sarah
goes above and beyond for her patients. I've told her to give
herself a break sometimes, to try to find a balance between her
work and home life, but she never quite manages it.

'Same as usual. Understaffed and overworked.' She snorts.
'I had an argument with Mum the other day. She said I need to

stop taking on so many extra shifts, and that Ivy spends more time with her than she does with me.'

'That's not true,' I assure her. 'Besides, you're doing the best you can. Anyway, I'm happy to have Ivy any time, you know that.' I tap my phone, and the picture of Alice Hughes lights up the screen.

'I know you are,' Sarah says. 'Thanks. Mum just doesn't understand that I need every shift I can get. Raising a child costs a fortune, doesn't it? Anyway, it might get Mum off my back if you have Ivy now and again, but it doesn't solve the problem of me needing to spend more time with my daughter.' She sighs. 'But I'm always there for her, aren't I?'

'Course you are.' I walk to the window and look across the garden. The lights are on in the office, and I can make out Max sitting at his desk with his laptop open. His hand is pressed to his ear, and I'm convinced he's talking on the phone.

'I just need all the shifts I can get,' Sarah is saying. 'Got to keep a roof over our heads.'

'Look, if you need—'

'Got to go,' she says, with no warning. 'Ivy's shouting for me. Knew it was too good to be true that she'd actually be asleep before eight! But according to Mum, she drifts off the second her head hits the pillow when she's there. Good old Grandma!'

'Go,' I urge. 'I'll call you tomorrow.'

I glance out of the window again; Max is still on the phone, throwing his arms around and shaking his head.

Turning away, I survey our bedroom. It's usually a calm, tranquil place, but Max's clothes lie strewn across the bed. The expensive navy suit crumpled in a heap. I pick it up and try to smooth out the creases. It's no use, but it's due to be dry cleaned anyway; it's been a few weeks since I last had a chance to go. With the dry cleaners being right across the road from Whispering Pages, it makes sense that I'm the one that chore falls to.

I check the pockets – nine times out of ten Max will leave

coins or receipts in there, and Demitri, who owns the place, always reminds me to check.

I place my hand inside the left pocket, surprised to find no loose change in there this time. My fingers clasp something, though – smooth and solid, like a bank card. I pull it out, surprised to see it's a plain white card. Not a bank card, or any kind of loyalty card.

On closer inspection, I realise it's a key card. And it's embossed with the logo of the River Walk Hotel.

TWO

I barely sleep, and when morning comes, my head is heavy, clouded with fog. Last night, I waited for Max to come to bed, ready to confront him with the key card. But before I could, Poppy had woken with night terrors and wouldn't sleep anywhere but our bed. So instead, I spent most of the night watching him, our little daughter pressed between us, nausea and anxiety invading my body, wondering how my husband could be linked to a murdered woman in a hotel room.

After dropping Poppy at school, I walk along Upper Richmond Road, heading towards the bookshop. When I'd first bought the business from Mum, I'd longed for the shop to be right on Putney High Street, where footfall is greater, and I'd assumed I'd attract far more customers. I'd scoured local estate agents, hoping that a retail unit would come up for rent or sale. Of course it would mean higher business rates, but I was willing to risk that for a prime position. But in the end, I'd listened when Mum had insisted that anyone who loved books would be willing to walk a few extra metres to experience the atmosphere of Whispering Pages. She'd baulked when I'd refurbished and added a small coffee bar, but she'd still given her blessing, admitting that it was up to me to do as I saw fit.

News travels fast, and the atmosphere around Putney this morning has changed; serious expressions on faces, clusters of people murmuring quietly. All of us affected by the death of a woman most of us won't know. The River Walk Hotel is on the other side of Putney Bridge, towards Fulham, in the opposite direction from the bookshop. But still I feel the presence of Alice Hughes everywhere, of what she's left behind.

The temperature has dropped further this morning, and with the clear blue sky, it feels more like January than November. I plunge my gloved hands into my pockets, finding the hotel key card. Fear seeps through my blood, cold and heavy. Tonight, after work, I'll confront Max. A coincidence; it has to be. There's a reason Max has that card. He found it. He meant to hand it in but hasn't had time. And then we'll laugh about it. How easy it is to jump to conclusions without context. This is what I tell myself, as the alternative is too heinous to imagine.

I'd tested the waters this morning, as we sat silently at breakfast. Poppy was with us so I'd had to be careful, but I'd asked Max if he'd heard the news about Alice Hughes. I'd studied his face for... what? Recognition? Lies? But he'd kept his eyes on his phone and shaken his head. A tragedy. That's what he'd said, before biting into his toast. And when I'd said it was funny how neither of us has ever been in that hotel, he'd frowned. 'We've had no reason to,' he'd said, his eyes still fixed on his phone.

Now, as I head towards the bookshop, I'm determined to find out for myself why my husband had that card in his possession. And why it's for the same hotel where a woman has just been murdered.

The shop door is already unlocked when I place my key in the lock. I push through, and immediately see Cole standing in the coffee bar. He smiles and lifts his hand in a small wave. 'Morning, Hannah.'

'I thought I was opening up today?' I say. 'It's your day to start late.'

'I was up anyway so thought I may as well come in. Couldn't sleep for some reason.' He sprays disinfectant onto one of the tables and meticulously wipes it down. He's wearing dark grey trousers and a thick black jumper with a shirt and red striped tie underneath. I've told him he doesn't have to wear a tie, and that as long as he's semi-smart, I'm fine with whatever he's comfortable in. Before me, Mum didn't insist on a dress code either.

I've never met anyone like Cole before. Everything about him is a contradiction. He's thin and tall, around six foot – the same height as Max – yet it's easy to overlook him in a room. While Max silently commands attention just by his presence, Cole seems to fade into the background, almost as if he's willing himself not to be seen.

'I couldn't sleep either,' I say. 'It's awful, isn't it?' I head across to the sales counter and set about opening up the tills.

'Yes, it is. I've been cursed with this insomnia since I was a kid,' Cole says.

I look up. 'I meant the woman in the River Walk Hotel.'

He stops cleaning and stares at me, his face blank.

'You haven't heard?'

'Nope. What woman?'

I tell him about Alice Hughes, and his face falls. 'That's terrible. Right here on our doorstep. Poor woman.' He resumes wiping tables. 'I just don't read the news, Hannah. It's too depressing. Isn't it better not to know about awful things happening? It doesn't do us any good, you know. Especially first thing in the morning.'

I open my mouth to disagree but stop short when the door

opens and an elderly woman walks in. 'Just browsing,' she calls, waving her arm around. 'Don't need any help.'

Cole glances at me, raising his eyebrows. 'Um, sorry, we're not actually open yet. It'll be another half an hour.'

She frowns, lifting her glasses and appraising Cole. 'The door was open. If you're not open, then why let people just walk in? It's confusing.'

'I'm sorry,' I chime in. 'That was my fault. I forgot to lock it. But it's fine – you're welcome to browse, but we can't run anything through the till until nine.'

She rolls her eyes and shuffles forward. 'I don't need any help,' she repeats. 'Just browsing.'

'Be sure to let us know if you'd like tea or coffee.' Cole plasters a smile onto his face and turns away from her. Thankfully, she doesn't see him scowling.

'Can you keep an eye on things for a sec while I pop upstairs? I need to put my stuff in my locker.' I pick up my bag.

'Take your time,' Cole says, his eyes narrowing.

As I head to the stairs, I feel him watching me. I always keep my bag in the office downstairs, stuffed in the drawer of my desk – only on rare occasions have I ever used my locker. And nothing escapes Cole's notice.

Upstairs in the staffroom, I close the door and head to the lockers along the back wall. There are only four – we've never needed more than three staff at any one time.

I press the code into my locker and open it, staring into the empty space. I pull the key card from my pocket and study it again, as if it will provide me with answers. I want to scream. *Why do you have this card? If you've never set foot in that hotel, then why is there a room key in your pocket?* It occurs to me that Max might look for the key card. And what will he do when he finds it missing?

Slamming the locker door shut, I lean against it and try to slow my breathing. Deep breath in, deep breath out. I can't let

Cole see that something is wrong – he's like a bloodhound and won't stop until he's found answers.

As if I've summoned him by thinking about him, the door opens and Cole peers in. 'Everything okay?' he asks, hovering by the door.

'Yep. Fine. Is that customer downstairs alone?'

'No. She left, so I locked up.'

I glance at my phone. 'Okay. Well, we've got a few minutes.'

'Coffee?' he asks. 'Normally it's the first thing you do. Is everything okay, Hannah?'

'I'm just a bit... This morning was hectic trying to get Poppy ready for school. It's been a bit full on. I'll have one now.'

He watches me closely. 'Is this about the woman in the hotel? It's getting to you, isn't it?'

I look away from him and root through my bag. 'No. Well, of course it's terrible. I just feel sad for her family.' I pull out lip balm and begin applying it, just so I don't have to look at Cole scrutinising me. My whole face feels too warm.

'If she had any. Some people don't have family, Hannah. Or family they can count on at least. Some of us aren't that lucky.'

'I know. You're right. I shouldn't make assumptions.' Cole's parents both died when he was in his twenties, and he's an only child. He never talks about it, but I know from my mum that he was married a long time ago, but is now divorced. They didn't have any children. He's only forty, though, so there's every chance he could be in a relationship, even if he makes no mention of it.

Cole nods, but stays by the door.

'Shall we go down, then?' I suggest, striding towards him.

He stares at me for a moment, not seeming to register that I've spoken.

'Oh, yeah.' He steps aside. 'I thought you were leaving that in your locker,' he says, pointing to my bag.

'Changed my mind,' I say. 'Come on, I need a caffeine fix.'

. . .

It's mid-morning before I have a chance to escape to my office. Katy hasn't turned up again, and neither Cole nor I can get hold of her, so I've been on the shop floor since we opened, while Cole takes care of the coffee bar. One thing I hadn't counted on was that some people would come in only for coffee, paying no attention to the books they're surrounded by, no matter how enticing I try to make the displays. 'You're either a book person or you're not,' Max always says.

Still, I'm grateful for any customers, whatever their reason for stepping inside.

While Cole assumes I'm doing a stock order and takes over at the till, I search the internet for everything I can find on Alice Hughes. She has a presence on social media, and the same photo that's been sprawled all over the local news stares at me.

From Instagram I learn that she was a personal trainer, offering private sessions at her home in Roehampton. I study the picture of her small purpose-built garden gym, and I wonder if somehow Max was having training sessions. But he would have told me. And he's never shown any interest in the gym. He runs occasionally, but mostly he's too busy to commit to any regular fitness routine.

I continue scrolling, soaking up information about Alice as if I'm her stalker. Is that what I've become? Obsessed with a woman who's no longer here. Is this what finding that hotel key in Max's pocket has so quickly turned me into?

It soon becomes apparent that although she was a regular poster on social media, there's very little of a personal nature in her posts. She's shared nothing that helps paint a picture of her, other than that she was huge on fitness and likes cats. It seems Alice had two Siamese cats – one white with piercing blue eyes, and the other mocha-coloured with green eyes. She clearly adored both of them, as her Instagram squares are as much about her pets as they are her personal training.

There's no hint that Alice was in a relationship with anyone, and nor are there pictures of her with any friends. Not a single one. *Strange.* Either she was fiercely private, or she wanted to keep the rest of her life hidden.

A knock on the door forces me to close my browser, just in time before the door opens.

It's a relief when Sarah appears, holding two coffees. 'I was passing and thought you might need one of these,' she says, sitting on the only other chair in the room. Never one for following rules, she's dressed in her scrubs, and her long, light brown hair drapes around her shoulders. 'Cole made me pay for these in case you're thinking I'm just here for free coffee.' She leans forward and lowers her voice. 'He doesn't like me, does he? All these years I've been popping in here and he can barely manage to make eye contact.'

'It's not you,' I assure her. 'I think it takes a lot for Cole to trust people. He's very wary until he gets to know you.'

'Well, I don't have time for that,' she says, rolling her eyes. 'Got enough to worry about.'

'Also, let's just say serving coffee isn't his favourite thing to do at work.'

'Not when he's technically the manager here.' Sarah laughs. 'I can't believe you let him have that title.'

'He works hard,' I say. 'I need him here. He knows this place inside and out. Even better than I do. He was loyal to Mum.' Something I'll never forget is that Cole has been here longer than I have, and used to work for my mother.

'He's just so *weird*,' Sarah says, stretching the word out to give it more emphasis.

'Are you working today?' I ask. As much as she's right about Cole, I will always defend him. Or anyone. *Innocent until proven guilty*. So why am I not applying that to my own husband?

She checks her phone. 'Yep. In exactly one hour. And this shift is going to be a long one. Actually, that's partly why I've stopped by. I've got a huge favour to ask. I really don't want to, but I don't have a choice. Mum was meant to be picking up Ivy after school and having her overnight. But can you believe she's just messaged me to say she's got her dates mixed up? Apparently, she's going out for dinner with friends tonight.' Sarah rolls her eyes again. 'I'm sure she only arranged it when she knew I needed help again.'

This does sound like the kind of thing Carol, Sarah's mum, would do. But innocent until proven guilty. 'Of course we'll have her,' I say, without hesitation. 'Poppy would love Ivy to come for a sleepover.' Even as I say this, I wonder how I'm going to confront Max about the key card with the two girls around. But at least Poppy will sleep well in her own bed tonight if Ivy is in her room with her.

Sarah smiles. 'That's amazing – thank you, thank you!' She jumps up and hugs me, sloshing coffee over the rim of my cup. 'Oops, sorry. Look, are you sure it's okay?' She sits down again. 'Won't Max mind? It's a school night and I'm sure the last thing he'll want when he gets home is to find the girls having a mini disco in your living room.'

'He'll be fine,' I say. But I'm already questioning why I've agreed to this when there's a hotel key that's linked to a dead woman in my locker.

Sarah studies me for a moment. 'Are you sure everything's okay with you and Max? I don't know what it is but I'm getting the feeling there's... I don't know – a bit of tension? Please talk to me, Han.'

I should tell her everything; Sarah would understand. She's been through enough in her life and she's always compassionate. I can always be myself with her. Yet my mouth remains firmly shut. How can I tell her what I found in Max's pocket? I need to know what it means first. 'We're okay,' I say, glancing at the door. 'It's just... he's been really off with me lately. Distant. Snapping all the time. I know it's work pressure, but it's hard to get through to him.'

Sarah places her coffee cup on the desk. 'Have you tried asking him how he's feeling? You've always said you two can talk about anything.'

Normally. But nothing about this is normal. Max's behaviour. The hotel key card. A dead woman. 'We've talked. He just says it's work stress. But it's affecting Poppy too.'

'Kids are resilient,' Sarah says. 'Look at Ivy. She's a little trooper. Takes everything in her stride. She hears all her friends talking about their dads and never questions me about Dean. She just knows he couldn't be with us. Plus, she's always being farmed off to Grandma's. So much disruption, but she's as happy as any other child. And as for Max, well, he loves you. It's as simple as that. Maybe you're just going through a rough patch. Remember when you were struggling with the baby days? That took its toll, didn't it? And look now. Those days passed, didn't they? And whatever this is, it will pass too. You just have to ride this storm and wait for sunnier days.' She chuckles. 'Jesus, it sounds like I've swallowed a self-help book! But it's true, though. I know it feels a bit crap right now, but you'll get through it.' She checks her phone. 'I'd better go. Patients need me. I'll call you later.' She stands, picking up her coffee cup. 'I'd better take this back otherwise PC Cole will be arresting me.' She chuckles.

At the door, Sarah turns back. 'All you have to remember is that Max is a good man.' She blows me a kiss before disappearing through the door, closing it behind her.

· · ·

At twelve thirty, I tell Cole I'm popping out for lunch. 'I need to get a few things,' I explain, before he can question me. It's a rare occurrence for me to leave the shop; my days are short enough with the school pick-up at three, so I rarely take a break. 'Need me to get you anything?'

He shakes his head. 'You know I always bring my lunch, Hannah.' And it's the same every day – a ham and cheese sandwich on wholemeal bread, cut into two triangles with some grapes, an apple and two digestive biscuits. Cole has never deviated from this menu.

He turns back to organising the shelves, but in the reflection in the doors, I see that Cole's turned around again to watch me leave. *He knows something is wrong.*

The November chill seeps through my clothes, piercing my skin as I make my way along the high street, towards Putney Bridge. I'm compelled to keep moving, even though I have no business walking anywhere near the River Walk Hotel.

I am a criminal returning to the scene of my crime – even though I've done nothing to this woman, and have never even met her.

I don't know what I expect to see when I get there, but it's quieter than I'd imagined it would be. There's one police car parked by the entrance, and a uniformed officer standing by the door. It's not the frenzied scene I've imagined.

Outside the hotel, by the railing, is a sea of flowers. Passers-by slow down for a moment and stare, and I imagine their relief that this tragedy isn't happening to them. Without much spectacle, they continue walking, their lives resuming because Alice was a stranger to them, her life nothing to do with theirs.

Somehow, though, it's got something to do with mine.

I, too, slow down as I get closer, and I can't tell whether it's because my whole body feels like a dead weight, or because I need to see what's going on. To find answers.

I'm on the other side of the road so I stop and watch for a

moment. I'm not doing anything different to other people who have gathered on the pavement to gawp. There's no sign pointing to me. The guilty one.

'Horrific, isn't it?' I spin around and there's a young man in jeans and a puffa jacket walking towards me. He looks around thirty, and his dark brown hair falls across his forehead. He pushes it from his eyes and stops beside me.

I need to answer him. Act normally. 'Yeah, it's terrible. So sad.'

'Do you live around here?' He's not wearing gloves, and shoves his hands in his pockets.

I nod, but don't offer him any information.

'Did you know her?' he asks.

I look across at the hotel. 'No.' My cheeks burn, even though what I've said isn't a lie.

'It's just that you look upset. I thought maybe you knew her.'

A flush of heat passes through my body. 'Who wouldn't be upset? A woman's been murdered in a hotel room.'

He nods slowly but doesn't respond, and I feel the heavy weight of his stare.

'Did *you* know her?' I ask. Turning this back to him will detract from my guilt.

'Nope.' He smiles. 'You have a nice day now.'

He walks off, heading across the bridge towards the high street, and I'm left feeling uneasy. It's not just what he's said, but the way he studied me so carefully, his eyes appraising me for too long. I watch him for a few moments, and he turns to look back at me. There's no longer any hint of a smile on his face.

Whoever that man is, it feels as if he knows exactly what I'm doing here.

THREE

Oksana Thomas: I'm so sad to hear about the woman who was found dead in the River Walk. My heart goes out to her family. I hope they catch who did it.

Comments:

Lee Broomfield: Terrible. Wife was one of her clients. Said she was a lovely person. I can't believe the CCTV wasn't working. It had gone down and the engineer was due today. Otherwise I'm sure they'd have a suspect by now.

Renee Curtis: Not being funny, but what was she doing there in the hotel? Apparently she lived up the road. Bit weird. Think she was having an affair. Not saying she deserved what happened, so don't have a go, but it's a bit weird.

Ajay Khan: It's someone who knew her. Has to be. The police will find him or her.

Nora David: Maybe she took her own life? Suicide is the number one killer of young people today. Terrible.

Ajay Khan: Don't think it's possible to strangle yourself and then climb into a bath unconscious, is it?

Nora David: No need to be nasty – I didn't know that's how she died.

Ajay Khan: It's someone she knows, I'm telling you. Always is.

Sarah Brooks: Can everyone just stop commenting on her personal life? It's disrespectful and none of us know anything about her. Just let the police do their job.

I leave work early and make my way to Poppy's school. I'll have a twenty-minute wait at the school gates, but at least I'm outside in the cold, brisk air. As much as I love the bookshop, today the air inside feels stifling, and Cole's questioning gaze on me is too much to bear. Perhaps it's paranoia, but it felt as though he was scrutinising everything I did.

There's a group of three mums I recognise huddled by the gate. I don't know their names – I'm always rushing to the shop after dropping Poppy so I can never linger long enough to strike up a friendship with anyone. Sarah – who I knew way before the girls started school – is the only mum I talk to here for longer than a brief hello. And now it's too late to forge friendships. Everyone huddles in cliques, closed to new members.

The three mums are so engrossed in their conversation that none of them look up as I approach. Even before I hear a word, I can tell what they're talking about. Alice Hughes. As if her murder is something they watched a documentary about on Netflix last night. None of them look upset; instead, their bodies and eyes are alight with excitement. The pull of gossip. And it makes me feel sick.

I stand back and pull out my phone, my ears tuning into their conversation.

'I heard she was a... you know... a *prostitute*,' one of the mums is saying. 'Meeting a client there. And it all went wrong. You hear about that kind of thing, don't you? They're vulnerable women, aren't they? Doing that kind of work.'

I glance at the mum who's spoken. She shakes her head sadly, but her eyes are bright with relish. I take in her heavily made-up face, the golden hair tied up in a neat bun. The heels that can't be comfortable when you're chasing after children. I have no doubt that she drove here, even though the school's tight catchment area means most of us live within walking distance.

'I don't think they call themselves *prostitutes* any more,' the mum with dark cascading curls says. 'I think they call themselves *escorts*.' She nudges the mum next to her. 'As if that makes a difference. It's the same thing, isn't it?'

'It does make you wonder what kind of life she was living to end up that way,' the third mum says. 'Thank God she didn't have any kids.'

I've heard enough. 'Haven't you got anything better to do?' I spit. 'It's shameful and disgusting to gossip about someone who's dead.'

Although they all stare at me, their lipsticked mouths hanging open, no one says a word. And with the silence hovering over us, I turn back to my phone, once again pretending to be engrossed in something.

'What's your problem?' the loud one with the mum bun says, after a few moments. 'We were just talking about it. Ever heard of free speech?'

'There's a difference between free speech and vicious gossip,' I say. 'How about just having some respect?'

She opens her mouth to respond but quickly changes her mind and turns away, tutting and shaking her head. The conversation resumes, but this time, fully aware of my presence, they turn their attention to discussing the upcoming PTA Halloween disco.

By the time the school gates open, the crowd of parents has expanded and we all move forward in unison, like a wave creeping up to the shore.

I stand apart from everyone else and wait for Poppy's class to come out. It feels as though everyone is staring at me. Of course they're not, most of the parents here are too consumed with the conversations they're having, or their phones, to pay any attention to me, yet guilt wraps around me, a flashing beacon, highlighting that I'm not like anyone else here. *Somehow I'm connected to Alice Hughes.*

I know something important about the case that the police should know. Yet I can't go to them. Not until I've spoken to Max.

I'm so distracted by these thoughts that I don't notice Poppy has come out until she's rushing towards me, her bunches flying in the air. 'Mummy!' she calls, throwing herself into my arms. It delights me that even in Year 1 she's still so happy to see me at the end of the day. I hold her tightly, cherishing that she's here in my arms. Keeping me grounded. This is my reality. I can't let anything else be. 'Have you had a good day, sweetheart?'

She nods. 'What snack did you bring?'

I reach into my bag and pull out a packet of strawberry Yoyos. 'Here you go. We're picking up Ivy today too. She's coming back with us for a sleepover.'

'Yay!' Poppy exclaims, darting back to where the teachers are still dismissing children. She and Ivy are in different classes this year, much to both girls' dismay. When we found out the classes would be mixed this year, I was concerned about Poppy missing her friend, but she's blown me away with how easily she's formed friendships with other children. Ivy, though, has struggled, and still seeks out Poppy whenever the two classes can mix at playtimes.

Ivy appears from behind her teacher, who points to me and lets her go. 'Am I coming home with you?' she asks. 'The teacher told me, but Mummy didn't say anything.'

'You certainly are,' I say, mustering all the enthusiasm I can manage. 'It was a last-minute plan. Isn't that great?' I hand her the spare packet of Yoyos I always carry in my bag, and she snatches it without thanking me. 'You're welcome,' I say.

'Thank you, Hannah.'

Ivy hands me her book bag and water bottle and grabs Poppy's hand. The two girls walk ahead of me, their heads bent together as they laugh and chat.

I'm forced to jog to keep up with them, and I'm so focused on not losing sight of them that I almost bump into a passer-by.

'Sorry,' I say, not daring to look away from the girls.

''S'okay,' a voice I recognise says.

I glance up, but he's already walked past and I can't see his face. But I recognise his clothes: the jeans and black puffa jacket. The ones belonging to the man I spoke to outside the River Walk earlier.

I turn to watch him. He can't be a parent at the school – surely I would have seen him before. But I don't have a chance to dwell on this; Poppy and Ivy are already too far ahead of me, so I sprint to catch them up before they reach the main road. Whoever that man is, I push it aside. I don't have the headspace to worry about anything else right now.

· · ·

Having Ivy at home with us is a welcome distraction. The girls' laughter floats around the house, forcing me to live in this moment and banish all other thoughts. And the more I focus on this, the less the key card seems real.

But it sits in my bag – waiting to be dealt with, so it's only a matter of time before reality comes crashing back.

'Come on, Ivy – let's play outside,' Poppy says, pulling on her coat and rushing out to the garden. Nothing keeps Poppy inside – not even icy winter temperatures. Ivy follows, running to keep up, her coat dragging on the ground behind her as they bound towards the sandpit. It's always this way with the girls. Poppy leading and Ivy following, unquestioning.

As I stand by the kitchen window, watching them playing in the garden, bundled up in their coats and gloves, I check the local news on my phone. Alice Hughes is everywhere on the local forums and news sites, and her smiling face silently pleads with me. To do what? I don't know anything.

But I can find out.

While the girls are busy, I slip into the garden office and close the door. The girls will be able to see me through the glass doors and low windows, but Poppy will assume I'm tidying up.

I pull out drawers and search through papers, but there's nothing out of the ordinary. No evidence of any hotel stays. Nothing but work documents. Max doesn't keep receipts. Everything is paperless, buried in his emails.

Max's laptop is password protected but I try anyway – entering dates and words that might mean something to him. Poppy's birthday. Mine. Our wedding anniversary. None of them work. Frustrated, I slam the laptop shut, leaving it on the desk.

As I scan the room, I become aware that something feels different in here. Max's desk is a mess, when usually he puts everything neatly in its place once he's finished working. There are papers left in a haphazard heap, and pens and pencils tipped out of his pen holder. He's been preoccupied lately, that could explain it. *Just one more thing he's doing that's out of character.*

I turn back to the window, my breath catching in my throat when I see Max striding across the lawn. It's only five p.m. Max is never home this early. Poppy calls out to him, but he just waves and heads straight towards me.

'What are you doing in here?' he asks, throwing open the door. His voice is calm, but his eyes are narrow slits.

'I thought I'd clean up a bit while the girls were playing. I can keep an eye on them from here.' My throat burns with the effort it takes to lie. I'm not good at it.

Max glances at the girls. 'You didn't mention Ivy was coming. It's a school night. Is this a good idea?' He sighs heavily, his eyes darting around. 'I came home early but I've still got a ton of work to do. I'll never get peace now. And why are they playing outside when it's freezing?' He doesn't wait for an answer. 'When's Sarah picking her up?'

'She's not. Ivy's staying the night. Sarah had to work and needed my help.' I stare at him, defiant.

Time stands still until eventually Max's face softens. 'Just make sure they keep it down,' he says.

I leave him to it and walk over to the girls. 'How about we make some pizzas for dinner?' I suggest. Glancing back as we make our way inside, I see Max opening his laptop, tapping his fingers on his desk while he waits for it to load.

'What's wrong with Daddy?' Poppy asks, as the girls spread chopped tomatoes across their pizza bases. 'He was a bit angry. Is he stressed again?'

'He's had a hard day at work,' I say, wiping tomato sauce off the black granite worktop.

Poppy sticks out her bottom lip. 'My daddy's always angry,' she explains to Ivy.

'I don't know my daddy,' Ivy says. 'He couldn't be with us.'

When Poppy asks her why, I intervene and change the subject. 'Right, let's get cheese on these pizzas then I can put them in the oven.'

This works, and the conversation is quickly forgotten. Once the cheese is piled onto their pizzas, I suggest the girls play in Poppy's room until they're ready.

With endless energy, they bound upstairs and I turn to the window and watch Max in his office. His head is still buried in his laptop, his fingers furiously tapping the keyboard.

Taking a deep breath, I head outside, feeling as though my legs are too heavy to propel me forward. *Is that fear? Of what? This is Max. My husband.*

I knock loudly on the door. I won't tiptoe around him.

He looks up, his fingers hovering over the keyboard. 'Sorry, Hannah, but I really need to get this done.'

'Just wondering what you want for dinner,' I say, stepping inside. 'The girls are having pizza in a minute.'

Max turns back to his laptop. 'I'm not really hungry. Sorry.'

'I haven't been able to stop thinking about that girl,' I say, walking over to him. 'Alice Hughes.' I perch on the arm of the spare chair, study him closely.

He doesn't look up, doesn't even flinch. 'Who?'

'The girl who was killed in the River Walk.'

He sighs. 'I know it's sad, but we didn't know her.' He resumes tapping. 'This kind of thing happens all the time. Why are you getting this upset about it?'

His cold words shock me. I really don't know my husband any more. 'It doesn't happen on our doorstep,' I say.

'Things can happen anywhere. Poppy's safe. You're safe. That's all that matters.'

I'd planned to wait until the girls were asleep, but I reach into my jeans pocket, pulling out the card. 'I found this,' I say, holding it up.

Max looks up for a second then turns back to his computer. 'What is that?'

'It's a key card. For the River Walk Hotel.'

The atmosphere becomes heavy as I wait for Max to reply. Seconds tick by and he stares at me. 'What? Where was it?' he asks, turning back. 'You should hand it in.'

'It was in your suit pocket.' I've said it now and there's no going back. 'Why was it in your pocket? You said you've never been there.'

'Actually,' he says, 'now that I think about it – I remember finding it on a seat on the train. A few days ago. I meant to drop it to the hotel but I must have forgotten.'

I know he's lying – I *feel* it. Without another word, I walk out and head back to the house.

The girls wolf down their pizzas then ask if they can have ice cream. Max still hasn't emerged from his office, but that's a blessing.

'You had ice cream yesterday,' I remind Poppy.

'But that was *ages* ago. And Ivy didn't.'

'I had cake,' Ivy says. 'At my grandma's house. Chocolate cake.'

My mind is too full to expend energy debating with Poppy, so I give in.

After dinner, with their stomachs full of ice cream, they beg to go outside to play. '*Please*, Mummy,' Poppy pleads.

I shouldn't let them – it's nearly seven, and the temperature's dropped another five degrees. But they're nowhere near ready for bed yet. 'Maybe just for five minutes.'

'Come on, Ivy, let's play football,' Poppy suggests, grabbing Ivy's hand.

I begin clearing up the kitchen. I'm tempted to leave the mess to see how Max will react. I've been tiptoeing around him for weeks now, and all this time he's been lying. Hiding things.

Something smashes outside. I run out, shouting Poppy's name.

'It was an accident,' she cries. 'Ivy did it by mistake.'

I take in the scene: the broken office window, cracks spread across it like a spider's web. Max yelling so loudly that Ivy covers her ears and runs into the house. Poppy in floods of tears, running after her.

'Look what she's done!' Max shouts. 'Jesus Christ! I told you this was a bad idea.'

I glare at him. 'Calm down. It was an accident.'

'They shouldn't have been out here this late. I told you.'

'You need to get control of yourself, Max,' I hiss. 'They were just playing. It was an accident.'

He takes a moment before answering, and slowly his face resumes its normal colour. 'I know. I could just do without this,' he says, heading back to the office. 'I'll apologise later.' My confronting him about the key card has clearly got to him.

Inside, the girls are holding hands, cowering by the kitchen door. 'Daddy was horrible to Ivy,' Poppy says. 'Now she's really sad.'

I rush over to them and give Ivy a hug. 'I'm sorry Max shouted at you. He shouldn't have. He's just shocked that the ball smashed the window. He was just trying to work.' I defend him only because it's the right thing to do for Poppy's sake.

'I'm sorry. I didn't mean to,' Ivy sobs.

'At least there's not glass everywhere,' Poppy says. 'It could have been much worse.'

'I know, sweetheart. Come on, girls. Let's get upstairs and ready for bed – you've got school in the morning.'

It's another half an hour before the girls are tucked up in bed, Ivy on a blow-up mattress on Poppy's floor.

I'll have to let Sarah know what's happened tonight; there's no way I'll keep Max's behaviour from her, and Ivy is bound to tell her anyway. As it should be. 'I'm sorry about Poppy's dad,' I say to Ivy, as I turn off the light. 'Are you okay?'

She smiles, her small teeth shining in the darkness. 'It's okay. I think he shouted because he's so sad.'

'Well, we will have to replace the window, but I don't think he's feeling sad exactly. More worried, I reckon.'

Ivy pulls the duvet up to her neck. 'Not sad because of the window,' she says. 'He's sad because of his friend who's dead.'

My body turns cold. 'What friend?'

'The one everyone's talking about. I think her name's Alice. Like Alice in Wonderland. Max must be sad because they were friends. And now she's dead.'

I walk over to Ivy and kneel beside her mattress. 'What do you mean, Ivy? Why do you think Max was friends with someone called Alice?'

'They *were*. I saw them together. When Grandma took me to Brent Cross. They looked like friends. They were laughing and holding hands. Like me and Poppy do.'

My throat dries up and I struggle to speak. 'Are you sure it was Max? I think it must have been someone else. Lots of people might look like Max.'

'No!' Ivy protests, thumping the bed. 'It was Max. And he was with the woman I saw on Mummy's phone. The dead woman.'

FOUR

The hiss of the coffee machine downstairs wakes me. I turn over and check my phone; it's only five past five, yet Max is up already. This is nothing out of the ordinary – his day always begins long before most people's, but what's different is that he barely slept last night. It's hard not to reach conclusions about what's weighing on his mind.

After I'd put the girls to bed last night, I went downstairs and confronted him about Ivy seeing him with a woman at Brent Cross.

'I haven't been to Brent Cross in years,' he said, casually shrugging. 'She must have mistaken someone else for me.'

'She was certain it was you. And you were with a woman.'

Max had laughed. 'Hannah, she's a five-year-old kid. Lots of people look like me. It's not like I've got any really distinguishing features. And you can't seriously be accusing me of cheating?'

No, what I was accusing him of was much worse, he just didn't know it.

When I woke at two a.m., my mind in conflict, I went

downstairs to call the police, but I couldn't do it. I need to be sure before I throw Poppy's life into turmoil.

What I don't want to admit to myself is that perhaps I'm stalling because he's my husband and I don't want to believe it. Is it just denial?

'You're up early,' Max says when I join him downstairs. He's standing by the window, a cup of coffee in his hand. I focus on the steam rising from his mug, force myself to stay composed.

'Couldn't sleep,' I say, grabbing a mug from the cupboard. I study his face and realise I'm staring at a stranger. He might look the same, but he's not. I know it. I *feel* it.

'I'll have to get that sorted out.' He gestures to the garden office. 'It's not safe. Poppy needs to stay away from it. I should take the glass out,' he says, almost to himself. 'That might be better.'

'You shouldn't have shouted at Ivy,' I say.

'I did apologise to her. And I'll call Sarah. Explain what happened. I'm sure she'll understand. She's not exactly a passive parent, is she?'

When Max puts his mug down on the island and reaches for me, pulling me towards him, I don't recognise the feel of his arms, or the scent of his body. 'I love you,' he whispers into my hair. 'I love you so much. Will you always remember that? No matter what?'

I'm frozen for a moment, unsure how to react, until a vision of Alice Hughes explodes into my head. I pull away and turn back to making my coffee. Max watches me closely, but he doesn't comment.

'I'll take the girls to school,' he offers. 'Maybe you can go back to bed for a bit. You never have a chance to lie in. I'm sure Cole can manage in the shop.'

His offer is such a shock I can't help but wonder why he's made it. 'You said you had a meeting.'

'Can't you just accept I'm trying to do something nice?' He

empties the rest of his coffee into the sink and stalks off without looking back.

It's a relief to be in the shop before Cole today. Even though I know he won't like it, I text him and tell him he doesn't need to come in until this afternoon. We're not likely to be busy, and the only company I can face right now is my own.

Upstairs in the staffroom, I take the key card from the zipped pocket of my bag, staring at the hotel logo as if it will disappear if I look hard enough. Then all of this will go away.

I need to take it to the police. Maybe it has Alice's finger-prints all over it, intermingled with Max's and now mine. I'm sure they have the technology to separate different sets. Those fingerprints are an invisible message. The answer to Alice's death. Sweat pools on my lower back. I slip the card back in my bag and take it downstairs.

I jump at the sight of a figure standing there, watching me.

'What are you doing? You scared the hell out of me!'

'Sorry,' Cole says. 'Are you okay?' He squints at me. 'You don't look okay.'

'Course I'm not. The door was locked and I wasn't expecting you to be standing there. What are you doing here? You're not meant to be coming in until later.'

'I know,' he says. 'It might get busy.' He peels off his navy trench coat. It's far too thin for this weather, but Cole waits until minus temperatures before he'll wear a warmer coat. 'And it's Katy's day off.' He snorts. 'Actual authorised day off, that is.' He lowers his voice. 'People are taking a bit of an interest in our little high street since the other night. It's swarming with people. I've never seen Putney so busy.'

'But those people are hardly going to be stopping in here to buy books, are they?' I snap.

'They might,' he says. 'It gives them an excuse to linger.' He raises his eyebrows. 'Aren't you glad of the company? You never know who'll walk in here. Don't you feel a bit creeped out? There's a murderer out there somewhere.'

'Whoever it was, I'm sure they're miles away from Putney by now.' My words stick in my throat, sharp like knives.

'Not necessarily. You read all the time about murderers sticking around to see what happens. Turning up at funerals. That kind of thing.'

I stare at him.

'I've read a lot of true crime books,' he says, shrugging. 'It all helps with research for my novel.'

Cole has been working on his novel for as long as I've known him. He doesn't talk much about it, but every now and then he'll throw out a reference to it. Just to remind people he's writing it. 'Anyway, I'm not scared,' I insist. 'The police think it was someone she knew. So there's no reason whoever did it would come looking for me, is there?' Saying this turns my blood to ice, and my voice sounds as if it belongs to someone else. Someone who's narrating my life.

'I thought I'd come in anyway,' Cole says, stalking off to the coffee bar.

All morning I feel his eyes on me, just like yesterday, and I wonder if his scrutiny is real or imagined. I'm relieved when the phone rings and he becomes too engrossed in a conversation to pay me any attention.

It doesn't last, though, and as soon as he's finished the call, Cole saunters over to me. 'That was my neighbour Nadia again. She asked to speak to you but I held her off.' He smiles. 'She's wondering if you can fit her book club in yet. She's still after Fridays.'

I finish rearranging the fiction chart shelves. 'She only asked again a couple of weeks ago.'

'I know.' He shrugs. 'She's just desperate. She lives for that reading club, and our flats just aren't big enough to host all her friends. Nadia's a very popular woman.'

'I'd like to help, but I've already told her we have a book club here. It's just not feasible to fit in another one.'

He nods. 'Shame. She's lived in Putney her whole life and knows a lot of people in the community. She could bring in new customers. Make them think twice about ordering on Amazon.'

I'm about to tell Cole that my hands are tied, but he speaks before I have a chance to respond. 'And you won't believe this, but she knew Alice Hughes.'

Time stands still for a moment, and Alice's name seems to echo around the shop. 'Did she?' I try to keep my voice casual, while my heart races.

'Yep.' Cole nods. 'Nadia's daughter went to school with Alice. They were good friends, apparently.'

I let this information sink in. It's the closest I've been able to get to finding out anything more about Alice. 'Maybe tell her I'll pop over tonight after work. I'm happy to go there – it will save her a trip out in this weather. We can go through everything then. I can't make any promises, though. And it definitely can't be a Friday.'

'Will do,' Cole says. 'Funny, it's not like you to change your mind once it's made up.' He shrugs. 'I wonder what happened to her cats. Poor things.'

'What?'

'Nadia told me Alice had two cats. I hope someone's taken them in.'

Harwood Court is a large, six-storey block of flats by the leisure centre, a short walk from the bookshop. I've known Cole for years, but I've only been in his building once before, so it feels strange setting foot in here now. As if something is out of place.

He'd invited Mum and me to have Christmas drinks here a few years ago, when Mum still owned the shop. I'd been desperate to leave after about half an hour, but with the patience of a saint, Mum made sure we stayed until well after ten p.m. 'Be kind to Cole,' she'd whispered, when he'd gone to replenish our drinks. 'I think he's lonely.'

This is what I think of as my shoes clack along the polished wood floor and I make my way upstairs to the second storey.

Nadia's door is directly opposite Cole's, reminding me of the flat Max and I shared in Brixton when we first got together.

'Well, I've been waiting for this,' Nadia says, ushering me inside. I've only ever seen her in the shop before, so it's strange seeing her in her own home. It's too personal, and I immediately feel guilty. Her curly black hair is tied in a low pony tail and she has reading glasses perched on her head. She must be a similar age to my mum, and just like my mum, it's clear that Nadia makes an effort with her hair and make-up. 'My ladies will be pleased. Finally. We're all a bit sick of being crammed in here every Friday night.' She lifts her arms up. 'See for yourself. Not enough space to swing a cat,' she says. 'And someone always ends up sitting on the floor.' She tuts. 'Would you like something to drink?'

I don't really want anything, but I need this visit to last as long as possible. 'Tea would be great, thanks.'

I follow her into the small galley kitchen, which, other than the pale green colour scheme, looks identical to Cole's.

'Cole said you've lived in Putney your whole life,' I say, studying the family photos she's arranged on her fridge. I quickly work out she must have at least three children.

'Yes, I have. Hmm. That makes me sound boring, doesn't it? But why leave somewhere you find perfect? And I've travelled a lot. I'm not one of these people who doesn't even have a passport.' Nadia pulls out a bag of cat food and pours kibbles into a bowl on the floor. 'You don't mind cats, do you? Not allergic or anything? Sorry, too late, even if you are. Pixie's fur gets every-where.' She rolls her eyes. 'But I love that creature to pieces. I keep telling Cole he should get a pet. Treat you far better than any human.' She smiles, but I sense that sadness lurks behind it. 'I think a dog would suit him, don't you?'

I nod, wondering which of her many questions I'm even answering.

'You're married, aren't you?' she asks, as she sets about making tea. 'Shame. I worry about Cole, you know.'

'Why? He's happy. He doesn't need anyone to make him feel whole.'

'Oh, I know all that. I miss my Mo. He died when the kids were quite young. My youngest was still in secondary school.' She pauses. 'We all need a bit of company, don't we?' She bends down to stroke Pixie, a ginger tabby cat, who has appeared from nowhere and starts munching kibbles by Nadia's feet. 'Even if it's company from a pet.' She studies me. 'And the way Cole talks about you—'

'What?'

'Oh, nothing. I just mean it's all a shame. Anyway, you didn't come here to talk about Cole. How about my book club then? Is that a yes to Fridays?' She hands me my tea.

'Um, actually, we can't do Fridays, but I'd like to offer you Tuesdays. Would that be okay?'

Nadia sighs. 'Hmm. It's not ideal. But it's better than doing it here. Okay. I'll take it. Thank you.' She smiles. 'Good job you've agreed as I've already told everyone. Oh, don't worry. I said it wasn't definite, but I did mention you were coming here to discuss it.' She wanders past me into the living room, gesturing for me to follow.

'Anyway, it makes a change from what we've been talking about the last couple of days. Poor Alice Hughes.'

'Yes, Cole said you knew her,' I say, sitting on her sofa. It's too soft and sags in the middle, forcing me to lean forward.

Nadia sighs. 'Yes. She was best friends with my daughter in secondary school. They drifted a bit after leaving – that happens, doesn't it? – but I know they kept in touch. Eloise is devastated. She lives in Canada now. Met her husband when she was working over there and decided not to come back. She visits, of course, but her life is there now.' She shakes her head. 'I don't like her being so far away. Especially when senseless things like this happen.' She bats away a tiny fruit fly that hovers around her. 'And have you seen all that stuff they're saying about poor Alice online? It's vile.'

It's clear that Nadia is a talker – something I can use to my advantage. 'I know. And I'm so sorry. It must be so hard for your daughter.'

She nods. 'And for me. I bumped into Alice a few weeks ago one morning at the train station and I noticed she was a bit off. She looked so thin. Frail. I know health and fitness is her life, but she didn't look well. She looked as if she hadn't eaten properly for months. And I tried talking to her while we waited for the train, but she just stared at me with this vacant expression, as if she wasn't registering anything I said.' She leans forward. 'As soon as I got home from work that evening, I called Eloise and told her to check in on Alice. She messaged her but got no reply. Which is strange, because Alice always replied to Eloise's messages. Maybe not straight away – but eventually.'

'That is strange,' I agree. 'Have you told the police all of this? It might be relevant.'

'Yes, I went down there straight away when I heard. I don't know what good it will do, but I had to let them know.'

'What do you think was going on with Alice?' I venture, hoping I don't sound too desperate for answers.

Nadia's eyes narrow and her lips straighten into a thin line. I'm overstepping and I need to be careful.

'I couldn't comment on that,' she says, suddenly guarded. 'I'm not one for gossip.'

Taking a risk, I push on. 'I read somewhere that she had a boyfriend,' I lie. 'Perhaps they were having problems?'

Lines appear on Nadia's forehead. 'Eloise mentioned there was an ex in the picture, but I think that ended a long time ago, so I don't think it was anything to do with that.'

If there was an ex, then Alice kept him out of her public sphere, which is unusual for someone her age. Even if she didn't want photos of him plastered all over the internet, none of her words even hinted that she had someone in her life.

Because he was married?

'Anyway,' Nadia says. 'About my book club night – when can I start?'

It's another hour before I manage to prise myself away from Nadia's.

Thankfully, Sarah offered to have Poppy over for a sleepover tonight, so there's nothing to rush home for. I have no idea where Max is, but I'm in no hurry to face whatever version of my husband he'll be tonight.

As soon as Nadia shuts her door, across the hallway Cole's opens and he peers out. 'How did it go? I'm betting she talked you into it. Nadia's very persuasive.'

Cole looks different dressed in jeans and a sweater – almost as if someone else has chosen his clothes for him. I've only ever seen him in smart trousers and shirts.

'Were you waiting for me?' I ask.

'No.' His cheeks flush. 'I heard voices and knew you must be leaving so I came out to see how it went.'

A wave of guilt washes over me. I shouldn't be hard on Cole.

'Come in and have coffee,' he says, smiling. 'I've just made a fresh lot. None of that instant stuff.'

I'm about to tell him I need to get back, but quickly reconsider. He looks so pleased with himself, and I'm in no hurry. 'Maybe just water for me,' I say.

Even though Cole's flat is identical to Nadia's, it feels completely different. While Nadia's is tastefully decorated with bright colour-coordinated accessories and ornaments, Cole's place is full of mismatched furniture and beige walls. Framed eighties film posters hang in the lounge, and there's a grey rug covering the parquet floor. I hadn't taken much of it in the last time I was here with Mum – I'd been too worried about whether or not Cole would easily accept me taking over the shop. Mum had assured me that he had no interest in wanting to buy the business himself – his grand plans of becoming a published author meant he was happy to be an employee.

'You didn't answer my question,' Cole says, as he gets my water and sets about pouring his coffee. 'Did Nadia talk you into it?'

'You're right – she's very persuasive. I told her it will have to be Tuesdays, though.'

He laughs. 'She's like a dog with a bone until she gets her way. Bless her. I know it's a pain, but at least she'll stop harassing us now. I'm happy to stay late on Tuesdays.'

'You already do more than enough. I'm fine doing it.'

'D'you know how I spend most of my evenings?' He doesn't wait for an answer. 'I go for long walks around Putney. Taking everything in. I know every inch of the place, while most people sleepwalk through their lives, barely noticing what's right in front of them.' He smiles. 'I don't mean you. You're not like that.' He looks away and stirs the coffee. 'I see things, you know.'

'What things?' Holding my breath, I force myself to look at him.

'Things people don't want me to see.' He hands me my mug. 'Anyway, shall we sort out this book club, then?'

A foreboding silence wraps itself around me when I step inside the house. It's nearly ten p.m. – Max should have been home by now. I call his name, even though I know the house is empty. His BMW wasn't in the drive, and he's never in bed this early.

'Max?' I repeat. 'Are you here?'

Nothing but silence, and the echo of my voice.

I check each room in the house, and then go out to the office, peering in through the broken window.

Walking back to the house, I call Max's phone, putting it on speaker. It goes straight to voicemail, an artificial voice telling me to leave a message. Uneasiness seeps through my veins – Max's phone is always on. *But was it when he was at that hotel? Did I ever try to call him when he was with Alice? If Ivy is right. She's a child, though – how do I know for sure?*

The doorbell chimes, loud and shrill in the silence.

I rush through to the hall, relieved, even though it's not like Max to forget his key. This is just one more thing that's out of character. Throwing open the door, I stop short when I register who's standing there. Not Max.

Two uniformed male police officers.

My insides feel as if they've exploded, and pain surges through my body. 'Poppy! Where's my daughter?' I clamp my hand to my mouth.

One of the officers shakes his head. 'This isn't about your daughter. Are you Hannah Chambers?'

'Yes.'

'I'm PC Collins and this is PC Jarvis. Can we come in, please?'

I hold the door open and they step inside.

'Is there somewhere we can all sit down?' PC Collins asks.

I lead them through to the living room, my whole body numb. *Is this about Alice Hughes?* 'I don't want to sit,' I say. 'What's happened?'

'We're sorry to have to tell you this,' PC Jarvis says, 'but your husband Max Chambers has been attacked. He's in intensive care.'

FIVE

My legs buckle as I stare at the two police officers. One of them – PC Jarvis, I think, although I've already forgotten which is which – is well over six foot, with hair that's a similar colour to Max's. His blonde, younger-looking colleague, although far from short, is dwarfed standing beside him. I fold my arms across my body, a gesture I seem to have no control over. Although their words are loud and succinct, they don't feel real. None of this does.

'He was attacked near his office,' PC Jarvis says. 'We're assuming he was on his way home.'

'This must be a mistake.'

The pitying smile on the taller officer's face tells me I'm wrong. 'Paramedics were able to identify him from the work ID in his pocket. IBM Financial Services. York Road.' His mouth twists into a half-grimace. 'Emergency Services would have called you immediately, but your husband's phone and wallet weren't at the scene.'

'Is he... is he okay?' I'm seconds away from throwing up.

'They're doing everything they can,' the younger officer says. 'We don't have any more details at the moment.'

'What happened to him? When?' Adrenalin kicks in and I stand up, unsure what I'm supposed to be doing.

'He was found in an alleyway near his office building. Early indications are that it was possibly a mugging, but it's too early to determine that,' the tall officer explains. His words might as well be straight from a television drama. Not my life. 'You might want to get to the hospital as soon as you can. St Thomas'. He was beaten badly. I'm sorry, but it looks like they left him for dead.'

Hearing these words should cause me to double over in pain, or force tears to flood from my eyes. But now all I feel is numb. 'My daughter. I need to tell Poppy.'

'Where is she tonight?' the shorter one asks.

'Staying the night at my friend's house. Having a sleepover with her best friend.'

The officers glance at each other. 'You might want to wait until morning, then, given the time.'

I nod, though this is the last thing I want to do. I need Poppy to be safe at home with me.

'We can give you a lift to St Thomas' hospital.'

Somehow, I manage to thank them before I grab my coat and follow them to their car.

Hospitals are strange places in the dead of night. For the most part, eerily silent, as if everyone's been abandoned. And any sounds are amplified, demanding attention. My trainers squeak too loudly on the floor as I make my way to the intensive care unit.

The two officers escort me, and when we get there I see another uniformed police officer outside. The three of them stop to talk in low voices, while I look through the glass panel in the door. Max is in the bed closest to the door.

Even though my heart aches for him, the man lying under

those stark white hospital sheets is no longer Max. Not the Max I love.

Without checking if it's okay, I leave the officers and step inside the room. A nurse at one of the other beds glances up. Smiling, she comes to meet me at the door. She's around my age with a round face that immediately puts me at ease. 'Can I help?' She has a soft Irish accent, infusing the room with warmth.

Shock at seeing Max lying here like this – at all of this being real – renders me speechless, but I manage to nod.

'I know it looks bad,' she says. 'But we've seen people pull through with even more traumatic injuries. Please keep that in mind.' She smiles. 'And don't worry about the police being out there. It's just a precaution until they find out more about what happened to Max.'

I stare at my husband, and my chest constricts. There's barely a patch on his face that isn't covered with black and purple bruises, and his head is tightly bandaged. His eyelids are enlarged and swollen; even if he could open them, he wouldn't be able to see clearly.

Despite everything, I feel the sting of tears welling in my eyes.

'The doctor will come and speak to you as soon as he can,' the nurse says. 'He's just dealing with another emergency.'

'Can *you* tell me?'

'We've done a CT scan and he has an intracerebral haemorrhage. A bleed on the brain.'

I gasp, staring at Max.

'Thankfully, it's small, and we're monitoring him. We might need to control his blood pressure. He also has a fractured clavicle – his collarbone – but he won't need surgery for that. It will eventually heal on its own. It will be painful, though.'

I try to take in these words, but it's too much – all I can do is stare at Max.

She glances outside. 'They've been waiting to speak to him, but we've told them they can't. Not yet. I know they've got a job to do but so have we – and our patients' wellbeing comes first. But you can sit with him. Even if he doesn't open his eyes right now, I'm sure it would help him to see you when he wakes up.'

The nurse might be sure of this but I'm not. I don't know what's been going through Max's mind these last few months. Or what he's been doing. Is it Alice he'll want to see?

I slip into the chair beside Max's bed and stare at him. Bodies are so fragile, so easily wrecked. Minutes tick by, but eventually his eyelids start to flutter. I look up, searching for the nurse, but she's gone now, tending to someone else who needs her.

Unsure what to say to Max, I don't move.

Slowly, he turns his head and looks at me, and even though it's hard to see the expression beneath his blood-soaked, bruised skin, I can tell he's confused. 'Hannah?' He winces.

Instinctively I take his hand, trying not to flinch at the feel of his rough skin. 'If it hurts, try not to talk.'

'What... happened to me?' His voice is frail – he doesn't sound like himself.

I take a deep breath. 'You were attacked leaving work. The police don't know who did it. They think you were mugged. Your wallet and phone were taken.'

'I don't remember,' he says.

'None of it? Do you remember leaving work?'

'No.' He closes his puffy eyelids again, and grips my hand. Again I fight the urge to snatch my hand away. 'I'm supposed to be in Lisbon for the conference,' he says. 'I can't be here.'

Now I am the one who's flummoxed. 'What conference?'

'The annual conference. I'm meant to be there with Peter. I've got to get to the airport.'

And then it makes sense. 'No, Max. That was in May. And Peter left straight after that conference. It's November.'

Max winces again and he tries to pull himself up. 'I have to go to Lisbon.'

I look around for the friendly Irish nurse, but she's disappeared. 'Stop! You've had a bleed on your brain. You can't go anywhere.' I stand up. 'I'll go and find someone.'

Outside in the corridor, around the corner and out of sight of the police officers, I lean against the wall and take a deep breath. I'm doing everything I should be doing as a wife, yet I can't trust the man who lies in that bed. After a moment, I compose myself enough to look for the nurse.

She's at the nurses' station, filling out some forms, and she looks up as I approach. I notice her name badge. Orla. A pretty name. And she's in a place that's far from pretty. 'Everything okay?' she asks, clicking her pen closed and placing it down.

'Um, he woke up. And he's saying that it's May and he has to be at a conference in Lisbon. He's trying to get up.'

The nurse frowns. 'Okay. I'm coming.'

'He went to that conference and he can't remember it,' I tell her as we're walking back to Max.

She nods. 'Retrograde amnesia is quite common after a severe head injury. The police will love that, won't they? I'll let the doctors know. Try not to worry.' She checks her watch. 'I need to do his blood pressure and pulse check now.'

I watch from the hallway as the nurse talks to Max, trying to calm him down and persuade him that he's not in a state to go anywhere.

And meanwhile, all I can think is that I wish Max's injuries and amnesia were the only things to be concerned about.

My throat is dry and I need to get some water, so I walk away, heading to the nearest vending machine.

And then I keep walking, ambling down corridors, navigating this maze of a hospital, getting further away from the ICU.

I don't know how long I walk for, but eventually I make my way back to Max, and stand by his bedside.

He's asleep again, his chest rising softly under the hospital sheet. I watch him for a moment, and tears pool in my eyes. *What have you done?*

Dabbing my eyes with my jacket sleeve, I leave him to sleep.

Sarah opens her front door within seconds and pulls me inside. She's dressed in black joggers and a loose pink T-shirt, her hair tied back in a messy bun, her face free of make-up. She already knows about Max – as I'd sat in the Uber on the way home last night, I'd messaged her to tell her what happened to him; writing it was easier than making a phone call.

'My God, Hannah. I can't believe this.' She hugs me so tightly I feel as though I'll suffocate. 'I'm so sorry this happened. Is he okay? And are *you* okay?' She barely pauses for breath.

I nod. And when I pull back and look at her, I notice her eyes glisten with tears. 'Max is stable. And I'm... doing all right, I think. I just need to tell Poppy what's happened.' I peer past her.

'The girls are playing upstairs. They're still in their pyjamas.'

'I know it's early. I just needed to see Poppy. Give her a hug.'

Sarah glances towards the stairs, lowering her voice. 'I haven't said anything. Thought it might be better coming from you.' She takes my arm. 'Come and sit down before you tell her. Take a moment. The girls can play for a bit more.'

We sit on Sarah's sofa, and I try to gather my thoughts.

'What exactly happened?' she asks. The information I gave her in my message was brief and vague, so it's only natural she'll have questions.

'Max was attacked when he was leaving work. He was

found in an alleyway. If someone hadn't noticed him, he could have...' I trail off, drowning in sadness as I picture Max, caught unawares as he made his way to the station. Something he's done a thousand times before. He would have been preoccupied, and not noticed anyone coming up behind him. Until it was too late.

'What do the police think happened?'

'Apparently, they've got CCTV images but they're not great quality. It was a male. That's about the only lead they've got so far.'

Without a word, Sarah moves next to me and hugs me, and I let myself be comforted by her silent gesture.

'And what have the doctors said?' Sarah sucks in her breath. She and Max have always got along. They might have bonded through me initially, but I've often thought that even if I wasn't in the picture, they would have been friends. I wonder if she knows about him shouting at Ivy the other night.

I recount every detail I can remember them telling me, comforted that Sarah will understand the medical terminology.

'I've dealt with a lot of head trauma like Max's. He's going to be okay. It won't be easy, but it could have been so much worse.'

'He woke up and spoke to me. He thinks it's May. He can't remember the last six months.'

Sarah nods. 'That's common after this kind of injury. It's awful for Max, and all of you, but he's alive. Try to focus on that.'

I lower my voice. 'I need to ask you something.'

Sarah leans forward and places her hand on my arm. 'Of course. I'll watch Poppy as much as I can. I owe you for all the times you've helped me by having Ivy. You don't want to be dragging her to the hospital every day. And it's not exactly close by. Mum will have her when I'm at work—'

'No, it's not that.' I hesitate, unsure whether to bring this up now. 'When Ivy slept at our house the other night, she told me she saw Max the day that Carol took her to Brent Cross.'

'Mum's always dragging her there. They went a couple of weeks ago.' Sarah rolls her eyes. 'She loves shopping. My daughter will turn into a shopaholic one day. All because of Mum.'

Carol has never met Max so there's no point asking Sarah if I can speak to her.

'Does Ivy know anything about Alice Hughes?'

Sarah's nose crinkles, and a deep crease appears on her forehead. 'The woman in the hotel? Why on earth would she? What's that got to do with anything?' She pauses. 'Oh, hang on... I was on the sofa reading about it on my phone the night it happened and didn't realise Ivy was standing right behind me. She insisted she'd seen her before. I didn't pay it much attention. Ivy might have just thought she recognised her from somewhere. Maybe one of the school mums looks like her. I'd forgotten all about it until now. Why do you ask?'

I study Sarah's face, wondering how much I should tell her about this. If it was anything else then I would have filled her in on every detail. But Max is my husband. This is my marriage. And I need to work it out for myself first. It wasn't my intention to drag Sarah into this, and I don't plan to say anything about the hotel key card, but I need to know if Ivy really did see them together. Carol might be able to verify if Ivy mentioned recognising anyone at Brent Cross.

'It's a bit weird,' I begin. 'But the other evening, Max shouted at Ivy for accidentally smashing the office window and—'

'I know all about that. Which reminds me – I'm paying for it.'

I shake my head. 'When I put the girls to bed, Ivy told me she'd seen Max with Alice Hughes at Brent Cross. She said he might be sad now because his friend is dead.'

Sarah's face wrinkles. 'That's weird. Max didn't know her, did he?'

'No.'

'Then Ivy must have got it wrong. I can ask Mum if Ivy mentioned anything at the time. It is weird that he'd be at Brent Cross with a woman. Very weird. But... maybe it was someone who looked like Max. Alice was a personal trainer, wasn't she? She'd have no reason to have any dealings with Max's company.'

'That's what I thought. I just wanted to check.'

'I don't know what to suggest. If I were you, I'd be going out of my mind. Worrying. Wondering. But then, I have trust issues, don't I? Maybe that's clouding my judgement. Let's think logically. Ivy's always saying stuff. She gets things muddled sometimes. You know, speaks before she thinks. I guess that's completely normal at her age.' Sarah pauses. 'Did you ask Max if he knew Alice Hughes?'

I swallow the heavy lump in my throat. 'He doesn't.'

'Then either Ivy saw Max with someone else, or she saw Alice Hughes with someone who looks like Max?'

'Maybe.'

Sarah jumps up. 'Only one way to find out.' She walks to the living room door. 'Ivy? Can you come here a sec, please?'

The girls thud downstairs, bursting into the room.

'Mummy!' Poppy says, running over to me and throwing her arms around me. 'I don't want to go yet. I haven't even had breakfast.' She flaps her arms. 'And I'm still in my pyjamas.'

'Sorry,' Sarah says, standing up. 'I was about to get them something.'

I pat the seat next to me and Poppy jumps on the sofa.

'Listen, sweetheart,' I begin. 'Daddy had an accident last night on his way home from work, and he's in hospital. He's doing okay, but he'll need a lot of looking after when he gets home. He's very hurt.'

Poppy stares at me for a moment before her face crumples and she bursts into tears. I hold her tightly and stroke her hair. 'I want Daddy,' she cries, her tears soaking through my T-shirt.

'He'll be okay,' I assure her, even though I'm not convinced of this myself. 'We'll make sure he is. We have to look after him together, okay?'

She nestles into me, her fingers clinging tightly onto my arms. 'Does this mean he can't go to work?'

'Not for a while,' I say.

Sarah comes over to give her a hug too. 'How about you go to the kitchen and choose some cereal for you and Ivy?'

Poppy rushes off and Sarah turns to Ivy. 'Listen, sweetheart. I need to ask you something and I'm going to need you to have a really good think, okay?'

Ivy nods.

'Did you see Poppy's daddy at Brent Cross when you were with Grandma? It would have been a few weeks ago.'

Ivy glances at me before nodding.

'And you're sure it was him? Was it definitely Poppy's dad?'

Once more, she looks at me before answering. 'Yes. I'm sure.' She shrugs.

'You don't seem sure,' Sarah says. 'Was it definitely Poppy's daddy?'

Ivy's nose wrinkles and she chews her lip. 'Yes, Mummy.'

Sarah grabs her phone from the coffee table and scrolls through it. When she's found what she's looking for she holds it out to Ivy. 'And was he with this woman?'

I catch a glimpse of Alice Hughes's blonde hair. The smile that forces you to notice her.

'That's her!' Ivy says. 'The poor dead lady. Poppy's daddy's friend. The dead one. We walked right past them.'

Sarah gasps. 'Are you sure? Absolutely sure?'

'Yes! I saw them!' Ivy stamps her foot, her face turning red.

'I'm sorry,' Sarah mouths to me before addressing Ivy. 'Did Grandma see them too?'

Ivy shrugs. 'Can I have breakfast, please?'

'It's okay,' I say, even though I'm desperate for answers. 'Don't push her.'

'Let me call Mum now,' Sarah says. 'Maybe she can shed some light on this.'

While Sarah makes the call, I get the girls' breakfast ready.

When Sarah comes back, we huddle by the back door, and talk in low whispers.

'Mum says she can't remember Ivy recognising anyone, and she's sure she'd remember that. Sorry, that doesn't really help, does it? All I can think is that it must have been someone who looks like Max.' Her eyes widen. 'Do you think I need to tell the police? Is it relevant that my daughter thinks she saw Alice Hughes at Brent Cross a few weeks before she was found dead?' She pulls out her phone and I stifle a yell. 'Let me just check what day it must have been.' She scrolls through her phone calendar. 'Oh, here. It was Sunday, two weeks ago. I got called in to cover and had to get Mum to look after Ivy. She wasn't too happy about it as she'd planned a day out shopping.'

Max had gone into the office that Sunday. He'd told me he needed to be at the office to work on an important presentation for a client. Something he couldn't do at home, he'd insisted, where Poppy had been running around the house. 'It definitely wasn't Max,' I tell Sarah. I can't have her suspecting Max, not until I've found out for myself. 'He was at home all day.'

'There you go, then. Problem solved. It definitely wasn't Max who Ivy saw. Good. Not that I thought for one second Ivy was right. I have no idea where she gets this stuff from. Sorry. You don't need this on top of what's happened to Max.' She places a hand on my arm. 'What can I do? Anything, just let me know.'

'Thanks. I'm sorry he shouted at Ivy. He's been under a lot

of pressure with work.' I take a deep breath. 'And now I don't know what's going to happen to him. Will he still be able to do his job?'

Sarah pushes my cup of coffee towards me. 'I wish I could answer that, but we'll have to see how he goes. It will take time. He might have to relearn things. I know that seems scary. But I'm here. I can help.' She hugs me again. 'It's funny, isn't it? Usually it's me coming to you for help. I don't think you've ever needed me for anything major. Is it bad that I'm actually glad I can help you for a change?'

'I understand,' I say. I glance at my coffee and realise I can't stomach anything, even a drink.

'You'll work it all out, though,' Sarah says. 'Most likely without any help from me. You always do. Somehow you always find a way.'

Only this time there might not be a way out.

I study her face, her kind eyes, always ready to do anything for me, as I am for her. 'Sarah, there's something—'

A cereal bowl crashes to the floor and Ivy bursts into tears. 'I didn't mean to!' she shrieks. 'It just fell.'

'Don't worry,' Sarah says, rushing to her side. 'Come on, let's clean it up.'

'Can *I* do it?' Ivy asks.

Sarah wets a dish cloth and hands it to her daughter, watching as Ivy mops up the milk.

'What was it you were saying?' Sarah asks.

'Oh, nothing important. Another time.' The urge to confess all to her has withered away.

'Actually, there's something I wanted to tell you.' Sarah pulls me away from the table, lowering her voice. 'I've been thinking I might try to contact Dean.'

Her comment is so unexpected that it takes me a moment to register what she's just said. 'Dean? Is that a good idea? Why now?'

'I've been thinking about it a lot. Ivy's five now and she's never even seen him. What if she needs a father figure in her life? It's been over five years since we last spoke, and he might have changed. He might want to be in her life now. What if he's divorced? His marriage was a mess anyway.' She sucks in her breath. I know it's hard for Sarah to talk about; it almost destroyed her when she realised she'd been sleeping with a married man.

'Then he knows where to find you. And how can you ever trust him?' I think of Max as I say this, and I know my viewpoint has been skewed. I'm not in a position to give any meaningful advice to Sarah. 'Oh, I don't know. Maybe we need to follow our instinct. Or our hearts. I have no idea if I'm ever doing the right thing.' I pause. 'If you think it's the right thing to do, then I'll support you.'

'I'm sorry, Han. Listen to me going on and on about my issues when you've got so much to deal with. I'll sort it.' She smiles. 'But if I've learnt anything from being your friend, it's that we get through stuff, don't we? To hell and back – right?'

But I notice doubt flicker across her face before she turns her attention to clearing the table. 'Let me have Poppy today,' she says. 'I don't need to be in work until tonight, so it will give you time to go back to the hospital to be with Max. I'll drop her to you on my way to work tonight. Mum will be here with Ivy.'

As much as I don't want to accept Sarah's offer when she's dealing with her own problems, I don't know how Poppy would cope seeing Max in the state he's in. And what kind of wife would I be if I didn't spend my time by Max's side? 'Thanks, I really appreciate it.'

'Don't mention it,' she says.

I explain the plan to Poppy and her eyes brim with tears. 'But I want to see Daddy.'

'I promise you will. He just needs a bit more time to get better. And then I'll take you tomorrow. How's that?'

Reluctantly, she agrees, and Sarah seizes the chance to distract her, grabbing her hand. 'Right then, girls, what shall we do today?'

There's a silver Golf behind me as I pull out of Sarah's road. I only notice it because it's like the car I nearly bought before I settled on this one. After a couple of minutes, I drive past my road, and it's still there.

And when I head through Battersea, towards Vauxhall, the car is right behind me, whichever turning I take, no matter how many lights I stop at or risk going through as they turn amber.

It's too much of a coincidence that the car would also be going to St Thomas' hospital from Putney. I glance in the rearview mirror and try to get a look at the driver, but all I can tell is that the person behind the wheel seems to be male.

The closer I get to the hospital, the more uneasiness creeps in. Has this got something to do with Max's attack?

Then just as I pull into the car park, the silver Golf speeds past me.

And I'm left wondering whether I'm panicking unduly, or whether I have more to fear than I've realised.

SIX

Extract from the *Wandsworth Times* online:

> Metropolitan Police continue to investigate the murder of thirty-year-old personal trainer Alice Hughes, whose body was found at the River Walk Hotel in Putney on Wednesday.
>
> DCI Michaela Spears, who is leading the investigation, urges anyone with any information to come forward as soon as possible. 'This is a particularly horrific crime,' she says. 'And we're doing all we can to support Alice's family. They just want answers.'
>
> DCI Spears confirmed that unfortunately at the time of the incident, CCTV cameras at the hotel weren't operational. Therefore, police are relying on witnesses to come forward and are carrying out extensive interviews with everyone who was staying at the hotel.

The hospital feels less bleak with daylight filtering through the floor-to-ceiling windows. It's a hive of activity this morning, unlike at night when most patients sleep, and the body language of staff suggests less urgency.

There's a different police officer outside Max's room, and he doesn't smile as I approach. I've been told it's for Max's protection; they're not sure if whoever did this to him will come back to finish what they started.

I've been severed in two; half of me wanting to run to Max and the other half wanting to run *from* him. I need to know how he's tied to Alice Hughes.

Max is asleep, hooked up to a drip, machines beeping around him. 'Do you know Alice Hughes?' I whisper, leaning close to his ear. He doesn't move, but I wonder if somehow my words will make it into his consciousness and stir up a dormant memory. If he opens his eyes, I will show him a picture of Alice, young and vibrant. Alive. And see if there's any flicker of recognition on his face.

'Morning.' A dark-haired nurse walks in and begins checking Max's blood pressure. She moves with purpose, brisk and skilful. 'He had a challenging night,' she says. 'He didn't sleep well, and got very anxious. He tried to leave several times, and ripped out his canula.'

'Is he... will he—'

'He's doing okay now. His body's finally given in to sleep. The doctors are concerned about the bleed, and that he can't remember the last few months, but that can happen with a traumatic head injury.' She doesn't look at me as she speaks, but continues checking Max.

'Will he start remembering?' *I need him to.*

Her mouth twists. 'Some do but others don't. There might be a permanent gap in his memory.' She looks at me, a thin smile on her face. 'He's doing okay, though.'

I nod, turning back to Max. 'I need to bring our daughter in to see him later. But I don't want her to be scared. Poppy's only five.'

'It's your call, of course, but maybe it's better not to shield kids from reality. I think they can develop more resilience by knowing the harsh realities of life.' She glances at Max. 'It might do him some good to see his little girl. He really is fighting against being here.'

For several hours I sit by Max's side, watching as nurses and other medical staff go about their business. *They have no idea about the man they're looking after.*

On my phone, I scroll through Alice's Facebook and Instagram posts, even though I know every detail of them by now.

Max doesn't open his eyes again. But when he does, I'll be ready with a picture of Alice.

Eventually I force myself up. It's time to bring Poppy here.

Later, Poppy clutches my hand tightly as we walk from the car to the front door. Her small hand is sticky, but I grip hold of it. Our elderly neighbour Morris shuffles past with his dog, smiling and wishing us a good evening. I nod to him, grateful when he walks past us instead of stopping for a chat as he often does.

'Is Daddy going to die?' Poppy asks as I open the door. 'He looks bad. He doesn't even look like Daddy.'

Taking Poppy to the hospital didn't go well. The second she saw Max, her face crumpled and she erupted into tears. We hadn't stayed long, but Max had opened his eyes and smiled when he saw her, lifting his bruised arm to try to wave.

'No, sweetie,' I say. 'It will take some time, but he'll be okay. We'll all be fine. You just have to try to be really brave for him. Do you think you can do that?'

After hesitating for a moment, she nods and steps inside, peeling off her coat.

I'm about to close the door when I see a man walking towards us. He's wearing a grey hooded top with a padded gilet over it, his hood pulled so far down I can barely see his face. Fear courses through my body.

He calls out, pulling back his hood and running towards me. 'Wait!'

'Go upstairs!' I shout to Poppy. 'Quick!'

I try to push the door shut, but he reaches out and lodges his arm in the gap, forcing it open.

And that's when I see his face clearly. The man who spoke to me outside the River Walk Hotel. The one I saw at the school. Is he also the man in the silver Golf?

'What do you want?'

'Just to talk. Please.' He holds up his hands.

I pull out my phone. 'You're scaring my daughter.' I try to shut the door again, but he grabs it, and I'm no match for his strength.

'Please,' he repeats. 'It's about Alice.'

My body freezes, even though I shouldn't be shocked. His presence here could only ever be about Alice Hughes.

He scans my face, and I have no idea what he's expecting to find. 'I wouldn't do this if it wasn't urgent,' he continues. 'Look, I know who you are. And I know why you were outside the hotel that day.'

I inch back. 'What?'

'I think you need my help.' He waits for that to sink in. 'Can we talk now?'

I glance back at the stairs, and see Poppy sitting on the top step, hugging her knees to her chest, watching us.

'I need to get my daughter to bed.' *And to buy myself some time to work out what to do about this man.*

'Please don't be scared of me. I want to help you. I *need* to help you – for both our sakes.'

I study his face, but there's no way to tell if he's genuine. *What choice do I have?* He knows something and I need to find out what that is. 'I need a couple of hours. And not here.'

He nods. 'Do you know that pub by the river? The Boathouse?'

'Yes, I know it.'

'Meet me there.' With a quick flick of his head, he pulls down his hood and walks off.

I watch him disappear, then close the door, pulling across the security chain, and leaning back to let out the breath I've been holding in.

'Mummy? Who was that man?' Poppy slowly walks down the stairs, clutching Whiskers, her cuddly toy cat, to her chest.

'Just someone who wants to see how Daddy is,' I say, because somehow this must be partly true. I take Poppy's hand and lead her back upstairs. 'Listen, I'm going to see if Leda can babysit for an hour – is that okay? And then I can go and talk to this man about Daddy.'

To my relief, Poppy instantly agrees. She likes Leda, a law student who lives across the road. Leda might only be eighteen, but she has younger sisters so always knows how to relate to Poppy.

I send her a message and pray that she's available.

It feels as though I'm in a fugue state as I step inside the pub. While my life is crumbling by the second, everything out of my grasp, normality flitters around me. A Saturday night filled with casual conversations and laughter. And I'm here to meet a stranger. I don't know what this man wants or what I'll say to him. All I know is that whatever conversation takes place won't be good. He knows something. About Max? My stomach lurches as I scan the room.

He's in the corner, with a pint of beer in front of him, staring at his phone. Under the table, his leg taps. He only looks up when I approach, and he slips his phone into his pocket.

'What can I get you?' he asks, standing.

'I don't want anything.'

He looks around. 'Might look a bit weird if you don't have a drink.' He shrugs. 'Water even. I'll get you one.' Without waiting for a reply, he makes his way to the bar. He's left his gilet hanging over his chair, and for a fleeting moment I consider checking his pockets.

But then I remember what happened when I checked Max's that night. And how I'd be living in oblivious bliss if I had never done it. *It's better to know, though. Whatever the cost.*

It's busy in here tonight, and I'm grateful for the loud hum of chatter. It makes this encounter I'm about to have feel less menacing. Whoever this man is, surely he wouldn't do anything in front of so many witnesses.

I watch him closely, making sure he doesn't slip anything into my water.

'Who are you?' I ask, before he's even sat down.

'My name's Taylor Stone.' He holds out his hand, but I don't take it. He shrugs and sits down. 'I already know who you are. Hannah Chambers. Your daughter's called Poppy, and your husband is Max. He works for IBM. You own Whispering Pages.'

Beads of sweat coat my palms and chest. I unzip my coat, but leave it on. 'That stuff isn't hard to find out anywhere. What do you want?'

'Sorry, I know it must make you anxious that I know all that, but I make it my business to know everything about anyone who impacts my life.' He lifts his glass.

I glare at him. 'I don't even know you. I'd never seen you before that day outside the River Walk.'

Resting his elbows on the table, he leans forward. 'It's interesting how people can be connected without even knowing each other. Brought together by events out of their control.' He takes a sip of beer. 'Ah, I see you're confused. Sorry. I'm just a stranger who's turned up in your life, so I don't blame you for not trusting me. But you're here.' He lifts his arms up. 'Why did you come?'

I don't answer.

'Is it because you know that your husband is linked to Alice Hughes? That's why you were at the hotel that day.'

My body becomes a furnace and I reach for my water, glugging it down so fast it scratches my throat. 'Who are you?'

'I'm Alice's friend. A good friend. Turns out, her only real friend.'

Even though I've expected this conversation to be about Max, these words floor me. 'What?' I ask, though I've heard him loud and clear.

He takes a sip of beer, and stares into his glass when he puts it back down. 'Alice was one of my closest friends. She had issues,' he says. 'Lots of them. But she was a good person. And I was the only one she could talk to.' He turns away, but not before I notice the tears pooling in the corners of his eyes. 'She didn't deserve this. All she did was fall in love with the wrong person.' He lifts his glass again, this time taking a longer drink.

My stomach tightens and I grip the edges of my chair, fighting the urge to flee.

'You know who I'm talking about, don't you?' he says, his words laced with accusation. 'Did you know your husband was having an affair with Alice?'

A scream dies silently in my throat, and I can't find any words to replace it. Haven't I suspected this since I found the key card? And since Ivy said she'd seen Max with Alice? It simmered on the edge of my consciousness, but I wouldn't let it fully in. I *couldn't*.

Taylor stares at me. 'Ah, I see maybe you didn't. Unless you're a good actor.'

'I didn't know.' My words are drowned out by the cacophony of other voices in the pub. But I know he hears me. I pull my arms out of my coat, and let it fall.

'Then I'm sorry. I know this is a lot to digest, and you might have trouble believing me, so let me show you this.' He pulls out his phone and scrolls through it, handing it to me when he's found what he's looking for. 'It won't be easy to look at.'

I take the phone, and stare at the picture of Max. His arms wrapped around a woman who isn't me. Their bodies so close it's hard to tell where one ends and the other begins. My husband and Alice Hughes.

Without a word, I rush to the toilets, only just making it to a cubicle before I throw up. My throat aches by the time I emerge, and I head to the sink and rinse my mouth. Once. Twice. The urge to keep rinsing is powerful. To rid myself of the toxicity surrounding me.

My reflection in the mirror is ghostly, drained of my usual colour. I stare at it for a moment, wondering who the woman staring back at me is.

Max, what have you done?

Everything has changed now, but despite the searing pain ravaging my body, I will not be a victim. Alice Hughes is the only victim here.

Back at the table, Taylor springs up when he sees me. 'I'm probably not handling this well,' he begins. 'I... It's... This whole thing has been a mind fuck. I can't believe she's gone. I keep going to call her, then I remember... I should have given you more warning. Are you okay?'

I slide into my seat. 'No, I'm not okay. But that doesn't matter. All that matters is Alice is dead.'

'I think you might need something stronger than water now,' he says, glancing at the bar.

There's no hesitation in my answer. 'Gin and tonic. Not too much ice.'

By the time he's back with my drink, I've managed to compose myself. Knowledge is power, and now that I know about Max, I can face this head on. No more second-guessing, wondering about his guilt. Doubting myself when the evidence is clear.

'Tell me everything,' I demand. 'I want to know all of it.'

He points to my glass. 'Don't you want to have some of that first?'

I take a long swig, wincing as it burns my throat. 'Just tell me.'

'Alice met your husband in this pub. Did you know he came here after work sometimes? Most of the time he just sat with his laptop in the corner, and only had coffee.' A thin smile emerges on his face. 'Alice used to laugh about how he was addicted to coffee. He'd take it over alcohol any day, she said.'

Somehow, hearing something Alice said about Max is worse than knowing they slept together. I drink some more gin. 'Max has never been able to work well in the house. Our daughter's quite... noisy. He needed space away from the noise.'

Taylor nods, as if he understands. 'I don't have kids yet, but I'm sure it can be hard. Well, whatever his reasons, that's how they met. According to Alice, she was a bit drunk and started talking to Max. I think he was trying to brush her off at first, but eventually something changed. Alice said they really connected.' Taylor grimaces. 'Sorry, this can't be easy to hear.'

More gin, slipping uncomfortably down my throat. Numbing whatever this is I'm feeling. Taylor might be right and this is hard to hear, but the more details I have the better I'll be able to face it. 'Like I said, I want to know everything.'

'That's how it started,' he continues. 'They saw each other a lot. I'm guessing Max had a lot of late nights at work?'

I nod, recalling all the times he'd come home shattered but would still go to the garden office to work. 'He has a high-pressure job. Not one you can easily switch off from.'

'I know. Alice told me. He's a financial analyst.'

Part of me wants to scream at him to stop talking about my

husband, while the other part desperately needs more details. 'You said Alice had issues. What did you mean?'

Taylor stares at the table, and it takes him a moment to answer. 'It was all in her past. She suffered from depression. Badly. But she'd put all that behind her and was rebuilding her life. Starting afresh. She'd set up her own personal training business and was making a success of it. Alice was all about physical fitness, not just to look good, but for mental health.'

'Yet she had an affair with a married man?'

Taylor lifts his glass but doesn't drink from it. 'She didn't know Max was married for months. He told her he was single. He didn't wear a wedding ring, did he?'

It's never bothered me that Max has never wanted to wear one. It was just a token. We were married, I didn't need him to wear something if he wasn't comfortable wearing it. Under the table I twist my own ring around my finger, suddenly wanting to rip it off. To leave it abandoned in this pub for someone else to find and do with what they like.

'By the time Alice found out, it was too late. She'd fallen for him. And he promised her they'd be together one day.'

Nausea burns my insides.

'She was happy about this. She told herself your marriage couldn't have been working. That he would have left you even if she hadn't come along.' He takes a long swig of beer. His glass is nearly empty now. 'But then she found out something that changed everything. I think she was leaving him that night she died. Because of something she found out about him.'

My head swirls. 'What?' I hold my breath; I already know that I won't want to hear what Taylor is about to say.

'Max loves Poppy, doesn't he? She means everything to him?'

'Yes.' Despite his irritability over the last few months, I can't fault Max's parenting, and his love for Poppy comes above everything else.

'I don't know how to say this, Hannah.' He pauses again. 'But Max was planning to leave you. And he wanted to make sure he got Poppy too. He told Alice that there was only one way this would ever happen.' Taylor reaches for his glass and downs the last of his beer.

It feels like minutes tick by before he finally speaks.

'He asked Alice to help him. He told her that he'd only ever get full custody of Poppy if you were dead.'

SEVEN

The noise in the pub crushes my head. I stare at Taylor, willing him to disappear, for this all to be something my stressed brain has conjured. 'No,' I say. 'No. That's not true.' I grab my coat and rush from the pub, ignoring all the stares and comments as I barge past people.

Outside, I try to steady my breathing, and wait for the cold air to get to my skin. I'm still coated in a layer of sweat. Alice was lying. Or whoever that man in there is, he's the one lying. Max would never want me dead. If he wanted to leave me, then he'd just do it. It would be amicable. We would co-parent and make the best of the situation.

Max loves Poppy, doesn't he? She means everything to him? These words storm through my head. Max's father left them when he was seven – not much older than Poppy – and he's vowed he would never leave any child of his without a full-time dad.

I feel a heavy hand on my shoulder. 'I'm sorry,' Taylor says. 'I had to tell you. I don't think you're safe, Hannah. And neither was Alice. You need to get away from him. Now.'

'Leave me alone!' I turn and walk towards the high street.

Taylor already knows where I live so it's not as though I need to hide in which direction I'm heading.

A middle-aged couple stops and the man comes towards me. 'Are you okay? Do you need help?'

I tell him I'm fine and scurry away, shame and shock hanging over me.

'Hannah! Please wait!' Taylor pleads.

I spin around. 'What? Haven't you said enough?'

'I need to know what you were doing at the hotel that day. Why did you go there?'

'It's called rubbernecking. I was curious. It's awful, but there you have it.' I resume walking, fully aware that he's right behind me.

'I don't believe you. You know something, don't you?'

'Stay away from me!' My shout is drowned out by the rumbling of a bus. It stops at the bus stop I'm passing, the doors hissing open. I'm tempted to jump on it, wherever it might be going. To get far away from here.

'I need to know what happened to my friend,' Taylor says, throwing up his hands. 'I'm going to the police.'

I stop, and the bus drives on. 'No. Please don't.'

'I would have already but then I saw you at the hotel. Why were you there? You know what happened to Alice!'

I grab Taylor's arm. 'I had nothing to do with it. I didn't know Max was having an affair until you just told me.'

'I don't know what to think. But it doesn't look good, does it? If Max was planning to harm you, then there's every chance he was capable of killing Alice. And I think there's a reason you went to the hotel the day after Alice was killed. You weren't just being nosy. You've got better things to do. A business to run. But you went out of your way to go down there. Why is that?'

A group of teenagers walks past, barely acknowledging us. Still, Taylor lowers his voice. 'Unless... Jesus. Did you know about the affair? Did you go there that night to confront them?' His eyes widen and he takes a step back.

'No! I'd never seen Alice in my life. Not before her photo was all over social media.'

'Why should I believe that?'

'What about you?' I counter. 'Maybe you haven't been to the police yet because it's you!'

'Nice try, but I was in Italy for work when Alice was killed. I only flew back that night. Landed at eleven fifty. I'm sure it would only take the police two seconds to verify that with the airline. And I haven't been to the police yet because my head's been a mess. I can't think clearly.'

I study his face, and I'm forced to make a judgement call. Whether or not I tell him the truth, he already knows Max and Alice were together. All he'd have to do is go to the police. 'I... I didn't know anything about any affair,' I insist. 'But... the night it was on the news, I found a key card for the hotel in Max's pocket.'

Taylor recoils again. 'What?'

'I confronted him and he said he found it on a train.'

'And you believe him?'

'No. I don't know. It's not as simple as that. He's the father of my child.'

Taylor shakes his head. 'I need to go to the police. For your sake as well as Alice's. This just proves he's linked to Alice's murder!'

'No, please. I have a daughter. It would destroy her. It would ruin her life. And Max is in hospital fighting for his life.' The exaggeration flies from my mouth. I'm protecting Max for Poppy's sake. 'Please just let me deal with him. I'll get to the truth.'

'He's in hospital?'

'He was leaving work and someone attacked him. The police don't know yet if it was deliberate or a random robbery.

They stole his phone and wallet. Please, just give me time. That's all I'm asking. I can't let my daughter's life be destroyed without more proof.'

Taylor stares at me. Seconds tick by and then eventually his face softens and he stares at his trainers. 'I have a little sister. She's fifteen now, but I looked after her a lot when I was younger.' He sighs. 'You need to get away from him. For your daughter's sake. And Alice's. Don't let her death be in vain.'

'Max might not even survive!' I'm compelled to say this, even though the doctors are sure he will pull through. 'And maybe he had that key, but that doesn't mean he killed Alice!'

But I'm not sure I believe my own words.

Taylor shakes his head and looks at me sadly. He turns and walks away. And as I watch him, I realise I've never known fear like this before.

Leda's sitting on the sofa scrolling through her phone when I get back. In the faint light from the lamp on the side table, I can tell something's wrong.

'Is everything okay? Did Poppy wake up again? She's been doing that a lot lately. I should have warned you she isn't sleeping well.'

Leda looks up, forces a smile. 'No, she's been fine. I haven't heard her at all.' She glances at her phone. 'I did go to check on her, though,' she adds.

I sit beside her. 'Are you okay?'

Her mouth twists. 'It's just this guy I've been kind of seeing. He... Oh, it doesn't matter. I'm fine.' She slips her phone in her pocket. 'You're home early. I thought you'd be longer.'

'Don't worry, I'll pay you for the whole evening.'

Her face reddens. 'No, no, it's not that. How's Max doing? Mum told me all about it. It's horrible. Why is everything going all weird? First that poor woman at the hotel, and now Max. I can't wait to see the back of this year.'

Normally I would warn Leda not to wish time away and tell her that it's too precious. But instead I can only think about Alice and Max. 'Do you ever go to the Boathouse by the river?'

'Yeah, sometimes. Why?'

'Have you been in the last few months?'

She screws up her face. 'I don't know. Yeah, I think so. My friend Sasha's birthday. Before we went clubbing. In September.'

'Have you ever seen Max in there?'

'No, why?'

I walk over to the bookcase, and reach for the pot I keep the babysitting money in. I pull out fifty pounds. When I place the pot back I glance at the array of books filling the shelves – a mix of both mine and Max's, entwined like our lives.

This can't be happening.

'Don't worry,' I tell Leda. 'It's nothing important. Here you go.'

She takes the notes and places them in her pocket. 'Thanks. Let me know if you need me again. I'm happy to help with Poppy when Max comes out of hospital. I need to save up as much as I can before uni starts. Course fees are crazy, and there's living expenses too.'

I see her out, then watch from the window to make sure she makes it across the road safely. Despite it being only a few metres away, normally Max would walk her home. A thought flashes into my head, and I wonder if it was just Alice he was with, or whether there were others.

Poppy wakes me in the night, tugging at my duvet.

'Mummy, I can't sleep. I want Daddy.' She clutches Whiskers, her cuddly cat, to her chest.

Clambering out of bed, I take her hand. 'Daddy is being looked after. The doctors and nurses are taking good care of him, I promise. He has a whole team of people.'

'But he might die.'

Taylor Stone's words run through my head. *You need to get away from him. For your daughter's sake.*

'Let's get you back to bed.' I lift her up and carry her to bed, the tear trickling down her cheek causing stabbing pains in my chest.

'Mummy, will you stay in here with me? In case something happens to you?'

'Course I will. But nothing's going to happen to me. Mummy is super tough, okay?'

'I thought Daddy was too,' Poppy says, as more tears meander down her cheeks.

'He is,' I say, my voice shaking. I stroke her forehead. 'Try to get some sleep. I'll be right here next to your bed.'

'For the whole night?'

'For as long as you need me.'

'Thanks, Mummy.'

When she rolls over, I sit back, leaning against her bed. I pull out my phone and google Taylor Stone, but there's no trace of him online. It makes no sense that a man his age would have no social media presence or any mention anywhere online.

When Poppy begins softly snoring, I leave her room and pull the door closed. In our bedroom, I open Max's wardrobe and rifle through his pockets. All I find is a receipt for a pair of shoes he bought recently.

How is it possible that I was so unaware of what he was doing? I've never understood how someone could miss the fact that their partner is having an affair, but now I know how easily it can happen. Because these people are consummate liars. That's what it comes down to.

But has Max done something far worse than having an affair?

Finding nothing incriminating in our bedroom, I head downstairs and ransack the living room, pulling out books, flicking through them in case Max has hidden anything in between the pages.

Even though I know what's in every cupboard and drawer in the kitchen, I rifle through them all, desperate for answers.

Then I go out to the garden office, shivering in my thin jumper, compelled to search it once again. Inside, Max's laptop sits on his desk, though we still haven't had the broken glass replaced.

I scoop it up and take it back to the house. There has to be someone who can help me get into it.

EIGHT

'What are you doing here? You don't work on Sundays.'

One thing I've learnt about Cole is that change troubles him. And my appearance in the shop this morning has caught him off guard. 'Katy's here already. Can you believe it?' He gestures to the coffee area, where Katy is cleaning the coffee machine. 'I hope you're going to ask her why she keeps letting us down.'

I sigh. There are bigger things for me to worry about. 'Why don't you take care of that?' I say to Cole. 'I'm not supposed to be here, remember?'

Katy waves. 'Hey, Hannah.'

I turn back to Cole. 'I've actually come to see you, Cole. Um, Max is in hospital.'

'Oh. Oh dear. Is he all right? What happened?'

Briefly I explain what happened to Max, leaving out the part about him having no memory of the last few months.

Cole stares at me. 'That's awful. Have the police arrested anyone?'

'No. They have a grainy CCTV image, but the man wore a mask over his face. They can't identify him.'

'That's awful, Hannah. But why are you here? Shouldn't you be at the hospital? I can look after the shop until Max gets better.' He glances at Katy. 'Especially if *she'll* actually stick around. Where's Poppy?'

'With Mum.'

'Poor little mite.' He smiles. 'Kids are very resilient, though. And Jacqui will take good care of her.'

'Thanks for offering to help, but I need to be here as much as I can. To take my mind off it all.'

He frowns. 'Well, I suppose distraction is good.'

'I'll go and see him this afternoon. But I need to ask you something.'

Cole beams. 'Ask away. I'll do whatever I can to help.'

'You're good with computers.' I pull Max's laptop from my bag. 'I've got an important document on here that I need to find, and I can't remember my password. Max and I share it and I hardly ever use it. But I really need to get in.'

'Hmm.' Cole studies me, and it's all I can do not to look away from his intense stare. 'It won't be easy. I'm no hacker. Although I can do a bit more than most people.'

'Great. So you'll help me, then?'

'I'll have a look at it. But I can't promise anything.' He smiles. 'Leave it with me. I'm not doing much tonight. Other than my usual—'

'Actually, I was hoping you might look at it now. It's kind of urgent.'

'Oh. I see. Um, what about the shop?'

'I'll take over. And Katy's here too. You can go in the office. Take all the time you need. We'll manage out here.'

His eyes narrow, and again I sense his mistrust. He knows I'm lying. Hiding things. 'Okay, I suppose. But like I said – I can't promise anything, Hannah.'

'All I ask is that you try.'

He holds out his hands and I pass him the laptop. 'I'll need coffee,' he says. 'It's hard work hacking into computers.' He taps his head. 'Takes a lot of brain power.'

'Fine. I'll make some when Katy's finished cleaning.'

Time seems to stand still while I wait to see if Cole can get into the laptop. The shop's always quiet on Sunday mornings, but today the silence is ominous. Heavy and suffocating. What will today bring?

By lunchtime, Cole still hasn't emerged from the office. I'm organising a new window display when the door opens and Taylor Stone walks in.

'What are you doing here?' I hiss. There are several customers browsing and I don't want them overhearing anything.

'I meant to give you my number last night. In case you need to talk to me. Have you got your phone?'

I take my phone from my pocket and tap in the number he recites.

'I can't even imagine how you're feeling,' he says. 'If you really didn't know about Max's affair, then this must have been a huge shock. I couldn't sleep last night worrying about it all.'

'Why aren't you online anywhere?'

'What?'

'I checked. There's no sign of you on social media. Twitter. Instagram. Nothing. How do I know you're who you claim to be?'

He nods. 'I thought you might google me.'

'Answer my question.'

'Because I'm a private person and I don't want to be out there. Is it so hard to believe that someone of our generation wouldn't have an online presence? Why do I have to be the same as everyone else? Why does it make me some kind of freak if I'm not plastering every detail of my life all over Facebook?'

He's right. And I, for one, don't put anything on social media, especially pictures of Poppy. 'Then tell me how I can trust you.' I glance around the shop, relieved that no one is paying us any attention, and Katy's head is buried in her phone.

'I work for a law firm called Sampson and Hedges. Call them and ask.' He pulls out a business card. 'Here you go. Feel free to check up on me.'

'I will.' I make a mental note to check the website.

'And in the meantime, maybe this will help.' He scrolls through his phone and hands it to me. 'Look at those.'

Glancing at the other customers, I take Taylor's phone. And what I see on it are pictures of him with Alice. In one of them, they're in a gym working out together. And another is a selfie, both of them pulling silly faces to the camera.

Without a word, I hand his phone back.

'I nearly went to the police last night,' Taylor says. 'It was doing my head in. You have evidence that your husband was in that hotel and you've kept it from the police.'

I look around the shop again. Katy's still staring at her phone and there's no one by the till. The office door remains closed.

'Why didn't you, then?'

He holds up his hands. 'Because of this. I know how much it must take for you to keep this business going. And for your daughter. She doesn't deserve any of this. My dad died when I was thirteen and it still affects me now.'

'Max hasn't left Poppy.'

'No. It's you he wanted to leave. Remember?'

'Just go. Get out. Please. If you're not going to the police, then there's nothing more to say, is there? We don't need to keep talking.'

'Don't you think I wish it was that easy? I'd like nothing better than to walk away from all of this. Pretend I've never met you. But we're tied together now, aren't we? Through your husband and Alice. My closest friend, the person I cared most about in the world.'

I glance at Katy and see that she's now serving coffee to an elderly man. 'I don't understand what you want from me,' I whisper.

'All I want is the truth, Hannah. I want to know what happened to Alice. And I won't stop until I find out. It involves your husband – I know that for certain now. And I think you know it too. You need to get away from him. Before it's too late.'

'Excuse me, can I pay for this?' We both turn and see a woman with a young son standing by the till, waving a book. She wasn't there a moment ago, and I hadn't even noticed her anywhere in the shop.

I plaster on a smile. 'Yes, of course.' I turn to Taylor. 'I have to go,' I tell him.

By the time I've got to the till, he's disappeared.

And Cole is standing by the office door, watching me. He waits until the customer has left, then rushes over to me. 'Who was that?'

'I don't know. Just a woman buying a David Walliams book for her kid.'

He rolls his eyes. 'Not her. The man you were talking to by the door.'

'He was just asking directions.' I turn away, hoping Cole will drop his questioning.

'I've seen him in here before. A few times.'

A cold chill runs through me. 'A lot of people come in here. Any luck with the laptop?'

'Sorry, no. But I know someone who'll be able to help. Went to school with him. He owns a computer repair shop. If anyone can sort it, he can.'

'Great. Where can I find him?'

'Oh, don't worry, I'll take it. He'll do it for me as a favour.'

'No,' I insist. 'I'm happy to pay. Can you just give me the address? I'll go there now.'

'It's Sunday, Hannah. Lots of independent shops are closed

on Sundays. I keep telling you, we're one of a kind. Leave it with me. I'll take care of it.'

Protesting too much will only inflame Cole's suspicion. 'Okay, thanks. Remember it's urgent, though. Whatever it costs.' I smile. 'Within reason.'

I sit in my mother's conservatory and watch Poppy playing with Peach in the large landscaped garden. The sun has made an appearance this afternoon, and Poppy's taken the opportunity to go outside in just her jumper. Houses in Richmond have more garden space, and normally I love coming here to see Mum. It's usually a place I can relax, while Poppy plays outside with the dog. Today, though, I'm on edge.

'Shouldn't you be at the hospital?' Mum says, studying me. 'I'm happy to have Poppy here if you don't want her to see Max like that again. She can stay the night. She's been asking when she can have another sleepover.' Mum smiles, and I marvel at how few lines she has on her face. Her tanned skin seems to only grow more youthful.

'Thanks, Mum, but we'll manage. I don't need to go again today. I just need to be with Poppy. Take her mind off it all. It's all too much for her.' Especially after she found me ransacking the house last night. It took a while, but eventually I'd managed to convince her that I was looking for something important.

Mum frowns. 'Well, that's a bit strange. Why wouldn't you want to be with your husband when he's been hurt so badly?' She frowns. 'This isn't like you. Max needs you. What's going on, Hannah?'

I've never been able to keep things from my mother, even as a child. She always had an uncanny ability to just *know* what was going on with me. She felt it, even if I didn't share a word of anything I was going through.

I leave my cup of green tea untouched, and ignore the plate

of biscuits she always puts out. It's only ever Poppy who ends up eating them. 'I think... Max was leaving me, Mum.'

'Oh, love. No.' She rushes over to me and throws her arms around me. 'Why do you think that? You and Max are... you're inseparable. You've been through so much together.'

Formulating the right explanation is difficult. Mum has always liked Max, and thinks of him as a son. 'Lately, we've... we seem to have drifted apart.' *But I haven't. I've been right where I've always been. It's only Max who's drifted.*

'Actually, I did wonder if something was going on,' Mum says. 'The last few times I've seen you together there seemed to be... I don't know... tension in the air. Something like that.' She sighs. 'I thought it was just work stress. That's what you told me. And Max has never said anything whenever we've chatted. And he does talk to me, you know. He's always been able to tell me things. About his past. I know all about the fight he got into when he was younger. And the boy he attacked who could have died. He talks to me, Hannah.'

Mum's rarely spoken to me about Max's past before, and I'm surprised she's doing it now. 'It wasn't just Max. There were a few of them.' Not that this excuses anything. Although Max claims they attacked these other boys in self-defence, he's regretted his actions ever since. At least that's what I've always believed.

'And it wasn't easy for him after his dad left,' Mum continues.

'I know. It wasn't just work stress. But it's fine. Poppy and I will be okay. We'll get through this.'

'Of course you will. You always do. But that doesn't stop the pain. You don't have to soldier on. It's okay to admit you're struggling.'

We both turn to watch Poppy throwing a large stick to Peach. She runs around the garden and the dog chases after her, the stick hanging out of his mouth.

'What makes you so sure he was leaving you?' she asks.

'Please don't, Mum. Can you just trust me?'

She's silent for a moment, watching me closely, trying to read me like she always does. She's desperate for answers. 'Maybe things will have changed after his accident. Things like this can force people to reassess their lives.'

'He doesn't remember anything of the last few months.'

'Maybe you were just going through a rough patch and he wasn't thinking things through. There's no way he'd want to be without Poppy.' She reaches for a biscuit, inspecting it before she takes a bite.

Her words turn me cold. It always comes back to that. There's no way Max will be without Poppy. 'You don't understand. He's lost his memory. The last six months. Completely erased.'

She finishes her biscuit and stands up, taking her coffee over to the conservatory door. 'Well, that leaves you in a horrible predicament. Do you tell him he was leaving you or do you carry on as if nothing's happened?'

While she doesn't know the full truth, what she's saying is right. Those are the only choices I have.

Unless I leave. Like Taylor said. Get as far away as possible from a man who could be a murderer. Who might want *me* dead.

Then I think of Alice. How, no matter what she did, she didn't deserve to have her life snatched from her. By a man she trusted.

'I'm going to carry on,' I tell Mum. 'For Poppy's sake. And if he regains his memory then we'll deal with whatever he wants to do. The main thing is he needs me right now.'

She squeezes my shoulder. 'I'm proud of you,' she says. 'And I would be whatever decision you made. It's important to talk in a marriage,' she says. 'Above all else. Communicate.'

I turn to watch Poppy outside. She's still running around

the garden, Peach chasing after her, barking. 'Actually, Mum. Would you mind having Poppy for the night? She's got some clothes and a toothbrush here, hasn't she? There are some things I need to do and I don't want to have to drag her around with me.'

'Of course. I'm happy to help.'

Poppy's delighted with this news, and rushes out to the garden again when I get ready to leave.

'She hasn't been sleeping well,' I warn. 'She'll probably wake up in the night. Maybe a few times.'

Mum tuts. 'Don't worry. I'll be there for her. I've done this before, you know.'

'And I think she's bottling it all up about Max. Trying to be brave and then falling apart at night. It's too much for her.'

Mum rolls her eyes. 'When your dad and I divorced, we got through it, didn't we? And you weren't much older than Poppy.'

I hug her, breathing in her comforting scent of Chanel N°5.

'Oh, I nearly forgot,' she says, when I'm at the front door. 'Cole called me earlier. He said he's worried about you and asked me to check how you're doing. That's kind of him, isn't it?'

Rain hammers against my windscreen as I drive home. It's dark already, and I turn up the radio and scream until my throat feels as though it will crack. And when I stop at the lights, I thump my fists against the steering wheel.

I glance in the mirror, my breath catching in my throat when I see a silver Golf behind me. Just like the one that was following me the other day. It's too close behind for me to see the number plate.

The lights turn green and I press down on the accelerator, veering into the right lane. The Golf does the same, and I squint into the mirror, trying to get a clearer view of the driver, but can only make out that it's a man.

For several miles he follows me; no matter which road I take to try to lose him, he's there right behind me.

Finally, after taking a long detour through Wandsworth and Clapham, I make my way home. I can call the police if he stops when I do.

But when I pull up outside the house, he screeches past, careering around the corner and disappearing. But I've memorised the number plate: *AF23 NKT*.

I pull out my phone, a layer of sweat coating my body beneath my jumper and padded coat. It feels as if I've been holding my breath the whole drive home, and I finally exhale.

I scroll to Taylor's number and press call.

'What are you doing?' I demand, the second he answers.

'Hannah? Is that you?'

'Why are you following me?'

'What are you talking about? I'm not following you.'

'It was you. You followed me home from Richmond. From my mum's house. In a silver Golf. Why?'

'Hannah, calm down. I don't even know where your mum lives, and why would I follow you? If I need to talk to you then I can just find you in the bookshop. Or at your house. You're not making any sense.'

'What car do you have?'

'A blue Audi.'

'But... but it was you.' Although I'm becoming less sure of this by the second.

'Hannah, listen. I'm at home. Can you hear the TV? I'm watching Netflix. Does it sound like I'm in a car?'

For a moment I listen to the sound of voices. An American film or box set. Not the sound of a car.

'And listen, I'm boiling the kettle now.' After a few seconds I hear the hiss of a kettle.

'Then who was it?' My breathing starts to slow, though my heart still races. 'This is the second time someone in a silver Golf has followed me.'

'Are you sure? They're fairly common cars.'

'Yes, I'm sure! What if it's got something to do with Max's attack? What if they're coming for me next?'

'I don't know,' Taylor says. There's a long pause. 'But you need to be careful. What if... what if Max wasn't planning to do anything to you himself?'

Panic swells in my stomach. 'What are you saying?'

'What if Max found someone to do it for him?'

NINE

Extract from police interview with Sue Leone:

DCI Spears: Can you tell us what happened on the 17th November, the day Alice checked into the hotel?

Sue Leone: Um, I remember I was covering the front desk on my own. My colleague felt sick so she had to go home. It was fine, though. I've been there a long time so I can manage. Um, Alice came in and I got her checked in and gave her a room key.

DC Langdon: And how did Alice seem?

Sue Leone: I'm not sure. Happy, I think. She was nice. Polite. Some people are... well, they can be a bit rude. But she wasn't at all. I told her my niece is called Alice too.

DCI Spears: Did anything strike you as unusual? Anything Alice said or did?

Sue Leone: No, nothing. That's what's so sad. It was just an ordinary check-in. And then... you know. She's dead.

DCI Spears: What happened after you gave Alice her room key?

Sue Leone: She took it and went up to her room.

DC Langdon: Did you see Alice leave the hotel for any reason? Did she come down at all or call for room service or anything?

Sue Leone: No. I didn't see her again or hear from her. Until... you know.

DC Langdon: Did Alice say why she was staying at the hotel for one night?

Sue Leone: No. And we don't ask that kind of thing.

DCI Spears: Of course you don't.

Sue Leone: But there is one thing I've just remembered. The overnight bag Alice had with her looked like it was empty. As if she'd brought nothing with her.

I sit by Max's bed, listening to the bleep of the monitor. His face is barely recognisable through the bruising, but the shape of his body under the sheet is familiar. And comforting, if I allow myself to forget what's happened. Black it out.

But I can't. I won't.

On my phone, I search Facebook for Eloise Costa, Nadia's daughter. She's on there – although her latest post is from July.

On Instagram she's much more active, and she's posted something this morning – a picture of her and a young man on a beach. Scrolling through her photos, I quickly realise that Eloise loves spending time outdoors. In every photo she's dressed in casual clothes – joggers and T-shirts – and I wonder if she still had anything in common with Alice Hughes. The woman my husband slept with.

Forcing this thought away, I start typing a message to Eloise. I explain that I'm a friend of her mum's and ask if I can talk to her about Alice. I know she lives in Canada, so might know nothing, but it's worth a try. As soon as I've sent the message, I wonder if I'm making a mistake. There's every possibility that Eloise could mention my message to Nadia, and then I'll be left to explain why I'm asking her daughter about Alice Hughes. Just as I'd asked her questions the other day.

'Hey, Hannah.'

Stefan, Max's boss, stands by the door, lifting his hand in a wave. I stand up and gesture for him to come in. 'It's good of you to come,' I say. 'I know how busy you must be.' It's out of business hours, so it's no surprise that he's turned up now.

Stefan holds out his hand. He's a large man in his mid fifties, with a head of thick light brown hair, and his palms are rough and dry. 'I can't believe this happened to him.' He gestures to Max. 'Has he been talking?'

'Not much.' I glance at Max, who's been asleep since I got here. 'He can't remember the attack.'

'Probably for the best. It's worrying that it happened so close to the office. Lots of people have said they feel unsafe walking home. What do the police think happened?'

'I spoke to them this morning. They're continuing their enquiries. Which I'm taking to mean they don't have any leads.'

Stefan shakes his head. 'Unfortunately, this kind of thing is all too common in London.'

'He can't even remember the last few months.' I explain to Stefan that when Max first spoke to me, he thought it was May and that he had their annual conference to get to.

Stefan's bushy eyebrows knit together. 'That's not good. Not good at all.' He glances at Max again. 'What have the doctors said?'

'That sometimes people can lose their memory with this type of traumatic brain injury.' I look directly at Stefan, knowing that he won't like this next part. As kind as it is for him to come here, work always comes first with this man. 'And often they never get it back.'

Stefan turns to Max and sighs. 'That's not good news for him. He was working on a huge project.' He places his hand on my shoulder. 'Anyway, now's not the time to worry about that. We just need Max to get better.' He looks at me. 'How about a coffee? I'll get them from the restaurant downstairs – can't stomach those tasteless vending machine drinks. Nothing but dishwater.'

I place my hand on his arm to stop him. 'Actually, would you mind if I come with you and we have it down there? I could do with a quick break from this room.' As much as I don't relish the prospect of spending any time with Stefan, there are questions I need to ask him.

'Totally get that,' Stefan says, looking around. 'These places aren't pleasant, are they? Still, it's where Max needs to be. Come on. He'll be okay without you for a little while.'

It's fairly quiet in the hospital restaurant, and we sit on uncomfortable plastic chairs, while Stefan fills the awkwardness with chatter about his son finishing university. 'It was touch and go for a while with Theo,' he says. 'Thought he was about to quit at one point. Can you imagine? We're not quitters in our family.'

'Can I ask you something, Stefan?'

'Shoot.'

'How has Max seemed to you over the last few months?'

Stefan frowns. 'Fine. Why? What do you mean exactly?'

'I mean, has he been behaving differently? Distracted at work? Anything like that?'

'Hmm. Not that I've noticed. But what's that got to do with—?'

'Oh, it's nothing to do with what happened to him. I was just wondering.'

He stirs his coffee. 'Look, sorry if this is a bit personal, but have you and Max been having problems?'

'Why do you ask?'

He focuses on his coffee. 'This is awkward. But a couple of weeks ago I was walking past his office and I heard him arguing with someone on the phone. I've never heard him like that before, and I know Max would never talk to a client like that.' He coughs. A thunderous chesty sound. Too many cigarettes, I assume. Finally, he looks at me. 'I caught up with him later in the day and asked him about it and he said he'd been arguing with you. He apologised and said things were a bit difficult at home.' Stefan grimaces. 'I'm sorry, Hannah. It's none of my business. I wish I'd never asked him. I don't like to get involved in my employees' personal lives. As long as they're performing at work, that's all that matters to me. But as he was attacked – I'm just wondering if telling you this might help.'

For the second time in the last few days, I'm floored by something someone is telling me about my husband. Max and I have never argued on the phone when he's been at work. Of course we've often had disagreements, but we'd never let it cross over into either of our work days.

'What exactly did he say?' I ask Stefan.

'Just that you were going through a bit of a rough patch, but he assured me you were sorting things out. And that it wouldn't affect his work.' He smiles. 'I'm sorry. It really is none of my business.' He puts his spoon down and shakes his head. 'I'm the last person to comment on anyone's marriage – I've been divorced twice, and Pria's been hinting about walking down the aisle but I'm done with all that.'

'She's never been married, though, has she?' I say this, hoping he'll work out that he might need to compromise if he wants to keep Pria in his life.

A sheepish expression crosses his face. 'I know, I know.'

'Sorry, I didn't mean to have a go at you. I'm just—'

'Please don't apologise.' He flaps his hand. 'You've got a lot going on.' He pauses. 'Max will pull through. You know how stubborn he is. He'll fight like hell to get better. And he always gets what he wants, doesn't he?'

This is exactly what worries me – how far my husband is willing to go for the things he wants.

'So there was nothing else unusual?' I ask, having a sip of tea so I can avoid Stefan's scrutinising gaze. 'Or out of character?'

He contemplates my question for a moment. 'Actually, there is something. I hadn't paid much attention to it, but now that you've mentioned it. It's about Paula.'

I place my cup down. 'Max's PA?'

'The one and only. They've always got on well and had a healthy working relationship. But lately Paula's seemed a bit off with him. Keeping interactions short. Not really looking at him when he's talking to her.' He coughs again. 'I'd assumed she was going through some stuff in her personal life, but now I come to think of it – she's been fine with everyone else.'

I take a moment to think about what this means. Someone else Max was having an affair with? I need to talk to Paula.

For the next few minutes, I sit quietly as Stefan moans about Pria wanting to spend too much time with him. 'I've got work commitments,' he says. 'She knew that when she met me.

In fact, she said my passion and drive is what drew her to me. So why, then, does she want to change me?'

I shrug; I'm only half listening. 'Just talk to her about it,' I suggest. 'Listen, I know it's a big ask, but do you think I could have Paula's number? She might want to come in and see Max. Even if they've fallen out or something, she'll want to keep him up to date with work.'

'I'm sure she will,' Stefan says. 'Whatever happened between them, Paula's worked with Max for years so I'm sure she'll put aside any awkwardness.' He pushes his empty cup to the side. 'But I can't give you her number. Data protection – you understand? What I will do, though, is ask her to contact you. Is that okay?' He starts tapping on his phone. 'I'll do it now,' he says. 'Just to put your mind at rest.'

It's better than nothing. I thank Stefan, then I tell him I need to get back to Max.

It's the middle of the evening when I get home. It felt safe being in the hospital, and now there's just emptiness and fear. I'd tried speaking to Max, but he barely registered my presence.

I double lock the front door and turn on all the downstairs lights. As much as I miss Poppy, it brings some comfort to know she's safe with my mum.

In the kitchen, I grab a knife and check each room. It doesn't feel like there's anyone in here, but the driver of the silver Golf was definitely following me, and it couldn't have been Taylor. There's no way he would have had time to park up and rush inside somewhere. Turn on Netflix. Prepare for my sudden call.

Once I've checked the whole house and locked all the windows, I grab a blanket and take it downstairs. I call Mum to check on Poppy.

'She's fine,' Mum says. 'We had a movie night. *Frozen* again.

I think I must know the whole script off by heart.' She chuckles. 'Thank goodness it's got some humour in it. Is Max okay?'

'He barely woke up. But the nurses are pleased with how he's doing. Stable. I don't even know what that's supposed to mean exactly.'

'It means be grateful. He's doing okay.'

We say goodbye, and fear grips hold of me as soon as she's no longer on the end of the phone, the silence smothering me.

I call Sarah, and it goes straight to voicemail, as it usually does when she's at work. 'Call me when you can,' I say. 'Nothing urgent. I just wanted to hear your voice.'

I'm buttering bread to make a cheese sandwich when someone taps lightly on the door, the shock of it causing me to drop the knife.

Grabbing my phone from the worktop, I head through the hall and look through the peephole. I've been telling Max we should get a Ring doorbell, but he's always made an excuse. *They invade our privacy. Easy to hack into. We don't need one – it's safe around here.* Now I question why he was so adamant.

With a mixture of relief and concern, I see that it's Taylor standing there, his hands in his pockets, shuffling his feet from side to side.

'What are you doing here?' I ask, when I open the door. The security chain is still on – I still don't trust him.

'I was worried about you. When you said that car was following you. I came to check on you. I would have come sooner but I had to look after my niece.'

'I'm fine.'

'Is your daughter okay?'

'Poppy's at my mum's.'

'Okay. In that case, can we talk?'

'I didn't think there was anything more to say.' I say this, fully aware it's not the truth.

'There's plenty. I need to know what happened to Alice.

And don't you want to know how your husband's involved? Either to clear his name or to know that he's guilty? How can you just bury your head in the sand?' His agitated tone puts me on edge. He's never going to let this go. *And neither should I. I need to keep Taylor onside.*

I hesitate for a moment, while my brain scrambles to make a decision. 'I suppose you can come in for a few minutes.'

'No, I want you to feel safe around me. Let's go somewhere neutral. A different pub to last time?'

Although I'm reluctant to let him in the house, I'm too exhausted to go anywhere. 'Just come in. It's fine. I've got plenty of kitchen knives, so don't even think about doing anything.'

He holds up his hands. 'All I want is to know the truth. I can't take not knowing who did this to Alice. And why. It's tearing me apart.'

I pull the chain from the door, all the while wondering if I'm making a mistake.

Offering Taylor a drink feels surreal. He's not a friend, not even an acquaintance. We're linked by the death of Alice Hughes.

'I'll just have water,' he says, following me into the kitchen.

I fill a glass each for us, and put them on the worktop. Taylor ignores the kitchen bar stools and stays standing, so I do the same.

'I've barely slept since Alice died,' he says. 'I feel guilty that I didn't show her how much I cared about her. They say that, don't they? That we take people for granted until it's too late. Well, that's what I did to Alice.' His eyes fill with tears. 'I should have told her how much she meant to me.' He drinks some water. 'Words cost nothing. But I never told her.'

'I'm sure she knew,' I say, even though I have no idea what Alice thought about anything. 'Let's go in the living room.'

'How did you meet her?' I ask, once we're on the sofa.

'Funny story. We met in Putney library. About... let me

see... It would have been seven years ago.' He smiles, and his eyes shine. 'She was studying for her personal trainer qualifications and she used to go in there to work. She shared a flat with a friend at the time and she said she could never get anything done at home. And I was there for similar reasons. Trying to work on my uni dissertation. The funny thing is I can't even remember how we started talking. It was so gradual. Organic. We were just both always there. Then we were meeting up, socialising. That kind of thing. It wasn't until then I realised Alice was struggling.'

'The depression?'

'Yeah. It was like a cloud hanging over her that she couldn't escape from. No matter what she did, that darkness was there.'

'Were you together?' This is none of my business, but somehow I feel comfortable asking it.

'No. I had a girlfriend at the time so it was never on the table. I'm not saying I didn't find her attractive, but I quickly saw how vulnerable she was. And what she needed was a friend.'

Silence floats between us and I think about everything Taylor's just said. I want to hate Alice, for her part in being with my husband, but all I can feel for her is pity.

'I know you must have a low opinion of her,' Taylor says. 'I guess I don't really blame you for that.'

'No. It was my husband's fault. He's the one who was married.'

Taylor looks at me. 'It takes a lot to see it that way. I admire that.'

'It's just the truth. Did Alice ever mention a friend called Eloise from school?'

He frowns. 'Not sure. Maybe. She didn't see many of her old friends. I don't know why. Why do you ask?'

'I know a woman whose daughter went to school with her. I sent her a message asking if I could talk to her.'

'And what did she say?'

'She hasn't replied yet. I don't think she'll know anything – her mum says they haven't seen each other for years, and Eloise lives in Canada now. I just wanted to get a picture of Alice.'

'I can tell you anything you want to know. But what good would it do?'

'Maybe it will help me understand why Max got involved with her. I know she was attractive, but Max has never been just interested in looks. There had to be something else about her that would pull him in.'

'I wish I had answers for you,' Taylor says. 'But I have no idea what was going through either of their heads.'

'Even if they were having an affair, what I'm struggling to believe is that Max would want... to hurt me.'

Taylor studies me for a moment. 'It's always someone else, isn't it? Someone you hear about on the news. It could never happen to us. But the truth is, this kind of thing does happen. All the time. I think more people are killed by someone they know than a random stranger. And why not you? Why not me, if I had a wife? And there's usually an affair involved. Research it yourself. The stories are out there. But they're not just stories, they're real life, Hannah.'

'He wouldn't. Max would leave me if he wanted to. He doesn't need me to be...' I can't bring myself to say it. 'Why would he risk everything? His job? His daughter?'

'People do this kind of thing because they don't think they'll get caught. And because something else is stopping them thinking clearly.'

I recall my conversation with Stefan at the hospital, how he'd overheard Max arguing with someone. 'Did Alice ever mention that she'd argued with Max on the phone? When he was at work?'

'No, why?'

I tell Taylor what I found out.

He listens carefully, his forehead creased. 'And it definitely wasn't you?'

'Don't you think I'd remember that?'

'Fair enough. So you think it was Alice?'

'Who else could it have been? Max is generally a calm person. Or at least he was. He'd never argue about anything work related. He gets along with everyone.' As I say this, I wonder when, or if, I'll hear from Paula.

'I don't know. It's possible, I guess. If they were in a relationship, then of course they could have argued. And Alice was definitely volatile at times. Anyway, it seems there's a lot you don't know about Max.'

'That doesn't mean he's a murderer!' I shout.

Taylor's eyes widen and he holds up his hands. 'I'm sorry, I didn't mean—'

'Forget it. This is all just...'

'I know.' He sighs. 'But you're focusing on the wrong thing. While Max is in hospital, isn't it the perfect chance to get away from him?'

My head spins. 'I need proof before I uproot Poppy. I can't just walk away until I know. I owe that to my daughter. He's Poppy's dad. He'll need a lot of care when he comes out. Even if you're right – and I'm not saying I believe it – he'll hardly be able to do anything to me while he's so frail. And he can't even remember.'

Again, Taylor sighs. 'Suit yourself. I'll just have to be here when you need my help. Because it will come to that. Look how Alice ended up. I can't let that happen to someone else.'

'There's no proof Max did anything to her, though, is there? I need to be sure.'

Taylor nods. 'Then we'll get proof. I'm going to see Alice's mum tomorrow. I don't know what I'll be able to find out, but I need to see her.'

'Do you think she knows anything?'

My phone rings before he has a chance to answer. 'Sorry, I need to get this.' I walk into the kitchen. 'Hi, Cole. Everything okay?'

'Let's just say this is your lucky day. My friend just called. He's managed to get into your laptop.'

TEN

'When do you think he'll get here?'

It's the third time I've asked Cole this since I got to his flat, and his patience is wearing thin.

'I told you – Eddie's not the most punctual of people. But if he says he'll be somewhere, then he'll be there. Remember he's doing us a favour. It's Sunday night – he's not supposed to be working. Eddie's very protective of his days off. That's why he won't open up the shop like we do.'

I stand and cross to the living room window. Outside, Upper Richmond Road is fairly quiet, and the only people I can see are two young men heading in the direction of the high street.

Cole joins me at the window. 'Are you sure I can't get you something? Water, even? You seem a bit... anxious. What exactly is it you need on that laptop?' His hazel-brown eyes seem to pierce into me.

Instinctively, I want to tell him it's none of his business, but Cole doesn't deserve that after everything he's done to help me.

'It's actually for Max. He was working on something important and his boss needs the document urgently.'

'Oh. Isn't it on the cloud? Most things are these days.'

'Stefan couldn't find it anywhere. That's why I need to get into the laptop.' I force myself to look directly at him.

Cole studies me, his eyes narrowing to slits. 'Okay,' he says, after a moment. 'Well, it's just a waiting game now. I'm sure Eddie will be here soon.'

It's another hour before Cole's friend shows up. He's a short, stocky man with small hands. His hair is thinning on top and it's flecked with grey.

Walking over to me, standing far too close, he hands me the laptop. 'I've reset the password to, um, *password*. Just so you don't forget it. I recommend you change it asap, though.'

'Thanks for doing this,' I say. 'How much do I owe you?'

'Nah, it's okay. Did it for him.' He jabs his finger towards Cole. 'He's a decent guy, that one. You could do a lot worse. I mean, I know some people don't get him, but—'

'No, we're not together.' I hold up my hand and flash my platinum wedding band. One of the tiny diamonds fell out a couple of years ago and I still haven't got it replaced. Perhaps it's a sign.

Cole's face reddens and he places his arm on Eddie's shoulder. 'Didn't you have to be somewhere?'

Eddie glances at me. 'Yeah. Okay. Nice to meet you, Hannah.'

I put the laptop into my bag while Cole walks his friend to the door. They talk in hushed voices for a moment, but I don't have the energy to care about what they're saying. No doubt Cole is admonishing him for embarrassing him like that.

When the front door closes and Cole comes back in, his cheeks remain scarlet. 'Um, sorry about that. I told him you were my new girlfriend and that I wanted to impress you – so he'd do it quickly. If I'd said you were just a friend, then he wouldn't have been in such a rush. You know, it being Sunday and everything. His precious day off.'

As much as I'm annoyed by what Cole has done, all that matters is the laptop. Now I just have to pray that there's something on there that will give me some answers.

'I have to go,' I tell Cole. 'Thanks for doing this.'

Outside in the parking bay, I look up at Cole's window and see that he's standing there watching me. He lifts his hand in a wave, so I do the same. But as I drive away, I can't help feeling uneasy.

At home, I sit on the sofa with the laptop on my knees, searching through Max's folders and documents. There are hundreds to look through, and anything could be lurking behind the façade of a work folder.

I diligently check each one until my eyes begin to blur and my head pounds. But I carry on until I've been through them all. Whatever Max is hiding, it's not on here.

I click on Google Mail, but I don't know Max's password. The only thing left is checking his internet search history, and I'm surprised to find it hasn't been deleted.

What does shock me is that all the websites he's visited in the days leading up to his attack are linked to Alice Hughes. News articles, Google searches. All of them about Alice.

Then in between them, I notice he's logged on to his online banking. It's not our joint account, but Max's separate account. There's nothing unusual about that, but something compels me to click on the link.

Around a year ago, Max had needed me to log in for him. He was in Italy and was having trouble logging in to make a transfer. It's likely he's changed his passcode by now, but I've got nothing to lose by trying.

My heart races as I type in the digits. It works, and I'm taken to Max's online banking home screen. I click on his current account, and scan each transaction. Nothing stands out until I come across a cash withdrawal of ten thousand pounds. Two weeks ago. I try to recall whether there's been anything big we've had to pay for recently, but nothing comes to mind.

I stare at the transaction, as if it will provide me with an answer, and then I call the first person I can think of.

'Hey,' Taylor says. 'Are you all right?'

'I don't know why I'm calling you. But there's a weird cash withdrawal on Max's bank statement. I don't know what it means. I... I don't know what to think any more.'

'Wait, slow down. Start from the beginning.'

The words tumble out of my mouth like an avalanche. 'Max took out ten thousand pounds from his account two weeks ago. That's a lot of money. I've been trying to work out what it could mean. I don't understand it!'

'Okay, let's just think about this.' Taylor's voice is calm and rational, grounding me. 'Did Max mention buying anything? Were you having work done on the house? Something to do with his car? Anything like that? Think carefully.'

I wrack my brain. 'No. There's nothing I can think of.'

'Maybe he owed someone?'

'Max is so careful with money. He'd never need to borrow. He doesn't even use his credit card. He hates owing money.'

There's a pause. 'I don't know what to say, Hannah. You're right – it doesn't make sense. But isn't this just one more thing he's keeping from you?'

That's when it hits me. 'The man who's been following me. What if you're right and he's paid someone to...' I can't finish the sentence. 'I have to go,' I say, ending the call.

I check all the doors and windows again, and set the burglar alarm downstairs. I've never put it on before at night, but it's the only way I'll get any sleep. As much as I miss her, I'm glad Poppy isn't here tonight.

. . .

I sleep fitfully, and it's a relief when morning arrives. It's seven a.m. and still dark outside but the sky is beginning to lighten. Turning on lights as I go, I check the house again, and in Poppy's room, I scan the road outside. There's no sign of any Golf, and I begin to wonder if I've been overreacting. This is Max. My husband. He's not a murderer.

But Alice Hughes is dead, and Max was having an affair with her. He's withdrawn ten thousand pounds from his account without mentioning it, and he's fallen out with his PA again without saying a word to me.

I pick up my phone to check my messages, and there's a reply from Eloise.

It's so sad about Alice. What did you want to know? I haven't seen her for a while. Did you know her?

Immediately I reply, though it's likely she won't see it for a few hours in Canada.

I just wondered when you last spoke to her? And how she seemed?

I send the message, then see that Paula, Max's PA, has contacted me.

Sorry to hear about Max. I hope he's okay. What was it you needed to talk about? I'm in the office today but can meet briefly at lunchtime?

Finally, I might get some answers.

I could navigate these hospital corridors with my eyes closed. It's only been three days, but I feel as if I know the place as well as I know my house. Max is awake and staring at the ceiling when I step inside his room. He doesn't even look at me as I approach.

'How are you feeling?' I ask. It's a pointless question – one look at him is enough to know.

'Like I've been run over by a lorry.' He still doesn't look at me. 'Visitors are coming in here wearing hats and scarves. It's meant to be May.'

'Max, you know—'

'I know!' He says this so loudly that a nurse looks up from the patient she's attending to.

'Shh. Calm down. I know it must be weird.'

'I don't even know who I am any more.'

Neither do I. And that has nothing to do with your attack.

He turns to me. 'I'm trying to find fragments of my life, and I can't grasp hold of anything.'

'It's bound to feel strange, but you'll get through it.' I pour him some water. 'Stefan was here – he's sorting everything at work so you don't have to worry about anything. And you might start to remember. This might not be permanent.'

He closes his eyes. 'Yeah.'

'Do you remember anything that was happening in the news?'

He screws up his face. 'Like what?'

'A woman was murdered in the River Walk Hotel. Her name was Alice Hughes. Do you remember hearing about that?'

'No.' His answer comes too quickly.

I pull out my phone and search for a photo of Alice from the local newspaper. 'This is Alice.' I show him the photo.

'I've never seen her.' Max's face is unreadable.

'And you've never been to that hotel?'

'No, why? Why are you asking me this?'

I sit in the chair beside his bed. 'Just trying to help you remember things, that's all.'

'I think I need to sleep,' he says. 'Do you mind? And I don't want Poppy seeing me like this. Please don't bring her again.'

I promise him I won't, and then I slip out of the room as he's drifting out of consciousness.

The café Paula asked me to meet her at is only a five-minute walk from the hospital. There's a biting chill in the air, and above me the sky is a blanket of charcoal. I walk faster, just to keep warm, pulling my scarf up so it covers my chin.

Paula is already outside when I get there. I haven't seen her since last year's Christmas party, and her chestnut-brown hair looks different. It's shorter now, just touching her shoulders, and she's wearing rimless glasses, which I don't remember her having before.

'Hello, Hannah,' she says, holding out her hand. Her voice is formal and gravelly, and there's no warmth in her tone. Was she always this standoffish? 'I don't have long,' she says. 'I'm sure you can appreciate how much pressure we're under since... since Max's attack.'

'Course. I know how hard it must be without him there. Especially since Peter left.'

Paula gestures to the door. 'Let's go in. Do you mind if I eat? I probably won't get another chance. You don't have to, though, if you don't want to. I'm comfortable eating on my own.' She doesn't wait for an answer but heads inside.

'I'm not hungry,' I say to her back. 'But I'll have coffee.'

An awkward silence hangs over us once Paula's ordered her food. She shifts in her seat and taps something on her phone, her long nails clacking on the screen. She's clearly trying to avoid having any kind of conversation with me.

'How's Max doing?' she asks eventually, sliding her phone into her bag.

'He's... he'll be okay.' I feel as though I'm talking about someone else.

She glances around, avoiding eye contact. 'That's good.'

'I know you don't have much time, Paula. Can I be blunt?'

She stares at me. 'Yes.'

'Stefan said he thought that things were a bit strained between you and Max at work lately. Did anything happen? Did Max do something to upset you?'

Again, silence wraps itself around us, heavy and uncomfortable. 'Please, Paula,' I urge, when she doesn't reply. 'You can tell me anything.'

She shifts in her seat, and finally looks at me. 'I never wanted anything to do with this,' she hisses. 'I told Max to talk to you. It's not me you should be having this conversation with.'

'Just tell me. Please. It's Max you're angry with, not me.'

There's a long pause before she speaks. 'A few months ago, I'd gone out with friends after work. I'd, um, had a bit to drink, but I knew what I was doing. I remember everything. Clearly. I was leaving the bar when I realised I'd left my house keys in my desk drawer at work. I'd had such a hectic day trying to get things organised for a presentation Max had the next day, so I was a bit careless. I'd never normally have forgotten my keys. I'm usually on top of everything.' She pours herself a glass of water. 'When I got back to the office, I saw Max in the car park, sitting in his car. There was a woman in the passenger seat and it looked like they were fighting.' Paula stops to take a sip of water. 'She was... clawing at his face and he was grabbing her wrists, trying to stop her. And then suddenly they were kissing. I turned away. I couldn't watch any more.' She stares at me. 'It made me feel sick, Hannah.'

More evidence. But still it cuts into me as if it's the first time I'm hearing that Max has betrayed me. It has to be Alice. 'What did she look like?'

'I don't know. It was dark. All I knew was that it wasn't you.

I think she had long hair but I couldn't tell you what colour it was. I'm sorry, Hannah. This must be hard to hear.'

I don't tell her that I'm getting used to it. That the more I learn about Max, the more immune I become. *I just don't want the father of my child to be a murderer.*

'Did you say anything?'

'Not at the time. I was shocked. I went inside, found my keys, and tried to pretend I hadn't seen anything.'

'Stefan said you were off with him, and that something had changed between you.'

'That's true. After a few days I had it out with Max. I couldn't keep pretending nothing had happened. I told him I'd seen him. He begged me not to tell you, and promised he'd talk to you himself. But days went by and he kept making excuses for not having talked to you yet. And I realised he was never going to. He was a coward. I could never look at him the same after that. I asked for a transfer but they wouldn't move me. Stefan said I was an integral part of the team and Max needed me. And all I could think was that I don't want to work for someone who could do that to his wife and child.' She lowers her voice, stares at the water in her glass. 'It's exactly what my husband did to me.'

'I'm sorry,' I offer. 'And thank you for talking to me.' I stand up. The walls are caving in on me and I need to get out of here.

'Wait, what about your coffee? It'll be here in a minute.'

'You have it. Sorry, I need to go.' I turn and head towards the door.

'This hasn't been a shock to you,' she calls. 'You knew, didn't you? What's going on?'

I keep walking and don't look back.

ELEVEN

Putney Community Group
Public Group, 10.7K members

Anna Field: Does anyone know what's happening with the Alice Hughes case? I can't find any info and I want to know that the police are actually doing something. I live right near the hotel and haven't been able to sleep since it happened. What are the police actually doing?

Comments:

Mark Taylor: Poor you – not being able to sleep. A woman is dead! Get a grip! And as for the police – let them just do their job. Just because you don't hear anything, doesn't mean they're not doing anything.

Anna Field: No need to be nasty. I was just saying. As a woman, I'm extremely worried.

Arnav Gee: This isn't just about women. Men get murdered all the time too.

Sue Leone: I work at the hotel and I'm the one who checked in poor Alice. She seemed happy. Not scared or anything. She was nice. Kind.

Bruce Halsted: Should you be saying stuff like that on here? Isn't it confidential or something? Just saying. And shouldn't the police be looking into her clients as well?

Tabby McClure: They are. I was one of her clients and they've already spoken to me. I've told them confidential stuff that I'm sure will help. The net's closing in on the person who did this.

For several days I avoid going to the hospital. By saying he doesn't want Poppy to see him the way he is, Max has given me the perfect excuse to stay away. And Poppy needs me. I can't keep leaving her with other people.

Poppy and I have settled in to our new routine, and I begin to wish it could stay like this. If I went to the police about Max, he would be out of our lives for good, and I would be safe.

I'm watching Poppy play in the garden on her trampoline, bundled up in her coat, scarf and gloves, when I resolve to do this. It's what I should have done in the first place. I leave my green tea on the kitchen table and hunt for my bag.

It's in its usual place in the hall, hanging on a coat hook. I take it down and open the zipped compartment.

My hands clasp fabric instead of the hotel key card. I tip the bag upside down and rummage through the contents. But the card isn't there. I check my wallet, and pull out every card I own. None of them are the white hotel card.

'Poppy?' I call, rushing to the kitchen and throwing open the back door.

'Yeah?' She carries on jumping.

'Have you been in my bag for anything?'

'No!'

'Are you sure? I've lost something. A white card. Have you seen it anywhere?'

She stops jumping and shakes her head. 'No, Mummy.'

With a rising sense of dread, I try to recall the last time I saw it. It was yesterday at work. I was in the office and I'd looked in my bag just to check it was still there. It's a habit I've formed since I found it in Max's pocket. It helps me remember this is all real.

And now the only evidence linking Max to Alice Hughes that night is gone.

I check coat pockets and anywhere else it could be, lifting up sofa cushions and hunting through drawers. My search is futile: it's nowhere in the house.

'Can I help you look?' Poppy asks, when I've already turned over the whole house. 'Is this what you were looking for the other day when you made a big mess everywhere?'

'No, sweetheart. This is something else. But it's not here. I think I must have left it at work.' *I didn't, though. I've been carrying it around in my bag with me for days. Unwilling to let it out of my sight. And then this happens.*

'We can go and look,' Poppy says. 'I'll help you, Mummy.'

As much as I'm desperate to find the card, I can't have Cole asking any more questions. He's already suspicious of me. My only choice is to go after the shop closes.

My phone rings when I'm making Poppy a sandwich for lunch. I put down the knife, loaded with peanut butter, and rush to answer it.

'Hi, Mrs Chambers? This is Hilary Clough, one of the nurses at St Thomas'.'

My heart feels like it's stopped beating and I suck in my breath.

'The doctors have just seen Max this morning, and they feel that he can be moved from ICU to a ward, with a view to discharging him on Monday. That's good news, isn't it?'

Seconds tick by before I can answer. 'Yes, it is. Are you sure he's okay to come home? He didn't look too good when I was there last. Doesn't he need to be there longer? What if something happens when he's at home?'

'He's doing well. He'll be ready to go home. He'll just need a lot of rest. We'll go over his discharge summary with you on Monday.'

I've been living in a bubble for the last few days – just me and Poppy. I'm not ready for it to end. Eventually, I find the words to thank her, and be the wife she'll expect me to be.

I'm numb as we end the call. I knew Max would come out of hospital eventually, but I hadn't expected it to be so soon.

Poppy runs in from the garden. 'Is lunch ready?'

I go back to making her sandwich. 'I just had a call from the hospital. They've said that Daddy can come home on Monday.'

She squeals. 'Really? Daddy's coming home? He's not going to die?'

I hug her close to me. 'He's not going to die, sweetie.' *But he might go to prison if he's guilty of what I think he is.*

'This is the best day ever! Is Monday tomorrow?'

'No, it's Sunday tomorrow. So the day after that.'

Poppy runs back outside and clambers onto the trampoline again. With one eye on her, I call Sarah.

'Oh, Hannah,' she says. 'I'm so sorry. I've been meaning to call you back. Work has been horrendous. I've done four twelve-hour shifts in a row. I'm about to die.' She falls silent. 'Bad choice of words, sorry.'

'It's okay. I was wondering if you wanted to come over with Ivy for dinner tonight?'

'D'you know what? I will not say no. I'm dreading the thought of cooking tonight. What can we bring?'

'Just yourselves. But I was hoping you could do me a little favour. I'll need to quickly pop to the bookshop to see if I left something there – would you mind if I left you all here for a few minutes after dinner? I'll be as quick as I can.'

'Is that it? Course. You don't even have to ask.'

The first thing I notice when I open the door is the large dark circles under Sarah's eyes. She smiles. 'I look a mess, don't I?'

'You've been working so much.'

'It's not just that.' She waits for the girls to run out to the garden. 'I called Dean. He'd changed his mobile number since we were together but he still works at the same place.'

I lead her through to the kitchen. 'What did he say? Are you okay?'

'He went silent to start with. He was really shocked to hear from me. But then he was... kind of okay. I asked if we could meet and he said yes.'

For a moment, I push everything that's been happening to me aside and focus on Sarah. This is a huge deal for her, and she needs me to be fully present. 'Are you sure about this? Is it opening a can of worms?'

'Who knows? But I need to do this. What if when Ivy gets older, she asks me why I never tried to contact her dad? Don't I owe it to her to try to help him be in her life?'

'When you put it like that, I guess.'

She pauses. 'I'm so sorry, Han. You don't need to hear all this. How are you doing?'

'Max can come home on Monday.'

Her eyes widen. 'That's great news. You must be so happy.'

'The thing is – I don't know what to expect. He can't remember anything and he won't be able to work for a while. I'm struggling to see how our days will look.'

Outside, Ivy pushes Poppy on the swing. Neither of them seems bothered by the light spattering of rain that's just begun to fall. 'Let Ivy have a go,' I call. Neither girl hears me.

'Why do they insist on being outside no matter how cold it is?' Sarah shrugs. 'Has Max remembered anything yet?'

'No.'

'What about the attack? Have the police arrested anyone?'

Max's attack has taken a backseat in my mind with everything else that's been going on. 'Nothing.'

She takes my hand. 'I'm here for you. Always. Got it?'

I open my mouth to tell her about the key card when her phone rings.

'I can't talk now... No, I'm out... Can I call you later?' She hangs up, and I notice her hand is shaking.

'Who was that?'

'Um, Dean.' She grimaces. 'He seems really interested in seeing Ivy. He's like a different person.'

'Just be careful. I'd hate for you to get hurt again.'

She nods, and rubs her eyes. 'Thanks for looking out for me.'

And everything else I was about to tell Sarah evaporates.

I feel like a criminal breaking into my own shop. I lock the door behind me and leave the lights off, using the torch on my phone to guide my way.

It's cold in here, but somehow my body feels sticky, too warm. In the office, I scramble out of my coat and scour the drawers and desk area, even searching underneath chairs in case the key card fell out. But if it did, Cole or Katy would have found it by now. Or the cleaners.

Cole would have told me if he'd found it. Demanded to know why I have a key card for the hotel where a woman has been murdered. And what answer could I give him? And as for Katy – she would have been broadcasting it to every social network she's on.

With each passing minute my anxiety grows. If I've lost that card then I have nothing to go to the police with.

Once I've finished searching the office, I go onto the shop floor and turn on the lights. The sudden stark brightness forces me to blink. I check behind the till, but there's no sign of it. I check the lost property box, but there's only a glove and an empty water bottle in there.

Despairing, I once again call the only person I can think of to talk to.

Taylor answers after a few seconds. 'Hey,' he says. 'I hope you're doing better than I am. I was listening to a song and it reminded me of Alice. It kind of broke me all over again.'

'The key card is missing. It was in my bag and now it's gone. I've looked everywhere.'

'Shit. Are you sure it was in your bag? Could you have put it somewhere else?'

'No. I thought about leaving it in a locker at work to start with but I wanted to keep it on me. I don't know why. So I knew it was safe? I've been keeping it in the zipped inside pocket of my bag. It's not there. I've looked everywhere.'

'Maybe it fell out?'

'I told you I've looked everywhere!' My words are loud and harsh. It's not Taylor's fault – I shouldn't take it out on him.

'Where are you?' he asks.

'At the shop. I've checked my house and came here to look. It's gone, Taylor. The only evidence we had.'

'Stay there. I'm coming.'

. . .

If it felt odd coming here after closing by myself, letting Taylor into the shop feels even stranger.

'I don't know why I'm doing this,' I say, ushering him inside and locking the door again. I've got used to feeling this way wherever Taylor's concerned. It's almost as if it no longer matters whether I trust him. I'm going along with it because I have no other choice.

'Doing what?' he asks.

'Letting you in.'

He shrugs. 'Probably because you know I can help you. I'm the only one you've told, aren't I? Same for me. I want to protect Alice's name. Have you seen the toxic things people have been saying about her online?' He sighs. 'Just because she'd booked a hotel room for the night. She wasn't doing anything wrong. And she can't speak up for herself to let everyone see who she really was.' His hands clench into fists. 'It makes me sick.'

Taylor looks so sad, I almost reach out to hug him, as I would Poppy. Then, like a switch turning off, I remember that he's still a stranger. I still don't know if I can trust him. 'I know it's hard for you too,' I say.

I walk back to the till and begin rummaging through the drawers again, even though I know I won't find the key card. Taylor watches me. 'Max is coming out of hospital on Monday,' I tell him.

'That's quick. What are you going to do?'

'I don't know. I'd made up my mind to go to the police this morning, and then I couldn't find the card.'

'I still have the photo. That would prove he was seeing Alice. And whoever she was in a relationship with is bound to be a suspect. It should be enough.'

'Okay.'

'But have you thought this through?' Taylor asks. 'All the consequences? You were the one who begged me not to go to the police. What about your daughter?'

'If Max is innocent, then the police will clear his name. And if he's guilty then he deserves to go to prison. I'll make sure Poppy's okay.' I think of Sarah – how everything she does is to protect Ivy. And she does it alone.

Taylor paces the shop floor, sighing heavily. 'I think you should take a bit of time to think about this. Whatever you do has life-changing repercussions.'

He's right. I'd acted impulsively before when I decided to grab the key card and go to the police. I can't make rash decisions. I need to think things through carefully.

'Max can't do anything when he comes out of hospital,' Taylor says. 'Physically, at least. And like you said – he doesn't remember. Could he be prosecuted when he has no memory?'

'Then we need irrefutable proof. So that it doesn't matter what he can or can't remember. That photo is what we've got left.'

Taylor looks unsure. 'I suppose. This is your call.' He smiles. 'Alice was a decent person. She would have respected your wishes. It tore her apart when she found out Max was married. She told me once that she wondered what you were like. She had it in her head that the two of you would get along. You'd chosen the same man, she said. I know it's an odd thing to think when you're sleeping with someone else's husband, but that's the kind of person Alice was. She wasn't like anyone else I've ever known. It really hurt her to think of what she was doing to you. I think that's why she was trying to leave him. She can't have had any idea what he was planning before that.'

Tears swell in my eyes and I swipe them away. I refuse to be a victim. 'I need a drink. Want something?' I ask. Cole always keeps some gin in the staffroom cupboard for some reason, even though he's not a huge drinker.

Taylor shrugs. 'Go on, then. I need a bit of help drowning out this day. Maybe it will help me sleep.'

'What happened today?'

'I've been with Alice's mum again. Seeing her so broken just crushed me. Come on, let's get that drink and I'll tell you all about it.'

We sit upstairs in the staffroom, under the glaring halogen lights. I text Sarah to say I might be a little while longer. Her reply is immediate.

Don't worry. We're watching a film. Frozen *again! Aggh!*

'Forgive me for saying this, but you don't look great,' Taylor says, when I hand him a glass of gin.

Something about this makes all my anger bubble to the surface. 'What am I supposed to look like when my husband's had an affair and is possibly a killer? Sorry if I didn't bother with make-up today. Sorry if I'm just wearing joggers and an old T-shirt. Sorry if—'

'No, I'm the one who's sorry. I didn't mean it like that. I just meant... I can see what this is doing to you.'

I brush off his concern. 'What happened with Alice's mum?'

'As I said, Molly was broken. Of course she was. Alice was an only child. It's unthinkable to lose a child in such a heinous way. Her dad died a few years ago, so Molly doesn't even have him for support. And then not to have any other children who need you, to help you to carry on.'

I think about Poppy, how losing her would be the worst thing that could happen to me. I don't know how I'd find the strength to exist in a world without her. When she was two, Max and I had talked about having another baby, but neither of us pushed for it. We were happy to be just the three of us. And Poppy had Ivy, who is as good as a sibling to her. I wonder now whether Alice's mum had chosen to have only one child, or whether that decision had been out of her hands.

'She couldn't stop crying to start with,' Taylor continues.

'But eventually she managed to speak. It was nice. We talked about all the memories we have of Alice. And I think it helped her to hear my stories. She told me stuff about Alice that I had no idea about. Her childhood. Alice never talked about it much. She used to brush it off and say it wasn't important. The past and future don't matter, she'd say. All we have is now.' Taylor smiles. 'I told her she must have been a Buddhist monk in a past life.'

Despite the situation we're in, I smile too. 'Did you love her?' I ask. The neat gin I'm drinking emboldens me.

He stares at his hands, flexing his fingers. 'Yeah. But not in the way you think. She was an attractive woman, I'd be lying if I said otherwise, but I saw deeper than that. Into Alice's core. And like I said before, once I knew her I just wanted to look after her.' He sniffs. 'Don't get me wrong – Alice wasn't helpless. She was fierce and determined. She was just struggling with too much.' He taps his head. 'In here.'

'Do you think Max wanted to save her?'

'I can't answer that. But maybe you need to look at what was wrong in your marriage to make him even notice Alice.'

'Nothing was wrong,' I snap. 'Except that I didn't need saving. I've always been independent, I've never leaned on Max for anything. But he knew that about me from the start. If he wanted a woman to save, to make him feel validated, why did he marry me?'

Taylor's mouth turns up at the corner. 'I wish I could tell you. All I know about Max is second-hand info passed on from Alice.' He takes another sip of gin. 'She said he's a very private person. Doesn't talk about personal stuff much.'

'It wasn't like that with Max and me in the beginning. We used to talk about everything.'

'Maybe he couldn't be like that with Alice because he had to hide a huge part of his life from her. You and Poppy. The less he said about anything, the better, I reckon. The less likely he'd get caught out in all his lies.'

My head starts to spin as I finish my drink. 'I need to go home. I can't think about this right now. I need to get back to Poppy.'

Taylor stands. 'You need to be careful. Don't trust him, Hannah.'

Downstairs, I watch Taylor leave, then immediately lock the door again. I need a minute by myself before I can face Sarah and the girls. It still doesn't sit right with me that I'm not telling my closest friend the truth, and instead I'm conspiring with a stranger. A man I don't even know I can trust.

It's started to rain when I lock up the shop; there aren't many people out, but a steady stream of cars passes by.

Someone is running towards me, shouting my name. It takes me a second to realise it's Taylor, and further seconds before I notice the blood trickling down his face.

'Someone stole my phone,' he shouts. 'I tried to fight back but there were two of them. They ambushed me!'

'We need to get you to hospital.'

'No. I'm okay. It's probably worse than it looks. But my phone had the picture of Alice and Max. Without that, we have nothing.'

TWELVE

Monday comes too quickly, and with it a tightening in my stomach. Now I have to face Max.

Poppy kept me distracted over the weekend, meaning I had little time to dwell on what happened to Taylor. I'd told him there must be a backup on the cloud, only to have the air sucked out of my lungs when he said whoever stole his phone had hacked into it and deleted it from the cloud.

The photo of Max with Alice has gone – Taylor was targeted deliberately for his phone. Someone wanted that photo of Max and Alice. The same person who's taken the hotel key card? What I can't understand is why. All of this is evidence pointing to Max, and he's in hospital so hasn't done this himself. *Who, then?*

'Do I have to go to school?' Poppy says while we're eating breakfast. 'I want to be here when Daddy gets home.'

I push my bowl of cornflakes aside, no longer able to force them down, and plant a smile on my face that feels as if it will crack my skin. 'He'll be here waiting for you after school, I promise.'

And when I wave Poppy off at the school gates, my stomach once again twists into tight knots.

For the rest of the morning, I'm on the shop floor, giving Cole a break so he can come in later when I leave to pick up Max.

'You must be thrilled to have him home,' Cole says, when he comes to take over. He glances at Katy, who is half-heartedly clearing away cups and plates from a table. I'm so used to her calling in sick or not turning up, it's surreal that she's actually here again.

'It won't be easy,' I say. 'There'll be a long road to recovery. He won't be able to work for a while.'

Cole lowers his voice. 'Has he started to remember anything yet?'

'No.'

'That's a shame. I can't imagine losing six months of my life like that.'

'I'll get going, then.' I pick up my bag. 'Don't be hard on Katy,' I say.

Max doesn't speak on the way home from the hospital. He stares out of the window, his eyes darting around. It's as if he can't quite place anything. Perhaps everything is familiar yet unknown all at once.

'It must feel good to be out of hospital,' I say, to fill the silence.

There's a sharp intake of breath before he answers. 'It is. But there are so many gaps. I just want to remember it all.'

I try to offer him comforting words, but he doesn't seem to register what I'm saying.

He's still quiet when we get home and I help him to the sofa. He brushes me off. 'I can do it myself, Hannah. I'm not helpless. Stop fussing!'

'I need to get back to work,' he says later in the afternoon, when he's woken up from a short nap. 'From home, I mean. I can't just do nothing.'

'Stefan said you don't need to worry about anything,' I say calmly, even though I want to shout my words. 'They're managing.'

'I'm calling Paula,' he says, ignoring me. 'She can fill me in on what I've missed.' He looks around. 'Could you pass me the home phone? I need to get a new mobile.'

I do as he asks and hand him the phone. 'Won't she be extra busy? Why would you want to burden her with having more to worry about? Just rest, Max. Everything will be taken care of.'

I sit next to him and pull out my phone. 'Do you remember this woman?' I ask, showing him the screen. 'She was found dead at the River Walk Hotel.'

He glances at the picture before looking away. 'How am I supposed to remember that when I can't even remember the last few months?'

'I know. I'm just trying to find ways to jog your memory. I feel helpless, Max. I just want to help you.'

He stares at me for a moment then takes my hand. His skin feels different. Rougher.

Everything is different.

Then he lets go, and slowly his eyes begin to close, the phone call he wanted to make forgotten about.

He's still asleep when I leave to pick up Poppy, so I slip out of the house, relieved to escape the stifling walls of our home. The prison it has become.

All the way back, Poppy talks about all the special things she's going to do for Max. 'I can draw him a picture. A rainbow. Will Daddy like that? I can make it sparkly.'

'He'll love anything you draw,' I say, gripping her hand tighter. It does nothing to stop tears pricking my eyes.

When we get back, Max isn't on the sofa where I left him. I call out but there's no answer.

'Where's Daddy?' Poppy asks.

'I don't know. Let's go and check.'

We find him in the bedroom, lying in bed with the laptop open on top of the duvet. There's a pained expression on his face. He's not ready for this. For work. Or any of it.

Poppy rushes towards him and tries to throw herself at him. 'Stop! Be careful,' I warn.

And even though he winces, Max slowly places an arm around her. 'I've missed you,' he says. 'And Mummy.' He glances at me. 'I hope you've been looking after her.'

Poppy giggles. 'No, silly. I'm only five. Mummy has to look after *me*.'

He looks at me, then turns back to Poppy. 'Yep, that's how it should be.'

'But you're sick, Daddy, so we both have to look after *you*.'

'This is all I need to get better,' Max says. 'A hug from my little girl.' He glances at me again, and there's something in his eyes. Defiance?

I walk out of the room and leave them to it. Neither of them notices I've gone.

Later, when Poppy's in bed, Max and I sit on the sofa eating dinner on our laps.

'Have you been using the laptop?' he asks, stabbing his fork into his chicken. 'I can't get into it. It's locked me out.'

'No.'

His eyes narrow as he looks at me. 'Maybe I did it before the attack. Can't see why I would have, though. I need to get into it. Without my phone I can't even check my emails.'

'You can use my iPad. And you can get a new phone. You shouldn't be worrying about—'

'I know. But it's not just work. It's my link to the outside world. I'll go crazy just stuck in this house. I need to know what's happening out there.'

'A woman is dead.' The words seem to shatter around us.

'Why are you saying that?'

'Never mind. I've had an idea. Let me take it to Cole. He might be able to sort it for you.'

Max screws up his face, wincing as he does and clutching the side of his head. 'Cole?'

'Yeah. He's always fixing the IT issues at the shop.' I stand up. 'I'll go and get it. Is it still in the bedroom? I'll ask Mum to come over for a bit while I'm gone.'

Max's face seems to fold in on itself. 'I don't need babysitting,' he says.

'It's not. She wants to come and see you anyway, and I can take the opportunity to sort out the laptop. Can you just humour her?' I plaster on the fake smile I've become good at presenting.

Max says nothing – he doesn't believe me.

'You want to get back to work, don't you? As much as I don't agree with it.' I walk off before he has a chance to object.

'I just want my life back,' I hear him mumble. 'All of it.'

I ring the doorbell, my chest tight with anxiety. Lying doesn't sit well with me, even though I know that's exactly what Max has been doing.

Taylor opens the door. There's a purple bruise over his eye and cheeks. 'Come in,' he says. He's wearing jeans and a hooded top, and his feet are bare.

Before finding that key card, I would never have envisaged that I'd so easily step inside the home of a virtual stranger like this. And put myself at risk. But the risk of doing nothing feels far greater.

'Are you okay?' I ask.

He touches his cheek. 'It looks worse than it is.' He smiles. 'You must be worried to come all the way to Chiswick.'

'It's not that far.'

'Here, let me take your coat.' Taylor reaches out his hand but I shrink back, pulling the belt of my coat tighter around my waist.

'I'm fine, thanks. I just need to warm up.'

'No worries. At least let me take your scarf. I've had the heating on and it's boiling in here.'

He's right – it is warm in here, but I won't take off my coat, make myself too comfortable. I undo my scarf and hand it to him. 'Thanks.'

'Want something to drink?' he asks.

'No, thanks.'

He shrugs, and drapes my scarf over a coat peg. 'Suit your-self. Let's go in there and sit down.' He gestures to a door on the right and heads through the narrow hallway.

It's a sleek and modern flat, with abstract art hung on several walls. It has a nice feel. Homely and cared for, even if it is minimal.

'Aren't you worried?' I ask. 'You were attacked and your phone's been stolen.'

He holds up a different phone. 'Using my old one.'

'That's not the point. Someone's taken the hotel card. It's got my prints all over it.' It's only now I'm allowing myself to voice these thoughts. It can't just be random. Coincidence.

'It couldn't have been Max, could it? He's been in hospital.'

'Then there's someone else out there who knows. Or... someone's doing it for him.'

'I'm trying not to jump to conclusions,' Taylor says. 'But it doesn't look good. You said someone in a silver Golf has been following you. Have you seen them again?'

'No. But I'm always looking over my shoulder.'

'Me too.' He leans forward, resting his elbows on his knees. 'I'm guessing Max is home now?'

It strikes me that it's easier to confide in this man I barely know than it is my closest friend. Sarah would be distraught to know how much I'm keeping from her. I sit down too, and fold my arms across my chest. 'Yes, he is,' I tell Taylor. 'And it's weird.'

He nods. 'You should have got away when he was in hospital. Maybe gone and stayed somewhere else while we find something to prove he's guilty.'

'No. How would that look? My husband's recovering from a traumatic brain injury. I can't walk away. Not until I know.'

'Not even if he's a murderer?'

'I don't *know* that. Having an affair doesn't mean he killed Alice.'

'I know.' Taylor buries his head in his hands for a moment. 'It's doing my head in. I just want to know what happened to her.' He jumps up and walks to the window, pulling open the blind and peering through.

'Max happened to her,' I say.

He walks back over to me and places his hand on my shoulder. 'I'm sorry.'

'Actually, can I have some water, please?' My throat is dry and hoarse.

In the kitchen, I put my bag on the worktop and pull out the laptop. 'I've brought this with me. I've gone through it, and didn't find anything other than that bank transaction. But maybe you could have a look too? In case I've missed something.'

He frowns. 'I'm no expert, though. If you didn't find anything then I doubt I will.'

'Can you just try?'

He looks at me for a moment. 'Yeah, sure.'

I perch on a bar stool. 'Max always has his head buried in it.

I know he's a workaholic, but this evening he was saying how lost he feels without his phone or access to his laptop. I told him I'd take it to my colleague to have a look and see if he can get in. I lied to him.'

'Not as bad as the lies he's told you, though. Guilt's a pointless emotion, Hannah. Especially where Max is concerned.'

I nod. 'I was thinking – what we need to do is work backwards. Start with why he might want Alice dead.'

'I've done nothing but think about that,' Taylor says. 'It can't be because she was threatening to tell you about the affair. Not when he was planning to leave anyway.'

My throat constricts. 'According to Alice. What if she was lying to you?'

Taylor fills two glasses with water, and hands one to me. 'It's possible. She would never need to, though. I never judged her. She knew that she could tell me anything.'

'And I thought Max could tell *me* anything. Don't you see? How well do we ever know anyone?'

My words float around us, infusing the air with tension.

'Do you trust me?' he asks, taking a sip of water.

'No. Do you trust me?'

He laughs. 'Not a jot.'

'Then at least we both know where we are. Maybe she was threatening to go to the police, then? About what he'd said he was planning to do... to me.' The words slice into my mouth.

Taylor continues browsing through the laptop. 'Possibly. But unless Alice had evidence, why would Max have been worried? His word against hers, and he'd just claim she was a woman scorned.'

There are too many unanswered questions, and the more we dig, the more we flounder in the infinite possibilities.

For over an hour, I sit and watch Taylor as he scans every inch of Max's laptop. His face is a blank canvas, expressionless, and several times I open my mouth to ask if there's anything, before deciding against it. I need to leave him to it.

'There's nothing on here,' he says, finally. 'But then why would he leave any evidence on his laptop? This isn't the place we'll find answers, Hannah.' He shuts it down and slides it back to me.

The truth lies with Alice. Even though the dead don't speak, that's where we have to look. I tell this to Taylor and his face creases.

'What do you mean?'

'I mean, I need to unpick Alice's life.'

The frown lines remain on his face. 'I don't understand.'

'I need to know everything about her. What was she like? How did she spend her days? How was she feeling? All of it. This is what we need to find out, Taylor, don't you see?'

He contemplates my words. 'I guess. But that's what the police will be doing.'

'But they don't know what we know. Nobody else knows about Max, do they?'

Again, Taylor silently considers what I'm saying. 'Apart from whoever stole my phone. What exactly are you thinking?'

'I need to meet her mum.'

His eyes widen and he stares at me for so long it feels as though he's consuming my thoughts. 'But how?' he eventually says. 'You don't know her. I can't just rock up with a stranger and let you start asking questions about her daughter. Molly's grieving. She's fragile.'

The idea crashes into my head. 'Tell her I was a client of Alice's. That will work. I got close to her when she was helping me train. Her death has devastated me and I just want to pay my respects.' I pick up my glass and glug water to ease my dry throat.

Once again, Taylor looks horrified. 'I don't know. It doesn't feel right. Lying to a woman about her dead daughter.'

'I know,' I admit. 'But we need to do this. You want to find out what happened, don't you?'

'Yes. But they were barely even talking when Alice died. Alice had become distant from everyone. What do you think Molly could tell us about Alice's life?'

'Like I said, I need every crumb. I want the truth, Taylor. I need to know what my husband did.'

We sit quietly with our own thoughts. All I know is that whether Taylor agrees or not, I'm going to speak to Molly Hughes.

Eventually, Taylor breaks the silence. 'I'll call her tomorrow,' he says. 'It's too late tonight. Not that she'll be getting much sleep.'

And with his words, I'm one step closer to the truth.

THIRTEEN

Extract from police interview with Tabby McClure:

DCI Spears: How long were you a client of Alice's?

Tabby McClure: Over a year. I'm very committed to my fitness goals.

DCI Spears: Great. And how would you describe Alice?

Tabby McClure: She was really kind. She took an interest in her clients. I always felt like she was listening to me. And she was good at her job.

DC Langdon: Did Alice talk about her private life much?

Tabby McClure: (pause) No, actually she never did.

DC Langdon: So you don't know if she was in a relationship with anyone?

Tabby McClure: She never mentioned anyone. And after a year, you'd think it would come out if there was someone in her life. I used to have sessions twice a week. I did wonder if she was with anyone, but I didn't like to ask.

DCI Spears: And how had Alice seemed to you over the last few weeks?

Tabby McClure: (*pause*) She was really off. Distracted. She kept cancelling my sessions, saying she wasn't feeling well. And she'd never done that before. She was like a different person. One time she cancelled on me, telling me she was really sick, then half an hour later I saw her on Putney High Street.

DCI Spears: And did you confront her about this?

Tabby McClure: No. When you know someone's a liar – what's the point?

Goosebumps coat my skin when I wake in the morning to a silent house. Max isn't beside me, his side of the bed unslept in. It's seven o'clock, and usually Poppy is tearing around her bedroom by now. Demanding breakfast. Asking to watch TV.

Like a bullet piercing my flesh, it all comes crashing back to me. Nothing is normal.

Max insisted on sleeping on the sofa last night. He'd keep me awake, he'd said. It was better for both of us if he stayed downstairs.

I pull on my dressing gown and check Poppy's room. It's empty, but her duvet lies on the floor, her cuddly toys scattered over it.

They're both downstairs, cuddled together on the sofa, watching a cartoon. Poppy looks up and waves before turning back to the television.

'How are you feeling?' I ask Max.

'Tired. I didn't sleep much. Couldn't get comfortable.'

'You should have slept in bed. I could have come down here if you needed space.'

'It wouldn't have made any difference. The pain's unbearable.'

He says all this without looking at me, and I silently question why he won't make eye contact.

'Can we have eggs on toast for breakfast?' Poppy asks.

'It's a school day. Eggs will take too long.'

'*Pleeease*,' she begs.

'I could do with eggs too,' Max says. 'The hospital food they forced me to eat was tasteless. I'd make it myself but...' He lifts his arms, then winces.

'I'll do eggs,' I say, turning to Poppy. 'But you'll need to get dressed for school while I'm making them.'

Poppy runs off, thundering up the stairs.

'I've told Cole I can't come in today,' I say.

'Why?' Max demands. 'I told you – I don't need a babysitter.'

'You have a head injury. You can't be alone in case—'

'In case what? If I was going to die, it would have happened by now. Anyway, Paula said she'd come over to go through some things with me.'

The image of Paula sitting in the café flashes into my head. Her words, full of indignation. *I don't want to work for someone who could do that to his wife and child.* 'She agreed?' I ask doubtfully. 'When you're supposed to be recuperating?'

'I'm her boss. She had no choice.' I've never heard Max utter such harsh words. He's never been one to pull rank and throw his weight around.

Without another word, I head to the kitchen to make scrambled eggs.

After walking Poppy to school, I'm tempted to head to the shop, instead of going home. The thought of being alone there with Max fills me with dread. *But I can't leave him alone for too long. Just in case. If anything happened to him, it would be all my fault.*

I run him a bath when I get back, and leave the room while he undresses. I can't bear to look at his naked body – not because of the bruises, but because all I can picture is Alice Hughes's hands wandering all over it.

'I'll be in the bedroom,' I say, placing a clean towel on the edge of the bath. 'Not because you need help.'

'Wait,' he says, reaching for my arm. But then he lets it fall and turns away.

'Do you know anyone who has a silver Golf?' I ask idly.

He looks up. 'No, why?'

'No reason. I just keep seeing one outside the house. It must belong to one of the neighbours.'

In the bedroom, I send a WhatsApp message to Taylor's new phone, asking if he's spoken to Molly Hughes yet. And then I wait.

It's only a few minutes before his reply comes. We can meet her at her house in Cricklewood at eleven, and Taylor offers to drive.

Feeling as though I'm having some sort of affair, I send him a thanks, then slip my phone in my pocket. This is what Max was doing to me for months, with the difference being his was a real affair.

Time passes excruciatingly slowly until the doorbell rings. I rush to answer, and Paula stands at the door. Her arms are folded, and when she forces a smile her mouth barely turns up at the corners.

'Hi,' she says, glancing past me. 'I guess he told you I was coming?'

I nod. 'He's in the living room.' I don't add that he's been staring out of the window for the last half hour, as if the only thing that matters is Paula turning up here this morning.

'Why did you come?' I whisper. 'After everything you told me.'

She peers past me again. 'Because I need my job. I like my job. As soon as he's back in the office I'll put in another transfer request.' She shakes her head. 'I'm not the one who's married to him. That's worse, isn't it?' She stalks past me, slipping off her shoes in the hallway.

I watch how Max reacts to seeing her, surprised at first that there's a smile spread across his face. Until I remember that he has no memory of her standoffish behaviour towards him at work over the last few months.

'Paula, it's good to see you.' He reaches out his hand and she takes it briefly, before settling into the chair opposite.

'I'll leave you to it,' I say. 'I'm just popping out to get a few things.'

Paula glances up and gives a barely perceptible nod.

'See you soon, darling,' Max says, smiling.

He never calls me that.

As I'm walking out, I set my phone to record and slip it onto the bookshelf by the money jar. Neither of them notices.

Taylor picks me up by the river, and I jump into his car, praying no one has seen me. How would I explain this to Max? To anyone? 'Drive fast,' I say.

The sooner we're away from Putney the better.

We pass the River Walk Hotel on our right, and both of us look out of the window but stay silent. Everything looks normal there now, as if Alice was never there.

It takes us an hour to get to Cricklewood, even though it's only a few miles away. 'I didn't think about how bad traffic would be,' Taylor says when we pull up in a tree-lined residential street. 'We're a bit late.'

Molly Hughes's home is a narrow Victorian terraced house with a small front garden. The grass is overgrown, and most of the bushes along the front have withered and died.

'She normally takes good care of the garden,' Taylor explains.

I do a quick calculation: it's been just under two weeks since Alice was killed. Yet what I'm looking at is months of neglect. It's winter, though – not a time when gardens are a priority.

Behind the net curtains, someone watches us; Molly, I presume. Taylor told me her husband had died, so I assume she lives alone.

So much tragedy for one family.

Molly disappears from behind the curtain and a few seconds later opens the door. Grey shadows surround her sunken eyes, and she's clutching a tissue in her hand. She's tall and thin, and can't be more than sixty, yet she appears as frail as someone decades older. Her shoulder-length hair is grey at only the roots; the rest of it is dark, almost black.

'Thanks for seeing us,' Taylor says. 'I brought you some of that loose tea you love.' He holds up a bag, offering a thin smile.

'Thanks,' she says. 'That's kind of you.' She speaks slowly, her voice husky, as if the exertion of forcing out words is too much.

'This is Hannah,' Taylor says.

I step forward and take her hand. 'I'm so sorry. Alice was a

wonderful woman. She really helped me.' Though there is
nothing true about my words, I find them easy enough to say. I
don't blame Alice for sleeping with my husband – it's Max who
should have walked away.

'Thank you,' Molly says, stepping aside.

She leads us through to the first door on the left of a long
corridor that feels too dark. Too claustrophobic. It doesn't help
that there's no natural light, and the walls are deep red.

Thankfully the living room is far brighter, and light floods
in from the large bay window. The room is warm and filled with
ornaments and photos, but grief and emptiness loom over it,
seeping into every corner.

Taylor sits on the floral sofa, and I follow his lead.

'Horrible thing,' Molly says, pointing a long, delicate finger
towards the sofa. 'Ugly. I've never liked it. But it was my mum's
so I've kept it. She loved the awful thing.' She sighs. 'I'm just
glad she's not around to know about all of this.' She sits in the
armchair across from us. 'It would have destroyed her. She and
Alice were so close. They were like two peas in a pod. Mischie-
vous twins we all used to call them when Alice was little. Both
of them as cheeky as each other.' A tear meanders down her
cheek as she turns to me. 'So you were one of Alice's clients?'

I nod. 'For the last six months. She was really helping me to
get my fitness back. It was difficult after I had my daughter – my
abdominal muscles split and I really suffered.' This much, at
least, is true.

Molly's eyes narrow and my face burns. It feels as if my lie
is scrawled across my forehead.

'Yes, childbirth destroys our bodies. But I'd do it all over a
million times to have Alice back.' She wipes her eyes with her
crumpled tissue. 'She really helped you, then?'

'Yes, definitely. She was good at what she did.' I glance at
Taylor, who gives me an almost imperceptible nod.

'I wouldn't know. She hardly spoke to me about anything these last couple of years. Not since...' She looks at Taylor. 'Well, I don't want to go into all of that. Not when Alice isn't here to speak for herself.'

'It's okay, Molly,' Taylor says. 'She was very open with Hannah. They talked about the difficulties Alice was having.'

Molly turns back to me, looks me up and down. 'She had problems with her... you know... mental health as a teenager. An eating disorder. Anxiety. Before that she'd been the happiest child you could ever meet. Always smiling. Playing. She had a ton of friends. Then it was like a switch turned off and all of that stopped almost overnight.' She reaches for a fresh tissue from the box on the coffee table and dabs her eyes. 'Why do children have to change so quickly? Lose their innocence? There was no reason we could see for such a change in her personality. We put it down to growing older. Becoming a teenager. Life's not easy at that age, is it? Anyway, after school everything seemed to smooth out for her and she really got her life together. Until a couple of years ago. It was like the old troubled Alice was back again. But there was a reason this time. Her dad died suddenly and Alice just seemed to spiral. It's like she had no coping mechanisms.' She pauses, once again dabbing her eyes. 'She just fell apart.'

'I'm so sorry,' I say. And I mean every word.

'Did she tell you she went off the rails?' She turns to Taylor. 'I'm sure *you* knew. You were very close, weren't you?'

He nods, and stares at his trainers. 'I just tried to keep her thinking positive.'

'I'm not even sure Alice ever realised what was happening to her during these dark times. She just became reckless. It was like she was searching for something she could never seem to find.'

Happiness, probably. Isn't that what we all want?

'She did tell me she felt a bit directionless,' Taylor says.

'Like I said, life's hard for young people,' Molly says, shaking her head. She studies me again. 'You don't look much older than her.'

'I'm thirty-five. Only five years' difference.'

'And you have a daughter?'

'Yes, her name's Poppy.' As soon as I've said this I wonder if I'm telling her too much. If it will come back to haunt me when the truth emerges about Max and Alice.

'How lovely.' Molly pushes her used tissues into her pocket and pulls a new one from the box. 'Alice will never get the chance to have kids now. That would have been the making of her.'

'I'm not sure Alice wanted kids,' Taylor says. 'She told me she had too much living to do and it would be selfish of her to have them. I think she felt she wasn't in a place to devote herself one hundred per cent to parenting. She had the cats – I think that was enough for her.'

'Still, things change,' Molly says. 'One day she might have changed her mind. I'll never be a grandmother. Never be a mother again.' She erupts into a flood of tears, her bony body shaking.

I rush over to her and throw my arms around her.

'Sorry,' she says, between sobs.

'It's okay. Let yourself cry.'

She clings to me for a moment until her tears dry. 'You're kind,' she says. 'Alice was lucky to have someone like you in her life.' She looks at Taylor. 'And you, of course. I don't know what she would have done without you.'

'She would have been fine,' Taylor says, his eyes welling.

'No, she wouldn't. You don't know what your friendship meant to her. I think you held her together.' Molly blows her nose on her tear-soaked tissue. 'Sometimes I used to wish that the two of you would get together.'

Taylor shifts in his seat, and I silently make a note to question him again later. He's told me that they never had a relationship, but now I wonder if anything physical happened between them.

'We just didn't see each other in that way,' he continues.

'I know, I know. Alice used to tell me that all the time. But you can't blame me for hoping. So many men out there are just... no good.'

Max. And I'd always thought myself blessed to have him in my life. 'When was the last time you saw her?' I venture, fully aware that my question is intrusive, not to mention unethical.

Molly sighs. 'It was on her birthday. In January. I wanted to take her out but she said she was busy. She had too many clients needing sessions and she couldn't afford to turn them down. It was a busy time for her after Christmas. With everyone making New Year's resolutions to get fitter and all that. You know, Alice never once asked me for money. Since she turned eighteen. She said she was determined to make her own way in life.'

These words fuel my sadness. And all I can picture is her dying alone in that hotel room.

'Once, I left an envelope with two hundred pounds in her flat. Do you know what she did?' Molly shakes her head. 'She handed it right back to me the next time I saw her. It breaks my heart to think of that now.'

'Do you mind me asking why you didn't see more of each other?' I'm precariously close to the line, but I need to know.

'I think she was hiding something.'

Taylor frowns. 'Like what?'

'I don't know,' Molly says. 'But I think she didn't want me involved in that part of her life. It was like she didn't want me to see what she was doing. Or what she was going through. It felt like she was cutting me out.'

'It was the same with me,' Taylor says. 'Over the last few

months, she seemed to be making more and more excuses not to see me. She was busy or tired, or already going out.'

Molly nods, and when I turn to Taylor, I wonder if he's thinking what I am: that Max has got something to do with this change in Alice.

'They'll never find the person who did this,' Molly says, smoothing out the pleats in her maxi skirt.

Taylor leans forward. 'Why do you think that? We have to try to be positive.'

'Because they have nothing. No leads. Zero. Sometimes cases aren't solved. Look up the statistics. That's what I've been doing.' She reaches for her phone and waves it.

And all the while I sit in this grieving mother's house, I'm harbouring a potential suspect. A wave of nausea slithers through my body. I can't let this woman suffer like this. She needs answers. We all do. This thought is quickly overshadowed by Poppy, and how devastated she would be if Max was wrongly accused of murder. I'm torn to shreds. I need to act quickly.

'The police will find who's responsible,' I say, placing my hand on Molly's arm. 'We have to believe that the truth will come out.'

When we leave, Molly stands by the door watching us. She lifts her arm in a semi-wave, then folds her arms once more.

Taylor and I don't speak until we're in the car. 'I think it helped her,' he says, fastening his seatbelt. 'To have some company for a little while. Someone to talk to about Alice. It's like it keeps her alive somehow. That's how I feel too.'

'But we didn't find out anything helpful, did we?'

'I did warn you that Alice hadn't seen her mum for ages. Molly wouldn't have a clue what was happening in her life right before she died.'

'Someone must.'

Taylor starts the car and we pull away from Molly's house. 'Yep. Your husband.'

'Who can't remember anything, even if I did come right out and accuse him.'

Taylor focuses on the road. 'Unless he's lying.'

'What?'

'How do we know he's really lost his memory?'

FOURTEEN

Paula's black Peugeot has gone from our driveway when I get home. Inside, the house is silent, and I wonder if she's taken Max out somewhere. 'Max? Are you here?' My voice echoes into the empty hallway.

I slip off my coat and leave my bag on the side table, calling Max's name again. My phone will give me the answers. But when I get to the living room and check the bookshelf, it's not there.

'Looking for this?'

I spin around to face my husband. He's sitting on the armchair in the corner of the room, holding up my phone. It's remarkable how quickly his strength is returning.

'Oh, yeah. I left it behind by mistake. Why are you sitting over there? Isn't the sofa more comfortable?'

'It was recording,' Max says, his eyes darker than usual, scrutinising me.

'Was it? I must have accidentally pressed something.' With my heart hammering, I walk over to him and hold out my hand.

He slowly places the phone in my palm. 'You should be more careful. I might have needed to call you urgently.'

'Thank goodness you didn't. Are you hungry?'

'No. Paula made me a sandwich.'

'That was good of her,' I say, heading into the kitchen.

'I deleted it for you, by the way,' he says.

Slowly I turn back to face him. 'Oh? What?'

'The video it was recording. You don't need that clogging up your phone, do you?'

Sweat coats my palms and the backs of my knees. 'Thanks.'

'I'll have coffee if you're making it?' Max smiles, but there's no warmth in it.

In the kitchen, I scroll through my phone, just in case Max is lying. But the video is gone. Then I check through my messages, making sure there's nothing on there that would alert him to what I'm doing. And what I know. But Taylor's number is saved under the name 'Kristina', and I constantly delete my call log. There's nothing he could have found out.

Taylor's words force their way into my head. *How do we know he's really lost his memory?*

I boil the kettle and fetch two mugs from the cupboard. I need to keep up the pretence of normality, or this all falls apart.

I carry the coffees through to the living room, and hand one to Max.

'I'll take mine upstairs,' I say. 'I've got some things I need to do on my laptop.'

'Sit with me for a bit,' Max says.

This is the last thing I want to do, but I do as he suggests.

'How did it go with Paula?'

'It went well. It was good to catch up on things. And Paula goes above and beyond for me.' He smiles. 'I don't know what I'd do without her. She said she's happy to come over any day after work if I need her.'

I study Max, desperately trying to read him. Either he's lying to me about Paula, or she was misleading me, making me think she can't stand being around him. Confusion clouds my mind, and I can't see my way out.

I can't trust anyone. Max. Paula. Even Taylor. That's the only way I'll get through this.

'Remember when we first met?' Max says. 'I felt like I'd always known you. It's funny how you can get that with some people, isn't it? And others you know you'll never connect with.'

I nod, unsure where he's going with this.

'And it's funny how one person can be everything to you. Your whole world.'

'But it isn't exactly like that, is it? We have our careers. Would you ever give yours up? Or is it just as big a part of you as I am?'

Max contemplates my words. 'Maybe you're right. But it's healthy to have more than one thing making you feel whole.' He stares at me. 'I remember the exact moment I knew I loved you.'

I raise my eyebrows. Max has never mentioned this before.

'We were watching *Titanic*. God, I hated that film. And you spent the whole time analysing it. Do you remember? You said there was no way that Rose and Jack could be in love – they'd only known each other for days. You said it set unrealistic standards for relationships. But still you watched the whole film, and your eyes teared up at the end.' Max smiles. 'I was looking at you, and suddenly I felt it. In that moment, I knew I loved you.'

'You've never told me that before.'

He ignores me. 'You're right that we needed more than just each other to complete us. But you're wrong about one thing. I would give it all up for Poppy.'

The doorbell rings before I can respond, and I jump up without hesitation – I need to get away from Max, even if just for a few moments.

'Hey, Hannah!'

Sarah's warm face beams at me, and it's all I can do to stop myself crumbling in her arms when she hugs me.

'How come you're here?' I ask.

'Florence Nightingale at your service!' She beams. 'I've taken the week off work, and I'm here to help you with Max. I'm fully qualified – references available on request – and I'm used to having no breaks. I'm also used to difficult patients.' She laughs. 'Seriously, though. You probably need to be in the shop and, to be honest, I could do with time off from the hospital. It's a win–win.'

'Thank you,' I say. 'If you're sure? How did you manage to get leave at such short notice?'

'My annual leave was piling up. I never take it, so they were happy to let me actually take some.'

I lower my voice. 'Max won't like it, though.'

'That's because he's a man and he doesn't like feeling help-less. He'll get used to it.'

At first Max's face brightens when he sees Sarah, but something changes when she tells him her plan to stay with him.

'I don't need looking after,' he grumbles.

'Have you forgotten I'm a nurse? I'm here to take care of your medical needs. Nothing else. You don't have to talk to me. I've got this.' She pulls a book from her backpack. 'The latest Adele Parks. More interesting than chatting with you, Maxy.'

He laughs, and I realise it's the first time I've seen him show any genuine happiness in a long time.

'I'll get to work, then,' I say. 'I've got a book club on this evening so I won't be home until later. I was going to ask Mum to pick Poppy up from school.'

'I'll do it. If you don't mind Ivy coming back here?'

'Thanks, Sarah.' I give her a hug.

'Now, get to work. Cole will be scaring off all the customers.'

Outside in the drive, I look in through the window,

suddenly aware that I'm leaving Sarah alone with a man who might have killed someone. I'm about to go back in when I notice Sarah is laughing, waving her arms about, perhaps regaling Max with one of her stories from life in A & E. And he's listening attentively. Still smiling.

All is fine. Max wouldn't hurt Sarah.

But I make up my mind to call and check in regularly.

'She's really done it this time,' Cole says, the second I set foot in the shop.

'Who? What's happened?'

'Katy just called and said she's not coming back. Apparently she's found another job.' He rolls his eyes.

I stare at Cole. 'What exactly did she say? She liked it here. Why wouldn't she even serve her notice?' This news has caught me off guard, but it's nothing compared to everything else that's been happening.

'She just said this wasn't the right place for her and she needed a change.' He sighs. 'I did suggest we should let her go ages ago. Remember?'

'Not now, Cole. I really can't deal with this at the moment.' I head to the office.

'We'll manage,' he calls after me. 'Don't worry.'

I call Katy's phone, but it rings until her voicemail kicks in. 'Katy, hi, it's Hannah. Can we talk about this please? I thought you were happy at the shop. Give me a call back when you can.'

Next I call Taylor, but he doesn't answer either. Uneasiness spreads through me: Taylor always answers my calls. I leave a message urging him to call me as soon as he can.

I scroll through the internet on my phone, soaking up all the latest posts and news stories about Alice. The police still have no leads. *Because Max isn't known to them.*

Cole appears in the doorway and suggests I go for some

lunch. 'If you're here for the book club tonight, you'll need to eat something.'

I wish I'd never agreed to it now, but I can't let Nadia down. Her daughter still hasn't replied to me, and I've chased her up too many times already.

When I call Sarah to check on Max, in a hushed voice she tells me that he's asleep. 'Good thing, too,' she says. 'After you left, he was trying to convince me that he'd be okay on his own, and that I should go. You know how stubborn he is. I almost gave in.'

'You won't leave, though, will you?'

'No. I told you I'd look after him, and that's what I'm doing. There is something I need to tell you, though.'

My chest constricts. 'What?' The trouble when you lie to everyone around you is that the avalanche can come crashing down at any moment.

'I said I'd meet Dean tomorrow.'

I stop holding my breath. 'Are you sure about this?'

'He's Ivy's dad. Whatever's happened, I can't change that.'

And that's exactly the same for me and Max.

'Thank you again,' Nadia says, taking my hand. 'Cole says you might be short-staffed?'

'It's fine. Just had Katy leave us with no warning.'

'Oh dear – that's not good. I hope it won't cause a problem for tonight?'

'Not at all. I'll be here for whatever you need.'

'Wonderful. I've had thirteen confirmations. Unlucky for some, but not me. Thirteen is actually my lucky number.'

For an hour I sit in the coffee area, on hand in case anyone needs anything. Although I'm listening to the ladies as they all animatedly discuss *This Is How We Are Human*, my mind is crammed with other thoughts. Max. Alice Hughes. The man in the silver Golf. Taylor. The ten-thousand-pound cash withdrawal.

Nothing makes sense; I'm locked in an escape room, with no idea how to solve the puzzles that will set me free.

'Hannah?'

I look up and Nadia is peering at me, frowning. 'Are you okay? You were miles away. We've finished. That went well, I think.'

'Sorry. Let me see everyone out.'

When everyone's gone, Nadia hovers by the door.

'Is everything okay?' I ask.

'Yes. Well, I'm not sure, actually.' She pulls on her red faux-leather gloves. 'I spoke to Eloise earlier. She said you'd messaged her. Asking all sorts of questions about Alice Hughes.'

Her loaded words hang in the air.

'I—'

'And then I remembered that you'd also asked me about her when you came to my place. Or tried to, in a roundabout way. What's going on? What are you doing?'

Thinking on the spot has never been a skill of mine. I've always liked to have time to process things, to think carefully before I speak. But Nadia leaves me no choice.

'You're right – I was asking questions. And it's... I'm ashamed to say it.'

'Go on.'

The lie plants itself inside my head, fully formed, impenetrable. 'I've always wanted to write a true crime book. And when Alice died, I just thought... what if I could write about it? I don't mean now. I mean in the future. I want to be respectful to her family. Please don't tell Cole – he's been working on his own book for years and I don't want him to think I'm trying to outdo him or anything.'

Nadia stares at me, her eyes wide. She appears to be struggling to find any words.

'You should be ashamed of yourself,' she says. 'Trying to profit from someone's murder.' She flings open the door and steps outside, letting in a huge gust of wind.

At least she believed me. The alternative would have been far worse.

FIFTEEN

Facebook reel from Molly Hughes:

I'm posting this video on Alice's Facebook page because I want it to stop. All the gossiping and speculation about my daughter. Well, it hurts. Do you people ever think about that?

Alice was my child. I know she was thirty, a grown woman, but she was still my *child*.

Long pause. Molly Hughes wipes tears from her eyes.

Alice had problems. But she did *not* kill herself, as some of you vile people are saying. It's clear from the police report that taking her own life in that way would have been impossible. And my beautiful daughter had everything to live for.

Whoever did this – you won't get away with it. The police will find you. Someone must know something. If you're hiding anything or covering for someone then you need to do the right thing. For my Alice.

Breaks into tears. Video ends.

· · ·

Taylor opens the door, his eyes swollen and red. 'Sorry,' he says. 'It's not been a good day.'

I step inside, peeling off my coat as I remember last time I was here I refused to remove it. I feel more comfortable being here this time. It's familiar to me. Safe. It no longer feels like that at home. 'Has something happened?' I ask.

'No. That's just the problem. I keep hitting brick walls. I have no idea what to do. We're stuck. There'll never be justice for Alice now.'

I take his arm. 'You can't think like that.'

He leads me through to the living room. 'How come you're here? Is something wrong?'

I tell him about Nadia, how she confronted me about my excessive interest in Alice. 'It's shaken me up. I need to be more careful.'

His mouth twists. 'It sounds like she believed your excuse, though?'

'For now. But if she does decide to talk to my colleague, he'll never believe what I told her. If I was writing a book, he would definitely know. Cole already thinks I'm acting suspiciously. I can't have him questioning me. He's much too hard to lie to. And I feel like he's always silently trying to work out what's going on with me.'

'You didn't need to ask her daughter about Alice,' Taylor says. 'I can tell you anything you need to know. More than an old school friend who hasn't really seen her in years.'

'I know. I made a mistake. And I can't afford to do that again.'

Taylor walks over to the window and peers through the blinds. 'What now, then?' he says.

I might not have known him long, but I've never heard him

so despondent. I join him at the window. 'The driver of the silver Golf.'

'What?'

'We need to find him. Whoever he is. He's the only person who can help us.'

'Why would he help us? He's been following you. Probably sent by your husband. I don't think helping you is on his agenda. That's not how people like that operate.'

'Maybe not, but anyone can change their mind about something if the price is high enough.'

Taylor stares at me, blinking. 'What are you suggesting?'

Perhaps the plan only occurred to me moments ago, but now the seed has planted itself, I'm convinced it's what we have to do. 'If Max did want to harm me and had hired someone to do it, that person knows the truth. And if I offer to pay him more than Max did, then I'm sure that will convince him to talk. It has to.'

Taylor's eyes widen and he shakes his head. 'You can't mess with people like that. Do you know how dangerous it would be? These people are found on the dark web, they don't play games.'

Through the window, I scan the street outside, wondering if I've been followed here. But there's no sign of a silver Golf. 'I don't have a choice,' I say. I turn away from the window and sit back on the sofa. 'I've got some savings. Fifteen grand. I'll use that. It's more than Max withdrew.'

'No! You can't do that. It's too much money. You're not thinking straight. I think we should just go to the police. I can't do this any more, Hannah. We're not getting anywhere.'

I force myself to remain calm, so that I can persuade Taylor I know what I'm doing. 'We can't go to the police. We've said all along we need evidence, haven't we? There's no key card. No photo. Nothing at all that links Max to Alice. This is the only way, Taylor.'

An urgent silence falls around us. 'Please, just let me try,' I say softly.

'I don't like this. I really don't think you should put yourself at risk.' Taylor sits beside me and takes my hand.

The shock of his gesture sends a frisson of electricity though my body. I pull away, unsure what I've just felt. What it means. 'I'm doing this,' I repeat, pulling on my coat.

The house is silent when I get home. I know Poppy will be in bed, and Sarah will have needed to get Ivy home long before now.

'Hello?' I call.

'In the kitchen,' Max says.

I make my way through the hall, stopping in the kitchen doorway when I find Max sitting in the dark, only the faint glow from the solar lights in the garden. 'When did Sarah leave?'

'Ages ago. I told her I don't need her or anyone else here.'

'I'm trying my best, Max.'

'You've been a long time. I thought the book club was only an hour.'

'I had to clear up after. And there were a few things I had to do before I came home.' I smile, confident in the truth of my answer.

'Okay,' he says, scanning my face.

'Any problems getting Poppy to sleep?'

'She's not here.'

I freeze. 'What?'

'I asked Sarah if she'd have her tonight. So we could be alone. We never get the chance, do we? Life always gets in the way.'

'It's late,' I say. 'I'm tired. And you need to rest.'

'Then we'll go up together for a change. Talk until we fall

asleep. Do you remember when we used to do that? Before we had Poppy.'

His words are sentimental, delivered gently. Yet they fill me with horror.

'Let's stay down here,' I suggest. Being in the bedroom would only make me feel vulnerable.

'Good idea.' He smiles. 'Why don't you pour us some wine?'

'You can't have wine, Max. You've just been in hospital. And what about your medication?'

He glares at me for a moment before speaking. 'You have some then. I'll have a Prime. There's some in the fridge. That's allowed, isn't it?'

'Yes.' I go to the fridge to get his drink, but don't get myself wine. Instead, I fill a glass with water. There's something off about Max tonight. Even more so than over the last few months. 'What's wrong?' I hand him his bottle.

He unscrews the lid and takes a sip before answering. 'What do you think is wrong?'

'I... I don't know.' I drink my water too quickly and it hurts my throat

'This, of course,' he says, waving his arms. '*I'm* all wrong.'

'I know it must be difficult. Not remembering. It's—'

'I've done a lot of thinking about that since I got out of hospital. And I don't think my attack was random.' He searches my face. 'I think someone was waiting for me.'

'Have the police said that?'

'No. But it's my gut instinct. I'm never wrong about things I believe, am I? All the times I've said something will happen – doesn't it always? Remember when you were pregnant with Poppy? I told you before you even missed your period, didn't I? I just felt it.'

This is true. We hadn't even been trying for a baby, but one day Max looked at me and said he thought I was pregnant. I'd laughed, of course. I was taking the pill, and my period wasn't due for a few days so I wasn't even late. But somehow he *knew*.'

I nod.

'And when I felt that Peter was going to leave. He hadn't said a thing to me.'

Again this is true.

'And I'm right now. I just can't prove it.'

'You really can't remember any of it? Nothing at all?'

'No. But I get the feeling that if I did, this whole conversation would be very different.'

I'm tempted not to ask Max what he means. The answer won't be anything I want to hear. But he'll tell me anyway. 'What does that mean?'

He looks at me for too long without saying anything, and it takes all my effort not to turn away.

'Just that all of this would be different,' he says. 'If I could remember. Wouldn't it? Like that film *Sliding Doors*. One second is enough to change lives.'

'I... I think I'll go to bed,' I say, picking up my glass of water.

'Good idea. I'll come with you.'

Max watches me while I change into my pyjamas. Before Alice's murder, I wouldn't have thought twice about peeling off my clothes in front of him, or walking around half dressed. Now I'm as conscious of his eyes on me as I would be if he was a stranger. *He is. I have to remember that Max is not the man I married. I can't lose sight of that.*

I get into bed and pull the covers up to my neck.

'Why would someone attack me?' Max asks. He's not going to let this go.

'Until the police say it was deliberate, I don't think we should dwell on that. You're here now. Safe.'

But am I?

He gets into bed. 'They've told me they can't rule out that someone targeted me.' He stares at me. 'And you're not safe anywhere if someone wants you dead.' He turns onto his side, and it dawns on me how he seems stronger than he was only yesterday.

'The truth always comes out,' I say.

He shakes his head. 'I think you're wrong. Sometimes it manages to stay hidden.'

Minutes tick by as I lie still and wait for Max to fall asleep. He reached for me a few minutes ago, and I tried not to flinch under his touch. He didn't push for anything, though, and now he's turned away from me, and I listen to the gentle rhythm of his breath.

My phone vibrates and I grab it, reading the WhatsApp message from Taylor.

> There's a silver Golf parked right across the road. Licence plate AF23 NKT. But now isn't the time to talk to him. We need to be sure first.

I sit up, my whole body instantly alert with adrenalin and fear as I start typing a reply to Taylor. Then I remember that he'd worried about me confronting this man. I delete the message telling him I'm on my way over there. Instead I tell him that he's right.

'Max?' I whisper.

When he doesn't respond, I slip out of bed, grabbing the clothes I've left in a pile on the chair. I close the door behind me, grimacing when the click echoes into the silence.

It's less than twenty-five minutes later when I get to Taylor's flat, and I've spent every second of the drive over praying that the car is still there.

But it's not. Instead, there's an empty space on the road

directly opposite Taylor's building where it must have been. I pull into it, feeling like the air's been sucked out of my body.

I lock the car and head into Taylor's building, rushing up the stairs to his flat. I knock on the door, the thud so loud in the silence. There's no answer.

'Taylor?' I call.

There's no reply, but the door opposite his flat begins to open.

'I don't think he's in,' a young man says, coming out and locking his door. He looks younger than Taylor, and has a small dog with him.

'Thanks,' I reply.

'Try calling him,' the guy says, disappearing downstairs.

My head spins as I call Taylor's mobile, but again it goes to voicemail.

My blood feels like ice as I knock again. What if he went out there to confront the driver? I call him again, this time leaving a message. 'Can you call me? I'm worried,' I say into my phone before ending the call.

I wait, time ticking too slowly, fear seeping into my veins. The Golf wasn't there. And now neither is Taylor.

After a while, I try to be rational: it's late – there's every possibility that he's fallen asleep. Morning is only a few hours away, and I can call him again.

But as I drive home, I can't shake the feeling that something's happened to Taylor. And that it's all my fault.

SIXTEEN

I've barely slept. My head feels as though it's being crushed, and every limb in my body aches, screaming to be healed.

Something must have happened to Taylor. There's still no reply from him, and he's mentioned before that he's an early riser. He's already been attacked once. And now I'm swimming in a sea of guilt. I'm the one who stopped him going to the police. If I hadn't, things would be very different now.

Beside me, Max still sleeps, even though he's usually up long before now. The toll his attack took on his body goes far beyond his bruises and memory loss.

Downstairs, I try to eat some buttered toast, just to ease the empty ache in my stomach, but I abandon it when the food lodges in my throat. Instead, I drink tea, hoping it will be enough to sustain me this morning.

I leave a note for Max, telling him I'm leaving early to run some errands before I get to the shop. Sarah will stop by after dropping the girls at school, and I still feel uneasy about letting her spend all this time with Max.

Then I message Cole to tell him I'll be in late. I still haven't heard back from Katy, but I doubt Cole will mind being on his own. He and Katy never seemed to gel.

It's quicker to get to Cricklewood this time, even though there's still a steady stream of cars on every road I take.

Doubts set in, heavy as cement, when I get to Molly's house. The more contact I have with anyone who knew Alice Hughes, the more I'm putting myself at risk. From the police. From the driver of that Golf. From Max?

She opens the door within seconds, as if she's been expecting me. But her face is a mask of confusion as she struggles to place me for a moment. She's wearing a long black cardigan today, and loose black jeans.

'Hi, Molly.'

'Hannah?' she says. 'What's going on?'

'I'm sorry. I'm meeting someone near here shortly, and I wanted to stop by and see how you are. Is there anything you need?'

'That's kind of you. But that police liaison woman's been helping with stuff. She's not here again today, though. Thank goodness. I want my own space.'

'That's understandable,' I say. 'I was also wondering if you've seen or heard from Taylor since we were here yesterday?'

She pulls the door open to let me in. 'No, I haven't. But I did message him last night. I wanted to see if he'd come with me to Alice's flat this morning. I can't bear the thought of going alone. The police went through it all after they found her, and now I can't stop picturing them rifling through her things, unpicking her whole life. Alice would have hated that. She was such a private person.'

'I can imagine how hard it must be.'

Molly rubs at a smudge she's noticed on the wall by the door. 'Anyway, Taylor didn't reply. And it looks like he hasn't even read my message.'

Again, guilt threatens to drown me. 'I'm sure he'll reply,' I say, unable to meet her eyes. 'I could come with you? To Alice's flat. If it would help you?'

Her eyes brighten, and I silently curse myself for lying to this woman. 'That would be... yes, please. It would really help me.'

'Would you like to go now?' I ask.

'Oh, are you sure? Don't you have to meet someone?'

'Actually, they messaged just as I got here to say they can't meet now. So it looks like I'm free for a bit.'

'Thank you. I'll just get my bag,' she says. 'I always keep Alice's spare key in there. Even after all these months when I've barely seen her. I just kept thinking, you never know when she might need it. Lock herself out or lose her key. You never knew with Alice. There was always some disaster or other.' Her eyes well up, and I want to offer her words of comfort, but nothing I can say would help.

Instead, I nod and step back outside, leading Molly Hughes to my car. 'I'm just there,' I say.

'No,' she says. 'I'll drive my own car. Otherwise you'll have to come all the way back here to drop me off. And you live in Putney, don't you? Right near Alice.' Her voice is quieter as she says this last part.

'It's no problem at all.'

'You're very kind. But you're already doing enough by coming with me. I won't have you being a taxi service too.'

All the way to Roehampton, I've wondered how it will feel to step inside Alice's flat. I've prepared myself for every emotion: guilt, fear, anger. Even sadness.

What I'm not expecting is to feel numb as I step into her small flat. As though this isn't happening. The first thing I notice is the stale smell. The unlived-in feel. It's been two weeks since there was life inside this flat, and the whole place feels gutted. A body without a heart. Even though it's still full of Alice's belongings.

'I need to open the windows,' Molly says.

To the left of us is a large living room, with a dining table at one end and a large grey corner sofa in the other. Molly heads to the window and opens it. 'I used to worry about Alice living on the ground floor. When she wanted to buy this place, I told her it wasn't a good idea. I really tried to put her off. It's not safe, I said. But she laughed. She said she would fight off anyone who tried to break into her home.' Molly bursts into tears. 'But she didn't, did she? At that hotel. She couldn't defend herself.'

I rush to Molly and put my arms around her. 'I'm so sorry. Maybe she did fight back?'

'If she even saw it coming.'

And that's when the devastating sadness hits me. For the woman who slept with my husband. Not just once or twice, but for months.

Why would Max want you dead? Were you trying to help me? To stop him doing something to me?

'Let me get all the windows open,' I offer, when Molly loosens her hold. 'We can close them when we leave, so the flat's safe.'

'Thanks,' she says. 'I can't bear the thought of getting rid of her things. Everything she owned gone.' She breaks down, burying her head in her hands and crying uncontrollably.

I take her hand and wait, silently fighting my guilt, hoping that I'm doing enough.

Most of the walls in here are white, but there's a dark blue feature wall to the left of the window, and on it are hung framed inspirational quotes. *Choose Happy. Dream. Inspire.* Somehow, given what I've found out about Alice, it feels as though she probably never quite believed these messages she was trying to get her brain to absorb.

Molly holds up a bag. 'I'm going to take a few of her things with me. To keep. So I've got something of hers.'

I tell her that's a lovely idea, and while Molly begins filling the bag, I make my way to the small kitchen, leaning over the sink to open the window. It's clean and modern in here, and looks as if the kitchen's been recently updated. There are two cat bowls on a silicone mat on the floor, still with kibbles in them.

'Alice's neighbour took in the cats,' Molly says, appearing behind me. 'I have terrible allergies so I couldn't have them.' She looks up to the ceiling. 'I hope Alice forgives me for that. They meant everything to her.'

'I'm sure she does.'

'I'm going to clean those bowls out,' Molly says. 'I can't leave them just sitting there like that.'

While she sets about washing the cat bowls, I go to Alice's bedroom to open the window in there. It's a large room, with two windows on either side of a small white wardrobe. There are more inspirational quotes hung over the walls, and a blush pink faux-sheepskin rug on the floor at the foot of the bed.

I stare at the bed, with its pink silk sheets, and picture Max lying on it. *Was he ever here? Or did they stick to hotel rooms?* I take a deep breath and force the thought away.

Opening the window, I glance at the door. I can hear the tap running in the kitchen. Quickly, I open the wardrobe door and peer inside. It's crammed full of clothes and I run my hands over them. Jumpers. Dresses. Skirts. Every imaginable colour.

As I'm pulling at them, trying to get a picture of how Alice dressed, I notice something stuck to the back of the wardrobe, behind the clothes. I lean forward to get a closer look. It's a white envelope – stuck on with brown parcel tape.

Glancing behind me, I pull it off and shove it inside the waist of my jeans. I'm sure Molly mentioned that the police had searched Alice's flat, so I'm surprised they missed this.

'That's better,' Molly says, and I jump.

'I was just... I heard something fall in the wardrobe, so I opened it to see what it was. I can't tell if anything's out of place, though.'

Molly's eyes narrow and she walks towards me. 'Let me see. Maybe the police have made a mess of everything.'

But of course there's nothing in there now except far too many clothes.

'I'll have to sell this place,' Molly says, as we go back into the hallway. 'After she worked so hard to get it. By herself. The only help she had was from the money her dad left her in his will. She wouldn't take a penny from me.' She points to the back door in the kitchen. 'She even got the garden gym installed herself. And now someone else will probably tear it down. Replace it with a shed or something. Or make it into an office.'

Molly's probably right. There can't be that much demand for a home gym, despite people wanting to believe they will sort their fitness out.

'Maybe you can ask the estate agent if you can meet the person buying her flat? It might reassure you. To get to talk to them and know the person who'll end up living here.'

She stares silently at me for so long that I wonder if I've said the wrong thing.

'You're right,' she says. 'I think I will do that.' She sighs. 'I don't want to take up any more of your time. You can go now if you need to get on. I'll be here for a while. I think I'll be okay now. I just wasn't sure if I would be.'

'I don't mind staying.' Even though the longer I'm here, the more chance Molly might find out I've stolen something of Alice's. The envelope rustles under my coat with every step I take.

'No, you get off. But thanks for coming with me.'

I give her a brief hug, then make my way towards the door.

'It's very strange that Taylor still hasn't replied,' she says. 'I don't think he said he was going away. I know he often does for work. Maybe he's just busy with his job.'

'Yes,' I say. 'I'm sure that's it.'

And then I leave Alice's flat as quickly as I can.

'How's Max doing?' Cole asks when I make it to the shop.

'He's frustrated he can't be at work, I think.'

'Yes, I imagine he's going out of his mind a bit.'

The envelope is in my bag now, and I'm desperate to open it. It might be nothing; I can't pin my hopes on it, but either way I need to know. 'I've got some accounting to do,' I tell Cole. 'Can you manage out here?' It's fairly busy in here this morning, and I wonder if we'll manage without Katy.

'No problem,' Cole says.

'You haven't heard from Katy, have you? I sent her another message and she didn't answer.'

'No. I'm guessing she's probably washing her hands of this place. It was never her thing, was it?'

Cole's right. 'I'll have to advertise her job. I just didn't want to do that without speaking to her.'

'Somehow, I don't think Katy will care,' Cole says. 'She's always going on about how she's a free spirit and all that.' He rolls his eyes. 'I don't think any of us are really, if you think about it—'

'I'll be in my office, then,' I say, walking off before I get stuck listening to Cole philosophising.

In my office, I pull the envelope out and stare at it, running my hands across it. I'm about to rip it open when my phone rings.

It's Sarah, and for a second my heart seems to stop. *Has something happened?*

'Just thought you'd want me to check in,' she says. 'I've

dropped the girls to school, and Max is in a right grump. I don't know what's going on with him.'

'I'm sorry,' I say. 'You don't have to stay. 'Really. Go home. Relax. You never get the chance.'

'Actually, he's asked if I'll drive him to work. He says he needs to see the place he was attacked.'

I sigh. 'Max has got it in his head that the attack was deliberate. That someone specifically wanted to hurt him and it wasn't just a random mugging.'

'Oh. Why does he think that? Have the police told him that's what they think?'

'Apparently there was an attack similar to Max's yesterday. In the CCTV footage it looked like the same man. Wearing a mask again. And it wasn't far from where Max was attacked. But Max isn't listening.'

'So should I not take him?'

'I can't see it will do any harm. Maybe it might trigger a memory?'

'Not sure it works like that, but you never know. Okay, I'll check in later.'

'Sarah?'

'Yeah?'

I pause. I want to tell her to be careful, but then I'd have to explain everything. Including why I haven't told her what's been going on. But my mind can't form the words. *I'm sorry.* 'Thanks for doing all this.'

When we end the call, I pick up the envelope, slowly tearing it open. I remind myself it could be nothing important. But why would Alice tape it to the back of her wardrobe?

I pull out the contents of the envelope, and stare at what I'm holding.

Photos. Printed on normal printer paper, as if Alice has done it at home.

Ten of them altogether.

And every single one of them is a photo of me.

SEVENTEEN

Extract from the *Wandsworth Times* online:

> *Police are still urgently appealing for information regarding the murder of thirty-year-old Alice Hughes, whose body was discovered two weeks ago in a hotel in Putney.*
>
> *Today they confirmed that they have been unable to locate Alice's mobile phone, but her car keys and purse were found in the hotel room with a weekend bag.*
>
> *Police have also confirmed that they haven't been able to find the hotel room key card that was issued to Alice when she checked in.*
>
> *DCI Spears, the lead investigating officer, has urged anyone who might know of its whereabouts to come forward.*

> WHAT DO WE KNOW SO FAR?

> *Alice spent the morning with her clients, but had the afternoon free from personal training sessions. She then checked into the River Walk Hotel at 3:24 p.m. She was wearing a knee-length*

belted padded navy coat and a light pink bobble hat, gloves and scarf.

She gave staff at the hotel no impression that she was meeting anyone, and she'd checked in for only one night.

Speculation has been rife on social media as to why she was staying at the hotel when her home address was only a few miles away in Roehampton, but police are urging the public to be respectful to Alice's family.

'Sometimes Alice just needed to be in a different space. To clear her head,' her mother told reporters, before begging people to stop speculating about her daughter.

A vigil for Alice has been held outside the hotel this morning, with attendees holding placards demanding 'Justice for Alice' and 'Make London Safe for Women', among others.

Confusion spreads over me like a wave crashing against the shore. I study the photos again, committing each one to memory.

There I am, leaving my house. Walking along Putney High Street. Waiting outside the school to pick up Poppy. Letting myself into the shop. There's even one of me behind the till.

My brain scrambles to work out what this means. Was Alice stalking me? This is all about Max, it has to be. Did she become obsessed with the wife of the man she fell in love with?

Taylor said he thought Alice was leaving Max. But it's possible she had been following me before she made that decision.

I grab my phone and call Taylor; once again he's the only person I can speak to about what I've found.

Just as I've expected, his voicemail kicks in again. There's little point leaving a message when he hasn't replied to my other ones. Or maybe he can't. Someone's been watching both of us, and it must have something to do with Max.

I need to put an end to this.

Grabbing my bag, I leave the office. Cole is busy with a customer. I wait for him to finish, but the woman appears to be in no hurry to leave, even though she's already paid and Cole has handed over her purchase.

I walk up to them, hoping she'll take the hint, but instead she keeps talking.

'Such a shame. I really did like that Katy. She was always so kind to me. Even gave me free refills sometimes.'

Cole nods. 'Unfortunately, she never really fit in here, though. I don't think books were her passion. Shame. I hope she finds a job she'll love as much as I love mine.' He glances at me and smiles.

I wait for the woman to leave, then tell Cole I need to go.

'Has something happened?' he asks, his forehead creased with concern.

'I just need to be with Max.'

'You go. I'll take care of everything here.' He frowns. 'Are you sure you're okay, though? I'm a good listener if you need to talk.'

'Thanks. I appreciate that. I'll muddle through, though.'

I walk away, wishing I could believe my own words.

I sit in the car for a few minutes and prepare to face Max. I'm parked further down our road instead of the driveway to avoid any questions about why I haven't come straight in.

This has gone on long enough. Being unable to remember doesn't excuse what he's done.

Taking a deep breath, I scoop up my car key and reach for the door handle. But when a black Tesla pulls up outside the house, I freeze.

And then Max appears at the front door, stepping outside and shutting it behind him. He doesn't notice I'm here; his eyes are fixed on the car as he rushes towards it. He leans in to speak to the driver before opening the door and climbing in.

It must be an Uber. But Sarah is supposed to be with Max, taking him to work.

The second the car drives away, I start my engine and pull out. It's not too far ahead of me, so within seconds I'm right behind it. If the man is a taxi driver, then hopefully he won't think twice about a car following him. I just pray that Max doesn't turn around.

I follow them as they drive along Upper Richmond Road and turn off towards Wimbledon. A tsunami of questions crashes through my mind, vying for my attention, but I can't give any of them my focus. What is Max doing? What am I about to find out?

And then I think of Taylor, surprised by the intensity of my need for him to be in the car with me, going through this with me. I brush it aside. I still don't know him that well, so I won't rely on him for anything. Besides, he's not answering his phone, and I have no idea where he is. Or what's happened to him. Something else I need to address.

We pass the Common, and the Tesla ambles on through Wimbledon Village, eventually pulling into Denmark Road. My instinct tells me to hang back, and I'm right to do this; the car stops outside a Victorian terraced house divided into two flats.

I've been calm driving over here, safe in my car, knowing exactly where Max is. But now fear grips hold of me. I have no idea what Max is doing here, or who he's come to see.

I pull up further down the road and watch Max get out of the car and walk up the steps to the first-floor flat. I slip out of my car, quietly closing the door behind me.

My chest constricts, and I force myself to take deep breaths as I get to the narrow garden path, just as Max slips inside.

I jog up the stairs and press the buzzer. After a moment, the door clicks open, and I'm torn between wanting to run as far away from here as possible, and staying to face Max and his lies.

I think of Poppy. How I need to see this through for her sake. I step inside.

When the door opens and Max stares at me, his jaw hanging and his eyes wide, I almost change my mind.

'How did—?'

I push past him, fearless in my pursuit of the truth. Whatever awaits me, I will deal with it. Yet my legs feel weak, my body fighting against my mind.

I spin around and face my husband. 'What is this place? Why are you here?'

Silence, so palpable it feels as though I'll be able to reach out and touch it, wraps itself around us. We're frozen in a moment, and both of us know there's no going back once we've crossed this line.

When Max finally speaks, everything changes. 'You followed me.' It's not a question, and his words are fused with regret. 'Why did you come here, Hannah? You shouldn't have come here.'

He walks through the hallway, into a large, bright living room. It's empty other than a sofa and a coffee table. There are no pictures or ornaments. Nothing personal. Just an empty shell of a place. 'Who lives here?'

He ignores me. 'We need to talk. Sit down.' His voice is louder this time, harsher.

'No. You haven't answered my question. What are you doing here, Max? Who lives here?'

He studies me for a moment. 'That's not how this is going to work,' he says.

It's funny how quickly I've got used to his bruised face. The scars that might never fade. I can barely remember how he looked before. And I'm scarred too, though mine lurk beneath my skin.

I reach into my pocket and feel for the smooth and reassuring glass of my phone.

'Please sit down,' he says slowly, as if he's talking to a child.

I'm glad Poppy's not here to see him like this. Would he hide it from her? I no longer know.

After a moment, I sit down. It doesn't mean he's won. I keep my hand in my coat pocket. 'Where's Sarah? Does she know you're not at home?'

'I don't have to answer to her. She's not there. I told her to go.' He sits down, far too close to me. 'We need to talk, Hannah.'

Max is my husband, yet I want the physical space between us to be as large as an ocean. 'Yes,' I reply. 'We do.'

I won't take my eyes from him, even though it's hard looking directly into his. How can those cold, harsh eyes belong to a man I vowed to spend my whole life with? The father of my beautiful child.

A murderer.

'I don't know who lives here,' he says. 'I found the keys in my desk drawer.'

Incredulous, I shake my head. 'I don't believe you.'

'They had the address on them.' He holds them up. 'Look.'

He's telling the truth – at least about that much.

'I thought they might be yours.' He slams his fist on the arm of the sofa. 'Do you remember on our honeymoon?' he continues. 'You said we should always be honest with each other. No matter what. That we'd get through anything, as long as we keep communicating.'

I turn away from him, stare out of the double-glazed window. A white van rumbles by.

'When did that stop?' he asks. 'When did we stop talking?'

'You remember, don't you? When did your memory come back?'

'Oh, Hannah. It was never gone in the first place.' He searches my face, and I wonder what he's looking for. What conclusions he's reaching in his twisted mind.

'Why did you lie?'

'I had no choice. I think you know that, don't you?'

'I don't know what—'

'Stop!' His voice shatters around us, piercing my ears.

He grabs my wrists. 'Why were you following me?' His voice is lower, but his grip burns my skin. 'What are you doing?'

'Let go of me.'

'Answer my question! You think I'm weak. Because of my accident? You're wrong.' He tightens his grip.

I tip my head forward and thrust myself into him, smashing into his jaw. He yells and reels backwards, clutching his already damaged head.

I'm at the door by the time he's scrambled up, and I rush outside, racing to the car.

With surprising speed, Max chases after me, shouting my name, banging his fists on the car window.

With no time to put on my seatbelt, I slam my foot on the accelerator and speed off, watching him become smaller and smaller in the rear-view mirror.

EIGHTEEN

For hours I drive aimlessly, my only goal being to keep away from the house. Away from Max. Every few seconds I glance in the mirror, relieved to find that no one appears to be following me.

Without giving it any thought, I find myself heading towards Chiswick. Sarah has messaged to confirm Max's story about him telling her to leave. And now she's meeting Dean. She's got her own stuff to deal with. I don't expect Taylor to be home, but at least it feels like I'm doing something.

I get to his apartment block and head upstairs to his flat, my legs feeling heavy and fragile at the same time. Just as I reach the top, my phone rings.

Taylor.

'Where are you?' I say, without any greeting.

'Sorry, I've only just got your messages. My mum got rushed to hospital.'

'Oh, I'm sorry. Is she okay?'

'She will be. It was a minor stroke. My brother's with her now so I came home.'

'I'm outside your flat,' I say, my cheeks burning. What will he think of me being here?

He doesn't say anything, but his flat door opens, and Taylor peers out. He's wearing a black roll-neck jumper and dark jeans. Blue trainers I've not seen him in before. 'I thought you were joking,' he says, smiling. 'Sorry, you must have been worried about me. I should have messaged you.'

I brush past him, strangely confident with this man I still barely know. 'Of course I was worried. One minute that silver Golf is parked outside, and the next you're missing. What was I supposed to think?'

'I know. I'm sorry. I got the call right after I got off the phone to you and everything went out of my mind. All I could think about was my mum. I thought she was about to die. And by the time I got outside, the Golf was gone.'

'I'm glad your mum's okay.' The truth is, Taylor doesn't owe me anything. We're not friends. Our worlds have just collided and we're bound together by a woman's death.

Taylor leads me through to the kitchen. 'Something's happened, hasn't it? What is it?'

I reach into my bag and pull out the photographs, spreading them out on the worktop. Then I watch his face as he slowly realises what they are.

'What is this?' he says.

'I found them in Alice's flat. Hidden in her wardrobe.'

He screws up his face. 'What? How did—?'

'Molly was trying to get hold of you, to ask if you'd go with her to Alice's place. I just happened to go round there to see if she knew where you were, and I offered to go with her.'

Taylor stares at me as his brain scrambles to keep up. 'That must have felt weird.'

'It did. But I'm so desperate for answers, I didn't think about anything else. Like the possibility that Max might have spent time there with her.'

He studies the photos again. 'And you found these in her

wardrobe?'

A shiver of shame runs through me. 'I was just looking at her clothes. I was curious. Clothes can tell us a lot about someone. The envelope was taped to the back of the wardrobe, hidden.'

Taylor smiles. 'She did like clothes. Probably never even wore half of them.' The smile quickly fades. 'I don't get what it means.'

'Neither do I. Except that she must have been following me. I have no idea why, though.'

'She never told me she was doing that. Why wouldn't she tell me?'

'You said she was distancing herself from people in those last few months. Only Alice knew what was going on in her life.'

'And your husband. He knows.'

'*Did* know,' I say. Then I remember I haven't told Taylor about the flat I followed Max to just now. And the fact that Max admitted he's been lying about losing his memory.

Taylor listens while I recount every detail of what happened with Max just now. And while I speak, his forehead is a maze of lines.

'There's one way we can find out about the flat. Come with me.'

In the living room, Taylor opens his laptop. 'What's the address?'

I tell him and he taps on the keys, staring at the screen the whole time. 'There. Kinleigh Folkard & Hayward.'

'What?' I stare at the estate agent's website.

'Look. Here's the flat. And it's showing as still available to rent.'

'Max said he found the keys in his desk drawer...'

Without a word, Taylor grabs his phone and dials a number. Seconds tick by. 'Hi, I've just seen a two-bed property I'm interested in renting on your website. 10A Denmark Road. Is it still available?'

More seconds pass. 'Right... Okay... Thanks.' He hangs up and lets out a deep sigh. 'That property's literally just been taken. Apparently, the person picked up the keys yesterday.' He shakes his head.

'So Max was lying again. He's just rented that place. But why?'

Taylor is silent for a moment. 'I don't know.'

And then it dawns on me, as clearly as if it were written on paper in front of me. 'Because he's leaving. And he wants to take Poppy with him.' Saying this, my heart feels as though it's being wrenched from my body. 'But if he wanted me dead, he and Poppy would be free to have the house. It doesn't make sense.' *And he'd been different last night, more open somehow.*

'You're right,' Taylor says. 'It doesn't add up.'

'Unless... Think about it. Max loves Poppy. He'll want her far away from memories of me. He wants to get her away from the house to protect her.'

Taylor considers this silently for a moment. 'Unless he's changed his plan. There are other ways to get someone out of your life.'

'Like what?'

'Make them seem like they're an unfit mother. I don't know. Make them look guilty of something?'

Alice.

The hotel key card with my prints all over it. The missing evidence linking Max to Alice. My whole body heats up. 'No. He can't. I was with Poppy that evening. And in the shop all day.'

'True. But it might be enough to cast doubt in people's minds. Enough for him to say he should have custody of Poppy. Maybe his plans changed because he's already killed someone and he doesn't want to risk doing it again?'

I've been holding it together for weeks now, soldiering on, fighting to get to the truth. But now salty tears prick at my eyes, and I feel myself crumbling. Losing all sense of what I need to do. The tears come hard and fast. Right here in Taylor's home.

He doesn't say anything, but tentatively reaches for me and holds me close, letting my teardrops spill onto his jumper.

I don't know how long we stay like that, but eventually I pull myself together, feel my strength returning.

'What will you do now?' he asks.

'I can't go home. How can I be under the same roof as him when I can't trust that I'm safe?' And I've already told the school that Max isn't able to pick up Poppy on his own, and that I need to be with him. Just in case he has ideas about taking our daughter.

Taylor considers what I've said for a moment. He chews his bottom lip and studies me. 'Stay here. At least until you sort out something more permanent. I'll go and stay with a friend so you and Poppy can have the place to yourselves.'

His offer takes me by surprise. 'I, um, I don't know. It doesn't seem fair to you. And would it be weird? We hardly know each other and you're doing this huge thing. Look how we met.'

He nods. 'I know. It's crazy. But it also feels like the right thing to do. I made things worse for you, I'm sure. Showing up in your life like that. I blame myself for a lot of what you're going through.'

'You didn't make Max do anything. This isn't your fault.'

'I still feel bad. The least I can do is offer you a place to stay.' He holds up his hands. 'No pressure, though. I'm sure you have other places you can go. But you and Poppy are welcome to stay here, and I'll get out of your way. Just for a few days. Not sure any of my friends would put up with me for longer than that.'

It feels like insanity to even consider Taylor's offer, but

Sarah has no space, and if I stay at my mum's then Max would know exactly where to find me. Mum wouldn't stop questioning me until she knows everything. 'Okay,' I say. 'Thanks. It will give me a chance to work out my next move.'

'You can have my room and Poppy can sleep in the guest room.' He stands up. 'Let me just go and sort out clean sheets. It's not a five-star hotel, but you'll be comfortable and safe.'

While he gets up to make the beds, I message Sarah to ask if she can collect Poppy from school and meet me at her place. She replies immediately.

That's fine. Saw Dean. Lots to tell you. Oh, and I just messaged Max and apparently he's gone into work now for the afternoon. I advised against it but you know Max!

And then I feel a huge swirl of guilt that I didn't even ask her how it went with Dean. Vowing to make it up to her, I go to find Taylor.

He's in the guest room, making up the bed. 'I need to get home quickly and pack some stuff. Max is out so I've got a small window.'

Taylor looks alarmed. 'What if he comes back and finds you there?'

'I'll lock the door from the inside. I'll be fine. It won't take long to throw some clothes in a bag. I'll be back later with Poppy. I don't know how I'll explain all of this to her.'

He nods. 'Be careful.'

As I'm leaving, it occurs to me that I've heard those words too much lately.

The second Sarah opens the door I can tell something's wrong. 'What's happened?' I ask. 'Are you okay?'

She throws her arms around me. 'Life's a bit weird at the moment, and I feel like I've hardly seen you.'

I hear the girls thundering around upstairs, shrieking and laughing. To Poppy, everything is normal. 'Let's sit down and talk a minute. Is this about Dean?'

Sarah has had so little of my time over the last couple of weeks, just when she needs me.

We go through to the kitchen, but neither of us sits. 'I wasn't ready for it,' Sarah says.

'To see Dean?'

'Yeah. Max had practically ordered me to go home again, and then Dean messaged to see if we could meet earlier, so I had the time to meet him. I would have said no if Max had needed me. I hope you know that?'

'I know. But that doesn't matter, anyway. What happened with Dean? And I'm sorry I haven't had a chance to talk to you about it.'

'It was the weirdest thing. I met him in Hammersmith. He wanted to meet in the West End but I said I couldn't. It's too far when I've got school pick-up at three. Anyway, when I got there and saw him, it was as if no time had gone by. He looked exactly the same. But kinder somehow. And guess what? He said he'd left his wife not long after we split up.'

'Oh. Then why didn't—?'

'I know. That's exactly what I asked him. If he left her, then why didn't he contact me and try to see Ivy?' She sighs. 'He said his head was a mess. He needed space from both of us.'

'That just sounds like an excuse, Sarah. Sorry.'

'You're right. I told him that. Or something like that anyway. But he was different, Han. It was like he'd grown up. He said he often thought about Ivy.'

I stifle all the words I want to say. How Dean would never be able to make up for the five years Ivy has lost. How I don't trust why all of a sudden he's finally ready to see his daughter. But of course I stay silent. Sarah needs me to support her.

'I showed him a picture of her,' she continues. 'And he asked if he could keep it. Then we started talking about meeting up. The three of us.'

'Okay. And are you ready for that? Is this what you want?' I don't know why I'm asking this when it's all Sarah's ever wanted.

'I just want Ivy to know her father.' She raises her eyebrows, waiting for my response. Is it approval she needs?

'Okay, well, you have to follow your instinct. And the truth is, Ivy is all that matters in this. So if it's best for her to have Dean in her life, then it's a good move.'

Sarah nods, but doesn't say anything.

'You don't seem happy, though.'

'I am,' she says. 'It was just something Max said the other day when I told him that I was talking to Dean. It kind of bothers me.'

The mention of Max's name makes me stiffen. 'What did he say?'

'He just said that once someone has done something to hurt you or betray you, there's no going back from it. If you forgive them then they'll do it again. Because they know they've got away with it. He said he couldn't remember this but Paula had told him his colleague Peter at work had left them in the lurch, leaving without giving his notice or anything. He said his boss would never trust him again, so there's no way he'd get his job back, even if he came begging. But we do it in relationships all the time.' She pauses. 'I guess that's just bothering me.'

'Don't listen to Max,' I say. 'He doesn't even know Dean.'

'But—'

'I'm leaving him.' The words fire into the room like bullets, stunning Sarah into silence.

It takes her a moment to recover. 'You're leaving Max? But

he's... Why? Hannah, what's going on?'

I'm at a critical juncture again, where I have choices to make that will impact so many people's lives. I've kept Sarah out of this so far, and for her sake I need to continue to keep her in the dark. Even if it means her perception of me will change, and possibly damage our friendship.

'Things haven't been right for a while now,' I begin. 'I didn't tell you this, but before his accident I was planning to leave him. We just can't carry on how things are.'

Again she's rendered speechless. 'I had no idea. I thought Max was just stressed at work.'

'He was. But it's more than that. And I can't do it any more.'

'What does Max say about it? He never said anything.'

'That's the problem. Of course he can't understand any of it. He can't remember the last few months. So I think he's a bit shocked.'

'Why now? Couldn't you wait until he's better?'

'If he's well enough to even think about work, then he can deal with this.' My words are harsh, delivered too sharply.

The look of disgust on Sarah's face is too much. In all the years I've known her, she's never looked at me that way. No matter what I've told her.

'I'm sorry, Han,' she says. 'But that sounds so heartless. Is there something you're not telling me?'

'No.' I swallow the lie, hoping that one day – when the truth is out there – Sarah will be able to forgive me.

She stands up. 'This is a bit of a shock. But... well, it's your life and I trust you've got reasons for walking away, even if I don't understand them. You're supporting me with all the Dean stuff, so I'll support you with this.'

I nod.

For a moment we're silent. It's the first time since I've known Sarah that there's ever been awkwardness between us.

'Can't you give Max another chance?' she says after a while.

'Talk to him and explain how you were feeling before the accident. You can't just throw your marriage away.'

I take my time to answer, search the maze of my mind for a way to help Sarah understand, without having to unbury the truth. 'When it's over, it's over,' I say, turning away from the mixture of confusion and shock on my friend's face.

'I'm guessing you haven't told Poppy yet?' she says.

'No, I'll tell her in the car. I've got somewhere we can stay so we can talk while we're driving there. I've packed some things for us.'

'You really have thought this through, haven't you?'

I've had no choice.

'Stay here,' she says. 'I know there isn't a lot of room, but Poppy can sleep in Ivy's room and I'll sleep on the sofa. It's less drastic than you having your own place somewhere.'

I stand up and hug her. 'Thank you so much. But I need to do this. It will make it easier in the long run.'

'I don't understand,' she says. 'Or at least stay with your mum, then.'

'I can't. This has to be a clean break. A friend is letting us stay at his place. He won't be there for a few days.'

'What friend?' She frowns, and I'm glad I can't read her thoughts. I know it would make me falter.

'Just someone I know from work.' I leave my lie as vague as it can be.

'Okay,' she says. 'Well, I know what you're like when you've made up your mind about something, so there's no point me trying to change it.'

I call out for Poppy, and tell her we have to go.

Surprisingly, she doesn't try to negotiate more playing time. Instead she yawns and rubs her eyes. 'Bye, Ivy,' she says, giving her friend a hug.

Poppy's compliance only makes having to break the news to her even more devastating.

NINETEEN

Extract from police interview with Finley Adams:

DCI Spears: Can you tell us why you didn't come forward when we appealed for help from anyone who knew Alice Hughes?

Finley Adams: I didn't know about it. I've been staying in Birmingham with my cousin. Helping him out and stuff. He's the one who told me.

DCI Spears: Yet you still waited for us to track you down. And we only managed to do that after finding emails between you and Alice from January this year.

Finley Adams: I've been busy. And I hadn't even seen her since April.

DC Langdon: Can you tell us the nature of your relationship?

Finley Adams: We just used to... you know. It was all casual. You know what I mean?

DC Langdon: Not really. Explain it to us.

Finley Adams: I mean, we were just meeting up whenever we felt like it. Nothing serious (*long pause*). It was just sex.

DCI Spears: And what happened in April?

Finley Adams: She just ghosted me. Like I didn't exist any more. No message or call or anything. She just suddenly disappeared.

DC Langdon: I see. That must have made you very angry. I would hate it if someone did that to me. Were you angry with Alice, Finley?

Finley Adams: Are you kidding me? The girl was a psycho. I was glad to be rid of her.

Something crashes into my back, forcing me awake. I roll over and see Poppy flailing around, still asleep. Confusion clouds my mind until I remember.

This isn't our house. It's Taylor's flat. And last night I had to deliver crushing news to my daughter, and watch her face crumple, her body sag as if her heart had been ripped out.

I tried to soften the blow, telling her that Max and I just needed some time apart for a while. But her five-year-old brain couldn't make sense of my words.

Unsurprisingly, she didn't embrace the idea of sleeping in a new place, a place without Max, and it was nearly midnight by the time she fell asleep.

'Poppy?' I gently nudge her. It's nearly seven o'clock and I need to get her ready for school. From here, the school run will be much longer.

Her eyes pop open. 'Where's Daddy?' she asks.

'At home. Remember? We're just staying here for a few days.' The truth is, I have no idea where Max is. He hasn't tried to contact me since I ran from that flat yesterday. But his silence only fills me with dread. 'We need to get ready for school, Poppy. We can call Daddy later. What shall we have for breakfast?'

Taylor bought a few groceries yesterday before he left, from the convenience shop across the road. I haven't checked what there is, and don't expect him to know what Poppy likes for breakfast, but I'm grateful for his kindness.

Poppy yawns and climbs out of bed. I don't know how she'll get through the school day with so little sleep.

While she gets dressed and brushes her teeth, I go to the kitchen to search the cupboards. There are Corn Flakes and Weetabix, bread and jam. A carton of milk. Everything we need.

'Mummy?' I turn around and Poppy's standing in the door-way. 'This feels weird.'

'I know.' I go over to her and put my arms around her. 'But we'll get through it together, okay? You and me.'

Poppy nods and forces a smile. She eats her breakfast in silence; normally, she talks more than she eats, and breakfast can take over half an hour.

Everything feels different when I open up the shop this morning. It's partly because I've driven here from Chiswick, instead of walking from my house. And it's also the fact that

Max is only a few roads away. I'm easy to find if he wants to. He knows how much this place means to me.

Cole arrives not long after me, when I'm immersed in sorting out a new delivery of books. 'Everything okay?' he asks, nudging me.

It would probably be easier not to mention anything that's happening with Max, but I've told enough lies to the people around me. 'Not really.' I say. 'Um, Max and I have separated.'

Cole stares at me for so long I wonder if he'll ever open his mouth. And when he does, he seems lost for words. 'Oh, um... Really?'

'Yes.'

And then his questions come thick and fast: Am I okay? What happened? How is Poppy feeling about it?

Too many questions, none of which I want to answer. 'It's a long story, but Poppy and I have moved out.'

Cole sighs. 'Right. I see. I'm sorry.'

'Thanks.'

'This kind of thing is never easy. My parents divorced when I was ten. Did I tell you that?'

I nod, even though I'm not sure he has ever mentioned it.

'Anyway, it was hard at the time, but as I got older I realised it was the best thing for all of us.' He smiles. 'I'm sorry, though. Where are you staying?'

'At a friend's place. Just for a few days until I can sort out what to do.'

'Hmm. Just be careful. Sarah's single, isn't she? She might not have your best interests at heart. Sorry to say that but you know me. I'm always honest.'

'Sarah's not like that,' I say. I won't put Cole straight about where Poppy and I are really staying. The last thing I need is him questioning me about Taylor. Jumping to conclusions, none of which have any chance of being correct.

Thankfully we're interrupted by a customer; having this

conversation with Cole is too much. It's served me well to keep my work and personal life separate, and I don't want to change that habit now. No matter how bad things are. Having this shop is what will keep me sane.

While Cole goes off to assist the customer, I take the chance to disappear to the office, delving into all the admin I haven't taken care of over the last couple of weeks because I've been so distracted.

Sarah calls to check on me at lunchtime. But there's something off about her voice. Or perhaps it's my paranoia. The doubt that's seeping into my mind like an infection.

'How are you and Poppy?' she asks.

'We'll be okay. Not right now, but eventually.'

Sarah sighs. 'I called Max this morning. He didn't answer.'

'Maybe it's hard for him,' I say. 'Because of our friendship.' But as I say this, my mind scrambles to find the real reason this might be. Does he assume I've told her about the flat? About his threatening behaviour when I followed him there?

'I suppose,' she says.

I wish I could tell Sarah that it's better this way. We both need Max out of our lives.

'I hope you won't be a stranger now that you're living in Chiswick,' she continues.

'It's not far. And anyway, it's only for a few days, until I can work out what to do.'

'I understand.' She pauses. 'I saw Dean again last night. He came over after you left. He just turned up. Said he was passing. I think he was hoping Ivy would be up. Luckily she was in bed, though. I told him we need to work on having a friendship and building trust before he comes into her life. I don't know if I'm doing the right thing.'

'He shouldn't have ambushed you like that. Listen, why don't you come over tonight? Say around eight? We can have a bottle of wine and chat all evening.' I have no idea how Sarah will respond to my offer – I only know I have to be there for her.

'I'd love to. I'll ask Mum to babysit,' she says, just as a message comes through from Taylor, asking how our first night in his flat went. 'Anyway, I'd better go,' she continues. 'I'll pop round and check on Max in a bit. I did take the week off work for him so I may as well make myself useful.'

I'm on the sofa, cuddled up with Poppy, both of us eating popcorn, while I try to distract her with a movie. So far it's working, but I know the minute the film finishes, she'll be silent again. Sadness that she isn't able to articulate swelling in her body.

The doorbell rings and we look at each other. 'Wait here,' I tell Poppy.

I get up and look outside the window, scanning the road for the silver Golf. *AF23 NKT*. The number plate is permanently engraved in my memory now. There's no sign of it, but that doesn't mean it's not close by.

I make my way into the hall, then hesitate for a moment. The chain is on the door – we're safe if I don't open it. 'Who is it?' I call.

'It's Taylor. Just checking you're okay.'

I slide the chain off and let him in.

'Sorry for turning up like this. I did message but you didn't reply. I called too. Got really worried.'

'I've been watching a film with Poppy. To cheer her up. I always put my phone on silent when we have a movie night. Sorry.'

'No, don't apologise. Okay, well, now I know you're okay, I can focus again. I've been messaging all of Alice's clients. Seeing if she might have said anything to anyone. I know the police will have already done it, but it helps to feel that I'm doing something useful. I'll leave you to it.' He turns away.

'There's something I forgot to ask you. It completely slipped my mind. Do you remember I told you about Alice's friend from school, Eloise? I'd forgotten this but when I was talking to Eloise's mum, she mentioned something about Alice having an ex. Do you know who it was?'

Taylor shrugs. 'Not really. Alice had a few short relationships but she never spoke about them much. She said people had a right to privacy so she wasn't going to gossip about her sex life as it was theirs too.'

'So there could have been someone? Earlier this year?'

'Yeah, but I don't know any names.'

'I wonder if it was Max.'

'I'm sure the police have investigated any men who've been in her life,' Taylor says. 'Anyway, I'll leave you to it. I've got more investigating of my own to do.' He gives a small laugh, but it's infused with sadness.

'Why don't you come in for a bit?' I ask. 'It's your place, after all.'

He glances past me. 'Are you sure? Will your daughter mind?'

'Maybe you should meet her. Given that we're living in your flat. Just come in.' I usher him inside, and close the door.

In the living room, Poppy looks up when we come in.

'Poppy, this is my friend Taylor. This is his flat he's kindly let us stay in.'

Her eyes flick between me and Taylor. 'Thank you,' she says.

'Don't mention it. So, what's that you're watching?'

'*Elemental*.'

'Is it good?'

She shrugs. 'Yeah.'

I put my hand on her shoulder. 'How about you carry on watching while I have a quick chat with Taylor in the kitchen?'

'Okay.'

'How's it been, staying with your friend?' I ask once we've left the room.

'Hmm. Sam's a good guy, but I'm not sure his girlfriend's too pleased about me crashing there. I get the feeling she likes to be there every night. Feel a bit like a gooseberry.'

'Sorry. Look, I've been thinking about it, and I need to go to the police. Poppy needs stability. She needs her routine. We've only been here one night and she's distraught. She didn't sleep until gone midnight last night. And it will probably be the same tonight.'

'I get that,' Taylor says. 'Look, I'm no expert in kids, but don't you have to give things a chance? Help them to build resilience? Or something like that.'

Taylor's probably right, but what's the advice for helping your child when their father's committed a heinous crime?

'Sam and his girlfriend are going on holiday this weekend, so that's another week at least that I'll be able to stay there.' He smiles. 'So there's no pressure to rush into anything.' He lowers his voice. 'That gives us time to find that driver. To get the evidence we need. Then you can go home and Max will be out of your lives. You'll have full custody of Poppy, and you won't have to live in fear any more.'

Taylor's describing the ideal scenario. But everything depends on me getting to that man, whoever he is. And now the clock is ticking, so loudly it drowns out everything else.

'We haven't seen the car for a couple of days. What if he's not following either of us any more? Or he's changed cars?' This thought has only just occurred to me, and anxiety floods my body.

'We'll get to him,' Taylor says. 'I don't think Max is finished with whatever he's set in motion.'

We continue talking in low voices, choosing our words carefully in case Poppy overhears, until I'm drained. 'Can we talk about something else?' I ask.

He raises his eyebrows. 'Yeah, course. Like what?'

'I don't know. Tell me about you. Your family. Anything.'

And while he talks, I let his words float around me, picturing the scene he's setting. His early childhood seems to have been a happy one. Two older brothers, summers in France with all his cousins. Parents who were happy together until his dad died. And while I listen, for just a moment I lose myself and forget everything that's happening.

When I look up, Poppy's standing in the doorway watching us. 'Mummy, I'm tired,' she says quietly.

'Okay, I'll put you to bed.' I turn to Taylor. 'I'll just be a sec.'

'No, don't rush. I'll leave you to it,' he says, standing.

'You don't have to go yet,' I blurt out, surprising myself, and clearly Taylor too from the way his eyes widen. But his presence here comforts me, makes me feel a little safer somehow.

He shrugs. 'Maybe just for a bit, then.' He crouches down so he's level with Poppy and holds out his hand. 'It was nice to meet you. Goodnight, young lady.'

To my surprise, Poppy takes his hand and giggles. 'I'm not a *lady*,' she says. 'I'm a girl!'

It takes a while for Poppy to fall asleep, and I begin to regret asking Taylor to stay. I'm wasting his time. Eventually, though, she succumbs, and I turn off the lamp and slip out of the room.

The doorbell rings as I'm shutting her door, and Taylor rushes out of the kitchen. 'Are you expecting anyone?'

That's when I remember I'd told Sarah she could come over tonight. I've been so distracted that it slipped my mind. 'I'm so sorry – I told my friend she could come round. I hope that's okay?'

'No problem. I want you to treat this place like your own.

Within reason, of course. I do quite like the ornaments my mum forced me to put up.'

I check through the peephole to make sure it's Sarah. She's reaching forward to press the bell again when I pull open the door.

'Hey,' she says, holding up a bottle of Prosecco. 'I thought we could both do with this. This week's just been—'

Her face falls when she notices Taylor standing behind me. 'Oh, sorry.'

'I was just leaving,' Taylor says, grabbing his coat. He holds out his hand. 'I'm Taylor. This is my flat usually. But happy to hand it over temporarily to Hannah. She's actually been keeping it a lot tidier than I do.'

Sarah shakes his hand, but her body seems to stiffen, and her lips are pursed. I don't know what she's thinking, but it won't be anywhere close to the truth so I need to set her straight. At least, as much as I can. 'She knows she's always welcome at mine if anything changes,' she says.

Taylor smiles. 'She's lucky to have a friend like you.' He points to the bottle. 'Wine glasses are in the cupboard above the sink.'

Sarah doesn't reply, but steps inside and gives me a hug. She waits for Taylor to leave before speaking. 'Who exactly is he? I don't think Max would like this. I know you said you met him at work, but how well do you know him? I've never heard you mention anyone called Taylor before.'

I wish I could erase the suspicion in her eyes, but she's right to be mistrustful. After all, I am lying about so much. 'He works for a publishing company. He's one of the sales reps.'

Her face softens. 'Oh. But you could have stayed with me.'

'I know. And I really do appreciate that.' I reach for the bottle. 'Come on, let's get this open.'

In the living room, we sit cradling our glasses, as comfortable as two people can be in the home of a stranger.

'So you haven't changed your mind then?' she asks. 'About Max?'

I shake my head, lifting my glass but suddenly not wanting to drink.

'Has he done something? This just seems so out of the blue. I feel like you're not telling me the whole story. We always talk about everything, don't we?'

'Like I said, I've been feeling this way for months. I'm sorry I didn't talk to you about it. You were going through your own stuff. Working so much. Worrying about money. Dean. How did that go last night?'

Her cheeks flush. 'Clearly I still have feelings for him. When I'm around him, I just... I don't know. Want him, I suppose.'

'I could have told you that's how you'd feel.' I pause. 'Does he feel the same?'

'I don't know yet. I'm just trying to suss him out.' She takes a sip of Prosecco. 'This isn't about me, though. It's about Ivy, and what's best for her. Dean doesn't have to want *me*, I just hope he wants his daughter in his life.' She looks at me. 'Anyway, how are *you* doing?'

'Not great. But I'll get through this.' I look at her. 'So will Max.'

'That guy. Taylor. He likes you – I can tell.'

Her comment takes me by surprise, and I feel my cheeks warm. 'No, he doesn't.'

'I'm not blind, Han. I saw the way he looked at you. Don't tell me you haven't noticed. Did you leave Max because of him? You can tell me. What do we always say?'

'Friends for life, no matter what.'

'So if there's something going on with that guy – please just tell me.'

I stand up, trying to stem my anger. No matter what she's saying, Sarah deserves my patience. 'I'm not interested in

Taylor. He's a friend. Anything else is the last thing on my mind.'

Her questioning eyes rest heavily on me. 'Okay. You've said it so I believe you.'

I turn back to the window to avoid caving in and telling her everything.

My chest tightens. The silver Golf is out there, parked across the road. *AF23 NKT*. I turn to Sarah. 'I need to run out and do something really quickly. Could you just stay here with Poppy? I'll be two minutes.'

'Yes, but what—?'

I've already left the room before she's finished her sentence.

I fly down the stairs, almost tripping over in my haste to get outside. The street is quiet, and the car is still there, a man sitting in the driver's seat, staring at his phone.

I hesitate at the entrance to Taylor's building, unable to move. I've never felt fear like this.

But the man in that car is the only person who can give me answers.

TWENTY

I've never seen him before. There's no stab of recognition as I stare at this man. He's at least forty years old. Dark hair flecked with grey. Hazel eyes spread too far apart. A nose that turns up at the end. Even sitting down and dressed in a hooded top, I can tell that he's muscular. Bulky.

He stares at me, his eyes bulging when he realises who I am. And that I'm right here in front of him. He mouths something: *What the fuck?* And then he's starting the engine, grabbing the steering wheel. The car lurches forward.

I bang on the window. 'Wait! Please! I just need to talk to you. Please!'

He ignores me and drives, so I have no choice but to jump on the bonnet, grabbing hold of the windscreen wipers. They'll snap off in a minute, and I'll be on the ground. Underneath this car.

'Crazy bitch!' he shouts, but still I hang on.

The car picks up speed, and again I wonder if this is it for me. But then we reach the end of the road and he slams on the brakes. My grip loosens and I'm flung to the ground. I land on my side, pain searing though my body. I'm only inches from the front wheels, and they're edging towards me.

I try to scramble up, but I sink back to the ground. I need to crawl away. But even if I can manage it, he'll just plough into me. I close my eyes, try to summon the energy to move.

This is how I'm going to die. And what will happen to Poppy now?

But then he kills the engine and silence falls. I hear the car door open and heavy footsteps approaching.

He crouches down. 'What the fuck were you doing?' His breath smells of cigarettes.

Only now do I open my eyes. He's tall, looming over me, my life in his hands.

'I need to talk to you,' I manage to say.

He shakes his head, then reaches down and drags me up. 'Get in the car.'

Every bone in my body hurts, and I force myself to roll onto my side, waiting for the dizziness to subside. Then I do as he says. I want answers. Even if I'm not around to act on them. I manage to hobble to the car, and as soon as I'm inside he speeds off, screeching around the corner.

'Where are you taking me?' I fumble around to fasten my seatbelt for fear of smashing through the window. He's driving way too fast for this residential road.

'You said you wanted to talk. So that's what we're about to do.' His voice is deep, and there's a hint of a regional accent I can't place.

'Where?'

'Away from here. That's all you need to know. Stop asking questions.'

I stay silent after that. I have no phone on me. No bank cards. I was in such a rush to get to him that I left with nothing on me. Not even my coat. But I'm not cold – I'm too warm.

Without warning, he takes a sharp left and pulls up outside an old church. There's a park on the other side of the road, empty at this time of night. And there's no one walking down either pavement.

He turns to me. 'Talk, then. What do you want?'

For a moment I'm frozen, my mind unable to compute that I'm in a car with this man. A man who wants me dead. Then I think of Poppy and I find my voice. 'Why are you following me?'

He stares at me, chewing gum. 'I do what I'm paid to do.'

'By who?'

'Do you really think I'm gonna tell you that?'

'Then why are you talking to me now?'

He reaches into the glove compartment and pulls out a packet of cigarettes, throwing his gum out of the window before he places one in his mouth. 'You came to *me*. Invaded *my* space. I have to put that right.' Opening the window, he lights his cigarette and takes a long drag. At least he has the decency to blow the smoke out of the window. 'I'm working out what to do,' he says. 'This wasn't supposed to happen.'

'You could have run me over just now. Why didn't you?'

He laughs. 'Really? Right there in front of all those houses? Did you see how many lights were on? All it would take is one person to be looking out. People are nosy. I've noticed that. No one minds their own business.'

I look around. This street is different to Taylor's. No houses. Just an empty church and a locked playground.

My pulse quickens. 'I'll give you fifteen thousand pounds,' I say, sickened by the large amount I'm offering. 'If you'll tell me everything and then stay away from me. Pretend you've never met me or my husband.'

He turns to me, but a few seconds pass before he responds. 'You must be desperate,' he says, inhaling on his cigarette. He turns to the window to blow out the smoke.

'Please. I know that's more than my husband offered you.'

He frowns. 'It is.'

My chest constricts, and I struggle to catch my breath. So this is real.

'Will you... will you take it, then?' I manage to ask.

'Where is it? I know you aren't carrying fifteen grand around with you.'

'I don't have that kind of money on me. I'll need to withdraw it from the bank. And not all at once. But you have my word, I'll get it to you.'

He grabs my wrist. 'Don't fuck me about. I don't like playing games.'

'I'm not, I swear.' I try to pull away from him but his grip is too strong. 'Let go of me!'

He drops my arm. 'You've got three days,' he says, blowing smoke into my face. 'No longer.' He flicks his cigarette out of the window. 'Get out.'

'Wait. Please just tell me what Max said.'

'Money first,' he says. 'Now get out before I change my mind.'

I open the door and clamber out, wincing in pain. I'm already dreading the thought of walking back this late along these cold, dark streets. But now I don't even know if my body will get me there.

I lean into the window. 'How will I find you? When I've got the money?'

'You won't. I'll find you. I think you know by now how easily I can do that.' He slams his foot down on the accelerator and I watch him disappear around the corner.

It takes me a moment to compose myself and I stand alone on an unfamiliar road, without my phone, and with only the vaguest idea of how to get back to Taylor's flat.

. . .

Sarah's looking out of the window when I make it back. I try to walk normally, so that she doesn't notice the pain I'm in.

When I get upstairs, she's holding the door open for me, pulling me inside. Shooting pains almost cripple me.

'What's the matter?' she asks. 'You don't look right.'

'I fell. Tripped over something. I'm okay, though.'

'Jesus. When?'

'Just now.'

'But where have you been? I've been worried! You've been gone for ages. You said you'd be two minutes.' She hands me my phone. 'And you left this. I was about to call the police.'

'I'm fine.'

'But why did you rush off like that? Where did you go?'

It occurs to me that Sarah might have been watching me from the window. 'I saw someone I knew. An old friend I went to school with. Sorry. She's not on Facebook and I haven't seen her for years.'

'Oh, okay.' She looks a bit doubtful but she lets it go. 'Poppy woke up as soon as you'd gone. She said she was thirsty, so I got her some water.'

'Thanks.'

'Then she freaked out because you weren't here, so I sat in there with her until she fell asleep. She's only just drifted off now.'

'I'm sorry. I would have messaged you if I'd had my phone.'

'Well, you're okay. That's all that matters.' She sighs. 'I'm not sure Max is okay, though. Sorry to say this but I have to be honest.'

'What do you mean?'

'He's not answering his phone or replying to any of my messages. When does Max ever do that? He always replies. He's anal about it. And I don't think it's just because I'm your friend.' She shakes her head. 'I'm sorry, Han, but I just don't get how you can do this. The man was attacked. He could have been—'

'Stop! Please. You don't... you don't know everything.'

Sarah studies me carefully. 'What are you saying?'

I usher her into the living room so we don't disturb Poppy. I sit down, but Sarah hovers by the window. 'What is it?' she asks. 'Just talk to me!'

'Max was having an affair.'

Silence falls heavily around us. I can't think of a time when Sarah's ever struggled to find any words.

'I'm so sorry,' she says. 'How do you know? Did he tell you?'

'No. He doesn't know I found out. And I don't want to go into details. But now do you understand why I'm leaving him?'

She nods, and joins me on the sofa. 'Yes. Who was it? Someone at work?'

'I don't know her name.' *Alice*. 'But most likely.'

'Shouldn't you tell him you know?'

'I've got to think about Poppy. I don't know what to say to him right now; all I know is I need to be away from him. To sort my head out.'

She frowns. 'I get that. But I'm still worried about him. He's not answering the door, or returning calls or messages. Has he even spoken to Poppy?'

'We tried him earlier. He didn't answer.' I swallow my lie.

'And you're not worried? I know you're probably angry with him, but what if something's happened to him? I know it's late, but maybe I'll pop over there on my way home. Just check he's all right.'

'Okay.'

I see Sarah to the door and give her a hug.

'I'll let you know how he is,' she says, before I close the door.

And I can tell – despite what I've just told her – that she's still wondering why I appear not to care.

. . .

I've just finished brushing my teeth when Sarah texts.

> *He didn't answer. No lights on. I can't tell if he's there. His car's still on the drive, but that doesn't mean much as he hasn't been driving since the attack. Messaged him again but no reply. Can you check on him in the morning?*

How can I possibly tell Sarah that there's no way I want to walk into that house if Max is in there? That I would be walking into a trap? I sit staring at my phone for a moment, starting and deleting messages before I settle on one:

Yes

TWENTY-ONE

Poppy grips my hand tightly as I walk her to school. Traffic on Fulham Palace Road was slow-going, and the only place I could park the car was at my house. The blinds were closed, and Max's car sat outside, exactly where it was when I followed him to that flat in Wimbledon.

Poppy had cried when she saw the house, begging to go inside to see Daddy, so I had to tell her he was away for a few days. She'd taken that well, and started suggesting all the places Max could be taking a holiday.

'Myah's mummy and daddy aren't together either,' she says, as we approach the school gates. 'And she said it's nice having two homes. She gets to spend loads of time with her daddy. Will I, too?'

I pull her close to me and wrap my arms around her. 'That's the plan,' I say. I long to tell her that of course she will. More than she ever has before; because isn't that the way it should be? But I won't make her that promise when there's no way it will happen. Not with everything Max is guilty of. And once I've paid the money and spoken to that man, I'll have everything I need to go to the police.

'Can we stay at home now?' she asks. 'If Daddy isn't there? Please, Mummy!' Tears stream down her cheeks, and it feels as though my heart is being wrenched from my body. I hug her tightly, and tell her I can't promise anything, but I'll try my best to see if there's a way to do that.

And now my own tears blur my eyes as I watch her trot through the gates, her bunches swinging. She turns around and waves, and I blow her a kiss, waiting until she's disappeared before I rush away. I don't want anyone asking me if I'm okay.

I walk home, though my house no longer feels like my own. I promised Sarah I'd check on Max so I have no choice now. Besides, I don't think he ever planned to hurt me himself, otherwise that man in the silver Golf would never have shown up in my life.

I pull out my key and open the door, calling his name. Most of the time it's obvious when houses are empty, and I know it now as soon as I step inside.

In every room, I open the blinds, taking in every detail. Max's slippers tucked under the sofa, where he always leaves them. The books on the coffee table neatly placed. Everything is tidy, exactly where it should be.

It's the same in the rest of the house. And there's nothing in the kitchen sink or the dishwasher. Upstairs, the bed is made, and all of Max's clothes hang in the wardrobe.

But downstairs, his coat, wallet and keys are missing. So, too, is his laptop.

I pull out my phone and call Paula. It rings for so long that I'm about to hang up when she finally answers.

'Hannah. Hello.' Her voice is laced with impatience.

'I'm sorry to bother you, but have you heard from Max?'

'Not since he came into work the other day. Why? What's happened?'

'No one's heard from him, and it looks like he didn't sleep at home last night.'

There's no response, other than a deep sigh. 'Is he with someone?'

'I don't know. But I've left him, so I'm not worried about that. Poppy needs to know where her dad is, though.'

There's a pause. 'If I hear from him, I'll let you know. I have to go now – I'm in the office about to go into a meeting.'

We end the call, and I notice it's nearly half past nine. I should have been in the shop well over half an hour ago, and I still need to get to the bank. I message Cole to tell him I'm running late but I'm on my way.

I feel like a criminal standing in line at the bank. Silently I remind myself that it's my money, and I'm free to do with it what I like. But that does little to ease my anxiety. I prepare myself to be interrogated, but to my surprise, the young bank teller barely raises an eyebrow. I have all of my identification, and within minutes the money is in an envelope inside my bag.

All the way to the shop, I clutch my bag tightly to my body. I'm taking a huge risk walking around like this, but I don't have a choice.

I call a greeting to Cole when I get inside the shop, and tell him I'll be right down.

'No problem,' he says, as I rush past him and the young male customer he's serving.

Upstairs in the staffroom, I pull out the money and slip it inside my locker, checking the door is locked several times before I leave the room. If there was a way to contact the man I'm handing it over to, I'd do it now, and get rid of the envelope before anything can happen to it. *Just like the key card. And Taylor's phone.* But I'm at this man's whim, forced to wait until he decides to find me.

'Is everything okay?' Cole asks, when I get back to the shop floor. 'I know it isn't, but you know what I mean. I mean, how are you doing?'

'I've been better. But I'm okay. At least I've got this place.'

'And you've got good friends,' Cole says. 'Don't forget that.'

'I won't.'

'Speaking of which, I know you're all sorted for a place to stay, but if you and Poppy want to then you're welcome to stay with me. I know it's not huge, but there are two bedrooms and two bathrooms so we wouldn't be in each other's way.' He smiles. 'Totally understand if you think it's a bit much working together and living together, though. I know I'm not everyone's cup of tea.' He looks down, staring at his shoes.

'If anyone thinks that, then you don't need them in your life,' I say.

He looks up, smiling. 'It's true what they say. Saying just one kind thing can make someone's day. Anyway, I need to order in some things for the café. Oh, that reminds me. We need to start thinking about a replacement for Katy, don't we? My niece Ella would be perfect. She's a student and needs a part-time job. She's just started at Roehampton uni, so she'll just be round the corner. It's ideal for all of us. And you've met her before – do you remember?'

I vaguely recall Cole introducing me to his sister and her teenage daughter in the shop a few years ago, but I wouldn't recognise the girl if she was standing in front of me. All my focus was on Cole's sister – how different she was from him. Confident and fashionably dressed. Easy-going and relaxed. 'I guess that's okay. Tell her to come in for a chat.'

Cole beams. 'Will do. My sister will be pleased. Brownie points for me.'

When I pick Poppy up from school, she's smiling as she walks out, hand in hand with Oscar, one of the boys she went to nursery with.

'Hi, sweetie,' I say, handing her an apple. 'Hi, Oscar.'

'Can Poppy come for a play date? My mum's just over there.' He points to a huddle of mums, and I recognise Andrea in the middle of them.

'Um, maybe not today, but another time.'

'Okay,' he says. 'Bye, Poppy.'

When he gallops off to his mum, I turn to Poppy. 'Have you had a good day?'

'Quite good,' she says, her mouth full of apple.

'Well, it's about to get better. We're off to Grandma's for dinner. She said she'll make us spaghetti bolognese – isn't that great?'

'Yay!' she says, and for the first time in days I see a glimpse of the Poppy she was before Max and I turned her life upside down.

'So that's it then? Mum asks, as she's dishing up dinner. 'You're just walking away.'

'It's for the best, Mum.'

This would be the time to tell her exactly what I told Sarah, to put an end to her questioning, her defending Max. But I won't. Mum would know I'm not telling the whole truth, and she wouldn't stop until she's got it all out of me.

Silently, I take the plates through to the dining room, placing them on the table.

She follows me, taking my arm. 'I know you, Hannah. There's something going on. Please talk to me.'

'I can't right now. One day. Soon. But not right now. Can you just trust me?'

With a sigh, she nods, heading back to the kitchen for cutlery. 'Poppy, dinner's ready,' she calls.

'There is something, though, Mum. Nobody's heard from Max for a while. He's not at the house and isn't answering the phone or replying to messages.'

'Can't say I'm surprised about that. He probably feels ashamed. You've left him, he doesn't want to face any of it.'

'But it's strange that his PA at work hasn't heard from him. He's been in contact with her every day since he got out of hospital. And suddenly nothing.'

Before she can answer, Poppy appears, carrying the dog. 'Can Peach sit on my lap while I eat?' she asks.

'No, she won't like that,' Mum says. 'Dogs aren't good at sitting still.'

Poppy sets her down and sits at the table.

My mum tries to distract her during dinner, asking her about the flat we're staying in, and how school is going.

Poppy answers politely, but she's quiet and not her usual self. She often talks at a hundred miles an hour, saying whatever she's thinking with no filter.

When it's approaching her bedtime, I tell Mum we have to get going, and she walks us out to the car.

'Maybe you should report him missing,' she whispers, when I've buckled Poppy into her car seat and walked around to the driver's side. 'If you're worried. I've been thinking, and that's what I'd do. You don't have to wait until it's been a few days. If it's out of character then it's important they're aware.'

She's right. Even though my instinct is telling me Max has disappeared on purpose. Why, I have no idea. All I know is that he's not going to let Poppy go. Ever.

I hug Mum goodbye and drive back to Taylor's, all the time hoping the silver Golf will appear in my rear-view mirror. It doesn't, of course, and this only makes me more nervous. Fearful. Because I have no control over anything.

. . .

When Poppy's in bed, lost to slumber, I sit in the living room with a glass of wine. I'm wearing a thick wool cardigan and two layers underneath it to save putting the heating on. Taylor's doing enough for us already – I don't want to take advantage and hike up his utility bills.

Thinking of him now reminds me I haven't told him about my encounter with the driver of that car. I reach for my phone and text him, leaving out the more harrowing details. And I tell him I've already got the money.

His reply is instant: *I'm coming over*.

He's here within half an hour, messaging me when he's outside the door so that he doesn't wake Poppy.

'Hi,' he says, when I open the door. 'I didn't want to use my key. I want you to feel that it's your place while you're staying here.'

I hold up my glass. 'I'm on the wine. Poppy was so tired she actually fell asleep quite early. Can I get you one?'

He laughs. 'Well, it is Friday night. And I'm glad Poppy seems to be settling.'

In the kitchen, while I'm pouring a glass for Taylor, I wonder how it's possible that he can make me feel so at ease, when everything I thought I knew about my life has been blown apart.

'You're not going to like this,' Taylor says. 'But there's a reason I came here.'

My back stiffens. 'What is it? Have you found something out? Is it Max?'

'No. Nothing like that. It's...' His face flushes. 'I came because I've already lost one person I care about. And I don't want to lose another. Sorry. You seem like the last person who needs looking after, but I'd never forgive myself if anything happened to you.' He takes the glass I hand him. 'I know you can handle yourself, but when you messaged that you'd talked to the driver of that Golf, I just...' He looks away. 'I'm sorry. This whole situation is crazy. I've only just met you... but I feel so comfortable around you.' He gestures with his free arm. 'Even with all of this going on.'

'Let's sit,' I say, pulling out a chair. Taylor puts down his glass and does the same.

I study his face, choosing my words carefully. This is something I've thought myself over the last few days. 'I'm not a replacement for Alice,' I say. 'And you're not one for Max. I don't think either of us can trust how we're feeling at the moment. This isn't a normal situation. But if there's anything there after all of this is... resolved, then that's a different story.'

Taylor considers what I've said, lifting his glass. 'Got it.'

'But I do know what you mean. About feeling comfortable. I mean, I do too.'

He smiles and nods. 'So, fifteen grand. That's a lot of money, Hannah. I really don't think you should do it. There has to be another way to get him to talk.'

'Money's the only thing people like him will listen to.'

Taylor sighs. 'I just don't like it. Not just that it's a huge amount, but that he's clearly a dangerous man.'

'He didn't deny he'd been sent to follow me. He pretty much said he does whatever he's told by the person paying him.' As I say this, I wonder how I can speak with such detachment. As if it's not me who my husband has paid a hitman to follow. But thinking of it now turns my blood to ice.

Taylor takes my hand. 'We need to go to the police, Hannah. Let them deal with this.'

'Let me speak to him first. He knows everything. And the police won't be able to ignore that, will they?'

Taylor shakes his head. 'At least let me be with you when you hand the money over.'

'Yeah. Okay. Thanks.' I pull away, because it feels too good.

'He's given me until Sunday, so I assume he'll just show up then.'

'Then I'll clear whatever plans I have and be around all day.' He squeezes my shoulder. 'It will be all right. I don't know how, but I have to believe it will.'

For hours we talk, finishing the bottle of wine and then another. And in that time our conversations seem to be about everything. Alice. Max disappearing. Taylor's work. My shop. We only notice the time when a message pings on my phone. It's three a.m. Ignoring the message, I tell him that I need to get some sleep. Cole is due in late tomorrow so I'm opening up the shop on my own.

At the door, Taylor gives me a brief hug. 'We'll get through this,' he says, disappearing down the stairs.

It's only when I'm in bed that I remember the text message. I reach for my phone and check it now. It's from an unknown number.

You're wrong if you think you'll ever be free. Keep looking over your shoulder, Hannah.

TWENTY-TWO

Putney Community Group
Public Group, 10.7K members

Lana Jankowski: What's happening with the Alice Hughes case? It's gone very quiet. We need justice for Alice.

Comments:

Sam Castle: Nothing's happening. No witnesses. No CCTV. Nothing. They'll never find out who did it.

Isabella Howard: A friend of mine was her client. She said Alice was definitely seeing someone. And she thinks Alice was hiding something. She started acting really weird. Cutting their sessions short because she was in a state. That kind of thing.

Sarah Brooks: Have some respect. You shouldn't be talking about her on here. If you've got anything to say then go to the police.

Nita Luthra: I'm Alice's neighbour and she was lovely. Always friendly. I never saw her with any man. But maybe that's because I mind my own business and get on with my own life.

Sitting opposite the young male police officer puts me on edge. I might have had nothing to do with Max's disappearance, but there's an avalanche of lies I've told waiting to take me under. And there's something about this uniformed police officer, the way his eyes narrow as he questions me. I need to be on my guard with him.

He looks around the house, silently taking everything in, noticing things any civilian would pay no mind to. I wonder how long he's had this job – if he has that desperate urge to prove himself to his older, more experienced colleagues. These are the people you have to watch out for. The ones who are hungry for success.

Thankfully Mum could have Poppy today, so she's spared from witnessing this.

'So you say you haven't seen him since Wednesday morning.' He does a quick calculation. 'Three days. Can I ask why you're only reporting it now?'

'I thought I had to wait. I didn't realise I could report someone missing straight away if they're not a child or someone vulnerable. I would never have waited otherwise.' It sickens me how easily lies roll off my tongue now.

He nods. 'The thing is, after his attack, he would be considered a high priority. Did you not realise that?'

My cheeks burn. 'Yes, I just... the last I heard was that there was another attack, so you thought it was the same person who attacked Max.'

'We try not to jump to conclusions.'

'I feel terrible.' I study the police officer's face, but there's no way to tell if he believes me.

He doesn't reply.

I answer the rest of his questions. Tell him how worried I am. That of course Max and I haven't argued, or had any problems in our marriage. And all the while I bury my guilt that I'm lying about everything, and Max is out there somewhere, safe enough to possibly be sending me threatening messages.

When PC Adams is happy he has all the information he needs, he asks if he can check the house. And with his words, my body freezes as the realisation dawns on me that Max could have got the driver of the Golf to steal the key card so he can hide it somewhere. In my things. So there's no doubt who it belongs to. With everything that's happened, my mind pushed it aside, but I'm convinced Max is the one who found it.

It's too late now. PC Adams is standing up, and I have no choice but to let him search the house. 'It won't take long,' he assures me. 'You can stay here.'

After an agonising wait, he finally comes back into the living room. I search his face, try to get a feel for what he's about to say so I can prepare myself. But his lips form a thin smile and he tells me he's all done.

'This will be logged on the system. Please let us know straight away if you hear from him or if he turns up. You'll be contacted by someone from missing persons.'

I'm tempted to stand by the window and watch him, just to make sure he's gone, but no doubt he'd notice me. Instead I go to the kitchen and fill a glass with water, drinking it all in one go.

And then it hits me, like a truck slamming into me: How am I going to explain to Poppy why her dad can't even call to say goodnight to her? And what if something truly terrible has happened to him this time?

. . .

The first thing I do when I get to work is check my locker. The envelope with the money in it is still there, but that does little to relieve my anxiety. I need it gone. I need some answers to go to the police with, so that they will put every resource they can spare into finding Max.

And then he'll no longer be out there, a threat looming over me, paralysing me.

'Everything okay?'

I slam the locker shut and turn to face Cole. 'Yeah, just, um...' I need something to distract him. 'Um, Max has gone missing. A few days ago. I was just at the house with a police officer.'

Cole looks shocked. 'Oh, that's... I'm sorry.'

'He's probably just avoiding me. Avoiding everyone. I'm sure he'll be back.'

'But aren't you worried? First he's attacked, and now this? Something feels a bit weird to me.'

'Then maybe you should channel that into your book instead of my life,' I snap. 'He'll be fine. He's cooling off somewhere. Getting used to the fact that our marriage is over.'

'Sorry, I didn't mean to—'

'No, I'm the one who should apologise. I shouldn't have said that.' The look on Cole's face makes me loathe who I'm becoming. I've never spoken to him so harshly before.

'It was a bit cruel,' he says. 'You know how much my novel means to me. I put everything into it. When I'm not here, that is.'

'I know, I'm sorry.'

That seems to appease him. 'Don't worry about it. Shall we get back downstairs? I had to lock the door, and there might be customers trying to come in. And it's not professional, is it? When we're open, we're open.'

I'm on edge for the rest of the morning, constantly on alert, my head bolting up whenever anyone comes into the shop. At least now I know what the driver of the Golf looks like. His face is permanently ingrained in my memory: the upturned nose and eyes set wide apart. Dark salt-and-pepper hair. Along with how, for those infinite seconds, he had my life in his hands.

Cole's having lunch in the staffroom when Taylor appears. 'Hey, are you okay?' he asks.

I glance around to make sure Cole hasn't suddenly appeared, relaxing an iota when there's no sign of him. 'The police were at my house earlier. I had to report Max missing. Otherwise, how would it look?'

'Yeah, I guess. What did you say?'

'I made it seem like we were fine, and that I was still living there. Otherwise they would have started questioning my involvement. And I'm sure he *is* fine.'

Taylor doesn't look convinced. 'How do you know that, though? The same person who attacked him could have—'

'I can't be sure, but I think he sent me this last night.' I pull out my phone and scroll to the message. 'He must have got a new phone.'

Taylor scans the message. 'I don't like this. He's not letting this go, is he?' He frowns. 'Are you sure you're being honest with me? There's nothing I should know?'

'No! What are you saying?'

'Nothing. Sorry. My head's just a mess. Since I was a kid, my mum's been drumming it into me not to trust anyone. It's kind of stuck.'

'Did you trust Alice?' I don't know what makes me say this, and for a second Taylor looks as shocked as I am.

Before he can answer, I hear Cole's footsteps on the stairs. 'Quick, you have to go. Cole's seen you in here before. He'll ask questions.'

'Meet me for lunch, then? How about Coppa Club?'

'Okay. Give me half an hour.'

Taylor makes it through the door just as Cole appears.

'I'll take over if you want your lunch now, Hannah,' he says, smiling.

'Yeah, I think I'll pop out for a bit. Clear my head.' I turn back to him. 'We really do need to get someone in to replace Katy. Any news from your niece?'

'Oh, yes, I forgot to tell you. Ella can come and see you this evening.' He smiles. 'Let's hope she does a better job at turning up than Katy.'

Taylor's already seated at a table when I get to the restaurant. I've been to Coppa Club before, with Max and Poppy on Max's birthday last year. Our food order had taken an especially long time, so Max had spent the whole of the wait playing noughts and crosses with Poppy. I could tell he needed a break, and I'd tried to take over, but Poppy had insisted that she had to play with Daddy. It was his birthday, after all.

I force this memory from my mind as I join Taylor. 'Did he see me?' he asks. 'Your colleague. Cole, is it?'

'Yeah. And no, he didn't. At least he didn't mention anything. Which is unlike him, so I'm assuming he didn't.'

A waiter comes over to take our order, and I'm surprised at how hungry I suddenly feel. I've barely eaten for days and it's bound to have caught up with me, no matter what stress I'm under. I order a Caesar salad and fries, and Taylor opts for a burger.

'You asked me whether I trusted Alice,' he says, when the waitress disappears to get our drinks. 'The truth is, I don't think I did. Not at the end. I think I've been struggling to admit that to myself.' He pauses. 'When someone dies, it's like you don't want to see any bad in them. And none of us are saints, are we?

We paint the dead as these angelic flawless people who did no wrong. But the truth is, I don't know what Alice was capable of at the end. She'd changed beyond recognition.'

'Do you still believe she was leaving Max? And that she wanted no part in what he was planning? That he wanted me dead so he could have Poppy?'

'Alice wouldn't hurt anyone. She was just troubled. I just don't know what she did to make him want to kill her.'

'Those photos of me, though. Why did she have those?'

'I wish I could tell you,' Taylor says. 'Sometimes Alice was hard to fathom.'

The waitress brings our drinks over. I'm only having apple juice – I need my senses on high alert.

'Please don't take it personally if I find the whole trust thing hard,' Taylor says.

'I won't. And I still don't trust you.' Even as I say this, I wonder if I mean it, or if somehow something has changed. It's hard to spend so much time with someone – under challenging circumstances – and not form a bond with them.

Taylor reaches for my hand, and for a moment I let him, because it feels good to feel something other than pain. And fear.

'One day we'll be able to look back on this with perspective, and everything will look a whole lot different,' he says.

I pull my hand away. This feels too intimate, and I'm not ready for it. I'm not sure I ever will be. I ask Taylor if he's heard from Molly Hughes, and our conversation resumes on safer ground.

'She's just frustrated that the police don't seem to be getting anywhere. They have DNA evidence apparently, but no one to link it to. Fingerprints from the room. But there are all the people who have stayed in that room before. It must be a nightmare for the police. Who knows how thoroughly hotel rooms get cleaned. And it's not exactly a five-star hotel.'

My heart beats faster. 'And here we are, sitting on information about Max. A possible suspect.' I tell Taylor what I've only just decided in the last few minutes. 'When I meet up with that man and hand him the money – I'll record our conversation.'

Taylor's eyes widen. 'That's risky, Hannah.'

'I know, but it will be enough to go to the police with. And maybe Max's fingerprints are all over the hotel room.'

'I don't like it,' Taylor says. 'But I don't think we have any choice.'

When our food arrives, I try to change the subject, but Taylor just pushes food around his plate. This is getting to him.

We've just paid the bill when I glance up and see a man standing by the bar, his back to us. Instantly I recognise him. The bulky body beneath a blue hooded top, the dark salt-and-pepper hair. Away from his car, he looks out of context.

Adrenalin courses through me. And nausea. 'Taylor. He's there. By the bar. He must have been following us.'

Taylor turns around, frowning. 'The man in the Golf?'

'Yes. That's him in the navy hoodie.'

'Stay here,' he says, springing up before I can object.

Unnoticed, he makes his way towards the bar. But it's only a matter of time before the man notices him. Everything seems to happen in slow motion. Just as Taylor reaches him, the man catches sight of him, jumping up from his bar stool and shoving him so hard that Taylor loses his balance. Then he is running for the doors, disappearing from sight.

Taylor manages to grab a bar stool to stop himself falling, and within seconds he's chasing after him, yelling at him to stop. But of course the man doesn't listen. I grab my bag and sprint after them.

I scan Putney Wharf, the indistinguishable crowd that floats in front of me, but there's no sign of either of them.

'Taylor!' I shout, but my words wither and die in the cacophony of traffic and voices.

And then I see him, walking towards me, clutching his stomach. Dark red blood drips from his head.

And then he collapses in a heap on the ground.

TWENTY-THREE

I sit in the hospital waiting room, feeling as though I have no business being here this time. It's not my husband in there being checked over by doctors.

But it's all because of me that Taylor is here now.

We've been here for three hours, and Cole didn't buy one word of my excuse that I'm not feeling well and had to go home. The lies are so tiring. I don't know how much longer I can keep it all up.

'But Ella's coming in at five,' he'd said, as if that could change the state of my health.

'You'll have to interview her,' I'd told him. 'Get her to fill out an application form and the job's hers. See if she can start tomorrow.'

'Are you sure about this? You're normally so fussy. I'd hate to—'

'Do *you* trust her?'

'Yes. One hundred per cent.'

'Then that's good enough for me.' I'd hung up, just as Taylor had been called in by the triage nurse.

Taylor walks towards me now, a large dressing covering the

cut on his head. 'They said I can go. But I'll need someone to stay with me for twenty-four hours. Concussion. Just in case something happens. Sam's away but I'll call another friend. I'm sure he won't mind having a night in for a change.' He pulls out his phone.

'No,' I say, placing my hand on his arm. 'I'll stay with you. It's your place. You should be where you feel comfortable.'

'Won't Poppy mind? I don't want to make things worse.'

'I'm sure my mum won't mind having her overnight. It's the weekend, so she won't have to worry about getting Poppy ready for school. And tomorrow is when the money is due.'

'Come on, let's get an Uber to my house to pick up my car.'

Night-time has crept up on us by the time we get back to Taylor's. He lies on the sofa, while I make tea.

'Shall we order pizza?' I suggest, and then I laugh at how ludicrous it is that we're talking about what takeaway to order when Taylor could have been killed. And when Max is out there, hiding in the shadows. *Planning what?*

'Yeah, anything,' Taylor says. 'I'm not that hungry, though. My head feels like it's been crushed.'

'He's a loose cannon, to say the least, isn't he? Whoever that man is?'

He nods. 'I told him you had the money. I was trying to make him stop. But he didn't want to listen to me. And you're about to give him fifteen grand.'

I ignore his comment. 'Do you think he's the same person who stole your phone and attacked you last time?'

Taylor considers this. 'Maybe. Probably. I don't know. When my phone was stolen, there were two of them, though. Maybe he has people he works with. I don't know what those people do.'

I order the pizza on my phone. 'What about Max?' I ask,

when I've finished.

'What about him?'

I try to organise my thoughts. 'What if I've got this all wrong? Max was attacked too. What if this is something to do with Alice?'

'You're not making sense. I know my head's foggy, but—'

'What I mean is – what if it was Alice who wanted to hurt me?'

'No. I told you she wouldn't hurt anyone. When I said I didn't trust her, I didn't mean that she could hurt people. She never would. This is a woman who would save ants if she ever found one in her kitchen. I'd tell her just to hoover them up and she'd have a go at me, tell me that they're all God's creatures. And why are we more important than an ant just because we're human?'

'That doesn't mean—'

'She was leaving Max, remember? That's the whole reason she's dead! Why would she want you hurt? Sorry, Hannah, but you're wrong.'

'What about the photos she had of me?'

He sighs. 'I know. I'm not saying she wasn't a bit obsessed with you because you're the woman Max chose to marry. Maybe he was messing her around in the beginning. Making her believe he would never leave you. I don't know, Hannah!' He closes his eyes for a moment. 'Let me see those photos again.'

I reach under the sofa cushion and pull out the brown envelope. He stays silent as he studies each one, and then he begins placing them in some kind of order.

When he's finished, he turns to me. 'Right. From what you're wearing in each photo, I've tried to put them in order. In some of them you're wearing a light jacket, others no coat at all.'

I look at the photos. Taylor's right.

'Notice anything?' Taylor asks.

And that's when I see what he's getting at. 'I'm not wearing my winter coat in any of them.' It's been colder earlier this year, so I've had my coat on since at least the middle of September. Which means none of these photos were taken after the summer.

'Alice stopped following me a couple of months ago,' I say.

Taylor nods. 'Looks like it. But we can't be sure why. Maybe Max told her he was leaving you and he and Poppy would have a new life together. With her.'

Even after everything I now know about Max, hearing this from Taylor cuts deeply into my flesh.

'And then Alice realised what he was going to do,' Taylor continues. 'It fits with the photos stopping. Everything changed.' He takes my hand. 'I know it's hard to face. And after everything, you still don't want to hear that Max could do something like this to you. I get that. It's horrific. But don't lose sight of that, Hannah. Don't crumble now. Hold it together or we'll never get to the truth.'

Nausea swirls around my stomach, snatching any words I want to say. All I can do now is wait to see what happens tomorrow. Will I get any answers from a man who is most likely capable of murder? Eventually I compose myself, just as the pizza arrives. But there is no way I can stomach any food now.

It's two a.m. and I've barely slept. Without Poppy here, on the other side of the bed, everything feels strange. Out of place. I pull on my dressing gown and grab the duvet, dragging it to the living room.

Taylor is asleep on the sofa, and I spread the duvet on the floor and lie down, closing my eyes.

'Hannah?'

'Yeah. Sorry, do you mind me being here? I couldn't sleep.'

'Not at all. As long as you don't snore.'

Despite everything, I laugh.

We talk for a while, whispering even though there's no one else here. Like two old friends. Only we're not. And maybe we never can be after all of this.

But when Taylor reaches down and takes my hand, holding it while he turns onto his stomach to drift off to sleep, I keep hold of it. Hoping that when I wake up, he'll still be holding my hand.

'I've made you coffee.'

My eyes snap open. Everything slowly coming into focus.

Taylor places two mugs on the coffee table and sits down. He seems better this morning.

'Thanks. But I should have done that.'

'What, because of this?' He points to his head. 'It was nothing. That guy just took me by surprise.'

'So he didn't say anything at all?'

'Nope. Too busy smashing my head with something. I still have no idea what it was.'

'You do know I can't let you come with me to hand him the money.'

He falls silent. 'I thought you'd say that.' He lifts his mug.

'I have to do this alone,' I say. 'Look what he's already done to you. Twice now. It must have been him who stole your phone.'

'Maybe. If he's working for Max then it makes sense he'd try and get all the evidence. What worries me is how Max knew about the photo of him with Alice.' He studies my face.

'It wasn't me. I know what you've said before, but you need to start trusting me, or we'll never get through this. And I suppose I need to trust you too.' I take his hand. His skin is warm and smooth. Different to Max's. 'There's something else. Poppy and I need to move back home. Max isn't there, and it makes no difference where I am. The driver of that Golf always knows where to find me. And this is the best thing for Poppy. She can't settle here – she's barely been sleeping and this is all really affecting her. Being in her own home might lessen the pain of Max not being around. Whatever's going on, Poppy comes first.'

Taylor nods. 'Does she know he's missing?'

I shake my head. 'Not exactly. I don't know how to tell her. But I will. Once we're back home.'

Taylor sighs heavily. 'You're doing the right thing. But promise you'll keep in touch. I need to know you're okay.' He looks around. 'And actually, I miss this place. There's nothing like home.'

'I'll bug you every hour of the day,' I promise. 'You might end up blocking me.'

'That won't happen,' he says. 'Oh, well. At least Sam will be happy to have his place back. So will his girlfriend.' He chuckles, but there's sadness behind his smile.

I'm in the shop by eight a.m.

All the way here, I checked the rear-view mirror, desperate to catch sight of the man who's been following me. Yet still I lock the shop door behind me, pulling on it three times just to make sure it's secure. I know I'll see him today, but I need it to be on my terms.

In the office, I call Cole. 'Take today off. To make up for yesterday. I insist. It's quiet on Sundays and I'll keep the coffee bar closed.' I brace myself for the objection.

'But I was just about to leave.'

'Do something fun for yourself. See a friend. Relax. I'm covering the shop today by myself. I'll see you on Monday.'

Cole doesn't say anything.

'Oh, how did it go with your niece?'

'Ella can start next week. She's just working on an assignment and doesn't want to get distracted.'

'Good. I look forward to meeting her. See you tomorrow, then.'

'I'd prefer to come in,' Cole says, just as I end the call.

All day I'm distracted, my head jolting up each time the door opens. It's never him, and by five o'clock, I wonder if he'll show at all.

With fifteen thousand pounds at stake, I'm confident that man will show up. Then it hits me that he could have gone back to Max and told him about my offer. Maybe he's demanded more money and Max is willing to pay it. All I know is that I can't afford to pay any more, and I'm not putting my business at risk.

That's when panic sets in. I'm in a maze that has no exit. *But I've got to find a way. For Poppy's sake.*

As soon as the last customer leaves, I lock the door. My phone pings – a WhatsApp message from Sarah asking if I've heard from Max yet. I put it in my pocket without replying, and stare through the doors. There's still no sign of that man.

I turn off the lights and head upstairs to the staffroom. There's a clearer view of the street outside from up there, and I'll wait all night if I have to. Going home isn't an option yet – I don't want to take that money out of the shop.

My stomach rumbles, reminding me I haven't eaten since breakfast. With another quick glance out of the window, I check the fridge to see if Cole's left any food behind. There's nothing in there, though – he never wastes food.

When I return to the window, I see a tall bulky figure across the road, standing there watching the shop. He looks straight at me but doesn't move. It's him.

I rush downstairs, almost knocking a chair over in my hurry

to get to him. Fear and desperation mingle but I don't slow down until I get to the door.

And see Cole right there smiling at me.

Across the street, the man has gone. It's as if he was never there in the first place.

'What are you doing?' I say, unable to keep the anger from my voice.

'Can you let me in? It's starting to rain. I think snow's coming, actually.'

I unlock the door and Cole comes in, rubbing his gloved hands together.

'Why are you here?' I step outside and scan the street. There's no one out there except a group of teenagers heading towards the Tube station.

'I was just passing. Having my usual walk,' Cole says. 'Didn't feel right not to stop by and help you close up.' He frowns. 'Are you okay? You don't look right, Hannah.'

'Did you see anyone out there when you got here? Across the road?'

Cole frowns again. 'Just those kids out there. Why? What's going on?'

Stick to the truth as much as possible. 'I was in the staffroom. I thought I saw someone watching the shop outside. Quite a tall, stocky man. Dark hair.'

Cole frowns. 'I didn't see anyone like that. Maybe that gang scared him off.'

Somehow I doubt that.

Cole watches me closely. 'Are you coming, then?' If there's someone watching the shop, we'd better lock up quick and put the alarm on. And I'm walking you home.'

Cole knows something is wrong. Everything I've been doing lately is out of character. And we've worked together for years. How long can I keep things hidden?

A clock ticks silently. And everything is about to unravel.

TWENTY-FOUR

Days pass, with no sign of the man in the Golf. Yet even though I'm constantly on edge, looking over my shoulder wherever we go, Poppy and I settle into a new routine at home. And slowly I see glimpses of the old Poppy.

The shadow of Max looms over me, but somehow I keep it hidden from her. To Poppy, Max is still a loving father; he just needed to get away from everything.

'Like a time-out to calm down?' Poppy had asked on the morning I'd told her we were moving back home. That had been the easy part, and then I'd had to break it to her that Max wouldn't be there.

'Something like that,' I'd replied. 'A grown-up version of a time-out. But he still loves you. And you'll see him again soon.' I'd tried to stem the flow of my tears, but they hadn't gone unnoticed, and Poppy had tilted her head, silently staring at me before wrapping her little arms around me.

Sarah has come to see us again this evening, as she's done every day since we moved back. Her concern for Max touches me, even though he doesn't deserve it.

'Are you sure you don't mind Ivy staying tonight?' she asks.

She starts a night shift at the hospital in an hour, and refused my offer of food, even though the meatballs and gnocchi are nearly ready. I've made far too much – I can't get used to cooking for only Poppy and me.

'Not at all. Ivy's welcome any time,' I say. *As long as I can keep her safe.* 'Are you ready for tomorrow?' Sarah is introducing Ivy to Dean tomorrow, which explains her lack of appetite.

She nods, but doesn't smile, and picks fluff from her hospital scrubs. 'It's all a bit overwhelming. I've really wanted this to happen for ages, and now it's just around the corner, I actually feel sick.' She places her hand on her stomach. 'Ivy's so excited. That's what's helping me see it through. And Dean's been... he's been great. He's changed so much.'

Sarah keeps insisting that Dean is a different person now. And people do change. Max did. But has Max reverted to the person he was long before I met him? Someone who could so badly hurt another person. Does he still have the capacity to harm people? I warn Sarah not to get sucked in.

'I won't.' She pauses. 'It's about forgiveness. I'm making a choice to let the past go. We all make mistakes, don't we? If we're sorry for them, why should we be punished?' She smiles. 'And it's Ivy who would lose out – not just Dean.'

'I know, you're right. Everything we do is for our kids, isn't it?'

She studies me carefully. 'I wish you'd talk to me more. I feel like you're putting up a wall. Is it because you know I like Max? I don't approve of what he's done, but isn't your marriage worth fighting for? Even if it's just for Poppy's sake?' She lowers her voice to a whisper. 'And what if he's done something? I'm really worried about him, Han.'

I freeze. 'What do you mean?'

'I mean like... killed himself. What if he just can't handle it?

Suicide's the biggest cause of death among young men in this country.'

A heavy lump lodges in my throat. I haven't considered that Max might contemplate ending his life. And these last few days *have* felt different. I haven't seen the man in the silver Golf, and there have been no more threatening messages. Everything is still and quiet. *The calm before the storm?*

'No,' I say to Sarah. I can't let myself believe that. I have to stay positive for Poppy. 'Max will be okay.'

There's a flicker of doubt on her face when she looks at me. 'I'm sure you're right. No point thinking the worst. Max will just be hiding out somewhere, waiting until he feels ready to come back and face everything.' Her mouth twists. She doesn't believe what she's saying.

'I'd better get going,' she says, checking her phone. 'See what A & E has in store for me today.' She sighs. 'Friday nights are the worst.'

'I hope it goes well with Dean tomorrow,' I say, as I see her out. 'I'm here if you need me.'

Once Sarah's left, and the girls are in bed, I go through the house checking the doors and windows are locked. I peer through the blinds, scanning the street outside. Everything is quiet. No silver Golf. A tight knot forms in my stomach.

I message Taylor to tell him I'm going to bed. This has become a regular habit with us: keeping in touch throughout the day, even when there's no news to share. I need to know that he's okay, and I assume he feels the same. He replies tonight within a few minutes.

> *Still don't like the thought of you and Poppy being alone there. You know where I am.*

In the kitchen, I make a cup of tea to take upstairs. The girls are both sleeping deeply when I check on them, and I make a silent promise to Poppy: *I'll be everything to you.* Just like Sarah is to Ivy.

Closing the door behind me, I turn off the lights and climb into bed, using my phone to set the alarm downstairs.

Sleep comes more easily tonight, and after only a couple of minutes, my eyes become heavy, closing until there's nothing but blackness.

A heavy thud wakes me. *One of the girls falling out of bed?*

I rush to Poppy's room and fling open the door, shining my phone torch into the room. But they're both there, lost to sleep. Safe.

With my heart thudding, I check the bathroom, then the spare room. Nothing is out of place. Nothing has fallen.

Downstairs is also undisturbed. But something's not right. It takes me a moment to work out what it is, and when I do, panic seeps through my veins.

The alarm down here isn't on.

I set it right before I fell asleep. I know I did. I pull out my phone, and click on the app. Disarmed. *I didn't press it properly, that must be it. It's easily done.*

But when I hear a noise – movement and breathing – I know that I'm wrong.

'I said you'd never be free, Hannah.'

I turn around and face Max. He looks a mess. Dirty clothes. His hair unbrushed. And then I notice the knife he's holding, glistening in the darkness. I try not to focus on it, and force myself to look at Max instead. There are so many things I want to say – need to say – but fear keeps me rooted to the spot.

'I'm taking Poppy,' he says. 'She needs to be with me.'

Finally I find my voice. I'll only get one chance at this.

'Max, please. We can talk. About everything. There'll be a way to sort this out.' My voice cracks. 'There's always a way.' *But how can there be when he's killed someone?*

He inches forward. 'It's too late for any of that.'

I want to back away but I don't. I have to believe there's still a tiny fragment of humanity left in him. 'Please, Max. Poppy's upstairs. And Ivy too. What if they came down now and saw you holding that?'

Max shakes his head. 'Everyone will understand one day,' he says. 'They'll see that I didn't have a choice.' He lifts the knife and I shrink back.

I glance around, but I can't see any way out of this. I turn back to him. 'There's always a choice, Max. You just have to make the right one. Isn't that what we always tell Poppy? To make good choices?'

He moves closer. 'Do you think I'm a kid, Hannah? That might work with her, but don't patronise me. Not after everything.'

I don't reply. I'm running out of things to say. Nothing is working; Max is steadfast, slowly moving towards me. He stares at me with wild eyes I don't recognise. How can this be the man I loved?

'I know everything,' I say, backing away from him. 'Your affair with Alice. I know every detail of it.'

He doesn't look shocked. 'I know,' he says.

'You were seeing her for months. It wasn't just a one-off mistake. *Months.*'

His eyes narrow. Confusion? As if he can't quite work out what I'm doing. Does this mean I have the upper hand? If only for a moment?

'How did you find out?' he asks. 'When?'

Max doesn't deserve to have me answer his questions. He's a murderer. I will keep all my knowledge to myself. For what he's done to Alice. And to Poppy and me. To our family.

'Answer!' he shouts, holding up the knife.

'Don't do this to Poppy. Please, Max. Let me call Mum to come over and look after the girls. We can go somewhere to talk. Away from here.'

'You must think I'm crazy,' he says. He looks desperate now, as if this is causing him pain. Because ultimately, I believe that he loves Poppy, despite what he's done. 'Answer my questions, Hannah.' He speaks quietly, as if he's already given up on me ever telling him. As if he's exhausted.

'Not until you tell me why you did it. Why did you kill Alice?'

He stares at me, and it feels as though the air's being sucked out of the room. Minutes tick by. *As soon as he speaks, this will be the end of everything.*

Slowly his mouth opens. It feels like no words are coming out as my brain struggles to compute what he's saying. All I hear is silence as his mouth moves. But he's talking, and slowly the words come loud and clear. 'No,' he says. 'No.' He shakes his head. 'I know what you're doing. It was *you*! You're the one who killed Alice!'

TWENTY-FIVE

Max's words explode in the air. And then everything I've feared becomes reality.

The missing key card. Taylor's mobile phone. All evidence that can be used to frame someone. I'm trapped and I need to get out of this.

'You killed Alice,' I say. 'And you've been trying to kill me.' I rush towards him, pushing him backwards with all the strength I can muster. He screams out, and the knife clashes to the floor.

I grab it before he's had a chance to recover, and rush upstairs to Poppy's room, slamming the door shut in my haste to separate us from Max. There's no lock, of course, but I'm hoping he won't risk doing anything in front of the girls.

Ivy's eyes pop open, and I struggle to regulate my breathing, but I need to stay calm for her sake. 'What's happening, Hannah?' she asks in a tiny voice.

'Don't worry, Ivy. I just need to make a call.' I dial 999 and tell them I think someone's in my house, trying to keep my voice calm so I don't scare the girls. I'm sure it's too late for that, though.

'Mummy? What's happening?' Poppy asks, pulling herself up and rubbing her eyes. It's always taken a lot to rouse her.

I finish speaking to the police and end the call. 'Everything's okay. I just thought I heard something downstairs.'

Immediately Poppy starts to cry. 'I'm scared,' she says, through heavy sobs. She holds out her arms and I sit on her bed and hug her tightly. 'I don't want anything to happen to you, Mummy.'

'It won't,' I tell her. 'The police will be here any second. They'll protect us.'

Ivy gets up from her mattress to join us, and I hug her too, silently apologising to Sarah.

'I want my mummy,' she wails, and the clash of both the girls' cries drowns out any noise from downstairs. I don't know what Max is doing, but I cling to the hope that his love for Poppy will override anything else, and stop him coming for me.

I try to calm them down, assuring them we'll be okay. 'I'm sure it was something falling downstairs,' I say, but neither of them seems convinced. They heard me on the phone. They're old enough to understand what it means that I was driven to call the police.

And when their crying subsides, I listen for sounds. But there's nothing.

We stay upstairs, huddled together on Poppy's bed in the torchlight, until finally the doorbell rings. I rush to Poppy's window and see the police car right outside our house.

'The police are here,' I tell them. 'We're safe now. Let's go and let them in.' I turn on the lights and take their hands as we walk downstairs. I notice Ivy's is trembling. 'Don't be afraid,' I say. 'They've come to check everything for us.'

There are two officers this time, one male and one female. The female officer, who looks around my age, asks if we're okay.

'Yes, we're fine. This is my daughter and her friend. They were having a sleepover.'

'Okay. I'm PC Everett. How about I stay down here with you all while my colleague PC Rowan has a quick look around?' She looks at the girls. 'Nothing to worry about. We do this all the time.'

They step inside, and PC Rowan disappears into the living room, while the rest of us wait in the hallway.

Max is long gone. There's no way he would have stuck around to wait for the police to get here. I feel as if I'm holding my breath while we wait for PC Rowan to come back. The girls are still clinging to me.

'All clear,' PC Rowan announces as he comes downstairs. 'Shall we go and have a chat? PC Everett can stay in the kitchen with the children.'

I watch as she escorts the girls to the kitchen, and prepare myself to tell more lies. I need to speak to the driver of the Golf first. I'll give him until tomorrow, and then if our paths don't cross, I'll go to the police. And I'll tell them everything that's happened since I found that key card.

'Why don't you talk me though what happened?' PC Rowan says, when we're sitting on the sofa, out of sight of the girls.

I've had a few minutes to rehearse this, but still it's not easy to lie to the police. 'A loud noise woke me up, so I checked on the girls then came downstairs. That's when I realised the alarm down here wasn't on. And I definitely remember setting it.'

'Do you always put it on at night?'

'Only since my husband went missing. He was badly attacked on his way home from work, and now he's been missing for over a week.' To my surprise, tears begin to trickle from my eyes, without me forcing anything.

'I'm sorry,' PC Rowan says. 'I appreciate this must be difficult.'

I nod, keeping my voice low. 'When I came downstairs,

someone rushed out of the front door. I didn't want to tell the girls that. They would have been even more scared.'

'Did you manage to get a look at this person? Were they male or female?'

'I don't know. I think male, but I can't be sure.'

'Okay. Have you noticed if anything's been taken? Or has anything moved?'

The kitchen knife Max was holding must have been one of ours. 'I don't think so,' I say. 'I haven't had a chance to check, though. But it didn't look like the person was carrying anything.'

'I notice you don't have a video doorbell or CCTV.'

'No.'

'And there's no sign of forced entry. How might someone have got in?'

I haven't considered this. Is this where everything comes undone?

'With my husband's key?' This idea crashes its way into my head. It's the perfect lie. 'Someone must have it!' Again, tears fall, and PC Rowan shifts in his seat. I sense that he isn't comfortable around a crying woman, although I can't be the only one he's encountered in his job.

'We'll keep all options open,' he says. 'Had your husband mentioned losing his keys before he disappeared?'

I dab my eyes with my sleeve. 'No. He's always careful. He doesn't lose things. And when he was attacked, they didn't take his keys. Just his phone and wallet.'

The officer nods. 'Okay. We'll send someone around in the morning to check for fingerprints, but there's not much chance anything will come up. People who break into houses tend to cover their tracks. Wear gloves. That kind of thing.'

I nod.

'Is there anywhere else you can stay tonight?' he asks. 'I assume the girls might be too scared to stay here.'

'It's late. There's nowhere we can go at this time. We'll be okay. I'm sure it's helped them that they've seen you check the house. And I'll double-lock all the doors and put the alarm on. If I put my keys in the front and back doors then no one can get in that way, even with a key. And I'm sure whoever it was won't try again tonight.'

'It's hard to be sure of anything when it comes to criminals,' PC Rowan says, and the way he's looking at me tells me he doesn't trust a word I've said.

Sarah looks shattered when she answers the door. I left it as long as I could this morning to bring Ivy home, but Ivy kept asking for her mum. Even my offer of pizza for lunch had no impact.

'Thanks for bringing her back,' Sarah says, while Ivy rushes inside. 'Are they both okay?'

I wish I could say with certainty that they are, but everything leaves a scar, even if we don't realise it has. 'I'm so sorry. Poor Ivy. She's been okay this morning but a bit quieter than usual, and she kept asking for you. I hope she'll be okay.'

'It wasn't your fault. I'm just glad you're all okay.' She lowers her voice. 'Do you think this is anything to do with Max disappearing?'

'I honestly don't know what to think.'

'It's just so weird that this stuff keeps happening. You must be terrified. Come in and we can talk about it?'

I've left Poppy in the car so that the girls wouldn't run upstairs and start playing. 'I need to get back. But we'll talk soon.'

Sarah looks disappointed. 'Are you sure you'll be okay? You can all stay here tonight. We'll squeeze in somehow.'

'Thanks for offering, but I think we'll be okay. I'll call you if not.'

'What did the police say?' Sarah asks, just as I'm about to leave.

I briefly turn back to check on Poppy. 'There wasn't much they could say. There was no sign of forced entry. None of our keys are missing.'

Sarah studies me. 'That's strange. Look, please don't take this the wrong way, but do you think maybe... Well, you've been so stressed lately and then all this stuff with Max's attack and him disappearing. Do you think there's a chance you panicked and just *thought* you saw someone? Our minds can do crazy things under pressure.'

I consider her suggestion. Maybe it's easier to let people think this is what's happened. Hannah is losing her mind. It's better than the truth coming out before I have evidence. 'I suppose it's possible,' I say. 'I was half asleep. I'm sorry Ivy got scared.'

'It's not your fault. And she'll be fine. Listen, I can hear *Numberblocks* on TV. That means Ivy is definitely doing okay. And so will you.' She yawns. 'Are you sure you won't come in for coffee?' She glances at the car. 'Is Poppy okay?' I know what Sarah's thinking: Poppy is normally desperate to spend every possible second with Ivy.

'She's just tired. None of us slept much after the police left. I grabbed our duvets and we all huddled up in the living room. Anyway, you're the one who needs to get some more sleep.'

On cue, Sarah yawns again. 'What are your plans this afternoon?'

Poppy and I are meeting Taylor in Leicester Square, but of course I don't say this. I gave Poppy the choice of either coming with me or going to Mum's, and she chose to come with me. The opposite of what I'd expected. 'Just some shopping with Poppy,' I tell Sarah, checking the car again where Poppy is staring out of the front window. 'Good luck with Dean tonight.' I lean forward and hug her.

'I'll need it,' Sarah says, but then she smiles. 'It'll be fine. It's *you* I'm worried about.'

When I'm with Taylor, there are brief flashes of time when I forget to look over my shoulder. When Max and the driver of the Golf seem like figures from a dream. People who exist in another time.

There's a crisp chill in the air this afternoon, but the sun shining through the cloudless pale blue sky warms us through our winter clothes.

'It's like summer out here,' Poppy says as we walk through Leicester Square with Taylor. Maybe it's wishful thinking, but she seems to have put the incident last night behind her. She grabs my hand; Poppy's at that age now where she's torn between wanting to cling to me, and needing to be free to explore the world on her own terms.

'It is,' Taylor agrees. 'I should have brought my shorts and T-shirt.'

'No, *silly*,' Poppy says. 'It's not *really* summer. We haven't even had Christmas yet.'

Taylor laughs. 'Are you sure? Okay then, you're right – silly me!'

Poppy giggles, and once again I marvel at her resilience. She hasn't seen Max, or even heard his voice, for days now, and has no idea when he'll be back. Yet still she's able to laugh with Taylor. To exist in only her innocent world.

'You should definitely have kids one day,' I say to him, when Poppy skips ahead of us.

'You think?' He shrugs. 'I don't know. I'd probably mess them up. I love my niece – she's like a daughter to me – but actually being someone's *dad*. Woah. That's a lot of responsibility.' He pauses. 'Hey, who am I kidding? I definitely see that in my future.'

My smile fades when the reality of our situation hits me. Nothing is normal here. Taylor is still little more than a stranger, and my husband wants me dead. He could also be trying to frame me for Alice's murder. Not to mention that I'm fast running out of options. 'I'm going to the police,' I say. 'Telling them everything. I can't do this any more. I've buried my head in the sand since the Golf driver disappeared, but I know something is just around the corner. I *feel* it. And having afternoons out like this, living in a bubble, won't change anything.'

Taylor contemplates what I've said. I'm the one who's been putting off going to the police. But I can't do that any longer. 'I know you're right,' he says.

'I can keep you out of it. They don't have to know we've ever met. You've already spoken to them, so I don't want them wondering why you didn't come forward with any of this before.'

'Then I wouldn't be able to come with you. To support you.'

'I don't need you to. I'm doing this alone. This is about me and Max. And Alice, of course, but... all I know is I have to do this by myself.'

Poppy runs back to us. 'Mummy, can we sit down for a bit? My legs are *so* tired.'

'How about over there?' Taylor suggests, pointing to a grassy area with benches in the centre of Leicester Square.

We all sit, but it's only a matter of minutes before Poppy runs off to play with a girl around her age. And while we watch her, Taylor and I talk about everything except what's happening. I've already told him that I'll be going to the police straight after this, and perhaps he's as relieved as I am that soon this will all be over.

'I hope we'll stay in touch after this,' he says. 'I can't believe I'm saying this, but I do think of you as a friend.' He laughs. 'Still don't trust you, though. But I'm working on that.'

And while I want to have Taylor in my life, it's hard to see how we'll ever be around each other without remembering all of this. Alice. Max. It's all woven into the tapestry of our connection, whatever that is. 'Who knows what the future holds?' I say.

Poppy runs back to us. 'Can I have a snack, Mummy? I'm really hungry.'

Taylor points to the other side of the grass. 'See that café over there? They have ice cream. If your mum says it's okay, that is.'

Poppy's eyes widen. 'Can I, Mummy? *Please?*'

I'm not about to deny my daughter ice cream when she's been through so much because of me. Because of Max. 'As long as you eat dinner later.'

'I promise!' she says.

By the time we get there a long queue has formed inside the café. 'I'll wait here and get it,' Taylor offers. 'No point all of us standing in line.'

'Chocolate and vanilla, please,' Poppy says.

'Coming right up.'

Poppy and I head towards a nearby bench. Before we reach it, a hand grabs my arm, and I spin around, my heart almost stopping.

But it's only Paula.

'Sorry,' she says. 'Didn't mean to shock you.' She looks at Poppy. 'Hello. I don't think I've seen you since you were a baby. You must be Poppy.'

'And I'm five,' Poppy says proudly.

'I know. And I'm Paula. I work with your Daddy. But I won't tell you how old *I* am.' She laughs, and I realise I've never seen Paula looking anything other than stern.

The smile vanishes from Poppy's face. 'My daddy's gone away. I miss him.'

Paula looks at me.

'Poppy, why don't you save that bench right there for us

while I talk to Paula for a second? You can do some colouring for a minute.'

Paula and I watch as Poppy settles herself on the bench and pulls her colouring pad from her small backpack. 'I'm glad you've left him,' she says. 'But where is he? He said he wanted to come into work and he never showed up. That's not like Max.'

'I don't know where he is,' I say. 'Probably avoiding me.'

Paula glances at Poppy. 'And his daughter? That's not like Max. Everyone knows how much she means to him.'

'Maybe he feels ashamed?'

'Yeah. Good. He should have thought about that when he... Anyway, it's funny bumping into you here. What are you two up to?'

It's strange that Paula's being so friendly. What Max did must have really affected her, and it's only now she's free of him that she can relax.

'We're just out with a friend,' I explain. 'He's over there getting ice cream and coffee.' I point to the café, where I can see Taylor hasn't moved much closer to the counter.

Paula stares at the queue. 'I don't fancy your chances of getting it any time soon. Which one is your friend?'

'The one in the black puffa jacket. Blue hat.'

Paula squints, then her face turns pale. 'That's Shane Roberts,' she hisses. 'What are you doing with *him*?'

I shake my head. 'No, my friend is Taylor Stone. I know him through—'

Paula turns and walks closer to the café. Within seconds she runs back. 'I don't know what the hell is going on, but that man is definitely Shane Roberts. He used to work for us!'

Her words don't make sense. I stare at Taylor, still convinced Paula's mistaken.

'Didn't Max tell you about him? Max had to fire him,' she says. 'And it all got nasty. First Shane said he was going to sue the company, then when that didn't get him anywhere he started threatening Max. He's a sick and twisted man. I don't know what you're doing with him, but you need to get as far away from him as possible.'

But I can't move. None of this makes sense. I glance back at Taylor, who's now moved closer to the front of the line.

'I'll show you.' Paula pulls her phone from her bag and scrolls through her photos. 'Here. This is from the Christmas party last year. Look. That's Shane!' She shows me her phone and on it is a picture of Max, Stefan, Paula, and a few other people I don't know.

And right next to them is Taylor.

Without another word, I run to Poppy and grab her hand, telling her we have to go now.

And then we run to the Tube station without looking back.

TWENTY-SIX

'What on earth's going on?' Mum asks, ushering us inside. 'Is it Max? What's happened?'

Poppy clings to my coat, and not even Peach, who is snuffling at her feet, can part her from me. All the way here she was asking why we had to leave without her ice cream, and I couldn't think of an answer. I'd stopped in a shop and got her a Magnum before we got home to get the car. I'd hoped it would help, and it did for a while, until her question changed to why we left without saying goodbye to Taylor.

'It's not Max, Mum. I can't explain now. Can you please have Poppy tonight? It's late already so I'll pick her up in the morning. There are some things I need to do.'

'No!' Poppy says. 'I want to come with you, Mummy!'

'What on earth is going on?' Mum asks again. 'You're worrying me, Hannah.'

In my pocket, my phone buzzes with another message from Taylor. Or Shane. Whoever he is. There's been a flurry of them since Poppy and I ran from Leicester Square. And I haven't read any of them, or listened to the voicemails he's left. 'Please, Mum. I need you not to ask any questions right now. I'll explain everything, I promise. I just need Poppy to be here with you.'

She stares at me for a moment, and I can tell she's trying to read me, as she always does, and that there is a multitude of questions buzzing around her head. 'Of course I'll look after Poppy. But this is all a bit strange.' She turns to Poppy. 'Why don't you see if Peach needs some water? She's been very thirsty today.' Mum turns back to me. 'Have you had dinner?'

'We haven't had a chance to eat.'

'Then stay for some. Surely whatever you have to do can wait an hour?'

'I can't. Sorry.'

For a moment Poppy doesn't move, and I wonder if I'll ever be able to leave her here, but then finally she hugs me and slowly wanders to the kitchen.

'Just one more thing,' I say to Mum before I leave. 'Please don't let Poppy out of your sight.'

It's hard to order my thoughts as I drive to Sarah's. It's dark now, and rain spatters against the windscreen. It's not just the weather that's changed, though. Everything I thought I knew has changed. Again.

There's a black BMW parked outside Sarah's house when I get there. Probably Dean's; she was introducing Ivy to Dean today.

I hesitate for a moment. This is an important day for Sarah and I'm about to go in and interrupt. But Dean will have been there for hours and Ivy will be in bed soon. This can't wait – Sarah will understand.

I ring the doorbell and wait. Seconds tick by, turning to a minute. I ring again. Finally she opens the door, a smile on her face that seems unfamiliar.

'Hannah! You're here! I was just talking about you.' She

lowers her voice. 'Dean's still here. We were just putting Ivy to bed.'

'I'm sorry for intruding. I didn't know he'd still be here.'

She smiles again. 'Neither did I. Anyway, it's fine – come in and meet Dean. Finally. You've heard enough about him all these years, so this is long overdue.'

I'm about to tell her that I need to talk to her urgently, but she's already hurrying to the living room. 'This is Dean,' she says, smiling proudly. 'Dean, Hannah. My closest friend.'

He's older than I've expected – at least in his late forties, and it occurs to me that I've never asked Sarah his age. Or much else about him. I dismissed him in my mind as soon as he cut her out of his life. There's an air of confidence about him, and I wonder if this is what attracted Sarah to him. She's so used to looking after people, being the one in charge, I wonder if he made a refreshing change for her. Someone who can clearly look after himself.

'Good to meet you,' Dean says. 'I've certainly heard a lot about you today. From both Sarah and Ivy.'

It hits me hard how awkward this is. What am I supposed to say to a man who's never bothered to see his daughter until now? For Sarah's sake, I force a smile. 'Sorry to turn up like this. I just needed to talk to Sarah quickly. It's kind of urgent.' Again, I smile at Dean.

'No problem,' he says, standing up. 'I need to get going anyway.'

'Oh.' Sarah's smile disappears. She'd never admit it, but she's not going to thank me for interrupting her evening.

'You don't have to leave,' I say. 'I can quickly talk to Sarah in the kitchen.'

But Dean is already pulling on his coat. 'No, no. I'll get out of your way.' He smiles at Sarah. 'I'm sure you've got a lot to talk about.' He kisses her cheek. 'I'll see myself out.'

Despite this, Sarah goes with him to the door, and they speak in hushed voices before I hear the door close.

I wait, pacing the living room, wondering how I'm ever going to get these words out.

'What's happened?' she asks, when she joins me in the living room.

'I'm sorry. I didn't realise I'd be interrupting—'

'Oh, forget that. He was probably about to leave anyway. And Dean's not important right now. *You* are. Come and sit.' She flops on the sofa and pats the cushion next to her. 'What is it, Hannah?'

I'm not sure I want to sit; moving is helping me to stay calm. I hesitate for a moment before joining her on the sofa.

'Okay, now you're scaring me. What is it?' Sarah urges. 'I know something awful's happened for you to be here now.'

And when I speak, the words tumbling from my mouth like a waterfall, it feels good to finally be confiding in Sarah. I start with the key card, sparing no details as I fill her in on everything that has happened since that night.

She listens carefully, and even though her mouth opens to ask a question several times, she waits until I've finished to speak. There's shock and disbelief on her face, and she stumbles on her words. 'I... I don't know what to say,' she says. 'I knew something was wrong. I've been asking you for weeks!' She quickly apologises. 'This isn't about me, sorry. I can't believe it.'

'Taylor's been lying to me since the second I met him. But why? What does he want?' I stand up. 'I know he must have been a friend of Alice's – I've seen photos of him and her mum knew him. So that much couldn't have been a lie.'

Sarah frowns. 'I don't get it. But it sounds like he wanted to get to Max. Ruin his life because he lost his job.'

'But how does Alice fit in?' I'm struggling to fit the pieces together – too many of them are missing.

'I don't know. But what if this Taylor has—?'

'Shane,' I correct. But how will I ever get used to calling him that? It sickens me to think that I was beginning to trust him. That somehow, despite the harrowing circumstances surrounding how we met, he was getting under my skin.

'Shane,' she says. 'Do you think he was trying to frame Max? Could he have put the key card in Max's pocket? I don't believe for one second Max could have killed anyone. What if it was Shane who killed Alice?'

And now, in light of what I've learnt about Taylor, my belief in Max's guilt is wavering. 'Max did have an affair, though. Paula saw him. And I saw photos of him with Alice.'

'On that man's phone. How do you know they're even real? Could have been a deep fake? It's easy to do.'

Sarah's right. I don't know they were real. And conveniently, those photos don't exist any more. Stolen, supposedly. Was Taylor lying about that attack? And the time he ran after the man in the Golf and we had to go to hospital? Was that something to do with him as well? Did he plan all of that?

'What if Max wasn't having an affair with Alice Hughes?' Sarah suggests. 'What if it was someone else?'

I don't know whether this makes me feel better or worse. 'So much still doesn't make sense,' I say.

'We need to talk to Max,' Sarah says. 'We need to find him. Tell him everything we know.'

Then it hits me. 'The last time I saw Max, he was threatening me with a knife. If he's innocent – why was he doing that? And that man in the silver Golf. Was he working for Max or Taylor?'

Sarah doesn't reply for a moment, sighing heavily instead. 'I don't know. But somehow this Taylor's got you thinking that Max wanted you dead.' She shuffles closer to me and places her hand on my arm. 'You *know* Max. He would never want you dead. It's ludicrous. You and Poppy mean everything to him.' She pauses. 'Even if he did have an affair. That's a completely different story to wanting your wife dead. And killing a woman you've been having an affair with.' She stands up, begins pacing the room just as I did moments ago. 'None of this adds up, Hannah.' She narrows her eyes. 'Well, I can't explain the photos Alice had of you. Or why Max had that flat in Wimbledon. Are you sure you've told me everything?'

'Yes. Everything I can remember. Wait, no, there's something else. Max texted me. Days ago. At least I think it was Max. With everything that's been happening, I didn't get to ask him for his new number. He said I'll never be free.'

Sarah frowns. 'Can I see it?'

I hand her my phone and sit beside her as she reads the message. 'That's the same number I've got for him. Did you reply?'

'No.'

'Then you need to, now. Tell him everything. You need to ask him to come home.'

I consider what she's saying; it does seem to be my only option. I start typing, telling Max that he needs to come home. It's about Shane Roberts. And that Poppy isn't safe.

The minute it's sent, I bury my head in my hands. I've held it together for all these weeks and now it feels as though I'm disintegrating. Sarah grabs my hand. 'You can do this,' she says.

It's all I need to hear.

'I'm going to the police,' I say, pulling away. 'To tell them that Taylor has wormed his way into my life, pretending to be someone else. Using a fake name. And that I think he's been trying to get to Max.' And as I say those words, everything is clear. 'I'll tell them it must have been him who attacked Max. They'll have to pay attention to that, won't they? Paula can verify that he's threatened Max before.'

'I'll come with you,' Sarah says.

'No, you can't. It's too late to call your mum to come and be with Ivy. I'll be fine on my own.'

'I can get Dean to come back and stay with her. Isn't it about time he started being a dad to her?'

'No, don't. Ivy doesn't even know him yet. I just don't trust anyone. I'll be fine on my own.'

She nods. 'Tell the police everything you've told me tonight. Max isn't guilty, so there's nothing to worry about.'

'I don't think I can tell them all of that. Not yet. I need them to focus on getting Taylor, not suspecting Max of anything, even if he's eventually cleared. Not without speaking to him first.' I check my phone, but there's no reply from him.

'Once you tell Max everything, he'll have an alibi for that night,' Sarah says. 'I'm sure of it. It can't be Max.'

'I hope you're right. He's Poppy's dad. I need to fight for my family. Even if there's nothing left of our marriage – this is about Poppy.'

Sarah nods. 'Now do you understand why I messaged Dean? And why I'm fighting to have him in Ivy's life?'

'I'm sorry if it felt like I wasn't supporting you.'

She shakes her head. 'Hannah, you never, ever have to apologise to me about anything.'

Sarah sees me to the door and I step out into the cold, small flurries of snow floating around me like confetti.

And as I drive, the strangest thing is that I feel Taylor's absence more strongly than anything else.

For hours I sit in the police station – on autopilot as I wait to be seen and make my statement – and it's nearly one a.m. by the time I get home. I message Mum to tell her I'm okay.

Being alone here should terrify me more than before, but for some reason I feel calm. I'm ready to confront whoever turns up, because I know someone will. Taylor's bound to know by now why Poppy and I disappeared, and why I'm avoiding his calls. He might have even seen Paula.

There are still too many unanswered questions: Who is the man in the Golf? Was it really Max who sent him? Or Taylor? And what happened to Alice?

Painful hunger pangs assault my stomach, so I make myself a hot chocolate to keep them at bay. My plan is to sleep downstairs again tonight; somehow, it feels safer.

I'm taking my mug through to the living room when I see him. Sitting in the chair by the window. Waiting for me.

'Hello, Hannah,' he says.

TWENTY-SEVEN

'Max,' I say, glancing at his hands. There's no knife this time, and he slowly stands up. Just as he was last time, he's dishevelled, broken, looking even weaker than after his attack. But still I'm on edge. *Trust no one.*

'I got your message,' he says.

'We need to talk, don't we?'

He nods, but doesn't move.

'I don't understand what's been happening,' I say.

'Neither do I.' He still doesn't move, and it's like we're strangers, skirting around each other. *This is Max. And I need to tell him everything.*

'You'd better sit,' I say.

'No, I'm fine standing.' He takes a step backwards, and I realise he's afraid of me. Or of what I'm going to say. And maybe he was the last time we spoke too, when he tightly clutched the knife.

'Please sit. We've got a lot to talk about.'

Silently, he does as I ask, sitting back in the chair, as far away from me as he can get.

'I think Shane Roberts killed Alice Hughes,' I begin. And

then for the second time tonight, I recount every detail of the last few weeks, leaving out nothing. The more I tell this story, the more detached I feel, as if this hasn't been happening to me.

Max buries his head in his hands when I've finished, and I wonder if he'll ever look up so we can face this together.

'I didn't think it would come to this,' he says. 'I didn't know what Shane was capable of. I knew he was... disturbed. And that he couldn't accept that I'd had to fire him.'

I wait for him to continue.

'It's such a mess.' He lets out a heavy sigh. 'I was Shane's boss. His mentor. I knew straight away that he doesn't have what it takes. It's hard in our industry. Cut-throat. But I gave him a chance. I tried my best to help him.' Max stares at his hands. 'It didn't work, though – he just kept making mistakes all the time. Not just rookie ones. He made a mountain of errors that could have cost the company a fortune. Not to mention damaging our reputation. I carried him for months, but in the end I had no choice. I had to let him go.'

This corroborates what Paula said. 'What did he do when you told him?'

'He didn't take it well. First, he begged me to change my mind. Give him a second chance. But it wouldn't have been a second chance. We were way beyond that number. He said he'd just bought his own flat and he wouldn't be able to afford the mortgage. He said the way things were at the moment, it would take him months to find another job. He was right, but I couldn't let that be my problem. It was stressful enough with Peter leaving.' Max studies my face, and I wonder what he's thinking. 'Shane tried everything to make me change my mind, and when that didn't work, he tried taking legal action. But all the evidence pointed to him being incompetent. So he began threatening me. Telling me he was going to ruin my life, just like I'd done to him.' Max shakes his head. 'He'd follow me everywhere. I'd leave work and he'd be there in the car park.

Just standing and watching me. Sometimes I even saw him outside our house. He'd bombard me with messages, but not from his phone. He was too smart for that.'

I wonder how I hadn't noticed all of this was going on. How did we drift so far apart that he couldn't share something so major? 'Why didn't you tell me?'

'I didn't want to worry you. I wanted to deal with it myself.'

This explains why Max has had such a short fuse over the last few months, and why I've felt that I've hardly known him.

But how does Alice fit into this? She and Taylor were friends, and I saw pictures of them together. I've met Alice's mother and Molly knew Taylor. Have I been wrong? Was Taylor just making me think Max was having an affair with her? I ask Max, and urge him to tell me the truth. And the faintest glimmer of hope plants itself within me.

Max falls silent, looking away. And that's when all hope disappears.

'I'm sorry, Hannah.' There are tears in his eyes when he looks at me again. 'I did have an affair with Alice.'

Even though this is what I've believed for weeks, hearing it from Max rips my insides. I'm conflicted. I want him to stop talking – he's said enough – but also I need to hear the whole truth from his mouth. No more second-hand accounts. 'Tell me everything.'

'I met Alice in the Boathouse. I'd gone there after work one evening, just so that I didn't bring home all the stuff that was happening with Shane. I didn't want you to see me worried. I thought if I put a bit of space between work and home each evening then that might help. So I started working in there instead of the garden office.' His eyes plead with me. But for what? To believe him? To accept what he's done? At this moment I don't know if I can do either of those things.

'I'd seen her in there a couple of times,' Max said. 'Usually with a friend. But the first night we actually spoke she was on her own.' I notice Max's hand is shaking. 'She kept trying to talk to me, and I was getting really irritated. I was even a bit rude to her. But she was persistent, and I'd had a shitty day.' He glances at me. 'I'm sorry. I bought her a drink, and that's how it started.'

Just like that. So easy for Alice Hughes to insert herself into Max's world.

'I take full responsibility for the affair. It wasn't her fault. I didn't even tell her about you and Poppy until much later. Maybe I was hoping she would end it if I told her. I was having trouble walking away myself.'

I try to quell my anger. 'And did she?' So far, everything Taylor told me about how they met seems to be true.

'No,' Max says, hanging his head. 'She said she didn't care. That she loved me and that was all that mattered. She said we can't help who we fall in love with.' He sniffs. 'It scared me. Nothing I did seemed to make any difference. I told her I'd never leave you and Poppy. Never.'

I stare at him, shock and disbelief clogging my brain as I struggle to make sense of Max's words. 'So Alice wasn't leaving you?'

'No. I was leaving *her*. She told me she'd booked a hotel room at the River Walk and begged me to meet her there at five. But I had no intention of going. I... I was a coward. I let her think that I would meet her, because it felt easier. And by the time she realised I wasn't turning up, I would have told you everything. That's what I was coming home to do. So Alice would have no more power over me if she threatened to tell you.'

'So you never went there? You've never set foot in that hotel?'

'Never. I was telling the truth when you asked me that. By the time I got home, ready to tell you – she'd been found dead.'

'But I found the key card in your pocket. If you didn't go to the hotel, why did you have it?'

'I don't know how it got there.' He lifts his head and stares at the ceiling. 'How do we know it was even Alice's card? It could have been a different one? Someone must have put it in my pocket. I don't know, Hannah! If I'd gone there and killed Alice, why would I have kept the card in my pocket? I would have got rid of it, wouldn't I?'

Max has a point.

Silence floats around us, uncomfortable but somehow peaceful along with it. A release. I look at him. 'When you came here that night, when you had the knife – I thought you were trying to frame me. I thought that's why you said I'd killed her.'

'I'm sorry. There's so much I'm sorry for, Hannah.'

'Do you think Shane is capable of murder?'

Max shrugs. 'I don't know. But it's too much of a coincidence that I met Alice randomly in a pub and she just happens to be a good friend of his. The colleague whose life he claims I've ruined.'

I let this sink in. It's true. It might be a small world, full of uncanny coincidences, but I can't believe for one second it was random that Alice met Max that night. 'He engineered it,' I say. 'He must have. He got Alice to approach you.'

Max frowns. 'Maybe. But he wouldn't have been able to force her to become obsessed with me. And that was real. I know it was. I felt the intensity of her. If he was just trying to ruin my life, all he'd need was one picture of us. For me to sleep with her once. But it went on for months.'

There are still so many unanswered questions. This is far from over.

'I don't understand why he'd want her dead,' Max says.

'Maybe she was going to tell you the truth about how she came into your life? I don't know, Max. He's the only one who can answer that.'

Max stands up and walks to the window, peering through the blind. 'She didn't deserve to die,' he says. 'For all her faults,

Alice was a good person. She knew who she was and she wasn't afraid to be that person, even if it wasn't who everyone wanted her to be.'

Somehow it hurts more to hear Max saying kind words about her than it does to know that he slept with her.

'What now?' he says. 'What are we supposed to do?'

'We go to the police,' I tell him. 'After that, I don't know.'

He turns to face me. 'I love you,' he says. 'That never stopped. I just lost sight of myself. Of us. I'll never forgive myself for that.'

'Are you asking *me* to forgive you?'

He stares at his trainers. 'I don't know what I'm asking. All I know is that I love you and Poppy. I want to be in your lives. I know it will take time, but I'll wait as long as it takes.'

I ignore him. I'm not ready to deal with any of that now. Perhaps I never will be. 'Where did you go after work that night she died?' I ask. 'You were late home that day. I remember Poppy and I were waiting for you. I'd made risotto. If you didn't meet her at the hotel, then where did you go?'

Max hesitates for a moment. Barely enough time for me to register a flicker of doubt on his face. 'I went to the Spotted Horse for a bit. Alice hated it in there so I knew she'd never turn up there. I wanted to prepare how I'd tell you. Plus, Shane had been threatening me and he was ramping it up. Telling me I didn't deserve to be alive. I wasn't ready to come home.'

'Someone there must have seen you? You'll need an alibi for the police, won't you? When we go and tell them everything?'

Max is silent for a moment. 'I'm ready to go. This has gone on long enough.'

Then I remember something that's been niggling me. 'What was that flat I followed you to?'

There's no hesitation in his answer. 'I... I rented it.'

'For you and Alice.' It's a statement rather than a question, because it's apparent that some of the things Taylor had said were true.

'No. I got it because... I was leaving you. After Alice was killed. I... I thought you did it. I thought somehow you must have found out about our affair. We weren't always as careful as we should have been. Alice always wanted to go out to places. We could have easily been seen. I figured you were playing some sort of mind game by not mentioning it. I thought maybe you just wanted revenge. And somehow you found out she'd be at that hotel and you went there and...' He hangs his head. 'I'm sorry, Hannah. I know you could never...'

I want to scream at him. Somehow, Max thinking I'm capable of killing someone is worse than anything else.

'I was going to get Poppy away from you. I really thought... I went over and over it in my head, and Alice just didn't have enemies. She kept to herself and only saw her clients. The only thing she ever did which hurt anyone was our affair.'

'And pretending you'd lost your memory?'

'I thought if I did that, then I'd be able to catch you out in a lie. I was looking for proof.'

Just as I'd been doing. I almost laugh at the absurdity of it.

'Do you think it was Taylor who attacked you?'

He nods. 'I didn't know for sure at the time, but it must have been.'

'There was a man following me. In a silver Golf. Did you pay him to hurt me?'

Max looks horrified. 'No! First you think I killed Alice and now—'

'You took ten grand out of your account. What was that for?'

He frowns. 'I helped Alice out. I loaned her some money. She said she needed to get some new gym equipment.'

I let this sink in. 'You must have really cared about her to hand over that much money.'

He doesn't answer.

'We need to go,' I say. Because what does anything else matter now?

We lock the door and stand on the doorstep. Max must know, as I do, that nothing will be the same after this.

He tries to take my hand but I pull away, and neither of us says anything about it.

'I don't know about you,' Max says, once we're in my car, 'but I feel the biggest sense of relief.'

But I don't.

Because even though I have some answers now, nothing feels right.

TWENTY-EIGHT

THREE MONTHS LATER

The sound of laughter floats upstairs, rousing me from sleep. I always sleep lightly now, woken by the faintest of sounds, and there's never a day when I feel energised.

I pull on my dressing gown and make my way downstairs, greeted by the smell of fresh toast and bacon as I reach the kitchen.

'Mummy!' Poppy says. 'We wanted you to have a lie in.'

'It is Saturday, after all,' Max says, as I reach for a mug.

'Want a toasted sandwich with bacon?' Max says. 'There's plenty left.'

The smile my mouth forms quickly withers away when I remember that this pretence of normality is only for Poppy's sake. Because she needs both of us, united we will stand.

So far, we've made it work. Max and I sleep in separate rooms each night, but still co-parent our daughter with gusto, eating meals together and taking Poppy on family days out. All to protect her mental health.

I can do this – just about – for now. And whenever I think of the future, there's nothing but a blank page, waiting to be written on.

'Can I watch TV?' Poppy asks.

'For a little bit,' I say, watching her run off before I've finished my sentence.

'I'll take her to the park this morning,' Max says, once we're alone. I notice his clean plate. His appetite hasn't suffered at all.

'You'll watch her carefully, won't you?'

Somehow, we've stopped mentioning Taylor. *Shane Roberts*. Neither of us has set eyes on him since he was arrested. The police couldn't charge him: his alibi was watertight – he was without doubt on a flight that evening – and there was no trace of his DNA on Alice.

It doesn't mean he's not guilty – only that he was clever enough to get away with it. And they haven't been able to trace the man in the silver Golf. A stolen car, belonging to an elderly couple who'd gone on a cruise and didn't even realise their car was missing from their drive. I doubt the police will find whoever he is now, but it's clear that the two of them are linked, and he's probably the one who killed Alice. For Taylor.

It still makes me sick how close I was getting to Taylor. That connection. Fabricated by him, but to me it felt real.

'I never take my eyes off her,' Max says, his words laced with irritation. 'Not when Shane is still out there. Free.'

The kettle boils and I pour water over my tea bag, watching the clear liquid turn dark. 'I know you won't.' I wonder if either of us will ever mention what constantly hangs over us: that Taylor isn't just going to leave Max alone suddenly. And what Max cherishes most in his life is Poppy. If Taylor didn't realise that before I met him, he knows it now. And he got to know Poppy, again through me. This thought makes me shudder.

'Have you thought any more about my suggestion?' Max asks.

Marriage counselling. Someone to help us stick a bandage over the gaping wound of our relationship. 'It's too late for that.

I'm moving forward now,' I say. It's what I tell him constantly, but every few days he tries again.

Max's shoulders sag. 'I understand,' he says, standing up and taking his plate to the dishwasher. Surely he can't blame me for feeling this way.

'I'll get to work now,' I say.

'You haven't had any breakfast.'

'Not really hungry this morning.' I lift my mug. 'This will be fine.'

He looks at his phone. 'Bit early to leave for work, isn't it?'

'I need to get a head start on the day.' I take a last sip of tea. 'Will you let me know how it goes in the park?'

He nods, assuring me he'll be hyper-vigilant. 'I won't even look at this.' He waves his phone.

'Are you worried?' I ask, as I stand in the doorway.

'Every single day,' he says. 'The police might have put it down to a random attack, but I know it was him.'

And there is nothing I can reply to that.

'She's great, isn't she?' Cole says, as we watch Ella chatting to a woman she's serving in the coffee bar. She's done wonders for this place. She's enthusiastic and charming, and it's never been so busy in here. Although the customers rarely buy books, it's good to have the place so lively.

'Yeah, she is.' I don't mention this, but I still miss Katy. As unreliable as she was, she was a part of the shop as much as Cole and I are.

'And best of all – I'm in my sister's good books. So it's a win–win.' Cole beams proudly, and I can't help but smile. 'I have to admit, it's a bit weird without Katy. And I never thought I'd be the one to say that.'

I laugh. 'Maybe you're human after all?'

The smile vanishes from his face, and at first I think I've

offended him until I see Sarah and Ivy making their way towards us.

'I'll leave you to it,' Cole says, wandering off and busying himself on the other side of the shop.

'There are my two favourite girls,' I say, hugging Sarah.

Ivy frowns. 'What about Poppy?' she asks.

'Oh, of course Poppy too,' I say. 'She's my extra special favourite.'

Sarah leans down to Ivy. 'Why don't you go to the children's section over there by Cole and choose a book? I'm sure he'll help you.'

'Really?' Her eyes widen.

Sarah nods. 'Yes. Special treat.'

Ivy trots off and I turn to Sarah. 'Not sure Poppy would be so happy to get a book. A toy maybe. Chocolate. Jelly.'

'It's been hard for her. I've not been able to get her much at all other than second-hand clothes and toys people have donated to us. But I feel that things are on the up now.'

'Dean,' I say. 'How's that going?'

Sarah blushes. 'Really well. He comes over almost every night to read Ivy a bedtime story, and then we take her out together on Sundays. You know, family time. And he's paying maintenance. A lot. I think he's trying to make up for the last five years when I've struggled by myself.'

'That's great. I didn't realise he was doing all that.'

Sarah winces. 'Sorry. It felt weird telling you stuff like this after everything that happened to you.'

'Whatever's going on in your life – good or bad – I want to know about it.'

She nods. 'Okay. And same goes for you.'

I swallow my guilt, forcing it away, just as I always do in Sarah's presence now. I should have told her right from the start. Would it have made any difference? All these months later and they still haven't found evidence to convict anyone of Alice's murder.

'How's Max doing?' Sarah asks.

'Still holding out hope that we can get back together.'

'And do you think you ever can?' Her words are laced with hope.

'No. It went on too long. I might have been able to forgive a one-night thing, but... there must have been something seriously wrong with our marriage for Alice to stand any chance of getting to Max.'

Sarah ponders my reasoning. 'I'm not sure life's as black and white as that. And if he had all this extra stress of what was happening with Taylor...'

Thankfully, Ivy runs over to us before I can respond. 'Can I have this book, Mummy?' She waves a book in front of Sarah.

'Good choice,' I say. 'Poppy loves Elmer too.' I turn to Sarah. 'I'll get that for her.'

'No, no. You've helped me out enough over the years. I'm getting this.' Sarah prises the book from Ivy's hand and clutches it to her chest.

'Can I see Poppy?' Ivy asks. 'Please, Mummy.'

'Oh, I don't know.' Sarah glances at me. 'I don't know what Poppy's plans are today.'

'Actually, Max is just taking her to the park. You can join them if you want.'

Sarah frowns. 'Are you sure that wouldn't be weird?'

'You and Max can still be friends. Our separation has nothing to do with that. And Poppy would love to see Ivy.'

'I'll give him a call, then,' Sarah says. She holds up the Elmer book. 'After I've paid for this.'

When I get home, the first thing I notice is the smell of freshly baked cakes. And then I hear Max and Poppy laughing in the kitchen. Domestic bliss. Max is doing this on purpose; forcing me to see how it could be if I ignored everything that's happened. Erased it from my mind, like something from an episode of *Black Mirror*. But I won't falter.

'Hey,' he says, when I get to the kitchen. 'Good day?'

'We've made cupcakes, Mummy,' Poppy says, before I can answer. 'Look!'

'Those look delicious,' I say.

Poppy beams. 'Daddy helped. But I did the hard parts. And we've made pizzas for dinner. Please can we have a movie night? And eat our pizza while we watch?'

'Okay,' Max says. 'As long as it's not *Frozen* again.' He places his hands together in prayer.

'No, not *Frozen* again,' Poppy says. '*Frozen II*!'

Max tickles her and she runs off, squealing.

'Please don't take this away from me,' Max says, when she's left the room.

'We can't stay living like this forever. We have to move on.'

'But Poppy...'

'She'll be fine. I can't talk about this now. I... I need space. Not to change my mind, but to sort out what I'm going to do.'

'None of us are safe,' Max says. 'Not with Shane out there, free to do what he wants.' Max's eyes fill with panic. 'Remember my attack? I could have been killed. He's probably just waiting for things to die down. For the police to forget about him. And for us to as well. And then—'

'Stop!' I cry.

'Mummy? What's wrong?'

I didn't hear Poppy come back in, but now she's staring at me, her eyes wide and curious.

'Nothing, sweetheart,' I assure her. 'Daddy and I were just talking about something. It's...'

But she's not listening, and rummages through the art cupboard, pulling out paper and some pens.

'Let's get this pizza in the oven, then,' Max says.

When Poppy's in bed, Max tells me he's planning to do some work in the garden office. He hasn't been out there for months, and I ask him about that now.

'Someone broke into it,' he says. 'Before. I could tell. It was a mess and I'd never leave it like that. It put me off for a while, but I can't avoid it forever. I need to go through everything and make sure Shane didn't take any work stuff.'

Guilt swells in the pit of my stomach when I remember taking Max's laptop to Taylor, handing it straight to him, to do with what he liked.

'I'll tidy up down here,' I say, surveying the mountain of toys. Despite having a movie night, Poppy still got all of her toys out to play with while she watched.

Max leaves me to it, and I almost call him back. But my mind shuts down anything I could say to him, so I turn away and focus on tidying.

I've nearly finished when I spot Poppy's pink Kidizoom camera under the sofa. Pulling it out, I realise it's still on. She loves taking pictures, and filming videos of people when they're not expecting it, and I scroll through it now, wondering if there are any of me on there.

The first video I see is of Max, and it looks like he's in the park. The screen moves and I see that Sarah is next to him, both of them laughing and urging Poppy to stop filming. Then the camera jolts, and all I can see is the sky, as Poppy laughs and runs off.

But the camera keeps filming, and although their voices are a bit muffled against the background noise in the park, I can make out every word Max and Sarah are saying.

'She won't change her mind,' Max says, while Ivy and Poppy shriek in the background, Poppy urging Ivy to push her.

'I've tried, Max. But Hannah's adamant. She can't look back, she just wants to get on with her life. I'm sorry. I've done everything I can.'

'Shane got what he wanted,' Max says. 'My life's over. Hannah will move out, or I will, and then I'll lose both of them. How can I live every day knowing I won't wake up and see Poppy?'

There's silence, and it sounds as though someone is crying. The noise of children continues to fill the background. Not just Poppy and Ivy. Voices of strangers.

'This is all my fault,' Sarah says. 'I'll never forgive myself.'

'It's not your fault I got involved with Alice,' Max tells her.

'You don't understand.' Her voice is quieter now, and I turn up the volume on Poppy's camera to make sure I can hear.

'What are you talking about?' Max says. 'How is this your fault?'

'Alice knew you were helping me.'

My throat constricts, as if someone has tied a noose around my neck. Confusion and fear mingle inside me. What the hell is this?

'You were just trying to help me.' Sarah's voice is quieter, as if she's struggling to get her words out. 'It's all because of me. Alice would have gone to the hospital and told them what I'd been doing.'

Their voices stop, and all I can hear is the shrieks of children in the playground. What if that's it and the video stops without me knowing what Sarah's talking about? This fear is greater now than any other.

'What?' Max says, finally. 'What are you saying, Sarah? Tell me!'

'Alice knew, Max. She knew what I was doing.' There's silence. Heavy and loaded. 'I saw you together. I followed you to her place so I knew where she lived. And then I went back another time and confronted her about the affair. I couldn't bear to think of what you were doing to Hannah.'

'I know. She told me.'

'She was obsessed with you, Max. She wasn't going to let you go easily. It didn't matter if you finished with her. That wouldn't have been the end of it. And I knew if Hannah found out, then she'd never stay with you. I couldn't bear the thought of Poppy ending up like Ivy. Having to live without her father being right there. It killed me to think that I was lying to my closest friend. Hannah's family to me – you know that.'

'What are you saying?'

'When I confronted Alice, and told her to end it with you, she told me she knew all about what I was doing. She'd heard us talking on the phone that time. When you were telling me to stop what I was doing. She knew everything.'

There's silence, and I try to picture Max, imagine what he was doing when Sarah said this.

'She said she was going to the police,' Sarah continues. 'I... I wasn't expecting that. I only went to her to tell her to end it with you.'

My head pounds, and it feels as though my skull is being crushed. Seconds of silence tick by.

'Alice knew all about the drugs I was stealing from the hospital to sell.' Sarah says. 'Don't act surprised, Max. She told me you'd talked about it. You should have told me she knew. It's okay, though, I know you defended me.' There's another pause. 'It felt awful to be confronted like that,' Sarah continues.

'You were desperate,' Max says. 'That's why I gave you that ten grand. So you wouldn't have to do that any more.'

'I *did* stop doing it. And I've been working every shift I can manage so that I can provide for Ivy. But it was too late because Alice knew. And she told me she couldn't let it go.' There's a pause. 'If Alice had gone to the police, my life would have been over. I'd have lost my job. My home. Ivy too.'

In all the years I've known Sarah, I don't think I've ever heard her cry. She's always soldiered on, putting on a brave face, refusing to acknowledge that she was struggling financially. I knew that stoicism wasn't good for her.

And now, she erupts into loud guttural sobs, and I can picture the anguish on her face. I'm angry with her – furious – but how can I be when she was only trying to protect me? And lying about Max's affair was to protect Poppy. I don't agree with it, but I too lied about huge things that were happening.

But what Max says next chills me to the bone.

'Did you go and see Alice? The night she died?'

Sarah doesn't reply straight away, and her silence speaks volumes.

'I... I just wanted to talk to her. To reason with her, and try and make her stop. To leave you and Hannah alone. To leave all of us alone.'

'What did you do?' Max says. 'What the fuck did you do?'

Sarah's sobs drown out the noise from the playground, and I can barely hear her next words. But somehow, it's as if she's shouting them.

'I didn't mean to kill her.'

TWENTY-NINE

There are tears in my eyes as I walk across the lawn. The short distance feels like miles, and my legs feel weighted down, as if they're trying to stop me getting to Max. I look up at the star-spangled black sky, and pray that somehow I've got this wrong.

He's engrossed in something on his laptop, and doesn't look up until I reach the doorway. I fold my arms across my body – I'm trembling, and it has nothing to do with the icy night temperature out here.

'What's the matter?' Max asks. 'Is Poppy okay?'

I haven't planned what I'll say; the words fall out, tumbling into the night. 'It was Sarah.' This voice I can hear doesn't sound like my own.

'What?'

'Sarah killed Alice Hughes. And all this time I thought—'

Max pushes his chair back. 'Why are you saying this?'

'I know, Max. I know everything.'

He stares at me. Seconds feel like hours. 'How?'

'Poppy's camera recorded you and Sarah talking at the park. I heard all of it.'

I've never seen Max's tanned skin turn so pale – not even

after his attack. 'I didn't know,' he says. 'I promise I didn't know until today. And I've been trying to work out what to do. I just don't know. It's my fault Sarah even knew Alice. I brought her into all our lives. I started this. What are we supposed to do?'

As distressed as he seems, Max has had hours to think about this, while I've only had minutes. 'I don't know. She... she killed someone.'

'She panicked. She was about to lose everything.'

Like Taylor has. And it was never him. 'You can't accidentally strangle someone,' I say, pushing away thoughts of Taylor.

Max stands up. 'I know. You're right. Sarah was trying to stop her going to the police. She... she... I don't know!'

My legs weaken, and I sit down on the chair in the corner. 'And all these weeks Sarah didn't say a word. She talked about Alice. Let *me* talk about her. And she acted so normally.'

'Self-preservation,' Max says. 'She had to block it out for her own sanity. It doesn't mean she was cold and calculating. This is Sarah we're talking about. Our minds do what they can to protect us.'

'Why are you defending her? Didn't you have any feelings for Alice? You must have. You can't spend that much time with someone and not care about them.'

He sits down again, his head flopping back against the headrest. 'I don't know how I felt about Alice. It was all too complicated.'

'She's dead. And Sarah killed her. That's all that matters.'

'I think we all just need to take some time to work this out,' Max says.

'We don't need to work out going to the police when we know a crime's been committed. Not just any crime. The worst type.'

'I know. You're right. But we need to give Sarah time.'

'How long?' I ask. 'A day? A week? A year? How long is enough time for her?'

Max shakes his head. 'I don't know.'

I stand up. With clarity, I see what I have to do.

'Where are you going?' Max asks.

But I don't answer, because if I don't do this now, then perhaps I never will.

The walls of this building have been repainted since I was last here. A lifetime ago. I should feel nervous. Frightened. But I feel neither of these emotions.

He opens the door and gapes at me, as if I'm an apparition, and he can't quite believe I'm standing here. I want him to say something, but he doesn't – he only studies me, frozen where he is.

'Hello, Taylor,' I say. One of us has to be the first to say something.

'What are you—?'

'I know you didn't kill Alice.'

He takes a deep breath, as if he's been waiting to exhale all these months. And then slowly he opens the door wider.

Inside, his flat feels cold, and I wonder if he's trying to save money on heating. The pay-out he got from Max's company will only last so long. Taylor gestures for me to sit on the sofa, and keeping my coat on, I do.

Finally, he speaks. 'Why have you come here?'

'For answers. You must have known I'd want them.'

'No. I assumed you'd never want to see me again. When you disappeared like that, I knew it was all over. Even before Paula came up to me.'

'What did she say?'

'Can't remember her exact words. Something along the lines of me being a despicable human being. She mentioned going to the police too, if I didn't leave you all alone.'

I walk across to the window, like I've done in this flat many times before. Even though everything feels different now, as I look outside, I half expect to see a silver Golf parked across the road.

'What did I do to you?' I ask, turning back to face him.

He stares at me. 'Nothing.'

'Max, though. You think he ruined your life.'

Taylor nods.

'But *I'm* not Max.'

'I know. I never—'

'Where did *Taylor* come from? That's not your name.' *Yet it feels like it is.*

'Actually, it's my middle name. Everyone calls me Taylor. Alice did. All my friends.'

'But not at work. You're Shane Roberts.'

'That happened by accident. When I went for my interview, I was so nervous – I didn't bother correcting them. I didn't think I'd get the job. I was up against hundreds of applicants. Those statistics weren't working in my favour. But then I got it. And it was too late to tell them I go by Taylor, not Shane.'

'That's good because I'm not calling you *Shane*.'

He raises his eyebrows, but doesn't say anything.

'You owe me the truth,' I say. I'm taking a big gamble coming here, but I'm banking on the fact that there was a connection between us, something I don't believe Taylor was faking.

To my surprise, he agrees. I didn't expect it to be this simple. All the ammunition I need to get him to talk is stored in my mind.

His voice is soft when he speaks. Gentle. If I closed my eyes, it could lull me into a deep state of relaxation. 'Everything I told you about my friendship with Alice was true,' he begins. 'All of it.' He looks down. 'What I didn't tell you is that I was the one who told her to talk to Max at the Boathouse. She did that for me. And it was the biggest mistake of my life.'

He looks up briefly, as if he wants to gauge my reaction, but then he stares at his hands. 'The idea was that she'd try it on with him. Entrapment. And then I'd get photos of them that I could use.'

'To destroy his life.'

He looks away. 'Alice didn't want to do it. She tried to talk me out of it. She said it was wrong.' He sighs. 'But she was torn because she knew how much I was struggling. I lost everything because of Max, and Alice was there picking up the pieces.' He flaps his arms. 'This isn't even my flat. I lost the flat I'd bought. Couldn't afford the mortgage. This is my friend's place. He's renting it to me while he's travelling for a year. When he gets back, I'm out of here.'

'Have you found a job yet?'

'Thankfully, I have now. But it's taken all this time for me to get anything. And the salary is nowhere near what I was earning at IBM. I spent years studying, got a fantastic position and worked hard to keep it, then Max knocks it down like a house of cards.'

There are many things I wouldn't defend Max about, but Taylor is wrong. 'It's not his fault you made mistakes at work. That you couldn't live up to what was needed for the job.'

He closes his eyes, lets out a deep sigh. 'So he's told you that same old lie?'

I blink. 'What? How can it be a lie?'

'Everything he told people at work was a lie. Max was my mentor. I looked up to him. Respected him. I was learning from him. But then, quickly I began to overtake him. Once I'd learnt everything I needed to from him, I was in a different league. I know he's good at his job, but I was hungry. Fresher. I could see things in an instant that he might take longer to work out. It's just how my brain works.'

Taylor's words are like a bomb exploding around me.

'Everything started to change,' he continues. 'Max felt

threatened. I'm not arrogant, Hannah, but with a few more months, I would have got a higher position than he had. It doesn't make me feel good saying that; it makes me feel sick now.' He pauses. 'Then the sabotage started. A whole campaign to try and make me look incompetent. Max would alter reports I sent to him, then point out to people how I'd made huge errors. He'd withhold essential info or give me wrong information. All of it made me look like I couldn't do my job. Then he'd take credit for my ideas, but I had no proof when it had just been the two of us present.'

Taylor pauses again, looks up at me as if he needs me to say something, but I don't know what to reply.

'Then he'd tell me things were urgent when they weren't – so I'd spend time working on that, only to find that I should have been prioritising something else.'

Finally, I find my voice. 'How can you expect me to believe this, when you've been misleading me this whole time?'

He nods. 'Do you remember when you brought the laptop to me? And I was going through it? I was able to send myself all the emails I'd sent to Max, with the original reports that he hadn't edited. There's loads of stuff on there. Proof. I'll show it to you.'

Without waiting for a reply, Taylor leaves the room, coming back with his laptop. He logs on and begins talking me through what he found on Max's laptop. Although I don't understand the financial reports, Taylor has meticulously cross-referenced his original emails with the documents Max had changed.

And it looks like everything he's told me just now is true.

'Why didn't you tell someone about this? When it was happening?'

'Because I didn't know Max was doing it until it was too late and I'd been fired. By then I had no access to my work emails. But Max had everything saved on his laptop. It was all easy to find on there. He must have assumed I'd never find all of it.'

'It was you who broke into our office at home, wasn't it?'

'I'm sorry, Hannah – I had to.'

'And the man in the Golf? Who was he? Max never wanted me dead, did he?'

'I was desperate. I didn't think just having an affair would have been enough to convince you to leave him. Some people forgive their partners, don't they?'

'It would have been enough.' I say this loudly. 'You didn't need to—'

'I didn't know you then! I'm sorry. If I could take it back, I would. All of it. I'd have told you right from the start and hoped that you'd believe me. But Max was such a good liar. He had everyone at work convinced.'

'You haven't answered my question. Who was that man? He nearly killed me.'

'His name's Archie. I lived next door to him when I was a kid. He wouldn't have hurt you. He's not a hitman. Not saying he doesn't do things he shouldn't – but he's not a murderer.'

'Did he attack Max, though? Or was it you?'

'It wasn't him. I know the timing doesn't look good, but I had nothing to do with that. It must have just been a random robbery. But I can't say I'm sorry it happened.'

I take a moment to consider what he's said. So many lies have been interwoven into the fabric of our connection, it's hard to know what to believe. But somehow, it feels as though he's telling the truth. 'What about when you were attacked?' I ask. 'You planned all of that. It was all part of trying to convince me to believe your lie.'

'Because I *know* Max killed Alice. When I made sure we met outside the hotel that day, it wasn't about ruining Max's life any more. It was about trying to prove he killed Alice. But I couldn't go to the police because I knew Max would say that I was trying to get revenge. They wouldn't have listened to me.'

'You had the photo.'

'I couldn't take the risk. Max would have won. He has anyway. He's got away with murder.'

Taylor's wrong, but I can't tell him who really killed Alice. I'm convinced Sarah will do the right thing, but out of loyalty to her, I won't force her hand. Not yet.

'Max hasn't won anything,' I say. 'Our marriage is over, and Poppy and I won't be living with him much longer.' And if there was the tiniest fragment of doubt in my mind before, Taylor has made sure that's eradicated. 'Now you've got evidence that Max was sabotaging you at work, what will you do?'

He takes his time to answer, and when he does, it's as if he's only just made up his mind in that moment. 'I'm moving on,' he says. 'I want to put all this behind me. I don't want to fight this battle any more. There's not enough evidence, so what's the point? And I have to believe that one day the truth will come out about him killing Alice.'

I study his face. It occurs to me how differently things might have worked out if I'd called the number of the law firm he gave me when we first met. But somehow in the midst of everything, it slipped my mind. 'That fake business card you gave me. I never called the number. But what if I had?'

'It was Archie's number,' he admits. 'And he was ready in case you did.'

A big risk. I could have lost it and googled the number instead. I tell this to Taylor.

'You're right. I just panicked and didn't think that through properly. I got lucky that you didn't call.'

We let that sit between us for a moment.

'You must have the key card,' I say. 'Max's fingerprints will be on there somewhere. That would have been enough to go to the police with, so why didn't you?'

Taylor shakes his head. 'I don't have the key card. I never did. I don't know who took it from you but it wasn't me.'

I contemplate his words. Could Sarah have found it in my

bag? There would have been plenty of opportunities. But how would she have known it was there? Aside from Taylor, nobody else knew about it.

'I can't take anything back,' Taylor says. 'But I want you to know that I did really start to care about you. We spent a lot of time together. I don't expect forgiveness, but I need to say that.'

'Same here, Taylor,' I say quietly. He will never be Shane. I stand up, checking my pockets for my phone and car keys.

Taylor walks me to the front door. 'Will I see you again?' he asks.

'Probably not.'

'I'll take that as a maybe.'

And as I walk towards the stairs, unseen by him, my mouth forms a faint smile.

THIRTY

I walk to the high street, my footsteps silent as they sink into the thick blanket of February snow. The tip of my nose is painfully cold, as are my fingers, even through my gloves. It would have been easier not to do this. To stay at home and focus on putting the house on the market.

Seeing Taylor last night helped me make this decision. For things to become clearer, people always need a voice. The chance for truth and honesty without fear of judgement. Or worse. I owe Sarah the chance to explain. And then I hope she will do the right thing.

As I approach the coffee shop, guilt burns inside me. It feels like I'm ambushing her, and I begin to waver. Perhaps I should have told her on the phone that I know. Given her a chance to prepare herself. But if I had, she would never have agreed to meet me. I slow down, despite being desperate to get inside and feel some warmth on my skin.

She's already there, in a seat by the window. She looks up and waves, her whole face lighting up with her smile. Since Dean's come back into Ivy's life, Sarah seems to be glowing, as if a heavy cloud has shifted and is no longer hanging over her. But now that she's told Max the truth, I wonder how she isn't worried that he'll tell me. Poppy and Ivy ran back to the park bench to grab the camera as soon as she'd admitted killing Alice, so I don't know how their conversation ended. All I know is that Max has kept Sarah's secrets before.

I push through the doors and try to smile when she stands and gives me a hug.

'What are you having?' she asks. 'Sorry, I couldn't wait. It's freezing. I've already got mine.' She points to the large cappuccino on the table.

'Don't worry, I'll get my own,' I say, walking off to the counter before she can argue.

Despite the early hour on a Sunday morning, the queue is slow-moving, but this only buys me more time to prepare. I glance back at Sarah while I wait. She's busy tapping on her phone and I wonder who she's messaging. Dean? Max?

When I get to the table, there's a wide smile across her face and her eyes seem to sparkle. Dean, then.

Everything will change when I start to speak.

'Dean's with Ivy,' she says. 'Can you believe it? It's the first time he's had her on his own. I can't believe this is all coming together. We're planning to introduce her to his other kids next week. Did I tell you? Layla and Oliver. They're a bit older than Ivy but we're hoping... Oh, it sounds so, I don't know. We're hoping they'll all get along.'

I nod and smile. It's only nine a.m., and I wonder if Dean spent the night so he could be around to take Ivy out. I'm not going to ask Sarah. It no longer feels important, or any of my business.

She looks at me, waiting for more of a reaction, but when I don't speak her smile fades. 'What is it? What's wrong? Are you still worried about Dean? It's been months now, and everything's working out well. Please don't worry.'

I take a deep breath. This will be the hardest conversation I will ever have, and half of me wants to pretend everything is normal. 'I know everything,' I say, my voice barely audible.

Her forehead wrinkles. 'Know what?'

'About Alice.' My breath catches in my throat, as it always does when I say her name. Everything freezes.

Sarah shifts in her chair. There's panic in her eyes. I've never seen her look frightened like this. 'Max told you. I... I didn't think he—'

'No, he didn't. I found out and confronted him.'

'How?'

'It doesn't matter right now. All that matters is the truth. I want to hear from you what happened. I promise I'll listen, and we'll work this out together.'

Tears pool in her eyes and she dabs them with a napkin. She tries to lift her cup but her hands are shaking so much that she places it down again. And my heart is aching. I want to reach for her, but I keep my arms by my side.

'I saw them together at the Boathouse. It must have been the May half term. I'd just finished a shift and Mum had Ivy. I just needed to switch off. They were outside the toilets. And they were... kissing.' She looks at me, her eyes emitting a silent apology, but she doesn't need to. I'm immune to this now.

'I'd just come out, and at first I could only see the back of Max and I thought it was you he was kissing. I was about to go up to you and make a joke about the two of you carrying on like teenagers. But when I realised it wasn't you – I felt sick. I didn't know what to do. What to say. I walked right past them, and neither of them even looked up. They were so...'

She doesn't need to finish her sentence – the picture is already clear in my mind.

'I hid by the bar. It was busy that night so they didn't see me, and I watched them.' Tears fall heavily now, smudging her mascara. 'When they got back from the toilets, they were more reserved. Just sitting chatting. Not even touching each other. I suppose Max was being careful in case he saw anyone you know. But you can tell when two people have something physical between them, can't you? They can't hide their body language.'

'I don't need to hear this part,' I say. 'Max has told me every detail of the affair.'

'Sorry,' Sarah says. 'I know it must be hard—'

'It's over with me and Max. I just don't need to hear it. This is about you and me. And Alice Hughes.'

Understanding floods her face, and she nods slowly. 'I stayed until they left, and then I followed them. Max drove her home to Roehampton, and I made a note of her address. He walked her to her door. It was raining and he took off his suit jacket and held it over her. Like they do in old films. It made me so angry. It was such an intimate gesture. My first reaction was to tell you. Of course it was. But then I thought about Poppy, and how she wouldn't be living with her dad any more. I knew you'd leave Max, and I didn't want to be the one to split up your family.' She shakes her head. 'I know that was the wrong thing to do. If I could go back—'

'We can't, though, can we?'

She coughs. 'Sorry. I think I'm getting a cold.' She reaches into her bag and pulls out a tissue. 'Then I thought about going to Max, and telling him to end it. If he did that, then maybe it would all be okay. You wouldn't get hurt, and neither would Poppy.'

'But you didn't, did you? He didn't even realise you knew.'

'Alice told him I knew. She didn't know who I was, but maybe he guessed from her description of me and showed her a picture to confirm it. I was expecting him to confront me any time, but he never did.'

'But you confronted Alice.'

She nods. 'I just need the toilet. Will you watch my bag?'

I watch her walk off, and count the seconds in my head. She takes so long that I wonder if she's left. Her bag's still here, but not her phone. I saw her put it in her pocket.

After a couple more minutes, I'm about to go and look for her when she appears, drying her hands with a paper towel.

'You were stealing drugs from the hospital,' I say, before she's even sat down. 'From your patients. How could you do that? Being a nurse meant everything to you. You could have come to me if you needed help with money.'

'I was ashamed. How could I have told you?'

'You told Max.'

'He's not you. It was easier to tell him. Especially when I admitted to him that I knew about his affair.'

'We tell each other everything.' As soon as I say this, I realise it's no longer true.

'I couldn't tell you. I was ashamed. And scared. Desperate. Max said he'd help me, so I kept quiet about his affair. It was like a silent understanding between us.'

Two of the closest people in my life lying to me, making sure I had a skewed view of my world.

'I would have lost my job if it all came out,' Sarah continues. 'It started slowly. Just one-offs now and again. Oramorph. Morphine tablets. Tramadol. Diazepam. I'd give the patients less than the stated dose, and keep what was left.' She stares at her coffee, which will be cold by now. 'Then, I'd sell to desperate people who needed pain relief. I realised I could make quite a bit, so I did it more. And it helped me pay for the essential stuff I needed for me and Ivy.' She stares at her trembling hands, and tries to still them. 'I broke down one day when I'd come to see you and you weren't there. I ended up telling Max everything. He was good to me. He told me I needed to stop and said he'd help me out with money.'

'He gave you ten thousand pounds, didn't he?'

She nods. 'I'm sorry. I'll give it back. Every penny.'

'I don't care about that. I would have given you any amount you needed. Any amount I could afford.'

'I know.'

'Max thought I'd stopped, but I hadn't. He had a go at me. Alice overheard us on the phone and that's when she said she was going to the police.'

'She didn't have to die for that.' I already know from the video on Poppy's camera what Sarah did, but I want to hear it from her.

Almost a minute ticks by before she speaks. 'I want to say that Alice wasn't the person she's being painted as. That she wasn't innocent. Kind. But that's not true. I think she was a good person – she just got desperate. She tried to cling on to Max with everything she had. Everything she did was driven by her need for him.' She looks at me. 'And for her need to protect people's mental and physical health. She said I was putting people at risk, and she couldn't ignore it. She said it didn't matter what I did – she was going to the police about me.'

Through the window, I see blue flashing lights. My body heats up. Sarah doesn't notice them – she continues talking, telling me every detail of the night she killed Alice.

But then the siren is too loud not to register. Sarah stops talking and slowly turns to look out of the window.

Her face drains of colour, and her eyes widen. She looks like a frightened animal.

I reach across the table and grab her hand, squeezing it gently. 'I'm here for you. Always. And Ivy. Whatever you need.'

I half expect her to bolt for the door, but she doesn't. She sits up straight, and begins pulling on her coat, and tying her hair up in a bun. 'Make sure Dean is the father he should be. Please.'

I nod. 'I will.'

'And can you call my mum and tell her where I am? Dean too?'

I can barely manage to say yes.

Sarah stands and walks to the door. She talks to the two officers waiting for her, before they lead her away to the car.

THIRTY-ONE

I've never felt so empty as I abandon my coffee on the table and leave the coffee shop, as if my insides have been hollowed out. I knew Sarah would have to face what she's done – I just wasn't expecting to have so little time with her before it was all over.

I'm proud of her that she had the strength to make the call to summon them here, because I don't think I could ever have done it.

Outside, I make the call to Carol, and I gently break it to her that Sarah's at the police station. She fires frantic questions at me, but I can't answer any of them. All I can tell her is to get down there as soon as she can.

Then I call Dean on Sarah's house phone. I don't expect him to answer – he doesn't live there – but to my surprise he picks up. Again, I tell him as little as possible, and he promises he'll look after Ivy until this is all sorted out. 'I'm sure it's all a misunderstanding,' he says. 'Sarah won't have done anything.' But his voice is tinged with worry. Perhaps he's realising how little he knows her.

It's still snowing as I make my way along Upper Richmond Road. The shop doesn't open until eleven on Sundays, so Cole will still be at home. There are some things I need to fill him in on, and I need to take care of it now. This feels like a day for closure. For laying the past to rest.

He looks startled when he opens the door and sees me standing there. I've never shown up unannounced at his flat before. 'Hannah! Are you okay?' He looks at his watch.

'Can I come in?'

'Yes, of course. But what's the matter?'

'It's nothing to worry about,' I assure him, glancing around. 'Can I come in, then?'

'Oh, sorry.' He opens the door wider and I step inside, greeted by the smell of freshly brewed coffee. Cole's very particular about the coffee he drinks, and I imagine he'd rather drink dishwater than instant from a jar.

'Will this take long?' he asks. 'I've got to get ready to open up.'

'I'll be quick, don't worry. Ella's in today, isn't she?'

'Yes. Um, have a seat, then.'

Only when I sit down do I realise why Cole is so flustered. He doesn't like anything unexpected. Someone turning up on his doorstep without an invitation will have pushed him out of his comfort zone. Even if it's me.

'Sorry to turn up like this,' I say. 'I just wanted to share some news with you.'

He frowns. 'Oh? That sounds intriguing. Nothing to worry about, I hope?'

'You know the last few months have been a difficult time for me. With Max and I separating. And his attack. All of that. Well, I've done a lot of thinking and I've made some huge, life-changing decisions.'

He leans forward. 'Okay. I'm listening.'

'I love Whispering Pages. You know I do. It's been in my life for years.'

'I know. That place has a lot of history.' He frowns. 'But where are you going with this?'

It takes me a moment to say the words. Until now, they've only been thoughts in my head. Something close by, but not quite here yet. 'I'm selling up.'

Cole's jaw drops, and he leans back, letting out a huge sigh.

'But I want to offer you first refusal. You're as much a part of that place as Mum and I are. It feels right that it should be yours.'

Cole stares at me for a moment. 'This is a bit of a shock,' he says. 'I… I don't know what to say.'

'I know you're working on your novel, and you didn't want to take on the responsibility when Mum was selling, but that was a few years ago now. I thought maybe you might feel differently now?'

He leans forward, smoothing his trousers. 'That's nice of you to think of me. I… um… It's a huge decision to make. You don't need an answer right now, do you?'

'No, of course not. I just wanted to let you know the decision I've made.' *And to cement it in my mind before I can talk myself out of it.* 'Take some time to think about it all.'

Cole huffs. 'Are you sure about this? You love that place. Won't it feel weird giving it up?'

'It hasn't been an easy decision, but I've thought about it for a couple of months now. And it's the right thing to do. For both me and Poppy.'

He nods. 'I understand. Your separation from Max must be hard. But what will you do?'

'Move away from London. I don't know where yet. Brighton appeals to me. And Poppy likes it there too. It will be her choice as well.'

Cole frowns. 'But your whole life is here. Everything. People who care about you. What about Sarah?'

'Let's just say I don't think our friendship will ever be the same. Sometimes there are things we can't forgive.'

He searches my face. 'You probably don't want to talk about it. But whatever's happened, I did always think to myself that she's not a good person.' He holds up his hands. 'Sorry.'

'Sometimes good people make mistakes.' I turn away, otherwise I won't be able to stop a flood of tears erupting.

Thankfully, Cole changes the subject. 'I suppose Brighton is close enough that Max can still see Poppy regularly. Well, it looks like I've got some thinking to do, haven't I?'

'Yep.'

'What if...? Oh, never mind.'

'No, go on. What were you about to ask?'

He takes a moment to answer. 'Okay. What if we ran the bookshop together? Partners. You'd get more time to do other things. It would be perfect. We already know we can work together, don't we?'

'That's true, but the whole point is I need to get away. There are too many memories here. Too much has happened.' *More than Cole knows.* 'I just can't stay here.'

'You're right. Then how about I come with you? We can set up Whispering Pages somewhere else. I can help look after Poppy too. It's not easy being a single mum.' He smiles. 'Let me help you, Hannah.'

His face is so full of hope and joy that I almost can't bear to let him down. 'I'm sorry,' I say. 'This is about me and Poppy.'

'Sure. Of course it is.' He checks his watch. 'How about a quick coffee, and you can fill me in on how it would all work if I buy you out?'

While he's in the kitchen, I walk around Cole's living room, studying the Impressionist paintings he's hung on the walls. I can't recall the names of any artists, even though Cole often mentions them.

I sit back down, moving the cushion out of the way. My

hand nudges something hard. I lift the cushion and see there's a phone there. I pull it out and I'm about to shout to Cole that I've got his phone when it hits me that this can't belong to him. I turn it over and study the case. A pink glittery case.

Confused, I realise where I've seen it before.

Cole comes back in, carrying two coffee cups. 'Here you go,' he says. 'Now tell me that isn't the best coffee you've ever tasted.'

I stand up and stare at him, all the words I want to say struggling to find their way out. 'What are you doing with Katy's phone?'

The colour drains from his face as he looks from me to the phone. 'I can explain,' he says. He places the cups on the coffee table, spilling coffee in his haste to get them out of his hands.

'Where's Katy? Why have you got her phone?'

'She... she left it in the shop. I meant to give it to her, but—'

'You're lying. I've been calling her. I told you that. I've called her loads of times.' And that's when I realise that Cole is the one who told me Katy had quit and wasn't coming back. I haven't heard a single word from her.

He turns to the door, his eyes darting around. 'I... I don't know...'

'What's going on?' I scream at him. 'What are you doing with this?'

Cole shrinks back. I've never spoken like this to him before, and it must take him by surprise.

'She was... she was in my business.' Droplets of sweat have formed on his forehead, and his skin looks hot and red. 'I had to stop her. It wasn't meant to happen. I had no choice.'

I've heard enough. Still clutching Katy's phone, I run for the door, leaving my coat on the sofa in my rush to get away from Cole.

THIRTY-TWO

THE DAY OF THE MURDER

As soon as her client has left, Alice sinks to the floor. This session was exhausting. Normally she can just guide her clients, and let the people she's training do the work themselves, but Tania always seems so needy. Alice has to do everything alongside her. Every lunge. Every squat. Every plank. She doesn't usually mind, it's just today it's drained her. Sucked out all her energy in one hour.

She sits cross-legged and takes a deep breath, forcing her mind to be calm. Lately there have been too many jumbled thoughts invading her brain. Most of the time, she can't make sense of them. One minute she's panicking about the business, then her brain flits to her mum and the guilt Alice feels for not having seen her in ages. Then it's Taylor, and how he's going on and on at her to finish this thing up with Max. He just doesn't understand. You can't help who you fall in love with, can you? And Max is right there in her head, always, overshadowing everything else.

Alice pulls herself up from the floor and stretches. Her muscles ache, and she needs to get out of these sweaty leggings and T-shirt and get in the shower. She checks her phone but there's nothing other than a message from one of her clients asking if she can reschedule her session tomorrow.

After replying that it's no problem, Alice's thoughts turn back to Max. She's sent him three texts already this morning, and he hasn't replied to any of them. He'll say she's harassing him, but when will he realise that if he just replies to her in the first place, she won't have to bombard him with more messages? Surely that's a no-brainer?

She finishes her stretches, then wipes down the mats and dumbbells, placing them back in the corner of the gym. As always, she sprays some White Company Flowers scent across the room, to freshen it up. There are no more clients today, and she always does this before she locks up.

Inside the house, she calls for Simba and Willow, and the cats come running up to her, their claws click-clacking on the wooden floors. 'At least you two love me,' she says. 'Or do you just want some food?'

They mewl at her, and she fills their bowls with kibbles, standing back to watch them for a moment. She'd be lost without them, even more so than she already is. Sometimes it's like she's swimming in a swamp, and every so often she reaches a patch of clear water, but it always turns back to the murky darkness. The tangle of vegetation, the thick mud and floating debris. This is exactly what's happening in her head. Once, Alice tried to explain it to Max, but he'd just looked at her blankly and told her she was beautiful. Right, like that's all a woman wants to hear.

When she hasn't heard from him by lunchtime, she calls his phone. He'll be at work and he'll be furious that she's calling him, but she no longer cares.

He doesn't answer. In desperation, she calls his work number. She's only done it once before, that time they had a huge row, and she promised him she wouldn't call him at the office again. But Alice is starting to give less of a damn with every passing second.

She's sick of being second best, of giving him all of her and getting nothing in return.

'Max Chambers,' he says, when he answers. His voice is professional. Different to the gentler voice he reserves for her when he knows she's on the other end of the line. Unless he's annoyed with her.

'I need to see you,' Alice says, smoothing a large strand of her hair. She does this when she's nervous. Max is always commenting on it, telling her it's distracting, but he can't see her now so she doesn't care.

'Why are you calling me at work?'

'We need to talk, Max.' She hates this phrase. It's bandied about so much; someone needs to come up with another way to say it.

'I'm at work, Alice.'

'I'm booking a hotel room for tonight. So we can talk properly. Away from my place. There's too much... history here. We need somewhere neutral.'

'I can't. I've got too much work on. You know how busy I am.'

She's about to protest, to try to coerce him into it, when he changes his mind. 'But you're right. We do need to talk.' He sighs heavily. She hates when he does this. He's always frustrated with her.

'So you'll meet me there, then?'

There's a long pause. 'Okay. At around five. I can't get out any earlier than that.'

'I'll book somewhere now and let you know where.' Alice tries to keep the excitement from her voice.

'Okay.' He hangs up without saying goodbye.

. . .

At three o'clock, Alice makes her way to the River Walk Hotel. She's booked this one partly to annoy Max, because it's so close to his home. Yet he hadn't protested when she'd messaged him to let him know.

She's decided to walk. It's cold, of course, but the sky is cloudless and she needs this thinking time to go through everything. To make sure she gets everything right. What she has to do is clear in her mind now. She won't let herself back out.

And by the time she walks into the lobby of the River Walk, she's ready.

The woman at the reception desk smiles at her. 'Hi. Are you checking in?' she asks. She has smooth brown skin and shiny dark hair. Perfectly shaped eyebrows. She looks like a woman who takes care of herself. Alice considers presenting her with a business card, but then she remembers she doesn't have any on her.

'Yeah, just one night,' Alice says. 'My name's Alice Hughes.'

'Ah, my niece is called Alice. Lovely name.' The woman smiles, and Alice glances at her name badge. Sue Leone.

Sue taps on the computer and prints out a sheet. 'Here you go.' She passes it to Alice. 'This is your receipt.' She takes a card from behind the desk, slotting it into a small paper wallet. 'And this is your key card. You're on the first floor – room twelve. There are no rooms on the ground floor, just the gym and restaurant. Dinner is from five p.m. – all the details are on the back of the card.' She turns it over to show Alice, as if she wouldn't be able to find it for herself.

'Thanks.' Alice takes the card.

'You're welcome.' Sue smiles. 'Have a lovely stay.'

Upstairs in the room, Alice flops down on the bed, spreading her arms out. She loves the feel of clean sheets. She sits up and opens her gym bag, pulling out a small bottle of Evian – the only thing she's brought with her. Alice doesn't drink coffee, and only has one cup of tea in the mornings.

Taylor always laughs at her. 'You fill your body with water all day – no caffeine – but if you go out in the evening you can drink me, or anyone else, under the table.'

She smiles to think of his words now. She misses Taylor. Despite how he's been acting lately, he's one of the good ones. But he hasn't spoken to her for months, not since she refused to end things with Max. She gets why he doesn't like it. Max hasn't been a good man at work. But Alice can't let that be her concern. She let Taylor have the photo – surely she's done her part?

Anyway, she's finally doing what Taylor wants – she's putting an end to all this. And she's going to tell Max's wife what he's been doing – it's not fair for her to be oblivious. Alice has to do this for her own sanity. Max will hate her, and won't want anything to do with her, but at least she will be free. It was a bit like that song by Selena Gomez. Alice needs to lose Max in order to love herself. She hums it now as she sends a message to Taylor, letting him know that she's ending her relationship. She presses send, then lies back down and waits, closing her eyes.

All that matters now is the truth.

At five o'clock, there's a knock on the door. Alice jumps up and checks her reflection in the mirror. Her clothes have to be just right for this. Relaxed and casual. Showing Max that she's not dressing up for him, not trying to keep him interested. And her make-up is minimal – just a dab of tinted lip balm. She looks fresh. Younger without a mask of foundation covering her skin.

Happy that everything is just as she wants it to be, Alice answers the door. And finds herself staring at Sarah Brooks.

'What are—?'

'Max isn't coming,' the nurse says, striding in and closing the door. She smiles at Alice, and her skin wrinkles. 'But you and I are going to have a chat.'

This is all wrong. This isn't how tonight was supposed to

work out. Max is supposed to be here so Alice can tell him that it's over. That she wants nothing more to do with him because she's come to her senses. But he's sent his friend instead. A despicable woman who's abusing her position as a nurse. Alice shudders.

'Get out,' she says.

'Don't you want a resolution to all this? One that works for all of us? I'm not here to argue with you or upset you. I just want to talk.' Her voice is pleasant, and Alice decides she should hear her out. What's she got to lose?

'Can I sit?' Sarah asks.

'If you like.' Whatever this woman has to say, Alice isn't going to make it easy for her. She's a criminal and shouldn't be trusted.

'Max isn't coming today,' Sarah says. 'He wants an end to this. No more sneaking around behind his wife's back. Who, by the way, is an awesome woman and mother. But you don't care about that, do you? Or you would never have—'

'I didn't know he was married when it started. I only found out later.'

'I get that. I really do. But you found out months ago. And here you are, waiting for him.'

Alice doesn't like the way she's being blamed here, especially when it's coming from a nurse who is stealing drugs to sell to people.

'Actually, it's all over.'

Sarah's eyes narrow as she looks at Alice. 'What do you mean?'

Alice senses fear in her voice. 'I asked him to meet me here to end it. And to tell him that I'm telling his wife everything.'

The woman's eyes widen and for a moment she struggles to find any words. 'I don't believe you. You're obsessed with him. He's told me everything.'

'I *did* want it to work, yeah. I loved him. I still do. But he's not good for me. I see that now. I'm moving on.'

Sarah looks around. 'I don't believe you. Why would you meet in a hotel room if you're ending your affair?' She glances at the bed. 'Oh, I get it. Were you going to give him one last fuck before you ended it? You're sick. You could have just called him or messaged.'

Alice blushes. Without wanting to admit it to herself, perhaps she'd envisaged that they'd spend one last time together. But this woman is right. It's sick.

'Because our relationship meant something to me. So I'm not going to end it with a WhatsApp message.' Or rather, Snapchat. Max had insisted this is how they should communicate so that there'd be no record of their messages.

'A pub, then,' Sarah says. 'Anywhere but a hotel room.'

'Max was fobbing me off. And sex seems to be the only language he understands. He might never have agreed to meet me otherwise.'

'You make me sick,' Sarah says, shaking her head.

Alice's cheeks flush with shame. How dare this woman speak like that to her? 'Who the fuck do you think you are?' Her voice is surprisingly calm. 'After what you've been doing.'

Sarah's face drains. 'What?'

'I heard Max talking to you on the phone the other day. I know all about you stealing drugs from the hospital. Selling them on to people who are desperate for pain relief. You're fuelling their addiction. It's immoral as well as being illegal. How can you live with yourself?' Alice spits these words out, disgusted by the mere act of having to say them. 'And Max is as guilty as you are for not saying anything.' This has fuelled Alice's desire to be rid of him, although she's fast becoming convinced she's handled this all wrong. Did she really need to do this after all?

It's obvious that Alice has thrown this woman off course –

whatever Sarah has come here for, she hasn't been expecting to be confronted with this.

'Our health is all we have,' Alice says, when Sarah doesn't speak. 'You're a nurse! You're supposed to heal people, not wreck them. And you've been doing it for years!' Alice stands up and moves to the desk, perching on the side of it. She's looking down on Sarah now, and it helps. 'Max didn't tell you that I knew, did he?'

The silence tells Alice all she needs to know.

'And you're probably wondering why he wouldn't, when you were so close. D'you know what I think? It's because it suited him. Everything Max does is to suit his own needs. But he did try and defend you, if that helps. When I told him I wanted to report you to the police, he begged me not to. He told me how you'd been struggling with money, even with all the extra shifts you were doing. I get that. You're raising your daughter on your own.'

'It's been so hard,' Sarah says.

'But now I know this, there's no way I'll be an accessory to it. I can't turn a blind eye. I'm all about healing people, not hurting them. Which is why I wanted Max to come here tonight. So I could explain everything to him. Right before I go to the police with what I know.'

Sarah stands up. 'No... please... I'm not doing it any more.'

'Did Max send you here?'

'No. He doesn't know I'm here. He just told me that he was supposed to be meeting you. He only mentioned the room number because it's my door number. He thought that was a funny coincidence. He's leaving you, Alice. All this time you thought you were in control of this. Max has no intention of coming here.'

Her words sting, but Alice tries to brush it off. She could be lying. Desperate people will say anything to weaken you. But if it's true, what does that matter now? 'You really do talk about everything, don't you?' Alice sighs. 'That's none of my concern now, though. I'm moving on. I need to be free of Max, and free of you.'

There's a shift in the atmosphere, and Sarah's demeanour changes. No longer confident and in control, she seems to shrink before Alice's eyes. 'Please,' she begs. 'Please don't go to the police. My daughter will lose everything. She's only five!'

Alice has to switch off from this. She knows it will all be devastating for the little girl, but that's not Alice's fault – it's Sarah's. 'I have to. I couldn't live with myself if I didn't. Can you go now? I can't be around someone like you.'

Sarah slowly stands up and heads towards the door.

Alice follows, so that she can shut the door on this woman, ensure she gets the hell out, but suddenly Sarah is turning around, rushing towards her and ramming into Alice, forcing her backwards onto the bed.

Shock paralyses her, and she struggles to pull herself up. Sarah jumps onto the bed and forces her down by sitting across her chest. And then her hands are reaching around Alice's neck, squeezing. 'I can't let you do this to me,' she cries, but her voice is too faint. Alice can barely hear it, and it only becomes fainter. She manages to make out something about not letting her do this to Ivy.

And then everything is silent and black.

THIRTY-THREE

Extract from the *Wandsworth Times* online:

Metropolitan Police have discovered the body of a twenty-four-year-old woman in Putney, southwest London.

The remains were found in a private garage at the back of a block of flats on Upper Richmond Road.

The owner of the garage, a forty-year-old man, has been arrested on suspicion of murder.

This is not thought to be linked to the murder of Alice Hughes, also in Putney, whose body was found at the River Walk Hotel in November.

THIRTY-FOUR

THE DAY OF THE MURDER

Alice's eyes pop open. Her throat feels tight and sore, the skin around her neck feeling as though it's been torn off. She lifts her head and sees that she's alone now. Sarah Brooks has gone.

Left her for dead.

Max was supposed to come here, not that woman. But it doesn't matter. All that matters now is that she can call the police. And now they can add attempted murder to the list of all the things that woman has done.

Alice hunts for her phone and spots it on the desk.

She pulls herself up and slides off the edge of the bed, wondering why her legs feel so weak when she attempts to stand.

There's a knock on the door. For a second she freezes. Has Sarah Brooks come back? But surely she wouldn't risk it after what she's done. It's Max. He's come after all.

Alice gets to the door, pulls it open, ready to tell Max what's happened, but she halts, frozen, as she stares at a man she's never seen before. He's tall and wears dark trousers and a smart winter coat. He must have got the wrong room.

'Hi, um, are you Alice?'

She's wrong, then. He's looking for her. He sounds so polite and unsure of himself. Almost shy. 'Yes.'

'What's happened to your neck?'

She lifts her hand to cover it. 'Who are you?'

'Can I come in?'

'No. Who are you?'

He ignores her and brushes past her.

'Hey, what the...? Get out!' She tries to push him but he grabs her wrists.

'I'm not going anywhere. You need to listen to me.'

Even though his voice is soft, gentle even, there's something about him that isn't right. There's a blankness in his eyes. Something she's never seen in anyone.

And then she has a flash of recognition. And knows where she's seen him before. He works in the bookshop Max's wife owns. Alice has been in there several times, browsing the bookshelves, checking out the woman who Max says he will never leave. Alice had been curious to know what had made Max fall in love with her, and want to stay with her. She knows she went a bit too far taking photos of the woman, but she couldn't help herself. She needed to study her in her own time, without fear of being caught by Max.

'You're here because of Max's wife,' Alice says. She can't bring herself to say her name.

'You've hurt my friend,' he says. 'And anyone who hurts Hannah needs to be punished.'

A nervous laugh escapes her mouth. Any second now, this man will smile and tell her it's all been a joke. But his eyes remain blank.

'You and Max,' he says. 'You both need to pay.' He looks around the room. 'And do you know what? I feel very lucky today. I would never have found you here if I hadn't been closing up the shop and seen Sarah.'

'What?'

'Yep, I followed her here and she led me right to you. She didn't even see me standing at the end of the corridor. Too busy running from what she'd done. At least she had the sense to slow down and walk when she got downstairs. Not that anyone was paying attention.' He pauses. 'That's the thing with these soulless places. No one pays any attention. So that's the first bit of luck. The second is that you opened the door and let me in. I wasn't expecting that. I was ready to tell you it was house-keeping behind the door.'

Alice looks down at his hands and sees he has thick leather gloves on.

'And looking at the state of your neck, it's not too much of a wild guess to say that Sarah tried to strangle you. I told Hannah she was no good. But still, even more luck for me.'

Alice whimpers. Then hates herself for it. She needs to outsmart this man, find a way to get out of this room alive. She needs to stay strong. She's been given a second chance. She's not about to die now. 'I was leaving Max tonight,' she says, trying to keep her voice from breaking. 'I swear. It's over. I'm telling his wife everything—'

'Hannah!' he shouts. 'Her name is Hannah. Say it!'

This man is clearly disturbed. 'Hannah,' Alice says. 'I was telling Hannah everything.'

'No.' He says this quietly, but there's still force behind his words. 'That would destroy her. I can't let you do that.'

'Why? What is she to you? If she's your friend, why wouldn't you want the best for her?'

'Because I don't want to see her in pain. Not for one second. I just want all the toxic people out of her life. Max. You. I'll deal with Max later. And here we are.'

'You're sick. You're obsessed with her. What makes you think you'd ever stand a chance—?'

'Don't you talk about her. A piece of trash like you doesn't deserve to even know her.'

Of anything this man could say to her, Alice won't stand for being called trash. 'I know my worth,' she says, rushing towards him and thrusting her knee between his legs.

He manages to grab hold of her wrists, even though she must have caused some damage to his groin. Alice has a lot of strength in her legs, but he's much larger than her, and now she can't extract herself from his tight grip.

And even though she fights with everything she's got, when his hands reach for her neck, and grip it far tighter than Sarah had, Alice knows that this stranger's face will be the last one she ever sees.

THIRTY-FIVE

Extract from the *Wandsworth Times* online:

> *Metropolitan Police have arrested a forty-year-old man for the murder of Katy Mitchell from Wandsworth.*
>
> *Cole Potts, from Putney, has admitted killing twenty-four-year-old Katy, and hiding her body in a garage at the back of his block of flats. He then used her phone to send messages to her family and friends, which explains why nobody reported her missing.*
>
> *While being interviewed by police, Cole Potts also admitted to murdering Alice Hughes, whose body was found at the River Walk Hotel in Putney in November.*

AUGUST

Poppy and I sit on the pebble beach, both of us mesmerised by the sea. It's almost thirty degrees this morning, and it's not even ten a.m. Other than a man walking his dog, we have the beach to ourselves. I take a deep breath, and slowly exhale, releasing all my tension and pain.

'I wish I could swim in the sea,' Poppy says.

'When you're a bit older you might be able to a little bit. But not too far out.'

'Because sharks might get me?'

I smile at my daughter's innocence. 'Not sure there are any sharks around here, but you never know.'

I look over at Brighton Pier, which is quiet now, but will soon be heaving with visitors. Moving here from London was the best decision I could have made for us, despite it being a huge change. It's peaceful, even when it's packed with summer tourists.

To my surprise, Poppy is excited to start her new school in a few weeks, and she constantly tells me how grown up she is to be in Year 2.

Most Fridays, Max comes to spend the weekend with Poppy, and she probably sees him more than she did before. I've suggested he can stay in our spare room when he visits, but so far he hasn't taken me up on my offer. Instead, he stays at the Grand Hotel on the beachfront.

I have no idea how he can set foot in a hotel after everything that happened to Alice, but clearly it's just me who will never be able to.

'There they are!' Poppy shrieks, pointing across the beach.

I turn around and see two figures walking towards us. Unsurprisingly, I feel a jolt of nerves. Although we've messaged a lot since it happened, I haven't seen Sarah since we met in the coffee shop that Sunday morning. The last image I hold in my head of my friend is her disappearing inside a police car, her eyes wide and terrified, but also resigned. I remind myself that today is about looking forward – I don't think either of us want to go back.

Poppy races towards them and throws her arms around Ivy. It's as if they've never been apart. *Friends for life.* Just as Sarah and I were supposed to be.

I follow more tentatively – I have no idea how this day together will pan out. And as I get closer to Sarah, I notice there are tears in her eyes, even though she's smiling.

We hug, just as we've always done, and for a fraction of a second nothing has changed. Then she speaks and it's clear that everything has.

'I nearly changed my mind about coming,' she says, as the girls run towards the sea. 'But... it would have broken Ivy's heart.'

I nod my understanding. 'It can't have been easy.'

She laughs. 'Hardest thing I've ever had to bloody do.'

I point to the blanket I've laid out across the pebbles. 'Shall we sit for a bit? The girls seem happy over there.' By the edge of the water, they're already pulling off their shoes and socks and dipping their feet in the sea, squealing when they realise how cold it is, even in this heat.

'Good thing I brought a towel,' Sarah says. And then she smiles, and I see a hint of my old friend.

We watch the girls for a moment, then Sarah turns to me. 'Do you forgive me?'

'I'm not sure it's up to me to forgive you. None of it was about me, was it? The only thing that matters is whether or not you can forgive yourself.'

She thinks about that for a moment. 'No, of course I can't. But I'm paying for what I did. I've lost my job, the only thing I ever wanted to do. Now I just have to try to put some good back into this world to counteract everything I did.'

'That makes sense,' I say.

We turn back to the girls. More people are appearing on the beach now, setting up blankets and chairs, peeling off layers under the burning sun.

'It's hard to live with what I did,' Sarah says quietly. 'It keeps me awake all night. I barely sleep. I know I didn't actually kill Alice, but... I thought I had. And I left her for dead. That's bad enough. I was a nurse and I did the worst possible thing to another human. I don't deserve to be here. Sometimes I think about en—'

'Ivy needs you. Whenever you feel that way, just remember that little girl over there needs her mum. She can do without anything else. Dean. Your mum. Poppy. But she can never do without you, Sarah.'

My words seem to sink in, and slowly she nods. 'I know that.'

'Is Dean still around?' I ask.

'Yes. For Ivy. Not for me, of course. Not now. He can barely look at me. But that's okay. I just need him to support his daughter.' Her mouth stretches into a thin line. 'Mum's barely talking to me.'

'Give her time.'

'But you're still here for me. You always have been.'

Not as much as I should have been.

'Shall we have a walk along the pier? Grab some coffee?' I try not to think about the last time we had coffee together. *Move forward, never look back.*

'Sounds good.' Sarah stands, and helps me fold the blanket. 'Can you believe I've never been to Brighton?'

'Well, I hope you like it,' I say, stuffing the blanket in my bag. 'You and Ivy are going to be here a lot.'

Poppy is exhausted by the time she sinks into bed. I read *The Magic Faraway Tree* to her, but before long her eyes droop and she fights to keep them open until the end of the chapter.

'Did you have a nice day?' I ask.

She nods. 'Yes. I've missed Ivy. And now I won't get to see her every day at school.'

'We'll see Ivy and Sarah all the time – I promise. And I miss Sarah too, so I know how you feel.'

Poppy turns on her side. 'You're besties too, aren't you?'

'Yes, we are. And do you know what's really important? Always telling the truth to our closest friends. And always making sure they can trust us and we can trust them. Never hiding things, even if you think you're doing it to protect them.'

'Mum?'

'Yes?'

'I'm tired.'

I smile, and hug her goodnight. 'See you in the morning,' I whisper, but Poppy's already asleep.

In the bedroom, I sit on the bed and pull out my phone. It's seven fifteen, so I've got a little time. I scroll through my emails, freezing when I see Cole's name. I haven't heard from him since I ran from his flat the day I found Katy's phone, and I'd pushed him far from my mind. As much as I could. But now his name stares at me, beckoning me to click the email.

I swipe to delete it, but I can't do it. I don't know if it's curiosity, or the fact that I need some closure, and to have some understanding of Cole's senseless acts. I tap to open it, leaning forward as I read his words.

Hannah, I know you must hate me. I hate myself. But I had to explain my actions. Because I know you, deeply, and I know that you won't put this to rest until you know why two women died at my hands.

Alice Hughes was disrespecting you. Making a mockery of your marriage, along with your husband, of course. And she would never have stopped. She wasn't going to let him go. I'm not going to try and say I did it for you – I care too much about you to do that. I did it for me. So that I could be at peace knowing your husband and Alice were no longer hurting you. Max should never have survived that attack. He was meant to die too.

But poor Katy, she was an accident. Collateral damage, I

suppose. She found the key card in my wallet. I'm sorry, I stole it from your bag. But that's the least of my sins.

Katy said she'd found my wallet on the shop floor and needed to know who it belonged to so she had a look inside. She was about to go to the police. I panicked.

I know Katy and I never got along – we could never see eye to eye. But she didn't deserve that. I'm sorry that happened.

But most of all, I'm sorry for losing you.

Your Friend,

Cole x

My forehead burns, and immediately I delete the message. I don't want it in my inbox. I want nothing more to do with him.

For ten minutes after reading Cole's words, I can't move. I sit on the bed and think about Alice Hughes, and Katy, and how they should both still be here, living their lives.

Eventually I compose myself. I change out of my shorts and vest and put on a dress. I haven't worn it for ages, and I'd forgotten how much I like it. It's orange with a flared skirt and fitted top, and pretty angel sleeves.

I leave my hair as it is, sun kissed waves floating around my shoulders. And I'm not bothering to redo my make-up.

There's a knock on the door. Two minutes late. I hesitate in front of the mirror – one last check. And then I make my way to the door, checking through the peephole before I open it.

'What time do you call this?' I say, smiling.

Taylor laughs. 'Actually, I've been outside for the last fifteen minutes.'

I smile. 'You'd better come in, then. Poppy's asleep so you won't be able to see her.'

'Ah, next time,' he says.

'Hang on. What makes you think there'll be a next time?'

He tilts his head. 'Won't there?'

'That depends how well this time goes. And just so you know – this isn't any kind of date.'

'Oh, I know,' he says. 'That suits me fine because I still don't trust you.'

'And I definitely don't trust *you*,' I say, pulling him inside and closing the door.

A LETTER FROM KATHRYN

Thank you so much for choosing to read *The Girl in Room 12*. As always, I really hope I'm still managing to create suspense with those shocks and twists you hopefully don't expect. I thoroughly loved writing this one, and I'm still thinking about the characters now. I hope you are too, and I really hope you've enjoyed reading it.

If you did enjoy the book, and would like to keep up to date with all my latest releases, please do sign up at the following link. Your email address will never be shared and you can unsubscribe at any time.

www.bookouture.com/kathryn-croft

The Girl in Room 12 really did take me in directions I hadn't foreseen. I love it when that happens! I hope this book entertained you, and offered you an alternative world to escape to. If you liked the book, it would be amazing if you could spare a couple of minutes to leave a review on Amazon, or wherever you bought it. Reviews are invaluable to authors as your important feedback helps us to reach other readers who are yet to discover our books.

Please also feel free to connect with me via my website, Facebook, Instagram, or X. I'd love to hear from you!

Thank you again for all your support – it is very much appreciated. Readers really do bring books to life!

Kathryn x

www.kathryncroft.com

facebook.com/authorkathryncroft

instagram.com/authorkathryncroft

x.com/katcroft

ACKNOWLEDGEMENTS

Book thirteen. Right from the start I had the whole 'unlucky' thing in my head: it was all going to fall apart, the plot won't work, the characters aren't right. Well, I'm pleased to say I was wrong, and by the time I wrote *The End*, I realised that absolutely nothing about my writing process this time was unlucky. And once again, it's all thanks to many people.

My editor, Lydia Vassar-Smith – it really is such a joy to work with you, and thank you for once again knocking this book into shape. I marvel at your talent, and you are the queen of conjuring up inciting incidents – thank you for the one that made this book happen!

My agent, Hannah Todd – thanks for always checking in on me when I've gone quiet and you haven't had an annoying email from me for a while. Your support and tremendous kindness, as always, is much appreciated.

The whole publishing team at Bookouture – thanks for making the whole process so seamless and efficient and for being such lovely people.

Everyone at the Madeleine Milburn Literary, Film and TV Agency – for me it's been a ten-year journey with the agency and I really appreciate everything all of you do for all your authors.

Lucy Jagger – thank you for that evening walk where you listened to my rough plot, answered my medical questions and helped me flesh out some ideas. This one is for you.

Dr Andrew Welch – thank you once again for all your help

with the detailed medical advice you gave me for this book to work. I feel as though with another couple of books, I should know enough to start a medical career! Seriously, though – I really appreciate all your help.

Michelle Langford and Jo Sidaway – thank you both for another highly insightful and entertaining chat about all the detailed police procedure I needed to know to help make this book authentic. It's always such a pleasure!

My parents, Dr Grace Mckee and Dr Phillip Mckee – thank you both so much for once again answering all my random questions and for always being there. And thank you again for giving me a childhood full of books!

My husband and children: Paul, Oliver and Amelie – you're always so patient and understanding when I have to write and when I'm 'in the zone'. I know it must be annoying but thank you for letting me be me.

And last but definitely not least, to everyone who has ever picked up one of my books to read or review and given up their precious time – no words can thank you enough, and you are the reason I can keep doing this job that I love so much. Thank you so much!

PUBLISHING TEAM

Turning a manuscript into a book requires the efforts of many people. The publishing team at Bookouture would like to acknowledge everyone who contributed to this publication.

Audio
Alba Proko
Sinead O'Connor
Melissa Tran

Commercial
Lauren Morrissette
Jil Thielen
Imogen Allport

Contracts
Peta Nightingale

Cover design
The Brewster Project

Data and analysis
Mark Alder
Mohamed Bussuri